For Michael, Guy, Joe and Rhian

Chapter 1

The grand opening of our third garden centre, 1930

We were late when I escorted Charles' widowed sister to the podium. Everyone had told me that social advancement was only possible in England today if I had a glamorous woman on my arm. John-Boy, her handsome eldest son, followed us about two steps behind. The brass band were playing 'Land of Hope and Glory' as I helped her up the wooden steps to the platform, where she sat down between her brother and our guest of honour today, her worship, the lady mayoress.

"Such a lovely outfit, my dear," her worship commented. "Where did you buy that then? Somewhere in Oxford Street? Well, I just love your hat!"

"Oh no, Fifth Avenue in New York," Charles' sister responded. "I tell you – it's the only place to buy clothes. It was the hat that made us so late. Frederic's dog sat on it, you see."

The lady mayoress made room for her to sit down and muttered quietly, "Fancy that now. So, late again, huh? Well, you Yanks only joined the war in 1917 when we'd already been fighting for three years... But, I tell you, I've been so busy with council business that I've never found time to visit Tin

Pan Alley across the herring pond."

My escort snarled at her and turned away after such an anti-American insult. I walked across to face everyone. The Garden City Band struck up a drum roll while I adjusted the microphone and John-Boy sat down quietly at my feet, right on the edge of the podium, to stare at the large, enthusiastic crowd. He passed me a folded note, which I clutched nervously in my hand.

"My lords, Your Worship the Lady Mayoress, Ladies, and Gentlemen," I said into the large chromium-plated microphone, "the staff have asked me to tell you how we started one of England's first garden centres. But first, in this glorious summer of 1930, let me welcome you to this, the grand opening of our third and largest garden centre. In a moment, I will ask our lady mayoress to cut the red ribbon and declare our new establishment open."

I paused for some polite applause and took a sip of water from the glass in front of me. I took a quick look at John-Boy's note, which said: 'Freddy I'm so bored - I need a real good rogering asap - JB.' I looked down at him, wagged a disapproving finger and frowned.

I was wearing a hired outfit from Moss Bros today. The collar of the shirt was too tight on a hot day like this. My top hat was too big and perched precariously on my ears. I tugged at it politely before turning once again to the rented microphone connected with the tannoy horns at the back of the crowd, and cleared my throat. John-Boy's message had made me completely forget where I'd got to in my speech. I looked at my notes again:

"Let me tell you briefly about those very early days. It was not long after Armistice Day at the end of the Great War..."

Of course, what followed was the approved version, suitable for polite English society, without reference to the tragic or steamier side of British life after the war. I had written it with the help of a friend from the local newspaper, who wanted to print an exclusive social diary page in the Garden

City Gazette. Naturally, it bore very little relation to the truth about what really happened. Everyone had taken great trouble for years to keep the facts out of the daily newspapers. For a moment, I wondered how many of the great and the good would be sitting here today if they knew the more sensational details... Actually, everything started quite innocently, during a thunderstorm, soon after I had returned from the battlefields of Belgium and France...

Somewhere in England, 1919

The shower turned into a downpour. There was a flash of lightning and a rumble of thunder. I loaded up the old wheelbarrow and headed back to the greenhouse. As I turned through the archway in the hedge, I found Master Charles sitting motionless on a bench in the corner. He was huddled in an Army greatcoat and crouching in the shelter of the privet hedge I had been trimming earlier.

"Sir," I said. "Sir! ... You are getting soaked. Will you not come in out of the rain?"

He turned to me with a pained expression. I had heard rumours that he was still having flashbacks to the trenches. We had been told to be patient if we met him now that he was safely back home. I put the barrow down and went over to him. He looked at me as if he had never seen me before.

"Sir! Will you come in out of the rain? You could catch a chill..."

He got up slowly. I pointed at the greenhouse at the end of the lawn.

"...I'm about to make a cup of tea, if it will please Your Lordship."

He looked more relaxed.

"That thunder," he muttered, pointing with a shaking finger, "it sounded just like the rumble of distant artillery... Yes, tea... I'm really not myself today."

I held the greenhouse door open and he came in, dripping wet.

"The heaters are on, Sir," I said calmly. "If you will give me your coat, I can hang it to dry for a while."

"Heaters?"

"The gas heaters to propagate the seedlings, Sir... "

"Ah, yes."

I helped him off with his coat. He looked around.

"So, is this your retreat?"

"From the rain, Sir."

I picked up the tea caddy and showed it to him.

"Freddy, is it?" he asked, staring at me.

"At your service, Sir."

"Wasn't there an older gardener here before I went off to war in 1914? What was his name now? Bill? Or Will... ?"

"He died, Sir. It was the dreadful influenza epidemic last year. We only read about it in old newspapers out in France."

"Ah yes, they told me... influenza is killing more people than all those who died during the Great War, but why? ...Why, Freddy...?"

He seemed lost in a train of thought for a while but then glanced at me again.

"...Was it God's judgement on mankind, do you think – all this nasty influenza? Now they say I should talk to the vicar... But what does that man really know...?"

I took the old battered kettle to the tap on the wall and filled it.

"...They tell me you served in Flanders, Freddy," he whispered as I returned to the gas ring.

"I was an officer's batman, Sir."

"Would I know him?" the young master asked, staring at me.

I opened the box of matches and struck one. It was damp and I tried another, which eventually spluttered into life.

"No, Sir. He was killed by machinegun fire... early on in the war... "

I lit the gas ring and put the kettle over the flames.

"... Then I spent some time as a stretcher bearer, Sir. There wasn't much else for us to do, except to pick up dead bodies – I mean whatever we could find, and there wasn't much of that sometimes."

We sat quietly and waited for the kettle while the rain rattled on the glass over our heads and Master Charles stared silently at the ground.

"My men died, Freddy... " he muttered eventually "...every one. Not a single man left, except me... You saved them on a stretcher... But... I killed them... "

"I'm sure you did your best, Sir."

"No, Freddy. It was not my best. I was an incompetent officer... I was quite hopeless... It was just as they say. My men were all lions. I was the donkey... I led them into a trap... The German machinegun post was there ready and waiting... ack ack ack... and they were all dead – every one, except me."

He turned to me as if he was reliving every moment. His hand was trembling again.

"What can I say, Sir?"

"Nothing, Freddy... nothing... My men were the best, the absolute best. They deserved a better officer... But...they got me, instead."

I took the tin of dried milk from under the bench and passed it to him, trying to change the subject.

"Do you remember this, Sir?"

"Army rations... yes, Freddy, as if it was yesterday... Was he a good man – your officer?"

"We all loved him, Sir."

"So, he earned your respect through valiant example."

"Yes, Sir. But now, looking back today, I ask myself where did it get him – all that patriotic flag-waving bravado?"

"Was he mentioned in despatches?"

"I expect so, Sir."

"I was too, Freddy, only Headquarters said I was a liability... 'to be relieved of duty at the earliest opportunity'... "

We sat quietly again as the kettle started to sing. He looked up at me and pointed out of the window with his thumb. His voice was still hesitant and trembling.

"...They don't know, do they... how it really was, Freddy? You know, because you were there... My father... His Lordship, and my mother... They only know what it was like from newspaper reports... and from my letters back home."

"I don't think anyone could know if they weren't there, Sir, how dreadful it really was."

The kettle started to boil. I put some tea into the cracked teapot and filled it with hot water. Master Charles followed my every move.

"I loved my batman, Freddy."

"He was lucky, then, Sir."

"No, I really loved him. In that bloody war, he was the only really honourable thing, Freddy. He was everything to me... but we came back from a sortie to find a German shell had exploded right on top of him... I can't describe... Oh, Freddy!"

Master Charles burst into tears. I let him cry. I'd seen it all before – the shellshock, the horror and the loss. I poured out the tea and stirred in the dried milk. He eventually pulled himself together and turned to me. Now his words came in staccato bursts, like the rattle of a machinegun.

"Sorry, Freddy... I'm still grieving... He was so handsome... There was practically nothing left... but I saved some of his hair in this little box... Now I keep it with me all the time... It has become the most precious thing."

He passed me an old Swan Vestas matchbox, where there was some hair just like mine. A clump of caked blood still clung to one strand. I closed it again and handed it back to him. Anyone else might have been shocked, but after my stretcher duties in the trenches, followed by endless grave digging, I was beyond that now. These days, I felt far more concerned about the living than the glorious dead – so we drank the tea in silence. Eventually he put his mug down on the bench.

"You are the very first person I have ever told... Nobody else knows about this."

He carefully replaced the box in his pocket.

"I'm glad I was here to listen, Sir."

"Can I come and talk to you again tomorrow? I can talk to you, you see. They tell me to talk to the vicar... or the psychiatrist... but how can they really know what we went through, Freddy?"

I tried to change the subject.

"Perhaps the new war memorial will help people to realise the wastage of war. In the end, you see, Sir, on our front at least, we gained only a hundred feet of territory but lost it two weeks later to the Kaiser again."

"Memorial? Oh, the vicar's new fund-raising exercise."

He seemed at a loss for words. I smiled at him and he stared at me.

"I will be only too pleased to have someone to drink my tea with, tomorrow, Sir."

"Do you play chess, Freddy?"

"Yes, Sir, I learned to play when I was recovering from my operation in the military hospital... to remove the bullet, you see."

"Are you any good at it?"

"Some people said I gave them a good challenge, Sir."

"Very good, Freddy. You and I will have a game tomorrow."

"What about my gardening duties, Sir? Her Ladyship expects the kitchen garden to provide extra produce now the war is over. She says everything is in short supply nowadays."

Master Charles looked up at me.

"Well, I tell you, England expected us to do our duty out in the trenches, Freddy, but sometimes chess was more important, when I could play with him... my dead batman... Oh God, I miss him so much...but it must remain our little secret, Freddy. Yes, I'll bring the chess set with me tomorrow. I'll deal with my mother."

He got up, saluted slowly and ceremoniously, as if to honour a fellow officer, took his coat and closed the greenhouse door behind him.

The following day it rained from late morning and Master Charles arrived, just as he had promised, with his pocket chess set. While the rain thundered down on the glass over our heads, he set out the wooden board on the table, where we sat on old kitchen stools. Then he lined up the hand-carved black and white pieces in silence.

"White always starts, Freddy," he said eventually, turning the board around.

"In our hospital ward, Sir, the whites were the British and the blacks were the Germans. The black king was always called the Kaiser. Other patients sometimes placed bets to predict the outcome of the whole war."

"Who usually won?"

"The blacks, Sir, just like they did on our battlefield."

I remembered a quick opening gambit I learned in hospital. Very soon I had captured several of his black pawns and one knight. Already I was within a couple of moves of putting his Kaiser in check.

"Ho ho!" he muttered. "I see you've played this game before, Freddy."

He took my white king's knight just as I had planned. I moved my castle. I looked up. Master Charles was just staring at me.

"Your move, Sir!"

But he had lost his concentration and moved a useless pawn two squares forward. My moment had arrived. I prepared for the coup de grace with my remaining knight while he continued to stare at me.

"Sir! Your move now, I think."

He moved another pawn but overlooked the danger under his nose.

"Check, Sir!"

Master Charles stared down at the board.

"Good Lord, Freddy... Now I think you've got me cornered. Yes."

"It might even be checkmate, my lord."

"Your tutor in hospital taught you well."

"There were some very long, boring days in the hospital, Sir. Then I found a playmate in our trenches."

"They sent you back after that?"

"Digging graves, Sir, or as a stretcher bearer..."

I pointed to the glass above us, where the torrential rain had been replaced by drizzle.

"...I should get back to work, Sir. The vegetable garden needs weeding again."

He picked up the chess pieces and fitted them into the box that he clasped in his hand.

"Splendid game, Freddy. Same time tomorrow?"

"Thank you, Sir."

"Good. I'll bring you something from the pantry."

I reached for his coat and gave it to him. As he got up, I held the greenhouse door open and raised my cap. He looked at me, smiled again, and saluted slowly, as if he was taking leave of a fellow officer.

"The rain is easing off now, Sir"

He turned at the door with a puzzled look on his face.

"That soldier in the hospital, Freddy – the one who taught you to play chess so well – are you still in touch with him now?"

"No, Sir, he died from septicaemia...his infection spread too far, you see. We had to bury him quickly in the summer heat."

I tugged at my cap, just as I had done before the war, and he turned away from me.

"Freddy... thank you... for... "

He seemed to lose his train of thought again and went out into the drizzle.

The next day it was raining again by the time he arrived at the greenhouse. He was carefully carrying a tin but no chess set today.

"Something for us... " he said, trying to be cheerful. "My mother made it. I told her all about you. She thinks I need somebody to talk to."

I looked inside the tin. There was a fruit cake with cherries on the top.

"I've felt so much better since we played chess yesterday, Freddy. I thought we might talk more today because I'd really like to get to know you better. We'll play chess again some other time."

"Glad to hear it, Sir... Another mug of tea?"

He nodded and sat down on the bench where he had sat before and looked at me intently. I lit the gas ring with a match and put the kettle on to boil again.

"You remind me of my batman, Freddy. I think that's what brought it all back... It was the sight of you standing on the stepladder to cut the privet hedge outside the other day... So, tell me, did you have a good war, Freddy? Perhaps it made a real man out of you... My psychiatrist thinks it should have made a better man out of me. That's what he's just told my mother, anyway..."

I smiled and he pointed with his hand in the direction of the Big House.

"...They don't understand, Freddy. It is just as you said. They were not there... They don't really know anything about it... How can they?"

"I thought His Lordship, your father, fought the Boers in South Africa in 1902."

"Yes, Freddy, but that wasn't modern warfare was it? That was a war fought by gentlemen. Ours was a war fought by obsessed maniacs – Haig, what did he really know about life in the trenches and the Big Push? ... But all the time that wretched man was sitting safely behind the lines at his posh desk in Army HQ...drinking cups... I wish, Freddy... How I wish. "

The young man put his head in his hands and sighed.

"Your tea, Sir."

He looked up, startled.

"That's just what my batman used to say... Your tea, Sir."

Now there were tears in his eyes.

"How old are you, Freddy?"

"I'm twenty-two, Sir."

"Well, I'm twenty-seven. Tell me, did you love your officer?"

"I respected him, Sir. It was my duty."

"Ah, ... duty... yes... duty... But one's duty is so different in peacetime, Freddy... It is not written down like the articles of war, you see... Now it is about habit, custom, social values, the duties of the ruling classes, noblesse oblige and subjective things like that."

He seemed to lose his train of thought again and we sat quietly for a while. I stirred sugar into my tea. Somewhere, rainwater was dripping through a cracked glass pane over our heads.

"They say I should get married," he continued eventually, pointing back at the Big House with his thumb. "My father wants grandchildren... "

I smiled but said nothing.

"... I was engaged in 1914 to someone my parents wanted for a daughter-in-law... 'Good child-bearing stock. You won't do better, Son'... "

He put his head in his hands again.

"...I can't stand the sight of her... Not now, Freddy."

"Perhaps you'll find another young lady, Sir."

"Gone right off 'em, I have... Listen, I'm telling you things nobody else knows. You must hold your tongue about all this, Freddy, please..."

He looked at me sadly. I finished my tea, put the mug down and waited. I had been waiting so long to hear the terrible truth which seemed to be ruining his life and not even the psychiatrist was allowed to hear:

"Ever since that day, Freddy. It was calm on our front – no gunfire, no shells, no gas, nothing. The sun was shining. So I said to my men, 'You go down to the river and bathe.' My batman went with them. Time passed by so I went to see what they were all up to. When I arrived on the riverbank, they were all splashing about. My batman was about to dive off the bridge. He was stark naked and the sun was shining behind him. Freddy, well, I tell you... He was the most beautiful sight I had ever seen... Next day, boom, and he was dead... just little pieces splattered all over the shop... If only I had stayed behind in the dugout to take care of ... The one person in the world... We just needed more time... Oh dear...!"

I looked at him in silence, waiting for the tears to come again, but he only stared at the ground.

"...It was the sight of him on that railway bridge, you see... with his arms outstretched like the crucifix in the church, his brown hair blowing out in the breeze... Freddy, I will never forget... How can I ever, ever forget? ...He was my first real... Yes, but I left him to clean my service revolver so it would be ready... How could I? I never even had a chance to say goodbye... Boom! ...and he was dead. Too late, you see..."

This time, I got up and put my hand on his shoulder when he started to sob. It seemed a friendly thing to do. He put his hand on mine and squeezed it tightly. I think that was the start of it all. That was the moment I knew the terrible truth that he seemed to be so anxious to hold back from his parents and the psychiatrist.

"There wasn't even enough to fill the coffin... Nineteen, he was... All his life in front of him... Freddy, I will never, ever forget... "

He squeezed my hand tightly.

"I know, Sir," I reassured him. "I picked up bodies, too."

"But there were only little pieces...and these tufts of hair."

I turned back to the teapot to see how much tea was left. That's when I heard the old familiar sound of the safety catch being released on a service pistol. When I turned back to look, the young master had removed the gun from his coat and was looking at it closely. I froze.

"I want to be with him again," he muttered, turning the gun towards himself. "I know he's on the other side, waiting... We talked, you see, Freddy, just like you and I are now. We were going to live together when the war was over... We meant that much to one another, you see. It was real love. I'm telling you so you know, why, Freddy... not the damned psychiatrist... He would never understand. He wasn't there."

"Sir!" I said, firmly, gathering my wits about me. "Pass me the pistol, Sir. Too many people have died. Too many good men have died so that France could be free and you and I could live in peace again... "

He turned to me, still holding the pistol in his hand.

"...Sir!" I insisted. "The pistol... please."

For a moment I was afraid it would be his last. Slowly, he lowered the gun and let it drop on the ground. Fortunately it did not go off. I stepped on it quickly before he could grab it again but he just stared at me. I picked it up, replaced the safety catch and shook the bullets out into the water trough behind me.

"Too many people died, Sir," I said again. "Now I think it's up to the rest of us to try and make something better out of the world, don't you? ... If you'll excuse me, Sir. I'll hang on to this until you have recovered yourself. "

When I turned back to look, he was staring at me intently again but saying nothing. Perhaps I should have helped him to go back to the Big House, where his parents could send for a doctor, but I knew drugs would not help. A doctor could only delay the crisis. Sedation would never prevent it.

The next morning I found a note on the greenhouse door. This was often how Her Ladyship communicated with the staff. Sometimes, if she was displeased, it meant to come and collect your cards. Other staff had been dismissed this way but where would I find a job now? So many ex-servicemen were out of work in 1919. I made my way to the back door of the Big House, where I rang the bell. Her Ladyship appeared in person with one of her dogs on a lead. That had never happened before.

"Ah, Frederic... Will you accompany me around the rose garden?"

I smiled, relieved that I was not about to join the growing ranks of the unemployed. We walked slowly. The dog started to pull on the leash and she handed it to me.

"...How long have you been with us?"

"A long time, my lady. Since I was junior under-gardener."

She stumbled on a stone, grabbed my arm and held on to it. We walked on slowly. I moved the dog's lead to my other hand.

"The parterre is looking better," she smiled, looking around. "It got so bad while you were away in the war. There was nobody here after the flu epidemic. We have you to thank... "

She slipped again and held my arm tighter. In the distance, the birds were swirling around in the air. The sky looked stormy again and the wind was getting up but we walked slowly.

"...Also, Frederic, we have to thank you for dealing with my son... I heard... "

I coughed politely and she turned to me.

"...No, no... You handled the situation very well. Like a conscientious soldier you are just cleaning his pistol... to be returned when the time is right."

"It will be my pleasure, my lady."

"No, Frederic, credit where credit is due. After talking to you my son is happier than he has been for a very long time... I just want you to know His Lordship and I do appreciate what you are doing."

"It is nothing, my lady."

"Well, we will see... Please say nothing about this to Charles. I don't want him to feel that we are spying on him... "

It started to drizzle and we turned back towards the Big House.

"...He desperately needs someone like you who was actually there, you see... Yes, I think you are the only one who will be able to help him now. Charles doesn't like our local vicar and won't go and talk to him. He says the vicar doesn't know anything..."

The drizzle changed into a downpour and we sheltered inside a stone monument known as 'The Temple'. This had been erected in memory of Her Ladyship's father. She sat down with me on the garden seat inside, away from the rain.

"...Charles needs someone special in his life who understands him, just like you, Frederic."

"I saw tougher men than Master Charles break down, my lady. One or two so-called cowards were executed by firing squad... But they were probably suffering from severe shellshock. Of course, that was officially dismissed."

"The doctors have tried to bring him out of it, you know – electroconvulsive therapy. Now that was cruel. They tried hypnosis but he resisted that. The doctor said he was trying to hold back something he didn't want anyone to know about. Some drugs seem to work for a while but..."

I looked outside, where rainwater was gushing from a broken pipe to the ground. Suddenly Her Ladyship turned and looked me up and down.

"...Frederic, what are we doing sitting here together in 'The Temple of Love'? We must be careful or they will start whispering belowstairs that Her Ladyship has taken a lover!"

"But there is nowhere else to shelter from the rain in this part of the garden, my lady."

"That's what my sister thought... She took shelter in her gamekeeper's cottage. You might have read about the scandal in that dreadful rag Titbits... Her reputation was ruined, Frederic. It was terrible. No respectable person would talk to her."

"I'm sorry to hear it, my lady."

"But do you know what my sister told me? She looked at that nude statue over there – the one my great-uncle Bartholomew brought back from Greece..."

She pointed at the Eros of Praxiteles outside.

"... Well, my sister said – perhaps I shouldn't tell you... She said that is exactly what her gamekeeper looked like when he took all his clothes off... But you must excuse me, Frederic. I am forgetting myself. My poor sister's downfall should serve as a warning to us all."

"I will clean the statue, my lady. The wood pigeons have been perching on it. I thought it was a modern copy. Nobody said it was the real thing from Greece."

"Well, I've never liked it. Whoever saw silly great wings like that on a young man? One of the hands was knocked off, years ago."

Her Ladyship looked around and patted me on the knee.

"Not like you, Frederic... I'll tell you something. I was looking out of the window the other day while you were working in the kitchen garden. After all that dreadful slaughter in the war, good-looking young men like you have become the latest national shortage... No, Frederic, I'm just being a silly old woman with romantic, paperback dreams about my poor sister and Her Ladyship's secret lover outside in the woods."

"I will say nothing, my lady! I learned to hold my tongue on duty in France after some of the things I witnessed out there."

She turned to look me up and down.

"Oh Frederic! ...What have we done? The war in France was supposed to be a brief operation to teach the Kaiser a lesson or two – Queen Victoria's no-good grandson had to be shown that Britain still ruled the waves. Nobody thought that almost all of the young men of your generation might be wiped out in the trenches."

"I was just one of the lucky ones, my lady."

"So was my son, only shellshock has ruined his life. He came home quite different from the confident young man who went off to war in 1914, you know. And when I remember all those other British, German and French mothers who lost brothers, husbands, sons... But, listen, I think if the women of the world were to get together and form an international league of motherhood, we might change things for the better... Do you know, when the Versailles Treaty was signed in June; the only women present made the tea, laid out the tables, and then had to leave the conference room to allow the male politicians to sort things out by themselves. But men haven't made a very good job of the world so far, have they?"

She smiled at me.

"...Not you, Frederic. What would you know about such

things?"

She patted my hand while I looked at the clouds, which seemed to be clearing at last.

"It has stopped raining now, my lady."

She got up but turned to look at me again with a smile. I felt deeply honoured. She was treating me as a friend already.

"Please take care of my son. He thinks the world of you, he really does. He talks about you all the time. You might change his life for the better, Frederic. Please think about it."

"I'll do what I can, my lady."

"Look, I think the sun is going to come out..."

I helped her down the step onto the wet lawn.

"... Tell me, what did you do in the war? My son hasn't said."

"Mostly, I picked up dead bodies, my lady."

"Oh, how awful... But what else would a junior under-gardener like you be able to do? No gardens to dig on the Western Front."

"Only graves, my lady...rows upon rows...thousands of them."

"The lost generation... Well, I'm sure you did your best, be it ever so humble. Still, you did come back in one piece... Frederic. I'm so glad."

We walked slowly amongst the dripping roses towards the Big House. Once again she grabbed my arm at the slippery stone steps. I said nothing and held the back door open for her. She paused as if to say something else but I handed her the dog lead and she turned to go inside.

The young master returned every day to the greenhouse at the same time for the rest of the week. By Friday, we were even laughing about some sillier moments in the trenches. Our war had cheerful times too.

"My officer," I said, "well, he decided that not much could be done about the state of the latrines. Every day it rained and they overflowed."

"We had latrines like that, too."

"So," I continued. "My officer said, if we couldn't do

anything about the problem, we should change the name. Henceforth, they were to be known as the honey stalls. 'Latrines? What latrines? We have a honey stall, what?' ... Anyway, I planted some red poppies along the top of the earth wall to make everything look more cheerful. Officers could now sit in there and look up at the flowers to take their minds off the stench, Sir."

For the first time, he laughed. I think that was the moment I realised just what I had achieved – far more than the psycho-analysis, the electric shock therapy and the rest. An attentive ear, a friendly soul and a sympathetic spirit had won the day. So I sat back and relaxed for one moment to smile at the young master.

"Can I see you again tomorrow, Saturday?" he asked, looking concerned.

"I don't work Saturday afternoon or on Sunday, Sir."

"Then, we'll meet down in the village pub, then, Freddy – same time, tomorrow. It must be my turn to stand you a drink after all the tea you have made for me – and very good tea it was, too... "

He looked me up and down closely.

"... But, mainly, thank you, Freddy, for just being here and listening and talking common sense... Thank you for giving me your valuable time... I could love... Yes, I really could... Oh, Freddy, I could love...so very much..."

His voice drifted away and he just stared at me. Already I knew what he wanted to say but I wasn't offended. I just felt flattered that people from the Big House had started to take some notice of me at last.

"I'll hang on to the service pistol for now, Sir. I think it is for the best, don't you?"

"Quite! You are right... of course."

"I can clean it for you, Sir. The barrel needs a good clean and the mechanism needs oiling, Sir... That's what I used to do for my officer, Sir."

"I know. My man did the same. That is, until... "

For the first time, no tears appeared. He got up, put down

the mug, saluted slowly as if he was acknowledging a fellow officer, turned, and walked out of the greenhouse, closing the door behind him quietly. I sat quietly, thinking. The war didn't end with the Armistice. For some men it could go on forever – even after the Versailles Treaty.

The following day we met at the pub, at the same time, as previously arranged. Now the sun was shining, so we sat outside on the bench while the rooks circled over the distant trees. He seemed to be much more cheerful today. I suddenly remembered what Her Ladyship had said. Sometimes simple and sympathetic human companionship is the most wonderful thing we can provide for another troubled soul – irrespective of social class or my lowly position on this estate.

"My father has been telling me about the new road, Freddy."

"Where is that, Sir?"

"The county council have decided to build a new trunk road – a 'first class road' they are calling it – through the estate, between the Big House and the village here. They think people will soon be wanting a new main road to London but bypassing the village – the streets are too narrow for char-a-bancs, I mean motor coaches, lorries and the like."

"So it will slice the estate in two, Sir? What does His Lordship think of that idea?"

"Doesn't like it, as you can guess... You see, the government increased the purchase tax on petrol for my father's Rolls Royce to raise money for better roads – like this new one across the estate. It was the Development and Road Improvement Funds Act of 1909, Freddy. So His Lordship's tax is actually helping to pay for the new eyesore... Ironic, don't you think?"

"Very likely, Sir. I guess His Lordship had something to say about that, as well."

Master Charles screwed up his face in a caricature of his father.

"'This damn country is going to the dogs, Son! To the dogs, I tell you! ... I blame Lloyd George, yes, yes.'"

For the first time, we both laughed together and raised our glasses.

"To the dogs, Freddy," he shouted at me.

"Yes, to the dogs, Sir...and David Lloyd George."

He turned to me with a laugh.

"But my father insists Lloyd George has just unleashed a bureaucratic monster on the world... It is called his new Ministry of Transport...to sort out Britain's travel chaos – with better roads in particular. But this new Minister may prove to be far more powerful than people like my blessed father, who actually own the countryside in England, Freddy."

Now I raised my glass.

"Then I give you another toast, Sir. To the new Ministry of Transport Act, 1919, this new trunk road through the estate, and David Lloyd George."

Once more we clinked glasses over the table and laughed.

"My father shouted abuse in the House of Lords about our notorious Prime Minister Lloyd George the other day, Freddy. He was even quoted in The Times, yes, in the parliamentary section."

"I know, Sir. He caused quite a stir. I read all about it, not in The Times, of course – just one of the cheaper ones."

"I keep forgetting you can read, Freddy. Lots of the yokels and country bumpkins round here can't, you know."

"But my newspaper claimed he used two 'bloodies' and the dreaded 'F-word' during the debate at the Upper House, Sir."

"No, Freddy, what he actually said was that Lloyd George should pack off to the Bloody Tower to get his nodding head chopped off."

I couldn't help laughing.

"The newspapers usually get things wrong, Sir."

"Yes, my father would line up a few newspaper editors at the chopping block as well..."

He raised his glass to clink with mine once more.

"...Well, Freddy, I give you another toast: to David Lloyd George, his so-called 'People's Budget' of 1909 and the dreaded Parliament Act of 1911. They are my blessed father, His Lordship's, three pet hates, you know – even more so than the German Kaiser! The poor Kaiser he might even have been forgiven by now, I don't know; but Lloyd George, never! My father says the Western Front may now be secure but, the home front is still being undermined by Lloyd George and all his damned meddling."

We both laughed. I had found a new friend.

Now, at last, I realised that what people said was true. The war had proved to be a great leveller of social status. Our generation had been divided into two classes – the glorious dead and the rest. We were the walking wounded – the shellshocked and the survivors. Only the glorious dead seemed to deserve a marble cenotaph in the Mall. I still felt rather disappointed because nobody had ever laid flowers at my feet.

"Look," he said, putting his glass down on the table. "Freddy, my dear friend, you must stop all this 'Sir' business... You and I fought a war... together, Freddy... different jobs and different battlefields maybe... but I don't think of you as an inferior. I have started to think of you as a friend and my equal... So, please, Freddy, stop all this 'Sir' business."

"What shall I call you, then?"

"What about Charles?"

"If it will please you."

"Yes, it would... my dear Freddy... very much."

"Thank you."

"My father, of course, must still remain His Lordship."

"Naturally."

"Only, right now I feel more for you than anyone else... alive or dead, Freddy. I look at you and I see so many possibilities..."

I didn't know what to say but smiled at him. I felt really flattered. Nobody from the Big House had taken much notice of me until now. Today it seemed that both Her Ladyship and her son were in need of a special friend. Charles stared at me straight in the eyes, held his breath for a moment and let out a long sigh.

"England is changing, Freddy. It has to. All that them and us stuff – it can't last. In the trenches there were good men and bad men. I used to think social class mattered, at first. But then I saw how bad, incompetent officers came from the old, so-called respectable English families. Freddy, you know. You are looking at one right now."

I said nothing, but watched the rooks circling the trees in the distance. I was wondering how I could tell him my news about the letter from the Palace. I decided that if we were to be friends now, then the old, pre-war, Edwardian social barriers must come down.

"Charles," I said.

He looked up and smiled.

"Charles, I have some news and I need your help. My British Army uniform, such as it was, became so tattered after the incident that I had to throw it away – it was the blood stains, you see."

He looked at me intently.

"What incident, Freddy?"

"I rescued an officer from no man's land. He had come down in a flimsy Royal Flying Corps biplane but his pilot died... I didn't know then, that this young officer was related to our royal family."

"A relative of our good King George? But he survived, I take it, thanks to you?"

"It was the German machinegun post, you see... Nobody could get out into no man's land without being shot at. But I could hear the moans getting softer – I knew whoever was out there would soon be dead."

"So what did you do, then, Freddy?"

"I waited until dark, covered myself in black camouflage – bootblacking on my face and hands and all that... Anyway, I lobbed two grenades into the German machinegun post and it went quiet, so I was able to get the officer out of the passenger seat... "

Charles sat with his mouth open but said nothing.

"... This officer was bleeding to death and I tried to carry him over my shoulder. He was too heavy so I had to drag him back to the English trenches."

"And this officer was related to our good King George the Fifth? Well, I never, Freddy! So he survived and is alive and with us still... all because of you... a humble gardener who used to be a junior member of staff on this estate. "

I reached into the pocket of my jacket and took out the letter that had just been delivered, and passed it to him. He opened the envelope and took out the contents to study it very carefully. Then he looked up.

"The Victoria Cross ... You? ... Good Lord! The VC, no less."

I nodded.

"What should I do, Charles? My uniform has been thrown away because it could not be cleaned. Anyway, it had holes in it."

Charles' mouth fell open.

"You mean the German machine-gunners? So they got you before you blew them up with the grenades?"

I nodded, and pointed at my leg from which a bullet had been removed.

"I am wondering what I should do, Charles. Shall I say no to the Palace because I can't go dressed like this! And there isn't much else. My Sunday suit I wear at church is threadbare. I can't wear that, not at Buckingham Palace."

"No, Freddy, you must wear mine. That is the least I can do! Why on earth didn't you tell me anything before?"

"It didn't seem right. Anyway, I didn't know then. This is the first I have heard about it."

"You must come for dinner with me and my father – His Lordship – and my mother... yes, tonight... always roast fowl on Saturday. There is bound to be enough for just one more. I will tell them you are my guest. Freddy, my dear friend, it is my honour to invite you to dine with us this evening... You actually managed to achieve something honourable in that bloody war where I failed so miserably... I really did, you know. My men would have been better off organising themselves but they're all dead now... yes, under gravestones on foreign soil, just like Drummer Hodge, beneath foreign skies in that poem, you know."

He stared at me but I said nothing. I could not imagine what it could be like to be burdened with so much guilt. Before the war, he had always seemed to be such a cheerful young man – playing tennis, croquet or riding his horse in the woods. He seldom looked at me, of course. I was just a humble member of the working classes who had to tip my cap whenever he passed by. It was quite different now, so it must have been the war.

"Freddy, please will you be my special guest tonight...?"

I nodded.

"... Well, your threadbare Sunday suit won't do for His Lordship at dinner tonight, either... Come with me now, Freddy. We can go up the back stairs... and you can try on my best dinner jacket and the suit for the Palace... No time like the present... "

He got up and saluted me again.

"...Freddy, I mean it!"

Now there were tears in my eyes.

I had never actually been inside the Big House before. Since I started as junior under-gardener in 1912, I had never been further than the back doorstep to deliver fresh vegetables to the kitchen. Now, it seemed like a dream, walking up the back stairs behind the heir to the estate. The Big House was not as grand as I had imagined inside. There were no tapestries on the walls, no gold ornaments on the tables and no vast works of art hanging around the landing. In the corner of the ceiling I noticed a damp patch. He must have noticed me staring at it as we walked by.

"We'll have to get that seen to," he said, hurrying me along the corridor. "It is always the cost... My father doesn't like forking out for the builders... Out in Belgium we were attacked by the Kaiser's guns but back home we've still got Lloyd George to contend with. The threat from the Kaiser is over but Lloyd George's so-called People's Budget of 1909 is still taking its dreadful toll on the aristocracy..."

I looked around at everything while Charles continued to lecture me about politics today.

"...So, Freddy, the homeland is under attack, not by the Kaiser, but from within... You don't know anything about politics, extra taxes on petrol, tobacco, tea, sugar or alcohol; our Land Value Tax, supertax or death duties, do you? But I'm forgetting, since 1918 Lloyd George has given both you and my dear mother the right to vote in the English elections."

"I could have a look at the hanging gutter if that's blocked," I said. "I had to retile part of the roof on my cottage after the storm. It worked, after a fashion."

Charles ignored this but pushed me into a doorway and locked the door behind him.

"You haven't seen my collection of souvenirs from the trenches, have you? I found this Kaiser William helmet in the mud..."

On the mantelshelf over the fireplace was a magnificent German helmet beside a copper shell case decorated with the family coat of arms. I really should have guessed that there might be other, and far more sinister, items in his collection – but these were not on public display.

"... While you are changing, I'll play a record my batman liberated from a German dugout. Have you heard this one, Freddy?"

He wound up the gramophone standing in the corner. From the horn came the scratchy sound of 'Lili Marlene' on a 78 rpm disc.

"...This is my wardrobe, here," he said, opening the first of a row of doors.

There were drawers marked Underwear, Neck ties, Socks; and behind the next door, a row of dinner jackets and trousers hanging over wooden hangers.

"...Would you like a bath first, Freddy?"

I didn't know what to say.

"...You can. I have my own bathroom... The water is heated by gas, too, just like the seedlings in your greenhouse."

He opened another door and pointed inside. I followed and he put a hand on my shoulder and we stood in the doorway together.

"I'm happy to wash your back," he said, taking a loofah down from a brass hook on the wall.

"I used to do that for my first officer," I said. "But he had a small tin bath with a bucket of hot water, when we were lucky. As for decent soap – there was always a national shortage of things like that!"

We both laughed together again and Charles patted me on the back.

"Now I will do it for you, Freddy... It is not every day someone on this estate is awarded the Victoria Cross. It will be my honour and, yes, my great pleasure to act as your batman this afternoon, huh?"

He studied me closely as I stripped off my clothes and left them in a heap in the corner of the bathroom.

"Gosh, Freddy... You are beautiful. Do you mind me saying that? I haven't insulted you?"

I was used to nudity at the public baths. It didn't bother me. I was just happy that my body hadn't been blown to pieces like the remains of so many young men I had buried out in France. However, I'd never been called beautiful before. I felt flattered.

"Not at all," I said. "I wish my first officer had paid me a compliment just once in a while – maybe 'thank you, Freddy, for a nice cup of tea' or if I managed to scrounge a bit of soap for his bath. But he just assumed it was my duty, you see."

"Duty... yes, duty," Charles muttered. "For God's sake, why does everyone keep talking about my duty?"

His eyes seemed to glaze over for a moment. I continued.

"I would have done anything for him, Charles. But he just ignored me... All I wanted was a smile or a friendly 'good morning, Freddy'. That would have been enough, just once. If only he had noticed I was there, once in a while."

"Good. If you don't mind, I will stay and sit here while you have your bath."

He sat down on a washing basket in the corner of the bathroom but I pointed at the geyser.

"You'll have to show me how to use this thing, Sir. I'm afraid of blowing up the whole house."

He came over to the bath and put one hand on my shoulder.

"Sleep with me tonight...Freddy?"

The question was just like that – so straightforward, without emotion. I said nothing. He ran his hand down my back to clutch my bottom. I turned and got into the bath.

"Sorry, Freddy. I have shocked you."

"No. I am surprised, that's all."

"Stand in the bath and turn around, now... "

He went back and sat on the washing basket again.

"...Beautiful... you're so beautiful, Freddy... just like him."

There was an awkward moment. I didn't want to upset him or risk driving him back into his state of depression. I'd always known I was different – not the marrying kind. Somehow he seemed to know that too.

"Look," I said. "Honestly – it's not a problem. There has never been anyone in my life... Nobody."

"Well, Freddy, there is now... for better or worse... Oh, yes! Yes!"

This kind of thing seemed to contradict everything I had learned before.

"But, Charles, we were always told there could never be anything between officers and the men... nothing," I insisted. "Not even a smell of anything... We had a lecture from the padre at Headquarters. They just didn't like it when we played football with the Germans on Christmas Day... Only one thing worse than fraternising with the enemy, we were told, and that was inappropriate relations between officers and their men."

"But the war is over, Freddy... we won it, remember."

"No," I said. "Some of you are still fighting it."

"That's true!"

"Anyway," I went on, "the Armistice was an agreement to halt hostilities. It was not really some great military victory, was it...? Apart from some rusty German battleships in Scarpa Flow."

"You are right, of course... The German sailors scuttled most of those. Not much use to us now they're all under water, what?"

"And my officer said that the Battle of Agincourt was a decisive English victory won by Henry the Fifth on Saint Crispin's Day, in 1415. But what will historians say about our recent battles in France and Belgium, do you think...? Ypres or the Somme?"

"I don't know, Freddy. I really don't know."

He seemed lost for words again. I looked around the bathroom. The white tiles smelled of 'Liquid Gumption'. The brass plumbing and the taps had been polished until they shone. I had to go to the public baths in the town once a week in order to find anything quite like this.

"But what about us – you and I?" he asked, after staring at me for some time.

"I don't know," I said, finally sitting down in the water and turning off the geyser. "Do you think it would work? Should you not try to find someone of your own class and position in society? I don't feel worthy of such an honour."

"Why not? Why should I have to follow the tired, old, snooty English traditions: the social conventions of boring marriage, stuffy upper-class expectations about life, child rearing... and all that kind of thing ... just to please His Lordship?"

"What about Her Ladyship?" I asked, holding out the loofah and smiling.

He got up from the laundry basket and came to stand by the bath. I stood up again and passed him the soap. He stared at my penis, which was swelling by the minute. I made no attempt to hide anything. I felt I was entitled to feel proud of myself – even after the trenches of the Somme, I was still fit, healthy and very much alive.

"Look, Sir," I said, pointing down. "Now my Junior Freddy here is saluting Master Charles."

He looked up and smiled at me again.

"Gosh, Freddy, what are we doing? My batman was the same. He loved me to touch him like this – just like you... Now my psychiatrist talks about sexuality, the subconscious, repression and English inhibitions. But my batman didn't know anything about those. He was just like you, Freddy, unspoilt by public schools and the traditions of the English upper classes. He was really sweet and innocent."

I laughed, he smiled and we both looked at my erection.

"I'm not so innocent, my lord."

"Good for you, Freddy. Yes, good for you."

"Perhaps we are making up for lost time, Sir – all those deadly boring hours in the trenches followed by a few minutes of sheer terror, and death, for some."

"Like my batman, Freddy?"

"Yes, and the pilot of that plane in no man's land... and the German machine-gunners in that emplacement where I tossed those grenades."

"We've earned this right, Freddy. We have fought for this freedom... Let's just be happy that we lived for this moment."

"Yes, why not? Let's have a bit of fun now it is all over."

"So will you sleep here with me tonight in my cold, lonely, four-poster bed?"

"If you really want me to, Sir. I suggest you lock the door again."

"Yes, Freddy, I do want you to... Nobody needs to know anything, do they...? Anyway it really is none of their business."

"Well, if you really want me, it won't be lonely for you tonight."

He smiled and seemed to relax.

"Thank you, Freddy. I might sleep better with someone

like you."

Now I felt really flattered that somebody actually wanted me.

"And I don't think there will be much chance of it being cold either, Sir."

"I have been having such bad dreams, Freddy – well, I'll tell you. The other night I woke up, convinced that gas shells were landing in our trench again. I couldn't find my gas mask, you see. But things like that might not happen if you were there. The psychiatrist suggested I might take my old teddy bear to bed as a sort of comforter, but I ask you, I'm far too old for a teddy bear now. I really need someone like you, Freddy."

"Perhaps we might have a cuddle instead and you could get back to sleep again."

Charles started to rub my back gently with the loofah.

"You are so beautiful... Freddy, I am so lucky... How do you stay so slim and athletic? I suppose it's all the hard work in the garden – lifting, carrying and so on."

"I lost weight digging holes in the ground to bury so many ... out in France and Belgium."

"But you're home again now. Freddy, I'm so glad."

"Now I do exercises down in my cellar."

"What's that?"

"I bought some old gym equipment in an auction sale a while ago. Anyway, I've converted the cellar under my cottage into somewhere I can do my exercises... It helps avoid back-ache in the garden, mainly."

"It is private, then, this cellar?"

He was rubbing my back vigorously with the loofah and applying more soap. I turned around in the bath. He slapped my bottom and I giggled.

"You're so gorgeous, Freddy."

"It's also quite dark," I said, "except for the oil lamp or a candle."

"I'd love to come and watch."

"Of course, any time."

"Good."

I had never been in love before, but I realised that this was exactly how I was feeling. Somehow, what with the war and everything else, I thought I would have to wait. But suddenly I realised that, after everything I had been through, perhaps I should grasp this opportunity and try out every new experience. I'd heard all about Oscar Wilde's illicit lust for Lord Alfred Douglas, of course, and even read 'The Ballad of Reading Gaol'. But now, when I was actually being offered the possibility of the very same forbidden love, I felt really excited about the idea of illicit lust and the social dangers that seemed to obsess some of the English upper classes. After everything I had been through, today in 1919, civilian life was safe but rather boring. In the Somme, I'd learned to thrive under bombardment and relished so many near misses in the trenches. I could handle wartime dangers, but could I handle England in peacetime? Besides, Charles was someone I respected and was growing to like so much. Now I decided to change the subject.

"Will you come with me to the Palace to help me collect my VC?"

Charles said nothing for a while but continued to wash my back slowly.

"I have a much better idea, Freddy," he said eventually. "Will you do something for me?"

"Of course... name it!"

"At dinner tonight please will you ask my father, His Lordship, to accompany you to the Palace? And my mother... she's actually related to the Royal Family – it is a distant connection. They've been to royal garden parties before, so they will know how things are done. Don't ask me, I don't know."

"But you must come, my lord!"

"If they will let me in, Freddy... I'm hardly the pride of the British Army, am I? ...when it said 'to be relieved of duty at the first opportunity'."

"Charles, I'll tell them. You are..."

"Your batman?"

"My second? No, you will be my companion. I will say I shall be pleased to accept and I shall be accompanied by my military advisor, His Lordship; my advisor in courtly etiquette, Her Ladyship; and my companion – that's you, Charles."

I stepped out of the bath. He took a towel off the heated rail and wrapped it around me.

"I wish this was the flag of St George... Look, it's all true, isn't it? ... You are not having some kind of joke."

"You have read the letter from Buckingham Palace."

"And it really did happen... the plane in no man's land and all that... "

I turned around as he held the towel, and looked straight into his eyes.

"...Say no more, Freddy. I believe you... Now we have to get my parents to believe it."

Suddenly he kissed me on the forehead. I smiled and he kissed me again. The gramophone had been repeating 'Lili Marlene' over and over. Now we were both fed up with it and he went outside to turn off the machine.

"So, Charles," Her Ladyship was looking at me through her lorgnette spectacles, "please introduce us to your charming young guest."

I bowed.

"Freddy, my lady, your gardener... We talked a few days ago."

She turned away, muttering.

"I didn't recognise you, young man. They do say that 'clothes maketh the man'."

"Mother!" Charles took his mother by the arm and led her into the dining hall, and chatted quietly to her so I couldn't hear.

"Charles has brought a guest tonight," she exclaimed to her husband, who was already seated at the table.

He got up, obviously expecting to see someone else.

"I have invited Freddy, Papa. Please be nice to him ... We

have something terribly important to tell you."

His Lordship sat down again and looked amazed when Charles held a seat for me to sit down. Then Charles grabbed the flowers from the vase on the side table and laid them ceremoniously at my feet while his parents turned to stare at one another. His Lordship's butler stood behind us with his mouth open, clearly convinced that the young master had now gone completely mad.

"We have a national hero in our midst, Father," Charles said loudly, while His Lordship put one hand up to his ear.

"What's that?"

Charles looked at me and nodded.

"Show him the letter from the Palace, Freddy."

I got up and passed the letter to His Lordship, who fumbled in his pocket for something.

"Pass me my spectacles!" His Lordship spoke harshly to the butler, who was waiting to serve the wine. Holding the metal-framed glasses, he read the letter.

"What's that, dear?" said Her Ladyship, who was trying to read the letter across the table.

"King George has just awarded our junior under-gardener with a Victoria Cross. I don't believe this at all."

Her Ladyship's lorgnette fell into her plate.

"Some mistake, my dear. How could our humble, junior under-gardener possibly deserve a VC?"

"Father, this was not the siege of Sevastopol in the Crimea," Charles insisted. "Nor was it Mafeking in South Africa. These were the trenches in the Somme, Mama. I have told you... Modern warfare produces new heroes... just like our very own Freddy here."

The old man passed the letter to his wife. She read it carefully and held the watermarked paper up to the light.

"This is George's paper, alright. I know the supplier in London."

She was feeling the writing paper to see if it was a fake.

"You think it's genuine, then?"

Charles smiled at me, glanced up at the ceiling and then

turned to face His Lordship.

"Father, please. Can't you just accept that Freddy here did his bit for his country, but what he did was something very special."

His Lordship turned to his wife.

"Seems he was the one who rescued your nephew from that crashed plane in no man's land, my dear. Why didn't the War Office tell us about it? They really should have let us know first."

Now the old man turned to me and smiled.

"Frederic, will you accept our apologies for being so rude?"

"Please, Sir," I reassured him, "think nothing of it. I didn't believe it myself until they sent me this letter."

His Lordship turned to his butler.

"Bring those last bottles of champagne up from the cellar... We must celebrate a national hero, and here he is in our midst, by Jove!"

Chapter 2

1930 – The grand opening of our third, and largest, garden centre

I LOOKED AT MY WATCH. I had been speaking for five minutes. One or two people in the front row appeared to be nodding off to sleep. John-Boy looked up at me and cheekily mouthed the letters F... U... C... K... M... E... N... O... W. I turned away. This was just too much. He seemed hell-bent on undermining my stately presentation today. Now I decided it was time to wake everyone up with a little joke.

"So," I said, "by the end of 1919 we had discovered a source to supply our famous patent bagged manure for purchasers to spread on their gardens in the first streets of our great garden city. Yes, ladies and gentlemen, it really was domestic sewage, suitably treated of course, and sweetened with fresh hay, heather and honey blossom..."

There were some whispers and a round of polite applause.

"...We were doing our bit to promote the cycle of nitrogen... but all in the name of economy at a time of national shortages and hardship after the Great War... My lords, ladies and gentlemen, Lady Mayoress: a boy scout asked me the other day if I could recommend a formula for success in this modern world. 'Young man,' I told him, 'only hard work and dedication to duty will lead to success in life and, as my grandma told me years ago, God bless her, remember this, young man : always go to bed early and early to rise. It will make you healthy, wealthy and wise.' ... That's the way to get on in the world today."

There was some more polite applause and I continued with the sanitised history of our horticultural endeavour. When I looked down at John-Boy, he made a point of sucking his thumb as if it was a blowjob. I quickly turned back to my notes. Of course, the actual truth was somewhat different and not for the ears of polite society. There were some things that were quite unsuitable for this afternoon's audience to hear, or to print in the Garden City Gazette. The actual truth was far too shocking and just had to be kept out of the papers.

1919

After dinner, Charles pushed me up the back stairs. My head was starting to spin after so much champagne. I just wasn't used to it. He led me through his door and locked it. I fell backwards onto the bed.

"Allow me," he said, untying my shoes. "These are mine, after all... "

I lay staring up at the canopy of the four-poster bed. He was pulling at my trousers. I was too drunk to protest.

"...I must say, Freddy. My clothes look so much better on you because you have the figure for them... As my mother might say, clothes really maketh the man."

"It must be all that hard work in the garden," I giggled.

He gently pulled off my pants.

"Gosh, you are so pretty... You look better still without any clothes at all... "

I said nothing as he started to kiss my thighs and tenderly around my groin. Then he took my prick in his mouth and started to lick my balls. I was getting hotter and sat up to take off the rest of my clothes.

"...Allow me. I insist... Stand up, Freddy."

I rose unsteadily to my feet. The walls were swaying about.

"I'm not used to champagne," I giggled as he undid the buttons of my shirt. I put my hands on his shoulders to steady myself. The shirt fell to the floor. He pulled my vest over my head. He stood back and looked at me.

"Anything wrong?" I asked, feeling rather dizzy.

"Nothing, Freddy. Absolutely nothing... I just can't believe this... You are so beautiful, just like him."

I smiled and sank backwards onto the bed again with my legs dangling over the edge. He placed his hands on my knees and pushed my legs apart and then started to rub the insides of my thighs.

"You have the most beautiful round thighs... "

He pushed my knees up into the air.

"...And the most beautiful round bottom."

He started to flick his tongue between my buttocks. My head was still spinning and I lay back on the eiderdown as he moved his hands between my legs to hold them further apart. I put my feet over his shoulders and raised my bottom up off the bed. He cupped my buttocks in his hands and held them apart.

"Have you ever been fucked, Freddy?"

I groaned but said nothing.

"I want to fuck you! Please? ... I don't mean rape. I mean a gentle, tender-hearted fucking."

I lifted my legs up off his back and supported my hips with my hands and rolled back so that my legs stretched up to the canopy over the bed.

"I'm going to fuck you, Freddy... "

He rubbed his nose between my buttocks and then licked my balls with his tongue.

"...I'm going to fuck you very gently."

Suddenly I seemed to come to my senses.

"I'm not ready for sex, Charles. It is just too soon."

"Well then...sometime, please. We could have fun."

He put one hand around my waist to grab my erection. I hooked my feet over the wooden canopy rail over the four-poster bed and started to lift myself up higher and moved my feet further apart so I was almost hanging upside down in a 'Y' shape. He thrust his face between my parted buttocks. I was almost on the point of ejaculation. Suddenly the canopy rail collapsed and I fell back in a heap, his head still buried between my thighs. He sat back, out of breath.

"Now for breaking my bed, you will get a good seeing-to, whether you want it or not."

Again he saluted me. All I could do was giggle and turn over to lie face down on the eiderdown. I watched him as he threw off all his clothes and left them scattered across the floor. He was slimmer and more handsome than I had imagined and his prick rose to attention as if that too was still on parade. I tried to sit up again and look at him.

"Look, Freddy," he said, "now, my Master Charles is saluting you."

"I'm not ready, Charles, honestly. One day perhaps. I've only just got to know you."

He sat back and sighed.

"Yes, I used to walk past you in the garden before the war. You were always with Bill, the old gardener."

"Charles, it would be too much, too soon."

"I'm rushing you..."

"Can you wait?" I muttered while the world spun around me. "I just need more time. Everything has happened so fast."

"Yes, Freddy, my dear friend, of course, but sleep here with me tonight, please. I need you. Your moment has come. I really need you."

Peace celebrations were arranged across Britain on 19 July 1919 but in our village at least, a sudden bout of influenza amongst children in the local school sent the village doctor into another state of panic. So, only a commemorative service was held in the parish church and the village fete was postponed because of fears of another epidemic spreading through the community. By September the influenza had subsided and the vicar agreed that the right moment had arrived. This grand occasion would be held on a Saturday afternoon in aid of his local War Memorial Fund. Our village fete would be graced by His Lordship and opened by Her Ladyship. She would cut a red, white and blue ribbon to unveil a plaster model of the war memorial to be placed on the village green when enough money had been raised. Soon the entertainment committee was reconvened. A marquee was hired. A steam fair with a roundabout, a coconut shy and a guess-the-weight-of-the-pig attraction were all arranged. There would be prizes for a fancy-dress competition. So everyone had high hopes that the target for the vicar's fund would be achieved in one day.

I decided to call in to see my grandma, who still lived in the village. She had been ill with the flu but had survived, unlike her close friend next door, whose funeral only took place the week before. I knocked but found that the front door of her cottage was open.

"Hello, Fred, is that you?"

The parlour was small and cramped. Grandma still lay on her bed, which I had brought downstairs while she recovered. She sat up as I closed the door behind me.

"Hello, Gran," I said, "how are you feeling today, then? I wondered if you wanted to go to the fair on the green tomorrow. Her Ladyship will unveil the model of the war memorial, you know."

I sat down on the chair by her bed.

"Do you think I should? The doctor doesn't know if my flu is still infectious. Best that I stay indoors, Fred, my lad. I don't want any of the boy scouts to catch it."

I took her hand and got the letter from the Palace out of my pocket to pass to her. She reached for her reading glasses and read it once, glanced at me and then read it once more.

"Oh Fred... What's this? Your father would have been so

proud. I had a card from them all in Canada. Did you see it?"

"Yes, Grandma, you showed me last week."

I told her all about the crashed plane in no man's land and the injured officer, who turned out to be a relation of King George V.

"Well, Fred, now what? You've got the rest of your life ahead of you. What are you now, twenty-two...?"

I nodded.

"...You've come home to His Lordship's estate. I bet the garden is a mess. Even the old gardener died of this dreadful flu, you know."

Now I looked at her and smiled. She had always been my favourite relative and much closer than either of my parents, who had never seemed to have much time for me. Anyway, they now lived in Canada.

"You and I, Grandma, we were made of sterner stuff. I survived the trenches of the Somme and you are getting over your nasty flu now."

"But I hear that His Lordship's son is still suffering from shellshock. What do you think, then, Fred? Have you met him yet?"

"Yes, Grandma. Master Charles has been talking to me in the greenhouse. We've started playing chess together."

"And who wins, then? I bet you tactfully allow him to win – the right of the landed gentry to rule the chessboard and this community, just as they have for generations."

"No, Grandma, I won fair and square."

"Good for you, Fred. Now make me a cup of tea, would you, love?"

I got up to put the kettle on the stove and stoked up the fire. Quite unconsciously I started to whistle.

"You sound happy today," she laughed. "I know...my grandson has found someone at last! I can tell by the twinkle in your eye. Who is she – a local lass?"

I put down the coal scuttle and sat down to take her hand once more.

"Grandma, you know me too well and you are right. I have

met somebody...but I can't talk about it. Anyway, it might all be over in a week."

She looked at me over her reading glasses.

"Oh, like that is it? Well, it can't be Her Ladyship's daughter. She got married to some Wall Street financier in America. No English boys round here good enough, I suppose... What a stuck-up little missy that one used to be! ... I should know, I ran the village school."

I smiled and patted her hand.

"...Well," she sighed, "I hope she is worth it, whoever it is. Fancy you getting the Victoria Cross, though..."

She glanced up at a sepia photo hanging over the fireplace. It showed my grandfather in his Royal Navy official portrait of 1900.

"...Fred, your grandpa would have been so proud of you. He got a gong from the King too, you know – look."

I got up to read the certificate in a frame on the wall beside Grandma's portrait of David Lloyd George, and then turned to her once more.

"Grandma, I have to go. You know Her Ladyship's telephone number, don't you now? She said it is quite all right for you to telephone the Big House if you need me urgently. Or send the boy from next door to get me. I'll probably be in the greenhouse."

"Do you have to go so soon? But pour me a cup of tea, first, Fred dear... Sure you won't stop a moment longer?"

"Things to do, Grandma. Have you got enough cash handy to last the week?"

"Yes, thanks to our David Lloyd George I've got my old-age pension now...and my own vote. So have you, Fred, now you're over twenty-one."

She waved at the portrait of her great hero of the working classes, which was nailed to the wall above her head.

"...Your grandpa never lived long enough to see the day we would all get old-age pensions, you know. I don't think he would ever have believed the British Government might start giving money away at the village post office...thanks to our wonderful Prime Minister..."

She sighed and looked at me as I hesitated.

"...Oh," she added, "I see it now. Mustn't keep the young lady waiting. Bring her to tea here soon, Fred, my love. I'd really like to meet her. Then I can write to your mum and dad in Canada and tell them what I think of your secret beloved. I bet she's pretty – just like you."

I leaned forward to kiss my grandma.

"It is not quite like that, you see, Grandma."

I passed her the cup of tea and went to the door.

"Why isn't it like that, Fred?"

I smiled at her and went out, closing the door behind me.

Charles decided that I should go with him to the village fair and we would both be in disguise, in case any questions were asked. He would be dressed as Lawrence of Arabia and I would wear an old smock with XXX painted on the front. He found a suitable old felt hat at the back of the barn for me to wear and I had a wheat straw to suck to give an air of verisimilitude. Footwear was no problem. My old gardening boots looked quite the thing when my breeches were tied up with string around my knees. Charles was absolutely certain we would win both first and second prizes. He never wondered whether the great T. E. Lawrence was ever likely to be seen side by side with a humble, English country bumpkin in Arabia, but this did mark the start of his recovery from shellshock. For the first time in my life, somebody would be taking me out as his partner in public, even if we were both unrecognisable. I was immensely flattered by Charles' concern and this marked the start of a new chapter in my life.

So the great day arrived but I looked at the sky. I could not remember ever seeing such ominous black clouds since my time in the trenches of the Somme. By lunchtime, the wind got up and extra tent pegs had to be hammered into the ground around the marquee. A local brass band turned up in a lorry and set up their instruments. The great and the good started to arrive in motorcars. Someone drew up with a pony and trap. They all pointed at the sky and said everything would be all right because there was a patch of blue on the horizon.

However, just as Her Ladyship stepped forward to cut the red, white and blue ribbon, the heavens opened and a hailstorm sent everyone running in search of cover. Charles' magnificent costume started to look like wet laundry on the washing line and I suggested the two of us should shelter in my cottage, which stood just across the green. There we waited, gazing out of the window, thinking the storm would pass, but it only got worse. The sky grew darker and I lit my oil lamp while the young master stared at me, just as he had done on that first day. I lit the log fire in my tiny fireplace and we managed to dry out over another hot cup of tea. He got very excited and came to put his arms around my shoulders.

"Freddy, why don't we both move in here – just you and I? ...Then we might be happy together."

I turned to him, quite amazed at this suggestion.

"His Lordship's son and heir living with the gardener from the estate? How long would that last, do you think? The Women's Institute would be out in force, protesting on the village green. Questions would be asked."

"Oh, well, it was a nice idea, Freddy. Please take off that ridiculous old smock. You are much too beautiful for anything like that. I'm sorry I ever thought of it."

"Well, Charles," I said. "I don't think Lawrence of Arabia would even have been seen dead in your outfit, now the rain's got at it. You look more like a squashed cabbage leaf than His Lordship's son and heir."

"You need a good spanking, Freddy!"

He had never been in my tied cottage before. Of course he wanted to see the cellar. So, he followed me down the steps as I went ahead, carrying the old oil lamp.

"Careful," I warned. "They are a bit slippery. It is a bit damp down here."

He sat down on the steps at the bottom and watched as I

went round lighting some candles I had placed around the walls.

"It looks quite pretty... " he said, smiling.

I took off my shirt and picked up some dumb-bells.

"... Pretty, like you, Freddy."

"I usually practice naked," I said. "Like the gymnasts in Greek or Roman times."

"Go ahead... "

I went up the steps to lock the cellar door. He watched intently as I stripped off the rest of my clothes and did some handstands against the cellar wall. Then I did some sit-ups on the exercise bench, followed by some slow arm-curls with the weights.

"Gosh... So that's how you keep in good shape now... "

I started to do some press-ups in front of him. He put his foot out to rub my bottom.

"Fancy a good fuck, do you? Watching your beautiful arse cheeks makes me want to fuck you again and again, Freddy."

I smiled and got up again.

"I think it could spoil everything," I insisted. "One day, but not yet."

"What about down here? Let's think of all the different positions you could hold while I fuck you... "

"A handstand?"

"We could try that one... "

"Lying on my back on the exercise bench?"

"Yes, that one, too... "

"Hanging by my feet from the ceiling... I've put straps up there... "

I pointed.

"Oh, like my four-poster bed, but you did break the canopy rail... "

"Sorry."

"No, I'll have it fixed back with proper brackets so it is stronger... just for you. You really must do that again. I would enjoy fucking you when you are hanging upside down... "

I did a handstand and put my feet into the straps on the

ceiling so I could take my hands off the ground.

"Gosh!"

"Take hold on my feet, Charles."

"I know what you need first... after breaking my bed... "

"What's that, then?"

"Your pert buttocks need a good, hard spanking... "

"Go on, then!"

"Can I?"

I nodded and watched as he went round behind me and started to rub his hands around my buttocks.

"Mm, gorgeous. I'm going to spank you... "

I closed my eyes. I had never been spanked before while hanging upside down from the ceiling. He put the fingers of his left hand between my buttocks to hold them apart and started to smack each one alternately.

"Freddy, you are sex on legs!"

He stopped smacking me and started to massage my legs. I groaned, preparing myself for a slap, but he stooped to pick up a leather strap lying on the floor.

"Not yet, Sir!" I insisted. "I'm not ready for that either... not yet... "

He smiled and laid the strap down again as I lowered myself from the ceiling to stand on the floor.

"Sorry, Freddy. Come and sleep with me again tonight? I haven't slept like that for ages. It was so lovely curled around you."

I turned round as I was pulling my vest over my head and smiled at him.

"Do you think we should?"

"Come at midnight. I'll wait for you by the door at the bottom of the back stairs. They'll all be in bed by then... "

Now, for the first time he kissed me on the mouth.

I felt like a burglar creeping across the lawn to the rear of the Big House that night. The back door was still closed when I arrived, so I waited in the shrubbery. In the distance the village clock struck twelve and then a shaft of light appeared across the grass. I crept towards the open door. Charles was in his dressing gown and slippers. He locked the door behind me.

"Thank you so much for coming, Freddy"

Now he kissed me tenderly on the forehead once again.

"I couldn't wait," I whispered.

He led me up the stairs to his room and locked that door too. He gestured towards two armchairs either side of the fireplace, where there was a table for a decanter and two glasses. I nodded and smiled.

"Look, don't worry," he said, putting one hand on my shoulder. "Nobody can hear us here. Everyone else's room is in the other wing of the house. Let's just relax and be happy... "

I smiled.

"...What you do for me, helping me to relax, find my feet and forget about the war and all that... Freddy, words cannot express... Listen, I love you. I shouldn't...but I really do. Now you know."

"Please, don't think about it."

He picked up a small box by the decanter on the table and handed it to me.

"I bought this to give to him... my batman... but I left it too late."

I opened the box. Inside was a jewelled tiepin. It looked expensive.

"Look," I said. "I don't think I can accept this. I'm not worthy of such a beautiful thing."

"Why not?" he insisted. "I've told you, I bought it for him. Won't you at least do me this honour... Back in 1917, I thought if I gave it to him and I was the one who got blown to pieces, he could at least keep it as a keepsake or sell it if he was short of cash ... Look, Freddy, I want you to have it... Please."

I thought for a while. I suspected it was a diamond. I had never held one in my hand before. The last few days had been something of a whirlwind. I was anxious not to appear too hasty, but I relented.

"Thank you. I will. Time for bed?"

"Not yet, Freddy. Now I need your advice... "

I sat back and waited while he poured out some of the wine and then turned to me.

"...It is my father, Freddy. He says it is time for me to get married."

"He has no right to expect that," I insisted. "This is something for you to decide, surely."

"But this is England, Freddy, and England expects every man shall do his duty..."

We sat quietly. Eventually he got up and sat down on the floor in front of me and leaned back against my legs.

"...I have decided," he said quietly. "You know, don't you? ... I have a duty to you, Freddy...You are the one I want."

I put my hand on his head and he smiled at me.

"But," I insisted, "It's not going to be easy for us, is it?"

I thought for a while.

"...Couldn't you go through with a marriage of convenience, just for his sake? ... Perhaps we could find some time together, once in a while."

"No, never! Never! Anyway, you might lose interest in me, too, Freddy."

I said nothing but continued to run my fingers through his hair. He looked up at me with another smile. At last he seemed able to relax.

"I'm going to teach you to ride, Freddy. You can have my horse. I can ride my father's mount. He won't mind. If you are with me, they won't assume I'm going off to hang myself from a tree somewhere."

We stared at one another. At least Charles was able to laugh about his attempts to commit suicide – because he loved me. Had the young master found a reason to live now?

"Yes, I'd like that, Charles."

"Would you really? I told my mother, you know. I said you were the best thing to happen to me this year. She nodded her head, Freddy. She loves you, just like I do. I really do, you know. "

"Thank you."

"Listen, Freddy. You and I could go through the rest of our lives and never find anyone else."

I said nothing but stooped down to put my hands around his shoulders.

"Bed? I'm ready... Are you up to it?"

"The canopy rail over the bed has been repaired and made stronger. You won't bring that down in a hurry!"

I had intended to leave before dawn, before everyone was awake, but realised that we had overslept. Suddenly, there was loud knocking on the door outside. Charles got up to see what it was all about while I put on some clothes. Then I heard some agitated conversation in the passageway. Charles turned to me from the doorway.

"The rain is coming through the ceiling over the grand staircase, Freddy. My father would like you to do something, if you can."

Charles was standing with the butler, who seemed very agitated and not the least surprised to see me in the young master's bedroom.

"The builders won't come, my lord," the butler complained bitterly. "I telephoned them but they say the last invoice is still outstanding. His Lordship, your father, hasn't paid them anything for months. They were most insistent, Sir."

Very soon I found myself up on the flat leaded roof of the Big House. The rain had eased off but there were large pools of water everywhere. The hanging gutter was still overflowing and water seemed to be disappearing down through a gap in the brickwork, into the house below. I had been warned that leaves often blocked the drain into the downpipe leading from the roof.

"What can you see, Frederic?"

Now Her Ladyship was leaning out from the shelter of the dormer window overlooking this section of the flat roof.

"I need something to clear away the leaves, my lady.

And there's a large dead rook or seagull that's stuck in the drainpipe."

"How about this bucket here?" I climbed over the puddles towards her while she held the bucket out through the casement.

"Frederic! Well, look at the pickle David Lloyd George has got us into! We've just had to pay this new Land Value Tax. That dreadful Welshman really has got it in for people like us. Now there's hardly anything left in the bank except my savings and I'm not spending those, no matter what His Lordship, my husband says! ...I won't do it!"

She laughed when I took hold of the bucket and reached inside for a shovel. It was rather too long to fit through the window and she chipped the paint trying to pass it to me.

"Dear Frederic, what would we do without you? We'll have to pawn the Beckstein grand piano next. It was my father's pride and joy, you know. I do wish the People newspaper could have proved their case in that juicy scandal about Lloyd George's private life. When was that? Oh yes, 1909. They said he paid twenty thousand pounds to keep his secret adultery out of the papers. Do you want me to come out and help you?"

"No, my lady, I will manage."

"I think it would have ended Lloyd George's political career before he could do so much damage to the landed gentry, you know. Now we're nearly ruined, but we're not the only ones..."

She was leaning further out of the window to see what I was doing but she carried on lecturing me about Lloyd George and his dreadful People's Budget of 1909.

"...Young man, I do hope you would never vote for a really nasty politician like that! Politicians are crafty folk, you know. Lloyd George assumed that by giving votes to people like you and me last year, it meant we would both start to vote for him and his radical politics. It all boils down to numbers of votes at the ballot box, Frederic."

"Quite possibly, my lady."

"I can see that our lovely piano will soon have to go before the rain gets into the music room as well. Please do what you can. Do you need Charles to help you clear the hanging gutter? I warn you he's no good at heights up here!"

"No, M'lady. I will manage. I've dealt with floodwater like this before – out in the trenches of the Somme."

"Oh, poor Frederic, how awful for you!"

I had to kneel down in the water to get my hands down into the drainpipe in order to remove the rotten carcass and leaves to pile them in the bucket.

"Can you do it, Frederic? Do you want me to fetch the butler to help you?"

"No, my lady."

Suddenly there was a loud gurgling noise and what was left of the leaves got sucked down into the drainpipe, followed by gallons and gallons of plunging water. I stood up again, holding the bucket.

"Well done, Frederic! You've saved the day!"

I went back to Her Ladyship and passed the bucket to her through the open window. She looked relieved but then took a look inside the bucket.

"Ugh! Maggots! So it was a large rook that blocked the drainpipe."

"I've seen dead bodies before, my lady."

"Now we'll have to wait for the plaster to dry on the walls downstairs. I'm so glad my father never lived to see the damage. He was so proud of this house... But it was the increased death duties we had to pay when he died – more implications of Lloyd George's so-called People's Budget in 1909. It was all his fault. David Lloyd George started it, I tell you, Frederic! And now the lords have had their powers trimmed with this Parliament Act, you know... Their lordships are permitted only to delay bills passed by the Commons but not to reject them."

I clambered in through the window and closed it behind me.

"... But your trousers are wet through, and your shoes. Oh dear!"

"You never saw our dugout in Flanders, my lady. I nearly got drowned in the mud down there! An exploding shell brought the earth wall down, you see."

"Oh, poor Frederic! Now give me your wet things – I insist! The butler will dry your shoes and I'll get your trousers washed and ironed... Well, if necessary, I'll do it myself. Put this coat on to hide your modesty."

She gave me the housecoat she was wearing.

After that, I gave up the idea of sneaking out of the house before dawn. The butler seemed to know exactly what was going on in the young master's bedroom during the night, but he'd served the family long enough to know how important it was to hold his tongue. A few days later he even woke us up with two cups of tea, first thing, when he knocked on the door. Charles got out of bed to unlock it.

"Excuse me, Sir," the Butler muttered. "His Lordship says the vicar has just telephoned again. The cesspit outside this house has polluted the stream running through the vicarage garden. Her Ladyship says to ask you to beg Freddy, of his goodness, to kindly see what he can do about the sewage as soon as possible. Our local vicar doesn't like it when ordure starts flowing through his garden, Sir. It is causing a dreadful stink."

"Where's the estate manager? Why can't he see to it?"

"Oh, he's no longer with us, Sir. He left on Monday – emigrating to Australia, Her Ladyship says. It's the financial situation, you know. More economies must be made. My job might be going next!"

The butler shuffled away down the corridor again. Charles leaned over me to put one cup of tea on the bedside table and then ran his fingers through my hair.

"Did you hear that...?"

I laughed and turned over. Charles kissed me tenderly and stared down directly into my eyes.

"...Freddy, you really are my dream come true."

"That's all we needed today," I said, thinking about the latest crisis outside. "But at least the state of the drains will give him some new topic to talk about – apart from you and me."

"Well, my education at Eton and Oxford never prepared me for estate management, Freddy. I learned about Latin and Greek, not effluent control. You'll have to do something. They all look to you, you know, after your triumph up on the roof. My mother has been singing your praises."

So I found myself standing beside the wrecked cesspit with Her Ladyship. She was wearing her Wellington boots and a raincoat today.

"Oh, Freddy, what a dreadful pong! No wonder the vicar doesn't like it. I suppose he will call this 'the devil's work' and shake his fist over us from the pulpit next Sunday."

We were looking at the broken wall of the cesspit, which had collapsed, allowing ordure to run down into the stream.

"It was the rain, my lady," I explained. "It just caused everything to overflow and break the earthen dam here."

She was poking at the ground with her walking stick and clearing soiled toilet paper to one side of the path.

"Now what do we do, Freddy? Well before you suggest it, I'll tell you – there's no money to pay the builders. I'm glad my father never lived to see this."

"But why was nothing done to modernise the drains, my lady? Mediaeval cesspits like this should have gone out with the ark."

"My father liked shiny new bathrooms, just like the ones in London hotels. So he ordered brass fittings for the latest patent water closets and spent his money on those in 1901. It never occurred to him to wonder what happened after he pulled the chain for the cistern to flush it all away... Yes, Freddy, my late father was a bit short-sighted, you see. You are looking at where it all ended up for the last eighteen years – no proper drains at all... What a mess! No wonder the vicar doesn't like this flowing through his garden."

She heaped up another pile of toilet paper with her walking stick.

"So, what now, my lady?"

"Oh, Freddy, please do something! You dug trenches out in France. Now is the time to dig some more!"

"But we need a proper foul sewer, my lady, lined with glazed earthenware piping, but where would it go to down there?"

I pointed down the slope towards the stream and the vicar's garden fence in the distance. There was toilet paper as far as the eye could see.

Behind me, Charles appeared, holding a spade. Her Ladyship turned to her son.

"Perhaps the local council could do something and connect us with their new sewage scheme," she suggested to him. "Well, they want us to start paying higher rates. Time for them to give us value for money, I think... Of course, His Lordship insists the town hall is a breeding ground for a lot of damned communists, probably led by Lenin or Trotsky, straight from Russia, of course. My husband seems to be obsessed with things like that these days."

Charles was staring at the scene of devastation in front of us.

"Looks like a bomb's gone off here, Mama."

She ignored him and was much more interested in my views about politics today.

"So what do you think, Freddy? Will the dreaded communism spread up here from Moscow after the Russian Revolution, two years ago in 1917? I was distantly related to the Russian royal family. It's so sad! I went to stay with them some years ago, before they were all brutally murdered, you know."

"Mama," Charles interrupted. "I think we've got more serious things to worry about here, don't you? This sewage could lead to the outbreak of disease like the dysentery we all had in the trenches."

I climbed up the slope again.

"I think you should telephone the council at once, my lady."

Her Ladyship took my arm and we walked together up the slope to the Big House, followed by Charles with his spade. She patted my hand.

"Could you talk to my husband about this? He would listen to you, you know, Freddy. If I told him what had to be done, he'd mutter something about damned suffragettes – that's me, by the way. But you know we bombed Lloyd George's house in 1913 when he was Chancellor of the Exchequer, don't you? What a pity that bomb wasn't a bigger one to do away with him, once and for all, eh, Frederic?"

When I arrived at the greenhouse the following day, there was a new note pinned to the door. I was invited to take afternoon tea with Her Ladyship at three o'clock in the summerhouse. I opened the door to enter the greenhouse, where there was a parcel on the shelf, wrapped up in brown paper and neatly tied with string. It contained an old tennis racket, a pair of white shorts, a vest and a pair of white canvas shoes. They smelled of mothballs. There was one of Her Ladyship's visiting cards with yet another pencilled note:

Just some of my late brother's things I thought you might like. Do me the honour of wearing them this afternoon, weather permitting.

I knew that money was getting tight on the estate. I had asked for a new wheelbarrow to replace the old one with a wonky wheel and nothing had happened. Now, some other staff were being let go and not replaced. Moreover, I had started sleeping with her son and this was surely grounds for dismissal, or worse. But if I was being summoned to collect my cards, this was a most unusual invitation. The weather cleared up during the day and so I did put on the tennis things and headed for the summerhouse at the time required. Here I found the butler arranging tea and cakes on a folding table. Her Ladyship waved to me.

"Ah, Frederic... Gosh...!"

She smiled, and muttered something to the butler, who bowed and walked away.

"Yes... yes, very handsome. We must be careful. They will gossip that I have taken a lover... except that you, young man, prefer the love that dares not speak its name!"

She laughed.

"My lady?"

"Do, please, sit down. Now don't look so worried... "

She pointed to the seat opposite and lifted the lid of the teapot to look inside.

"...It is not Earl Grey... well, never mind. I should have done it myself..."

She turned to me.

"...Young man, you and I must have a very serious talk... "

I coughed.

"...Yes, I know! Don't deny anything... I know all about it...!"

She started to pour milk into the cups. I had no idea what to say now.

"...Frederic, yes, I do know about the footprints in the shrubbery and the mud on the back staircase. I even know how the rail of the canopy over my son's bed was broken... "

She put down the milk jug and turned to me.

"...Tell me, can you really hang yourself upside down from your toes?"

I shifted uneasily in my chair.

"...Sorry, that was unfair... "

She lifted the teapot and started to pour out the tea.

"...Help yourself to some scones and jam – I made them myself. The strawberries are the ones you grew in the garden... Oh, come now, Frederic, it's not every day a mother has the chance to talk to her son's secret lover. This really is quite exciting!"

"My lady, do you wish me to leave and find another job?"

She put down the teapot and turned to me.

"Enough of that! Now, Frederic, if I wanted you to leave,

would I have invited you to afternoon tea?"

"Perhaps not, my lady."

She reached forward to put a scone on her plate.

"Frederic, do eat something... "

I smiled.

"...Those tennis things were my brother's, you know. They fit you beautifully... I knew they would. He was like you – of the Oscar Wilde set. It runs in my family... But my father was afraid of the scandal and drove my brother abroad, where he died fighting in South Africa... But do you know how many died on our side in the fighting, which ended in May 1902, Frederic?"

"No, my lady."

"Well, I'll tell you – five thousand seven hundred and seventy-four. My brother was one of those, but sixteen thousand more died from disease. I think that was dreadful, don't you? Sixteen thousand died from the lack of proper medical care, Frederic. So, our government incompetence was staggering, just like the Crimea War, where Florence Nightingale made her mark and sorted out the problems in Scutari Hospital. It needed a woman, you see."

"We had dysentery and pneumonia in the trenches, too, my lady. I had to bury too many. In the military hospitals, English nurses did what they could. So often, my stretcher cases were beyond help... But, please, I want to forget all about the past. Now I have learned to look forward to the future and to smile at people again... It is high time to look after the living, don't you think?"

She reached forward to place a hand on my arm, and patted it.

"Yes, I do see what my son admires about you."

"Thank you, my lady!"

She withdrew her hand from my sleeve. I placed a scone on my plate and picked up the knife.

"That's not solid silver... just EPNS."

I didn't understand but smiled.

"A sign of the times," she continued. "Now in my father's

day, we had solid silver. How times have changed... "

She sighed and I spread some butter on my scone.

"...Frederic, look, what I really wanted to say is this... My son is going to need someone special... Yes, I know he will never get married. Now, are you that special person, Freddy?"

It was the first time she had ever called me Freddy.

"Now, listen, young man. Scandal must be avoided at all costs. I told you about Lloyd George, didn't I? ... Well, we haven't got twenty thousand pounds to keep your name out of the popular newspapers."

"Sorry, M'Lady."

She laughed and smiled at me.

"Well, perhaps it will never come to that. Anyway, if that horrid Lord Queensbury hadn't interfered, then Oscar Wilde might have lived happily with his lover Lord Alfred Douglas. And, if my father hadn't interfered, then my brother might still be alive. Now listen, young man, I have decided it is time to keep this thing in the family... I am going to make it your personal responsibility to ensure that no scandal – not a whiff or a rumour – comes out."

She leaned forward.

"Do you understand, young man?"

"Yes, my lady, I understand."

We sat quietly and ate our scones and jam. Her Ladyship flicked at a troublesome wasp that was buzzing around her, and changed the subject.

"Will we have a good crop of strawberries again this year?"

"I don't know, my lady. It has been so wet!"

I reached for a slice of cake.

"Listen, young man," she said, looking at me closely. "I am going to trust you. There's no alternative, but we can't have any more muddy footprints up the back stairs. That just will not do, will it?"

"Sorry, my lady."

"No, you misunderstand me. I'm not criticising!"

I said nothing.

"...You must move out of your damp little cottage. It may soon be demolished to make way for the road scheme, anyway. Why don't you come and live with us?"

I put down the plate to stare at her.

"...Oh, don't look like that... Look, dear Freddy. My son has suddenly found something to live for... and that's you. I used to think he might find a young lady to love and to take care of him but, well, Freddy..."

I smiled at her and for the first time she smiled at me.

"...You have given him whatever it took to make him happy again... a raison d'etre, as the French would say... You fought for France during the war, so you must know some French. You have given him what no woman could."

"I thought His Lordship wanted grandchildren – that's what Charles is afraid of."

"My husband has got grandchildren – lots of them – in America. My daughter has an enormous family. We may be going out there to stay with them soon, when my son gets better, and that may well be up to you, Freddy. Once His Lordship, my husband, sees all his American grandchildren again, I think he will take the pressure off my son to get married, don't you?"

I put my plate down again.

"Please have some cake, Freddy. I made it myself, specially for you, you know."

"Thank you, my lady."

"My husband may be selling half of the estate to the developers for new housing on the other side of this new trunk road everyone is talking about. Your cottage will just have to go anyway... They call it progress. Well, the motor car is no longer preceded by a man with a red flag, is it? Now everybody wants one and Henry Ford will make sure that his production lines produce Model Ts that are cheap enough for anyone to buy... And this new Minister of Transport is duty-bound to improve the British network of public roads, no matter what my husband might have to say about it in the

House of Lords."

Her Ladyship waved her hand in the air as if she was appealing to the old guard in the Upper House. I put some cake on my plate.

"...Well, Freddy, will you come and live with us... to look after my son, day and night? If you sleep with him – that is what he wants, after all – nobody would need to know, except me. The two of you could have the old nursery in the west wing. There are two rooms with an interconnecting door, where nanny used to look after us. You didn't know that, did you? This house has been in the family a long time, you see."

"What would His Lordship have to say about that, my lady?"

"The doctors have recommended my son should find a loving relationship... Frederic, there are things you really must know. That business with the gun... Well, there have been other suicide attempts. My son has only just started to recover, thanks to you. The doctors prescribed drugs, sedatives, sleeping pills and so on, but you have done more good than any of them, and so fast."

"Thank you, my lady."

"Now, what with your Victoria Cross – yes, I telephoned the Palace and asked, just to make sure, you understand. They confirmed that everything is genuine and you really are a national hero, unlike my son."

"May I have another slice of cake?"

She waved at it.

"Frederic, will you do us the honour of coming to live in the Big House... ? Even my husband has commented on the difference you have made to his son... 'That boy's like a new man, I tell you. Must be the pills that new doctor has given him! Jolly good, what?'"

Now she mimicked His Lordship's pompous voice beautifully and we both laughed.

"...Only, he doesn't know where you fit into all this, does he, Freddy...?"

She patted my knee again and smiled.

"Well, what do you think? ... Needless to say, the garden will still need your attentions during the day, but you can eat in the hall with us and stay with my son all night and nobody will know... If anyone asks I will say you are doing extra work as his attendant. I'm sure they will understand, that is, if it is really any of their business."

"I'd like that, my lady. I really think he loves me."

"And what about you, then, Freddy? No girlfriend in the village? No simpering sweetheart to bring you a ploughman's lunch – all tied up in a pretty, pink ribbon – for you to munch together under the old oak tree." She laughed. Clearly, she already knew the truth about my non-existent love life.

"There has been nobody, Ma'am...until now."

She smiled at me, but then thought of something new.

"And one other thing."

"Yes, Ma'am?"

"Do you know anything about motor cars? There's something wrong with the old Rolls Royce. The chauffeur swings the starting handle but often nothing happens. He says we need to get the local automobile engineer to service it but there's no money to pay for anything like that. Well, it was the Land Value Tax, you know. Anyway Lloyd George has put up the tax on petrol..."

"Yes, you told me all about it, Ma'am."

"Did I?"

"When you and I cleared the dead rook out of the downpipe up on the roof."

"Oh yes. Let's hope we get some hot weather to dry out all the plaster downstairs. Now, Freddy, about the Rolls Royce – could you help the chauffeur to get it to start? What do you know about the ignition system, fuel supplies and dirt in the carburettor?"

"I used to drive the staff car for my second officer, Ma'am, after my first officer died. I went on a special Army training course out in France."

"Did you, by Jove?"

"Yes, we had to know what to do if it broke down and how

to get it started on the battlefield."

"What kind of car was that then, Freddy – some clapped-out old Ford truck or a Sentinel steam wagon?"

"Oh no, Ma'am. It was a Rolls Royce Silver Ghost. My second officer had it shipped out from England – it was his own, you see. He didn't like the standard Army staff cars. Unfortunately, the Rolls shone so brightly in the sun, being bright silver paintwork, the German gunners used it for target practice. We had several narrow escapes!"

"What fascinating stories you have to tell, Freddy. No wonder my son loves you so much! He really does, you know!"

"But one day some of our chaps poured sugar in the petrol tank. It was April the first, you see. Oh dear, the Rolls broke down!"

Her Ladyship was trying to remember something.

"Oh, of course, Freddy. Sugar caused the sparking plugs to soot up, I remember! I watched my brother clean the spark plug of his motorcycle. I looked and learned, you see. Now His Lordship thinks I'm just a silly, ignorant woman with anarchist tendencies... like throwing another bomb at Lloyd George, probably."

She patted me on the arm again and I continued to talk about my experience with the Rolls Royce that broke down.

"Well, my lady, it took me a while to find out what was wrong with my officer's car, but in the end I did get it started before the next bombardment began. After that, I fitted a locking petrol cap to prevent any more sabotage."

She stared at me with her mouth open.

"Well now, Freddy, you don't say! You know His Lordship's chauffeur is about to retire. Anyway, he knows more about horses. He's been here since my father's time. He used to be the groom."

"I did hear some talk, Ma'am."

"Could you take over, Freddy?"

"Me, Your Ladyship?"

"Yes, to get the Rolls Royce going again and drive it for

me and His Lordship. Your Army training course might come in handy. I think there's dirt in the carburettor. His Lordship says I cannot possibly know anything about these things. But that's what I think, anyway. My brother's motor-cycle was always getting blockages in the carburettor. He had a two-and-a-quarter horsepower tricycle, you know. I still remember. He paid sixty-four pounds in 1901 for the Country Gentlemen's Association to supply it. I even learned to ride the thing! ...Well, I tell you, Freddy, it was so exciting! That is, until my father found out – then I got banned! I was only allowed to ride my horse after that."

"I'll do what I can, Ma'am."

"Good! Bless you, Freddy...Take some of the cake with you."

She got up and brushed the crumbs off her dress.

"By the way, could you have a look at the old tennis court? Tell me how much it will cost to get the net working again. You must learn to play tennis with my son – to get him active and moving about again, like the doctor said. You never know, I might even be tempted to get my old tennis outfit out from all the mothballs."

"I will look forward to seeing it, my lady."

"Can you actually play tennis, Freddy?"

"Yes, Ma'am. Out in France, my officer was billeted in a magnificent commandeered chateau. There was a tennis court right outside. I learned to play tennis there, you know, during quiet times at the front line. The doctor recommended it after I was wounded in my leg."

"Where? Show me, Freddy!"

"I can't, Ma'am. It would be rude!"

She laughed and tapped me on the arm

"My son, now... Does he know where your war wound is?"

"Yes, my lady."

"But he sees you naked all night, I know. What a lucky boy! Tell me, young man. Is Charles really any good in bed? That bit didn't get shot away or anything...? You should know...!"

I laughed but did not know what to say now. She'd completely taken the wind out of my sails. I'd heard about emancipated women but, really! To hear such language from Her Ladyship! I just smiled.

"...Only, you are too polite to tell me to mind my own business... Do you know, Frederic? If I were younger and you were looking for a wife... So many young men of your generation were killed in the war – the lost generation, they call it. Really handsome young men like you have become the latest national shortage! You could take your pick of the young ladies of England, if you wanted – yes, even the most glamorous debutante presented at court this year. That is, if you didn't prefer the love that dares not speak its name."

By now, I realised that it was in her nature to be like this. She actually approved of me.

"I'll take that as a compliment, my lady."

"And I'll tell you something else. Back in 1903 I even joined lovely Emmeline Pankhurst and her Women's Social and Political Union – that is until my father found out. Well, Freddy, he nearly disowned me and threw me out on the street! I had to give it up, just like riding the motorcycle..."

Now another wasp was buzzing around me. I flicked at it.

"...Anyway, Freddy, Papa died before he could stop me becoming a militant suffragette. But the point is, Freddy, men seem to be making such a big mess of the world. I'm so glad that Lady Nancy Astor has stepped forward to become England's first woman MP, hopefully representing Plymouth in the by-election. Well, I ask you, if it had been left to the women of England and Germany, would we really have gone to war in 1914? And what exactly has really been achieved?"

"Vast acres of gravestones, my lady. I helped to bury too many."

I sniffed. She placed her hand on my knee again.

"Yes, I know. I'm insensitive and often speak my mind inappropriately. Listen, if you and my son really love each other, then...well, you and I can at least be honest with one another. His doctor said only yesterday just how much more confident Charles has suddenly become – less withdrawn, less gloomy, less depressed about everything. It is you, isn't it? He's found someone to live for and somebody to love. I'm glad it was you, Freddy – someone we can trust – not some ignorant farm boy who will sell his sensational story to the newspapers."

"Thank you, Ma'am."

"So handsome. You are every woman's dream but they just don't know the truth, do they? And that is how it must remain... Freddy...another thing, my brother used to use one of the attic rooms as his gymnasium. Heaven knows whether any of that old equipment is still any use to you, but why don't you have a look? Get Charles to take you up there and see – but watch out the leather straps won't snap with age in case you might be tempted to hang upside down from the ceiling. It even has gas lighting... Anyway, it might be more comfortable than your damp cellar."

She knew it all. I had no secrets left.

"Thank you, my lady."

The butler appeared behind us with a telegram on a tray. She took hold of it and waved him away again.

"I hate these things, Freddy. I always assume they contain more bad news – just like the war..."

She read it carefully and turned to me again.

"This is from my nephew, yes, the one you rescued from his crashed plane in no man's land. He's coming here tomorrow to see you. He wants to meet you face-to-face at last. He says he owes you just about everything – because you, alone, bothered to save his life..."

I must have looked shocked.

"But how should I address him, my lady? Now do I say 'Highness', 'Your Honour' or just plain 'Sir'? Should I still salute him and remember the conventions of Army discipline?"

"Well, I talked to him on the telephone the other day. He wants you to call him John. Well, that's his name. Can you cope with that? He doesn't like ceremony. He says good men who served in the battlefields are of one class. He certainly speaks highly of you, even though you've never been formally introduced..."

She looked at me.

"... Freddy, now what's wrong?"

"I just don't feel worthy, Ma'am."

"Hush now! He wants to meet you, that's all."

"But what should I wear, my lady?"

"What you're wearing now... Keep it... It suits you. You have the figure for it and my son is a very lucky young man to find you in his bed. Listen Freddy, I'm so glad that you and I get on. This is a promise – if you will be honest with me, then I will be honest with you. I look back now to all the times I used to see you working in the garden before the war. I know, I never even said hello. But I did not know you then – you were just a boy. Now I do know you and I'm glad we have become friends. You know, Freddy, the war has achieved one thing at least – it has made a really gorgeous young man out of you!"

So, the following day I found myself once again sitting beside Her Ladyship on the lawn. I should have suggested that Charles might join us but he had gone to see the specialist about the results of his latest psychiatric sessions. We saw a car sweep down the driveway. An elegant young man stepped out and came towards us. His face lit up when he saw me, and started to run.

"Freddy! ...Freddy!"

I stood up as he approached, and bowed. I did not know what else to do.

I was amazed when he bowed in front of me. Now we both laughed.

"...Freddy, I had no idea. The War Office is so secretive. They wouldn't tell me anything! It was only when my aunt, here, telephoned that I knew anything about you. Why, oh why wouldn't they tell me who you were...?"

He went over to Her Ladyship and kissed her warmly.

"... My fiancée sends her greetings, Auntie."

He sat down in the seat next to mine and took my hand to shake it warmly. Instead of letting go, he kept hold of it. Her Ladyship passed him a plate.

"Have a sandwich, John."

He ignored her and just held on to my hand, staring at me.

"Dear Freddy, I have never had the chance to thank you... I told the War Office I just wanted to know who you were so I could say thanks. Look, the war is over now. It is time you learned the truth. You rescued more than me from that crashed biplane. You don't know this and if anyone asks, you never heard it from me – it is still hush-hush, you see. I was on a secret mission to deliver the latest codebook... The Kaiser's cryptographers had broken one of our secret codes – they even started to read our weather reports. High Command were all at sixes and sevens."

"I heard rumours, Sir – all of us did."

"Well, dear Freddy, I was delivering the new codebook to our front-line HQ. It was sewn into the lining of my flying jacket. You rescued that as well! That was the reason the War Office were so grateful. It could so easily have fallen into enemy hands. I tell you, Freddy, you were a national hero...but nobody was allowed to say anything about this incident until the war was over. Secret codebooks weren't supposed to be flown around in flimsy biplanes over enemy territory. Believe me, I really was in hot water. The War Office was not best pleased – at best a court martial offence, but they knew I was related to the King, you see. The result was a diplomatic problem, which had to be kept out of the newspapers... But it is all over now, thank goodness, what with the Armistice, eleventh of November last year... Now you know, Freddy. That is why your VC had to be delayed – my fault. I'm so sorry."

Her Ladyship had been listening intently. She stood up and smiled at us both.

"Fascinating! Now I'm going to make another pot of tea. Anyway, you two should have some private time together."

We watched her walk away, flicking a wasp, which was buzzing around her. John turned to smile at me again. I felt deeply honoured.

"So, you work for my aunt as a gardener... Are you happy here?"

"I've known nothing else, Sir – apart from the war."

"Oh do call me John... You of all people have that right. Well, without you, I wouldn't be here. I have no doubt of that."

"I don't know what to say."

John looked around the garden.

"How many gardeners does my aunt employ here?"

"I was one of two but the head gardener died in the flu epidemic."

"So you have to do all this on your own?"

"I'm glad to have my old job back. Others were not so lucky when they came home from the trenches. Her Ladyship made this jam with strawberries I grew in the garden over there."

"But, Freddy, she told me you learned to drive and service a Rolls staff car out in France. Look, here is my card. Call me if you want to try something new. Well, take it anyway. I'm starting my own network of motor garages – for petrol, servicing and motor car sales. I think that is the business to make money in England today and I'm already talking to Rolls Royce about a franchise in north London. We could do with good people like you with proper training. Well, anyway, please think about it."

"I'm happy here. I want to stay."

"Well, I owe you absolutely everything, Freddy. You can call in any favour, any time. That is a promise and I mean to keep it – remember that."

Her Ladyship reappeared with the teapot. She smiled at us and sat down.

"So you two have had a while to get to know each other?"

"Yes, Auntie. I've asked Freddy to come and work for me any time if he wants a change. And he must come to my wedding. Please bring him with you, Auntie. Well, without him, there would have been no wedding, only a funeral... That is if anyone had found my body before the ruddy plane blew up."

We sat quietly while Her Ladyship poured out fresh tea.

"So, John... What do you think? Doesn't Freddy look handsome? A woman in my position might be tempted to take a lover... Well, look at him – absolutely gorgeous!"

"Auntie, really, how could you? Now you know what happened to my poor mama, your sister; and our naughty gamekeeper!"

We all laughed and Her Ladyship smiled at me.

"Look, Freddy is blushing, bless him!"

"I must go, Auntie. My chauffeur is still waiting. Things to do, you know... Don't forget to bring Freddy with you to the wedding. My fiancée will never forgive you otherwise. He will be our guest of honour. He is her hero and I wish he'd come and help me to build up my Rolls Royce franchise."

John shook my hand again and dashed off to his car waiting outside.

Her Ladyship pointed at the seat and I sat down again.

"So will you be leaving us now, Freddy?"

"I must think about it, my lady. Good offers of work are hard to find these days and he gave me his card."

"Well, if my nephew is offering you better pay and more exciting work elsewhere, what right do I have to stand in your way? You have no contract here but we would all miss you, dear boy."

1930 – Grand opening of our third garden centre

The wind was getting up and making strange noises in the microphone. The people in the front row were nodding off. John-Boy yawned. He looked up to suck his thumb suggestively at me again and pointed dramatically at his watch.

Well, I never was much good at public speaking, so I picked up my notes from the improvised music stand in front of me and stuffed them in my pocket.

"My lords, ladies and gentlemen... Lady Mayoress... The time has come to ask Your Worship now, if you would, of your goodness, to take the golden scissors from this silver tray and to cut the red ribbon before the wind blows it all away."

The Mayoress's hat was about to lift off in the wind. She grabbed hold of it and stepped forward to take the scissors from the tray I held up for her. Then, while a drum rolled, the dear lady snipped at the ribbon. But nobody had checked these scissors and they proved to be rather blunt. Charles' sister seemed to be on the point of hysterics behind us.

"Sister!" she muttered. "I should have brought you some decent shears from the States!"

We ignored her and her worship tried once more without success. So, did this foretell bad luck, just like the ocean liner that promptly sank on its maiden voyage after the champagne bottle stubbornly refused to break on its prow at the launch? There was some tittering in the crowd. Now I stepped forward to hold the ribbon, to stop it escaping from the blunt blades of the scissors.

"Third time lucky!" shouted the lady mayoress into the microphone.

"About time too!" Charles' sister muttered behind us. "Do you need some more help from the Yanks again now, dear?"

Her worship politely ignored her and turned towards the crowd:

"This time I really do declare this new garden centre open, and invite everyone to help themselves to refreshments at the garden party inside."

I pulled the ribbon tight to give the scissors a helping hand. At last the ribbon was cut and fell to the ground either side of the path while the crowd cheered, just as the Garden City Band struck up 'Rule Britannia'.

So I took the lady mayoress's hand to help her down the steps from the podium.

"Who was that dreadful Yankee woman?" she asked quietly. "I don't think she likes me at all."

I took the mayoress aside.

"She's Charles' sister," I explained. "She's still a bit upset. You see, not long ago, her husband jumped out of the window..."

"To get away from her? Frederic, I'm not surprised he jumped out of the window!"

"No, you misunderstand me," I insisted. "He was a financier on Wall Street until the big Wall Street Crash, last year. His office was in a skyscraper on the twenty-seventh floor... twenty-eighth of October 1929, 'Black Monday', you know."

She stared at me as the full horror sunk in.

"Oh God, and he jumped out of the window? Poor lady – no wonder she's still feeling rather embittered. Frederic, I wish you'd warned me! But sometimes it is better not to know the whole truth, don't you think? So who was that young man sitting there, all that time, at your feet? He was the one who seemed to be expressing himself with, what one might call, Californian self-expression."

I took her worship aside so he wouldn't hear.

"John-Boy is their eldest son – he's eighteen now."

"But isn't he a bit old to suck his thumb like that?"

"He happened to be in his father's office at the time and tried to talk him out of it – on the window ledge, you know."

"Oh no!" The Mayoress gasped.

"Yes, but the ticker tape machine brought more bad news... and..."

"Oh God!"

"John-Boy has hardly spoken a word about it since then, and now follows me around everywhere like a doting admirer."

"Real life can be too shocking and we just don't know what some folk go through to make them the way they are... I think we have yet to hear the truth about the Wall Street Crash."

"His Lordship lost everything he'd invested over there."

"Frederic, I often wonder about what we read in the

English newspapers, like this business recently concerning Mahatma Gandhi in India and the British salt tax he's been protesting about. Well, didn't a tax on tea start the American War of Independence? How can we trust English newspapers to tell us the truth about Gandhi, I wonder, hey? ... Let alone the facts about what actually happened in the USA last year... Frederic, you must write a book and tell us all the truth, one day."

Charles' sister happened to be passing us. The lady mayoress grabbed her arm and smiled at her.

"Sister! Well now, Frederic really should have phoned you to say those scissors were so blunt! I bet they sell ones that really work on Fifth Avenue! We're still a bit primitive here in the old country, you know... Now let's go and see if the English can actually make a decent cup of coffee, and let me treat you to a fancy custard tart..."

She looked down and pointed at her own bright yellow dress.

"...Well, as we say over here, Honey, it takes one to know one!"

Charles' sister burst out laughing. So they went off to find the refreshments, exchanging more cheerful banter and giggling with each other.

Charles nudged me on the elbow.

"Freddy, I think you've done your best to patch up Anglo-American relations since the war. My sister still misses him, you know – just as much as I and John-Boy, here, would miss you."

I gave my top hat and my gloves to his nephew to carry and we walked off together. John-Boy seemed to have given up all hopes of sex today. He had obviously decided just to be useful now and followed us, once more in silence, to the refreshment tent.

Chapter 3

1919

AFTER SUCH AN EXCITING day, I fell asleep in my cottage. I was still wondering if I might do best to take up the offer of a job in the new Rolls Royce franchise. Charles and I had already spent several nights together and, even without penetrative sex, I'd had more peaceful nights and was feeling extra tired. So I didn't go to meet Charles at the back door on the strike of midnight from the clock over the stables as I had done before. Unfortunately, I had absolutely no idea about the consequences of this change in routine. It was three o'clock in the morning when I was awoken by loud banging on the door downstairs. Someone was calling. I opened the window to look down onto the pathway outside.

"Master Frederic, it is urgent, yes, most urgent!"

By the light of the moon I made out the face of His Lordship's butler carrying a lantern. I closed the window and went downstairs to see what it was all about. I had never before been addressed as Master Frederic and this was most intriguing.

"His Lordship wishes you to come to the Big House at once."

I found my boots plus a coat, and followed the light from his lantern.

"There is an emergency," he continued. "Everyone is most anxious about Master Charles."

Eventually we reached the back door, where Her Ladyship was waiting. She dismissed the butler, took me into the laundry and closed the door. She seemed to be shaking.

"Thank goodness!" she muttered. "Tell me, Frederic, time is short. A lot hangs on your answer to this question. Be honest with me now – do you really love my son?"

"Yes, I do, my lady," I said without hesitation.

"Well, now is your chance to prove it, young man... "

I leaned back against the mangle. She came closer.

"...Charles has built himself a bunker under the dining table. He says the Hun are arriving any moment. He's been in the Gun Room. There's a lot of ammunition missing. We think he's got a rifle and a shotgun with him under the table. I'm afraid he's gone mad. We called the doctor, who says it is now time to sign the papers."

She sniffed.

"What papers, my lady?"

"To have him confined to the lunatic asylum... But the doctor needs two signatures, so he's gone off in his car to fetch another doctor in the next town, in order to declare Charles insane... Now, Frederic, you must decide if you really want him, then you've got to get him out from his bunker before the straitjacket is fitted on him. If you don't, then he will probably be declared legally insane and confined in the asylum for the rest of his life... This is no joke, Freddy. Yes, I know you've done your best for him."

"I don't believe it, my lady. He was alright when I saw him last."

"Look! You must believe it. If you are as brave as the Palace says you are, it is up to you to get him out, but I warn you, the shotgun is primed. He's already fired it at his father but fortunately he missed... Charles never was a crack shot."

"How long have I got?"

"I don't know how long it will take the doctor to drive into the town, find his colleague and come back again."

"Half an hour at most... so we've got to be quick."

"You'll try then?"

"Yes, my lady."

"Good boy."

I followed her up the stairs and along the corridor to the dining hall, where His Lordship was sitting on a chair by the door. He was now wearing the magnificent German helmet from Charles' collection. Somehow, I didn't think this was such a good idea under the circumstances – not that it was my duty to comment. I was considering the effect this might have on someone bordering on insanity.

"Looks good, doesn't it?" His Lordship said, tightening the chin strap. "Reminds me of my time out in Africa, what? ... Well, I thought it was better than nothing."

"Frederic is going to try to get Charles out," his wife whispered to him.

"What will you do?" he asked me quietly.

"There is only one way," I replied. "Charles won't fire the gun at a naked man."

His Lordship glanced at his wife.

"Now what, Frederic? ... I warn you, Charles says he's got a live German grenade with him under the table but I think the pin is stuck – probably rusty, you know. Well, you've got to be quick."

"Pardon me if I strip," I said, taking off my coat.

Instead of leaving, even Her Ladyship stayed put. I ignored them both.

"Are the lights on in there? He must see me before he fires the gun or tosses that grenade... He needs to see that I am obviously not in uniform."

"Now I follow," His Lordship looked up. "Good idea... Yes, the lights are on."

"Do you think this will work?" Her Ladyship asked, looking worried. "Shouldn't you have some sort of shield to protect you?"

"Hush, my dear," His Lordship muttered, turning back to his wife. "Frederic knows Charles so much better than we do."

I ignored them and finished taking off all my clothes. I opened the door of the dining hall slowly. Her Ladyship let out a deep sigh.

"Charles?" I said loudly.

"Who's that?"

"It's me. Freddy."

I pushed the door right open and looked under the dining table. At once I saw a double-barrelled shotgun pointing at me through the piles of furniture and cushions heaped beneath the table. I remained in the doorway, where he could see me.

"The Germans are coming, Freddy. Get back!"

"No, Charles... the war is over. It's 1919... we talked about it, remember?"

"Come closer."

I stepped through the doorway and moved slowly towards the gun barrels.

"Why aren't you in uniform, Freddy? Where's your helmet?"

I moved much closer so he could take a better look. Halfway along the table he had left an opening in his bunker. I didn't think he would be able to shoot me if I were to shelter in there. I played for time.

"Charles, are you listening?"

"I hear you, Freddy."

"I tell you, the war is over. The Germans have signed the Armistice. We don't need to shoot them any more. Do you understand?"

"It must be one of their tricks, I tell you... There's a Hun in a German helmet right outside the door there."

"In that case, Charles, I shall need to take cover with you. Will you let me in?"

A pile of cushions was moved aside. I crawled into the space. Inside the makeshift bunker a hurricane lamp was turned down low but I could see Charles in full British Army uniform. He was still holding the shotgun but it was fortunately pointing outside. The rifle lay at his side next to a box of ammunition.

"Hello, Freddy, where have you been?"

"I've just got back from the river," I whispered. "I've been diving off the railway bridge. The others are still splashing about... They will be here soon... You gave us permission to bathe, Sir."

I moved closer to Charles so he could see me better by the light from the lamp.

"Gosh, Freddy. You are so beautiful."

I put my arm on his shoulder.

"Come to bed please, Charles. The war is over, I tell you... Let me take the shotgun."

"Is the war over now? Then, tell me, why is that man out there wearing a German helmet?"

I pointed at the loaded shotgun.

"Pass me that thing, Charles. I'll clean the gun and oil it for you."

"No, we've got to defend our position to stop the Hun breaking through the line."

He picked up the old blunderbuss from the Gun Room, which lay on the floor between us. I wasn't expecting this and had underestimated just how disturbed Charles could become when he was so upset. I sat back to think for a moment. What was my virginity worth today? If he had fired the gun at me, I might have been dead by now. I shuffled closer to him.

"I'm ready, Charles. I'm ready for you."

"Do you think you could throw this hand grenade in their German position, then? I thought I'd give the Hun a taste of their own medicine."

Charles pointed at a rusty German grenade behind him.

"No," I said, "I want you to fuck me! You've wanted to do it for ages. Now is the time, Charles."

He was slowly coming to his senses at last. I put my arms around him and he smiled.

"Gosh! Has my mother seen you like that with no clothes on?"

"Come to bed, Charles, please. I want you to fuck me."

"Can I? You've always said no before."

He sat back. I had shocked his mind back to reality. He

looked around us at his construction of cushions under the dining table.

"What have I done, Freddy? It is 1919. The war is over, as you said. So it is time to turn the swords back into ploughshares. Who wrote that – Shakespeare?"

"Come to bed, Charles."

"Have I told you how beautiful you are, Freddy? But they told me at dinner that you might be going to work for my cousin. My father said it was none of my business what you did with your life. That's why I was going to toss this grenade at him, Freddy. He was so rude.'"

I was trying to back out through the gap in the cushions, dragging both of the guns as well. At the mention of a grenade I froze.

"What have you done with it?"

"This one, Freddy, I brought back from France?"

"Yes."

"Well I tried to pull the pin out but it has jammed."

I retreated into the makeshift bunker again, where Charles held the rusty grenade and was trying to pull out the pin once more. I shuddered. We were both staring death in the face. Fortunately, the rusty pin was still jammed.

"Charles! Give me that!"

"Freddy...do you know where the Hun is hiding?"

"Charles, give me that grenade...carefully now!"

He passed me a rusty lump of metal. This was no replica and I did what I could to hold the pin in place while I backed out through the cushions.

"Charles, stay here and secure the gun post, just as HQ ordered."

"What are you going to do with that grenade now?"

"I'm going to throw it outside."

"The Hun can't have gone far, Freddy."

"Be quiet, Charles, or the Hun will hear you!"

I took a run for the door of the dining hall. Suddenly it seemed to be so far away and I shouted through the door.

"Open this door, my lord! I'm coming out."

The door opened slowly.

"Quick, my lady, open that window overlooking the garden! This thing could go off at any minute now!"

Her Ladyship struggled with the window latch. Her husband reached forward to wrench the handle open. I hurled the grenade outside. There was stony silence.

"Get down, my lady! Stand back from the window, my lord."

We waited. His Lordship stepped forward again.

"It must have been a dud..."

Suddenly there was an explosion outside. The broken glass from the window flew in. We all dived to the floor.

"Good God!" muttered His Lordship. "Now what, Frederic?"

"That was no dud, my lord. There may be others, I don't know. Now I must go back and bring out the guns. And please take off that helmet, Sir. It has persuaded Charles that you are the Kaiser himself."

"Oh yes, how silly of me, Frederic! I never thought."

I opened the door into the dining hall again. The cushions under the table were pushed aside.

"Freddy, is that you? Is the Hun dead now?"

"Are there any more German grenades, Charles?"

"No, Freddy, that was the only one."

"Are you sure?"

"Yes, Freddy. These guns in here need cleaning, I think. "

I approached more cautiously this time, wondering if Charles had gone insane at last, but I could not see gun barrels pointing at me any more and relaxed.

"Come to bed, Charles... Will you let me in?"

Suddenly Charles burst into tears.

"Oh, Freddy, what have I done?"

I put my arms around him and he sobbed on my shoulder. I reached for the guns behind him. In the darkness I had no idea whether they were loaded and primed but took another chance and grabbed them both.

"Where are you going now, Freddy?"

"Stay there!" I shouted.

Slowly I got up while he was still kneeling under the table. I intended to make a rush for the door with the guns.

"Freddy, what about this Mills bomb, then?"

I froze.

"Charles?"

"Yes, Freddy."

"You said there were no more German grenades."

"This Mills bomb is one of ours – much better kit than the Huns' stuff. These never fail to go off properly."

I retreated backwards under the table. Charles took the Mills bomb out of its wooden case to pass it to me. I turned it over and stared at the saw-tooth patterns invented by Sir William Mills to make deadly shrapnel that might have ripped our flesh to ribbons at any minute. Fortunately, Charles hadn't tampered with this one, nor had it been armed, so it was safe. I sighed with relief.

"Oh God, Charles. You could have blown up half the house. What were you thinking of, for goodness sake? Best to replace this thing in its protective casing again."

I was staring death in the face once more. Charles passed me the wooden case and I carefully replaced the bomb inside. Then I grabbed both the guns by the barrels in one hand and the Mills bomb in the other. This wasn't easy but I didn't trust Charles' fevered mind not to regress to trench warfare again. Then I made a dash for the doorway, dragging the guns to point away from me. His Lordship was now watching us.

"This Mills bomb here is safe, my lord."

He passed it to Her Ladyship to take hold of while I passed him both the guns. She was staring in fascination at the lethal package in her hands.

"Don't drop that, my lady," I insisted. "It might be the last thing you do."

I thought she would be terrified of it but she held the box confidently in her hands, while His Lordship rushed off down the corridor to lock up the firearms in the Gun Room.

"Best to lock this bomb up in the safe, Freddy," she whispered. "I'll see to it. You forget, I've dealt with bombs before... I've got a confession for you..."

She waited a moment in case her husband was about to return.

"...Listen, Freddy, I was the brains behind the one that Mrs Pankhurst's suffragettes tossed at Lloyd George's house back in 1913. Yes, I was the one who got away from the police! ... Just our little secret, young man..."

She'd completely taken the wind out of my sails and I had no idea how to respond to this. She looked at the Mills bomb.

"...I wish we'd had one of these. This might have done the job properly. Mine only broke a few windows of Lloyd George's residence. Now go and get Charles out of there, then take him to bed, Freddy!"

Her Ladyship pointed at the dining room. I walked towards the door slowly, wondering if her son had now found anything worse under the table to throw at us but he was standing inside, watching everything.

"Do, please, take him to bed, Freddy, for God's sake," Her Ladyship said loudly.

She smiled as I led Charles out through the door.

"Look, Mother, doesn't Freddy look beautiful, so incredibly handsome – just like a Greek hero in the arena – don't you think?"

In the emergency I had actually forgotten I was completely naked.

"So," she sighed, "are you Freddy's Achilles' heel, then...?"

I had no idea what she meant by this. My education did not include the classics.

"...You are very lucky, Charles," she added. "You really do not know how lucky you have been."

Now I pushed Charles ahead of me and stood beside Her Ladyship, who seemed not the least embarrassed but patted me on the arm.

"Leave it to us," she whispered. "My husband and the

butler will get everything cleared away. By the time the doctor gets back, there will be nothing for anyone to see. Take him to bed, Frederic. This time, don't let him out of your sight! Now where's he gone?"

Charles had disappeared up the corridor. I assumed he'd gone to the toilet but he soon returned, carrying the old, dusty flag of St George, which had been hanging on the wall in the hall.

"Cover yourself up, Freddy!" he muttered, wrapping the red and white flag around me, laughing. "You might frighten the natives! Not Mama, of course. She looks ready for anything...!"

I was starting to relax after so much stress but Charles took me aside to whisper earnestly in my ear, "Freddy, the sooner we get that Mills bomb away from my mother and securely locked up the better. It might give Mama fresh ideas about another political assassination – Lloyd George, you know."

I gasped. Even Charles seemed to know about it. Were there no secrets in this house? He led me up the stairs to his room, where I collapsed on the four-poster bed and fell asleep at once, totally exhausted, and far too tired for sex.

"Frederic !"

I opened my eyes. There was daylight in the room. I looked up. I was naked apart from the flag, which now hid very little. I was still lying on the bed. Charles was in his British Army uniform and asleep, snoring, beside me. Her Ladyship was standing by the bed. She smiled as I gathered the flag around myself.

"The doctor gave Charles a sedative and he will be asleep until lunchtime. I thought you might like a cup of tea."

She pointed at the tea tray on the bedside table and sat down on the edge of the bed beside me.

"Don't you think I should put on some clothes?" I said, smiling. "Or else they really will start to gossip that you have taken a lover..."

She laughed and reached for Charles' dressing gown from

the back of the door.

Memories of the night before suddenly came flooding back.

"...What have you done with that Mills bomb, my lady?"

"Now stop worrying, Freddy. Women over thirty got the vote last year. Lloyd George is quite safe now – well most of the time, and from me, at least... Besides," she laughed, "I'm getting too old for that sort of thing these days."

"So where is it then?"

"Locked up in the safe, Freddy. His Lordship will take it back to his regimental headquarters at the next reunion dinner. No questions will be asked, I'm sure."

"Thank goodness for that."

"Look, Frederic," she whispered, handing the dressing gown to me. "His Lordship and I would like to talk to you... Come when you are ready. I'll go and make you some breakfast afterwards. The senior cook has had to go, you know."

I left the tea and followed her quietly down the stairs. As I passed the grandfather clock I noted that it was already eleven o'clock. His Lordship was waiting for us in the library, where he pointed to other chairs around a table. It was the first time he had ever invited me to sit down. Her Ladyship closed the door behind us.

"We will always be grateful for what you did last night, young man," he began.

"The Palace was right to give you a VC," she added. "You proved yourself worthy of it once more last night. I'm sorry I ever doubted it."

"Yes, service beyond the call of duty," added His Lordship, smiling at her. "My knowledge of explosives is rather out of date."

"What happened afterwards?" I asked. "I'm afraid I fell asleep."

"The doctor came back," Her Ladyship continued. "Fortunately, the other doctor refused to come out in the middle of the night, so the forms were never signed. Our son will not be sent to the lunatic asylum, and mainly thanks to you, Frederic."

"But we need to discuss what to do next," His Lordship added. "Clearly our son is only compos mentis when you are around. He is a different person. Do you really love one another that much...?"

I nodded, smiling, not knowing quite what to say. Even His Lordship now seemed to know everything.

"And do you really appreciate what you will be taking on? He can be quite a handful... but, well, I don't need to tell you that."

Her Ladyship giggled but her husband frowned at her. I decided to change the subject.

"Now may I ask you both a question?"

They nodded.

"Very soon, I must go to the Palace to collect my VC. May I ask you to come as well? Charles suggested that you, Sir, could be my military advisor and you, my lady, could advise me about etiquette at court. I want Charles to come as well in his military uniform as my companion. I believe that it is permitted for a senior officer to accompany a junior rank like me."

They looked at one another.

"Dear Freddy, we will be delighted to come."

"Deeply honoured and very proud," added His Lordship. "I once hoped my son would win some honour in the war... What?"

"I think the experience might help Charles to come to terms with everything, don't you?"

His Lordship got up from the table and put his hand on my shoulder.

"What we owe you, Freddy... Words are just not enough."

He seemed upset and left me to talk with his wife.

"My husband is rather sentimental... But, listen, Freddy. Clearly you must come to live here from now on. This would never have happened if you'd been here last night."

"I was packing and got tired, so I stayed at home. I needed

a good night's sleep."

"Charles couldn't understand why you didn't come to the back door at midnight. He sat on the doorstep and cried. I found him there."

"I didn't know he was expecting me."

"Well, he was and he got so upset, I think that's what started it all. He was afraid you'd gone off with my nephew to start a new life in the motor business."

"Sorry."

"Now, enough of that... Look." She put a hand on my arm. "Move in now. Bring all your things. I'll send the butler to help you. You must stay tonight. That way we'll all get some sleep and you'll make Charles happy again. But, Freddy, this is a big step you are taking. Are you really prepared to look after my son day and night? Are you sure you won't want to get married one day? I know we joked about it the other day. Do you really not want a family of your own?"

"I'm certain, my lady."

"Well, I'm sorry for you and all those eligible young ladies of England. However, I'm really glad for my son. Perhaps you are what he needs, after all... "

I smiled and said nothing.

"...By the way," she giggled again, "I haven't told you how handsome you are with no clothes on! All those simpering debutantes don't know what they're missing. I can quite understand why my son would want you between his sheets! So, you and I have one thing in common, don't we, young man? We're both social rebels. My sister was another one. Perhaps it runs in the family because Charles is much the same."

"How so, my lady?"

"Well, I made the bomb for the suffragettes to blow up Lloyd George in 1913. My sex-mad sister ran off with her gamekeeper into the woods, and now neither of you seem to care two hoots for England's sexual manners and conventions today, when you are making whoopee with my son..."

I couldn't help smiling.

"...So we must all be subversives at heart, Freddy. That

must be why I like you so much. Other men of your kind, like Oscar Wilde, Alfred Lord Douglas and my dear brother were thought to be weak and affected characters – limp-wristed or inadequate in some way, but you, young man, are quite different. A national hero, no less. "

I could think of nothing else to say.

"Thank you, my lady!"

"Well, we all have our secrets, Freddy..."

She looked at her watch.

"...Charles must be waking up now. Perhaps you ought to go and see if he is all right. Well, he's all yours now. You told me that you loved him."

I went upstairs to find the young master.

Charles was still in his Army uniform, lying on the bed asleep. I sat down on the edge. He seemed so peaceful. There was no sign of all the drama during the night before. But I realised that I was at a pivotal moment in my life. A shiver went down my spine. Did I really want this man, sleeping here so innocently? Did I want to become his plaything, his teddy bear now come to life? If I didn't, then I was at liberty to go back downstairs and tell Her Ladyship I had made a mistake – perhaps this was not what I really wanted to do with my life. But what else would I do with my adult years? Her Ladyship and I had made a joke of it but I really didn't want a wife. I had no wish to breed a family of sons to be slaughtered on the battlefields of the next war – and I didn't think the terms of the Versailles Treaty would keep the Germans quiet for long. As somebody laughingly suggested when we were demobbed from the Army depot in north London: one coat of grey paint and they'd be at it again; or the Russians, to dominate the world in the name of the communist ideal. Charles stirred, opened his eyes and looked at me. He held out his arms to hold me.

"Freddy... Oh, Freddy! I was dreaming about you, not chlorine gas, my faulty gas mask or high explosives landing in no man's land. You were there, leading me by the hand, back from the brink. I wanted to live because you said you loved me..."

This was too much. I sniffed. He pulled me closer and put his hand inside my dressing gown.

"...You were so gorgeous last night. Like a beautiful Greek hero in the arena, completely naked, you came to save me... Now go and lock the door, Freddy. You said you were ready for me last night."

He was rubbing my thighs and my groin to give me an erection, just as he did that first night when I said I wasn't ready for sex. But he had been the very first person to say he loved me. Yes, I had now made up my mind. I did want this handsome man. I would be his sexual partner. I needed this new experience. I wanted to feel a man's sexual excitement inside me. I got up to lock the door and threw the dressing gown down on the bed beside him as if I was laying down a challenge. He sat up.

"Oh, Freddy, come here! You're gorgeous...so beautiful..."

He reached out to run his hand up between my thighs. My erection seemed longer than I had ever seen it before. He clutched it in his hand.

"Look," I said, "Junior Freddy is saluting Master Charles once again."

"Yes, it is wonderful, like the rest of you... "

Now I knew. This was what I really wanted. I had waited twenty-two years for this moment. My life would never be the same again.

"...I love you, you know that, don't you, Freddy? Can I really fuck you now? You've always said no before. Are you really ready for me today...?"

I leaned forward to kiss Charles – this man I had saved from the rusty German grenade, the Mills bomb and the secure ward of the local lunatic asylum. Now this handsome aristocratic man was really mine. He ran his fingers between my thighs once more.

"...You are the most beautiful living thing I have ever seen, Freddy – not only gorgeous on the outside but kind, considerate, brave and so heroic on the inside. You came to save me

– you really did, just like my cousin in his crashed kite in no man's land. You are just as my mother said last night. We really do not know how lucky we are today... I think heaven sent you to save us in our hour of need."

"Oh, shut up, Charles," I giggled. "This is the time for action, not more silly words. We've had enough of those."

He got up and threw his Army uniform on the floor at my feet, as if he was returning the challenge. Charles stepped out of his underpants. We stared at one another while his erection grew to what seemed like twice the length of mine.

"Look," I said, "handsome Master Charles is saluting his Junior Freddy."

"Come here, you sexy gardener boy...Your time has come...a long, slow, tender-hearted fucking just for you, Freddy."

I bent over the bed in front of him and he mounted me from behind. He put his hand gently around my swollen penis and I ejaculated at once, within seconds. With that enormous relief seemed to come the release of years of stress – from the day I joined up in 1915, when I was only just eighteen. "Your country needs you!" declared Lord Kitchener on the poster, but he had drowned when his ship was sunk on the way to Russia. So, Lord Kitchener had become one of the glorious dead – listed somewhere in cold stone on a war memorial. Today, my passionate, throbbing, handsome lover and I were very much alive. We were two of the walking wounded – the shellshocked and the survivors. Now Master Charles desperately needed me and I really wanted a tender-hearted fucking. Through this unique human experience he would leave part of himself inside me - a marker and a token of another man's lust and tender-hearted love. Now I knew I had survived for this moment, even if it wasn't exactly what Church and State had wanted. Charles withdrew from me slowly. We kissed. I lay down on the bed to take him in my arms and we fell asleep together. After the last twelve hours I was quite exhausted but I knew that I had never been so happy.

The following day Her Ladyship appeared at our door, carrying the morning tea herself. She came in and sat down on the side of the bed while Charles was still fast asleep beside me.

"Listen... More bad news, Freddy. I telephoned the local council about the drains outside... No, Freddy, I was humble and polite. You would have been proud of me. I made no insensitive joke about the Russian Revolution spreading from Petrograd to our local town hall. And before you ask, Freddy, the Mills bomb is still locked up in our safe downstairs. I haven't chucked it through the window of the council chambers...but I was sorely tempted, young man. Old habits die hard you see – once a suffragette, always a suffragette, you know..."

She laughed. I sat up and she put the tea tray down. Her Ladyship had never talked to me like this before.

"...Have another biscuit, Freddy... Now would you believe it? The council have decided they will not dig the trench to bypass our cesspit. Nor will they pay for any of the drainpipes which we talked about in order to connect with that new intercept sewer they are building. According to the plans, it will run beside the stream through the vicar's garden, you know..."

I took another Garibaldi from the plate she passed to me.

"... The vicar now says he will take us to court if nothing is done about the dreadful smell. Well, Freddy, I said – so much for his Christian charity! I nearly told him to get someone else to open the next bloody garden fete!"

We laughed at one another.

"So, what do you want me to do, my lady?"

"Get Charles outside to help you with his spade and dig the trench yourselves, please. Well, you dug plenty out in France! ... Sorry, Freddy, that sounds unfair but what else can we do? You know about the dreadful money situation. Anyway, it would do my son a lot of good to do some useful work. Look at him...!"

She pointed at Charles, asleep and snoring loudly beside me.

"Useless lump! Why couldn't he have been like you, Freddy? England is really proud of heroes like you... But I'm forgetting, you really do love one another, don't you? I can see that quite clearly. If you did not love him, you would never have risked your life like that..."

I reached for my cup of tea from the bedside table. Her Ladyship looked more serious for one moment.

"...Do you know, Freddy? There was a moment I thought we ought to let them lock him up in the secure mental ward, just to be free of the responsibility. But you said you loved him... That made me think again... I was thinking of you, you see... "

She got up from the bed with the empty plate and turned around to look at us both.

"...Freddy, I hope you know what you're taking on, that's all...!"

She pointed at her son again and smiled at me.

"...Did he have sex with you again last night? I'll give you some of my soothing bath salts. I always used to have a long soak in the bath afterwards... Look, you've exhausted him... His father was just the same, years ago..."

She winked at me and pointed at her son once more.

"...Does he really know what an incredibly lucky young man he is? Anyway, if I can tell the vicar that construction of our new foul sewer will commence soon, I think I can put off his legal action."

"I'll do what I can, my lady."

She smiled and put her hand on my arm.

"Bless you. If I telephone an order for the drainpipes, the caulking and so on from that advert in our Country Gentleman's Estate Book, please will you dig the trench and lay the sewer with Charles? It is time for us all to unite and to get things done. One day England might actually be a land fit for heroes, Freddy."

"Yes, my lady, we'll see to it."

"Well, I'll go and fetch the bath salts and my vaginal cream. You might find that useful next time."

She reached down to touch my face with her hand and looked at her son again.

"You are so beautiful... Now, get him up and doing things, Freddy. Give him energetic things to do!" She laughed. "Well, I mean, apart from sex with you..."

We laughed at one another. Emancipation really was here to stay. One or two more pre-war, Edwardian social barriers had been battered down in England on this sunny morning.

"...Now, can I go and tell the vicar that construction work on the trench for the new foul sewer will start today?"

I smiled at her and she picked up the tea things to go downstairs while I marvelled at the extent of women's emancipation today. Did Emmeline Pankhurst really know what she had started back in 1903?

So we started digging a trench from the old cesspit down to the line of the council's new intercept sewer by the stream. It was hot work. I took my shirt off and put on some tatty old tennis shorts Her Ladyship had found for me. While we shovelled earth out of the trench, I told Charles just what his mother had said about him while he was asleep.

"Did she really say that about me being a useless lump?"

I nodded.

"And she said she might have allowed them to take you away to the secure mental hospital if it wasn't for the fact I said I loved you."

"Did she really, Freddy? But you two do get on like a house on fire, don't you? There don't seem to be any secrets between you at all."

"She's given me her vaginal cream to make it easier for you and I to have sex."

Charles gasped and leaned back on his spade.

"Shut up, Freddy. I think the vicar is down there and looking up at us over his garden fence. I hope he didn't hear anything."

We both waved at him.

"Good morning, Vicar!" I called out. "Lovely weather today."

He waved at me to come and talk, so I scrambled down the slope towards the stream.

"I read about your VC in the local paper," the vicar shouted. "Well done, my boy, and a local lad too!"

"Thank you," I muttered, turning round to look at Charles, who was up to his chest in the trench we had dug. "Another trench, Vicar, just like the ones we used to dig in France."

"Splendid work. I see you've even got Master Charles at it. Occupational therapy, what? Best thing for him, too, my boy. It was the damned smell, you know. The memsahib, my wife, just couldn't stand the pong any more, but we used to live in India, you know. I think she's forgotten how to live with smells like this."

"I've dealt with latrines before, Sir."

"I'm sure you have. Well done! Come and show me your VC when you get back from Buckingham Palace. Tell you what? Come and tell our new Women's Institute all about it. The good ladies of this parish started everything in 1915, you know, while you were moving up to the front line, probably."

"They sent us Balaclava helmets they'd been knitting, Sir."

The vicar laughed.

"Well then, young man, you must tell them how grateful you were. All my ladies are salt of the earth and they will love you! It will give them all a thrill to look at someone as young and handsome as you. Too many brave young men from this village died, you know – not that you'll be dressed like a half-naked Indian fakir wonder-worker like that, of course! God bless you, my boy."

We both laughed again and I climbed up the slope to continue our excavations. Just as I'd been taught in Flanders, we set up strings on sticks to determine the line of the trench, and used a spirit level on a plank to set the incline for the drain. Her Ladyship appeared with sandwiches and beer from the cellar.

"Good Lord!" she said, looking at our mound of earth beside the earthworks. Charles stuck his head up above the trench.

"This is real fun, Mama. Last time I did this we were under bombardment from the Kaiser's shells but now we've just got Lloyd George to deal with."

Then the butler appeared and coughed politely.

"The boy has come from Master Frederic's grandmother, my lady. He says she needs him to go to her cottage in the village at once."

So I made my excuses and hurried off to see what the trouble was. The front door was open when I arrived.

"A rat," muttered my grandma. "Frederic, it was as big as that..."

She held out her hands.

"...It ran into the scullery. You know how I hate them, Fred."

I armed myself with a poker from the hearth and went outside. Grandma picked up the shovel and followed me. We looked around the scullery and the yard outside but there was nothing to be seen.

"We should put poison down," I suggested. "I'll bring some next time from the greenhouse."

"Stay for a cup of tea, Fred. Why don't you...?"

So we returned to the parlour and she placed the kettle on the hearth.

"You've been neglecting me," she complained.

"Was that it, Grandma? I don't believe there was any rat."

She looked upset.

"Now Fred, would I send the boy to find you if there wasn't a good reason. You've been avoiding me."

We sat quietly for a while as the kettle started to heat up.

"Yes," I said, "Grandma, I should have popped in to see you last week. We've been so busy, what with leaky roofs and flooding drains."

"So when am I going to meet your beloved – your girl-friend, then?"

"It is not quite like that, Grandma."

She leaned forward.

"Why isn't it like that, Fred? You are handsome, fit and strong. Any young man like you needs a girl."

"Grandma, you just don't understand."

The kettle was boiling. She poured water into the teapot and reached up to the mantelshelf for the old tea caddy.

"What don't I understand, Fred? Surely you can tell me."

"One day, Grandma, but not yet. Have you got your pension from the post office this week? Did your National Savings book arrive?"

She turned to salute the portrait of Lloyd George on the wall.

"Our Prime Minister looks after his people, Fred. Now humble women like me have got the vote. I never thought the day would come. I would vote for Lloyd George again..."

She stirred the teapot and poured me a cup of tea.

"...Now this young lady – your sweetheart, Fred. When am I going to meet her, then?"

I decided to say nothing but blew at my cup to make the hot tea cool down. I didn't think it would be long before Charles got bored with digging the trench and gave up for the morning. Grandma shrugged her shoulders when I looked at the clock on the wall.

"I ought to go, Grandma," I insisted. "I'll bring a rat trap from the greenhouse when I see you next."

"Oh well," she sighed. "I hope she's worth it and doesn't let you down. That's all."

When I returned to our earthworks for the drains, Charles was still hard at work. His Lordship then arrived with bottles of beer. His wife was carrying sandwiches.

"Give me that!" he said, pointing at my shovel. "All well with your grandmother, Frederic?"

"She saw a big rat, Sir. I said I'd put down poison and a trap from the greenhouse."

He rolled up his sleeves to start shovelling the earth aside and it was he who actually discovered the remains of the old ice well hidden for generations in the side of the slope down to the vicar's garden.

"What on earth is this?" His Lordship called out when his shovel struck something under the leaves. His wife went to have a look.

"Freddy, come and look at this!"

I scrambled out of our trench to take a look. In the ground about six inches down was an old iron trap door. I told Charles to bring up the pickaxe to use as a lever. Together we lifted the door, to reveal a cavern reaching into the hillside. His Lordship dropped a stone through the hole and we heard it echoing as it bounced along the brickwork inside.

"Good Lord!" muttered Her Ladyship. "I heard about this from my brother, years ago. This is where our family used to store meat on ice blocks gathered from the lake during the winter, back in the old days."

"North facing slope, my dear," added His Lordship. "No sun ever got here. Makes sense, what? Charles, where's that hurricane lamp got to – the one you had under the dining table the other night?"

"Back in the Gun Room, Papa."

"Freddy, would you go and fetch it? Here's the key..."

He stooped down to whisper in my ear.

"...This key is new. I changed the lock. Don't let my son have this one, whatever you do."

So Charles and I soon found ourselves exploring the ice well with the lamp while his parents stared down through the trap door. It was completely empty. There was no rubbish or water in the bottom. None of the sewage seemed to have found its way down here, fortunately, and the brickwork was all in original condition except one brick high up which had fallen out and was lying at my feet. I thought nothing of it.

"We could divert the sewage into it," His Lordship suggested, "to use it as one of these new septic tanks I keep reading about. Freddy, what do you think, then?"

"What do we do when it fills up with ordure, my lord? Aren't we just delaying the problem? Supposing the smell upsets the vicar again. This is even nearer to the vicarage. Anyway, how can the men get their cart down here with the pump to suck it out every three months?"

Her Ladyship smiled at her husband.

"Freddy's got a point, you know."

"We had these problems in France," I continued. "Once we regained territory from the Germans, only to find it contained their new septic tank and it was full and overflowing. Army HQ wasn't amused at all, my lord. It cost us thirty-seven dead and severely wounded, for what purpose, I ask myself today."

"Dulce et decorum est, pro patria mori," muttered Charles sarcastically behind me.

"Freddy won't understand that kind of sarcasm," His Lordship snapped. "I really don't think it was appropriate to say anything like that, do you, Charles?"

"Wilfred Owen, Sir," I replied. "And I read some of Rupert Brooke's war sonnets as well out in the trenches. They are both part of the lost generation, many of whom I buried, because Rupert Brooke wasn't the only one to die needlessly of blood poisoning, my lord. But, thank God, your son and I did not. Now I think it is time to look after the survivors and build a better world, don't you?"

"Quite right, Freddy," His Lordship agreed with us. "Abandon plan B for a septic tank and we'll resume the trench for plan A as before."

He turned to his wife, who was fascinated.

And so Charles and I completed the trench for the sewer pipes. It was the first time we worked on anything like this together. The next day I pushed him out of bed early.

"Ah, time to dig new trenches for the front line before the Big Push, what?"

"Something like that, Charles, but I thought officers didn't dig trenches."

"We had to if all our men got killed, Freddy... Sometimes there was nobody else to do the spadework."

I was pleasantly surprised by Charles' stamina with the garden fork. The sun came out and we were soon down to our shirtsleeves. He seemed glad to find something practical to do and I said how much easier it was to dig the soil when there was someone special to do the digging with. That seemed to please him and we carried on until mid-morning.

"Time for tea?"

"Yes, Freddy. This time, I'll fill the teapot."

We put down our forks and found our way back to the greenhouse, where I sat down and watched while Charles took control. Somehow our roles had become reversed and now I knew for certain: it really was all because of the war.

"What is to become of the estate?" I asked. "If half of it is sold for building houses, do you think the rest would still be viable?"

"Well, Freddy, what do you think?"

"I've been thinking about what people will need when they move into all the new houses on the other side of the road. They will all have gardens at the front and back."

Charles left the kettle to boil and came to sit by me and put his hand on my knee.

"You mean plants for the gardens?"

"Precisely, Charles. We could make a list of things new residents might want to buy. We could start growing them here."

"You mean like a horticultural supplier?"

"Yes, that sort of business – growing seedlings for sale, rose bushes to plant, bags of compost, leaf mould and the like. It might help to balance the books and pay the builders to mend the roof of the Big House."

"My father would like that."

We sat quietly thinking for a while. The sun had come out for the day. Perhaps summer had arrived at last. Charles looked at his pocket watch.

"Freddy, I'm taking you for a ride on the horses. You can take young Stanley. I'll take the bigger one: my father's mount. There is somewhere special I really want to take you today. I just need to get away from sewage, drains and this damned smell."

So we abandoned digging for a while and fetched the horses from the stable. As Charles had promised, he had already taught me to ride and fortunately I fitted one of his old tailored outfits with the waist drawn in.

"You and I could start our own business," I said, as we road side by side along the old drove road. "We could use the greenhouses to force seedlings, shrubs and so on for sale to the new residents on the estate. The new road would help to bring extra trade from other areas. You never know, it might actually work. It might be something for us to do together."

The horses seemed to enjoy their outing today. They'd been shut up in the stables for too long.

"Charles and Fred, Horticultural Suppliers... how about that?" he suggested, turning his horse through a gate into the woods. "I don't like the words 'horticultural suppliers'. Do you? I think it sounds too much like a wholesaler for council parks departments, market gardens and so on."

"I know," I said. "Look, there are town centres, village centres and signposts directing you to places like that. I think we should take a leaf out of my officer's book and choose the right name for the place – to make it sound more pleasant and friendly."

We were following a bridle way, deep into the woods, and in the far distance, through the trees, I could see what looked like some ancient ruins. Was this the young master's secret hideaway?

"You mean like changing the word latrine to honey stall, Freddy?" he said.

"Precisely. Instead of calling it a horticultural supplier, how about calling it a garden centre?"

"What else would you want to buy if you were out for the afternoon with your young family shopping for things to grow in the garden?"

"A lawnmower?"

"Possibly... How about some horse manure for the roses?"

"A garden hose to water them with?"

"Yes, if it is dry in the summer."

"Some flowerpots?"

We rode on slowly while making suggestions to one another. Both horses seemed to know the path towards what turned out to be the remains of a castle.

"Right," I said. "You and your young family have bought all the things you need for the garden and your Model T Ford is down low on its springs. We must remember to include a car park! ... What else might you want before driving home and planting everything?"

"A cup of tea and a bun... "

"I can't see Her Ladyship handing out cups of tea through the kitchen window."

"It's not the done thing, old boy, what?"

"And the children will need somewhere to go to the toilet... "

"Honey stalls, this way!"

"Precisely. That's not really the sort of thing you would find at a horticultural supplier, is it?"

"What about donkey rides for the children while their parents are selecting the roses?"

"His Lordship could do all that. What do you think?"

"Then he would know the country really has gone to the dogs."

We raised imaginary glasses and clunked them together in the air, laughing, while the horses walked on slowly.

"To the dogs, Charles!"

"To our garden centre, Freddy! Now I must show you a special place that you've never seen before."

Charles dismounted and tied his horse to some old iron railings, where I also tied my reins. I followed him through a ruined wooden doorway.

"My secret place, Freddy. Watch your head on that branch there."

He turned into another doorway and led me down some broad stone steps into the ruined cellar. Beautiful brick arches still held up the ceiling and the ruins above us.

"What was this place, then, Charles?"

"Henry the Eighth had it built for one of his friends, until they fell out and he had his head cut off. Something like that, anyway, Freddy. But I wanted you to see it. Everything is so quiet here – like a retreat away from the twentieth century. I thought I might give you another tender-hearted fucking in my special place here."

I looked around the cellar.

"What if somebody comes?"

"The horses will make a noise. They always do. Stanley will shake his bridle. Anyway, we won't be long."

Charles started to undo my riding breeches. It was very romantic. I suddenly wondered what other illicit romances had passed undiscovered in this building over the centuries. He pushed down my pants to find my penis already erect and standing to attention.

"So," Charles said, "Junior Freddy is already on parade."

"Always at your service, Sir."

He laughed and looked around for somewhere we could fuck in comfort. There was a large old wooden crate and I bent over that. He did not need much sexual arousal today and Charles climaxed inside me tenderly within just a few moments. We dressed in our riding clothes once again but then he surprised me by getting down in front of me on one knee.

"Freddy, I really brought you here for another purpose ...to offer you this."

He put one hand in the pocket of his riding jacket and took out a small box, which he passed to me. I opened it. There was a gold ring inside.

"Well, Freddy, try it on then."

I stared at my lover. This moment was usually traditionally reserved for the moment when the young lord and master, heir to the estate, was proposing marriage to his future duchess. My sex and anatomy were all wrong for such an honour but I comforted myself that if I had been born female, Charles wouldn't love me at all.

"Charles, I can't take this..."

He seemed upset.

"...It just isn't right, is it?"

"Why not, Freddy?"

"Marriage is for men and women. How can I wear your ring on my finger? Whatever will people like my grandma think now?"

"It is just a plain ring, Freddy. How are they to know who gave it to you...?"

I looked closely at it. I was afraid the family coat of arms might be stamped on it, or some motto to declare that I was just one of the young master's goods or chattels now.

"...Listen, Freddy. I would like you to wear it – just like that tiepin I gave you ages ago. You wore that in church last Sunday. Nobody said anything, did they? Only you will ever know who gave you this gold ring..."

I suddenly opted for a dumb witness for the commitment I was about to undertake, and turned to bring one of the horses inside.

"...Now where are you off to, Freddy?"

"Wait a moment," I insisted, "please."

His Lordship's horse was too tall to fit through the doorway, so I brought in my own mount, which just managed to get down the steps into the cellar, where it stood obediently to observe the proceedings. Charles was still kneeling and holding the box with the ring.

"Oh, I see," he said. "I thought you were about to run off in disgust. So, you wanted a witness which couldn't speak."

"Now, Charles," I said. "What is it you wanted to ask me?"

He smiled and held up the box for the horse to see. It seemed to nod its head.

"Dearest Freddy, I want you to take this ring and be my partner in life, through thick and thin, as a gesture of our love."

He held the box open for me to see the ring. I held up my finger for him to slide it on. So, I was his now. Yes, I would be my master's lover. Charles took my hand and kissed it. An illicit and most secret union had been blessed today, but at least this dumb horse could never give evidence in a court of law.

After such unconventional excitement there could be no honeymoon. We resumed our digging the next morning but we stopped for a rest in the hot sun. Charles and I continued to suggest ideas for our garden centre but by the end of this conversation it was time for tea. As His Lordship had taken his wife out in the old Rolls Royce to visit her friends, she had left sandwiches for us to eat in the greenhouse. By now I had taken off my vest and was getting a bit sunburned around the shoulders.

"Gosh, Freddy, you look good enough to get fucked once more before we pack up for the day."

I giggled.

"Well?" he insisted.

"I know just the place, too."

"Where's that, then, Freddy? Is this your favourite place? You've seen mine."

"The old boiler room – not quite so romantic, Charles."

"I thought the greenhouses were heated by gas."

"They are now but years ago when I started here we had to stoke a boiler to keep the frost off the plants. Sometimes I would be in the boiler room all night to make sure the fire didn't go out if the late frost was really bad."

"I never knew that, Freddy. Anyway I was always away at boarding school. But I do remember being home here one summer holiday and wandering into the hothouse. Do you remember the oranges?"

"I also remember the heat and the humidity. I had to work in there."

"Yes, and you used to take your vest off. I used to come and spy on you because you were so handsome even then... very fuckable."

"I was about sixteen, probably."

"Yes and the old gardener used to tell you to put your shirt back on again."

"That's right, Bill was a stickler for correct dress in the hothouse! But why didn't you say anything to me? I would have done it with you, even then, you know."

"But I didn't know... about myself. I was still confused, Freddy..."

He smiled at me, shrugged his shoulders and changed the subject.

"...So this old boiler room is just the place, then."

I nodded and pointed round the back of the greenhouse. We abandoned the garden tools and the wheelbarrow and he followed me down some old stone steps. The door of the boiler room was stiff after all these years but there was still a key in the lock and it worked. A shaft of sunlight filtered down through the grating from the sky above. The boiler was still there but rusty and cold now. A heap of cinders still lay underneath it. Otherwise the room was the just the same as I remembered it years ago. Even the wooden bench where I sometimes sat all night remained and I brushed the cobwebs off with my hand while Charles looked around.

"Another secret dungeon, Freddy?"

"Hardly, Charles, and nowhere near as romantic as the castle ruins yesterday."

He put his hands on my bare shoulders, kissed me on the forehead and pulled me towards him.

"You are so warm and sexy, Freddy."

"I really should have cleaned this place up first."

"Too late now."

He unfastened the leather belt of my trousers and pushed them down over my hips. Gently he slid his hands down the back of my pants to clutch my buttocks.

"Very sexy... Gardening keeps your bum firm."

He kissed me again and I put my arms around him as he lifted me up off the ground.

"Just for you – a long, slow, hard fuck... to say thank you Freddy for saying yes, yesterday."

"I'd prefer another tender-hearted fucking."

"Now lie down on the bench, Freddy... "

I sat on the bench and he stooped to pick up my legs in order to undo my boots and pull off my trousers and pants.

"...Now lie back and relax."

As I lay back on the bench I suddenly remembered the cold lonely nights I spent here before the war while looking at the flames through the door of the boiler. On the brick ceiling above the bench was the pattern of noughts and crosses I had scratched during one particularly long night of boredom. I smiled at it as Charles gently pushed his erect penis between my parted buttocks and penetrated me. I pushed my feet up to touch the low ceiling.

"Oh yes," I muttered, smiling at him. "We could put leather straps up there so I could hang upside down... "

"I've been looking at you all the morning thinking that you needed this!"

Charles' rhythm grew more vigorous.

"Careful! I wanted another tender-hearted fucking."

"Freddy, you are so sexy!"

Charles collapsed on top of me as we both climaxed quickly together.

"The best yet!"

"It was hardly long or slow but I needed that!"

He tenderly kissed my neck and around my ear. Now I kissed him in return.

"Just what the doctor ordered... that I should find someone to love, Freddy."

I giggled.

"Charles, I don't think this is quite what the doctor had in mind."

"I don't care. You are fantastic... Better than all the pills... More effective than any bottle of medicine... much more relaxing than all the therapy, and even more invigorating than all the exercises... Freddy, you are fantastic."

"And hungry, Charles. You make me hungry. We'll wash first and eat. Look, there's the tap where I used to top up the boiler with the hose. I'll get some soap down here and clean the place up a bit. It can be our new secret rendezvous... We'll do this again tomorrow... yes?"

"Freddy, I love you... Do you know that?"

I started giggling again.

"More than just a long slow fuck?" I teased him.

"Seriously!"

"Yes, Charles. I do know! Now let's have food before I fade away, but we'll wash first, yes?"

After all this, I thought it would not be long before I was summoned to an interview with His Lordship. It seemed only a short time before news would spread of what his son and I got up to in the old boiler room behind the greenhouse.

"Ah, Frederic... Please shut the door..."

His Lordship was sitting in his estate office this morning to deal with the accounts. I stood to attention in front of the desk, just as I had always done when collecting my wages.

"...Have you had a chance to look at the Rolls Royce, then? I know the ashtray was overflowing by the back seat."

I relaxed but felt worried about the news I would bring. At least he was not about to sack me for having sex with his son.

"May I be honest, my lord?"

"Yes, well ... young man, my wife tells me you are always honest with her."

I decided to ignore this challenge.

"I've never seen a Rolls Royce Silver Ghost in such a sorry state, Sir. I think that was why Your Lordship's chauffeur didn't want me to examine it."

"Well, my father-in-law bought it, Frederic...in 1909. The tyres are a bit worn, I know. And it didn't help when that brick wall sprang out in front of us on the way back from the regimental reunion dinner."

"No, my lord, but I don't think Henry Royce would be happy with it now. Charles Rolls died in 1910, Sir, so I don't know what he would say."

"Yes, yes, Frederic! ... Surely the village blacksmith could hammer out the dent in the front. Could you put on some fresh paint to hide it?"

"My lord, forgive me...and with all due respect..."

"Well?"

"I will start at the back axle, my lord. When I examined them, the rear brakes had not been serviced for years. The brake cables are slack. The brake unit on the offside rear does not work at all – it needs immediate replacement. The hand-brake only functions on one wheel. The Dunlop pneumatic tyres are bald. The fabric is poking through the rubber in several places and so is the inner tube. The rear suspension has been terribly neglected. One of the leaf springs is broken. Another is cracked and unsafe."

"Anything else?"

"I found the road anchor, my lord."

"What of it?"

"Well, my lord, the old rope attaching the road anchor to the chassis of your Rolls is terribly frayed...and should be replaced."

"It's always worked before."

He stared at me defiantly.

"But, with all due respect, Sir, nowadays the careful driver is encouraged to depend on the brakes – even on a steep hill."

"You'd call that progress, I suppose?"

"Yes, my lord... And the red tail lamp by your rear bumper has no wick and cannot be lit as the law requires...after dark, my lord."

"And what else?"

He stared at me as if I was about to read the riot act or to report him to the new Minister of Transport.

"The nearside front axle is cracked, the suspension is buckled and the wheel bearing is broken, my lord. It was probably due to the impact of the brick wall. Anyway, the tyres are unsafe and have no tread at all."

"Well, go and buy two new Dunlop tyres, then."

"But, my lord, the front wheels are so out of alignment that new front tyres would quickly wear out. It would be a waste of money until something is done about the steering geometry."

"Geometry, Frederic? ...What do you know about geometry?"

"I learned about it during gunnery practice in France, Sir... when we had a quiet spell at the front."

"Did you, by Jove? Well, did you find anything else wrong with my Rolls Royce, then?"

"My lord, do you want the good news or the bad news?"

"Good news first, I suppose."

He tried to smile at me.

"I have cleaned the muck out of the carburettor. The engine will start now, well, most of the time; and I have emptied your ashtray, my lord."

"So what's the bad news, then?"

"There was hardly any lubricating oil left in the sump of the crankcase. What there was ...turned out to be thick black sludge. I don't think it had been changed or topped up for years, Sir."

"Well, replace the engine oil, then."

"But I found white metal in the sludge, Sir, where the big end linings have started to wear away on the crankshaft. That would explain the knocking sound which so alarms Her Ladyship."

"And?"

"Otherwise Henry Royce's engine seemed to be alright, if a little rusty, my lord, but the radiator is leaking where the bricks..."

"Anything else?"

"Unfortunately, the nearside headlamp will only shine on the ground, that is if the acetylene gas burner, the reflector and the glass lens had not been fractured."

"That brick wall again? Why do they always build them on blind corners? I think we did them a favour by knocking it down!"

"Most likely, my lord."

"So, Frederic...what do you recommend? Wouldn't the village blacksmith be able to do something?"

"But a Rolls Royce is like a precision instrument. That is what we were taught in France, Sir. It will last many years if it is properly serviced by trained mechanics with the correct tools. The British Army was proud of its training programme even under battlefield conditions."

"Yes, yes! ... So, Frederic, are you telling me my Rolls is now kaput?"

"It could be made into a new hen house for the chickens, Sir."

"Was that some sort of a joke, Frederic? ... But, I know, you have recently become one of the family..."

He looked sadly at me.

"...So now it is time for me to be honest with you... My father-in-law bought this Rolls Royce the same year as Lloyd George's People's Budget – 1909... Well, the House of Lords was in uproar about the Chancellor Lloyd George's new death duties, his outrageous Land Value Tax and supertax. We refused to pass his budget and sent it straight back to the House of Commons. Anyway, the whole affair later resulted in a General Election. Then my father-in-law treated himself to this brand-new Rolls Royce, before the Treasury could drain all his funds by way of devilish new taxes, Frederic."

"So I understand, Sir."

"Everybody at the club was saying David Lloyd George should go – to the Tower, probably. Nobody believed the House of Commons would invent the Parliament Act in order to get their wicked way...and that, Frederic, was when, if you'll excuse the expression, the shit really hit the fan... "

He laughed.

"...Yes, a bit like the vicar's garden, Frederic!"

We both laughed. My employer was actually talking to me as if I was another human being. Now I knew for certain – it must have been the war.

"Her Ladyship told me all about the People's Budget, Sir."

"We, in the House of Lords, all thought that Lloyd George would be thrown out, but he became British Prime Minister in 1916, with the support of the working man behind him. That gave him a mandate for more social reform...with renewed zeal to undo the English landed gentry and promote the rights of the working classes. He was Welsh, you see – embittered, twisted and, I think, he really hated the English aristocracy for exploiting the Welsh for so long..."

His Lordship sat back and smiled at me. I felt deeply honoured.

"...Frederic, it didn't help that English landowners had paid such low wages to Welsh coal miners, I know. Mine safety was neglected. Too many Welsh miners had died in explosions or by breathing coal dust. Then, Welsh coal was being exported to England and only Englishmen made a big profit out of it."

"And the Irish nationalists don't like us either, my lord."

"That's what I think, Frederic. But threatening Sinn Feiners with the Black and Tans won't do us any favours, will it? Lloyd George has got that wrong, I think. Perhaps it has been our fault, I know, but we certainly nurtured that Welsh viper in our midst. Anyway, my father-in-law left me the car, no money and a stack of death duties to pay. So that's why we're broke, Frederic."

"But David Lloyd George gave us old-age pensions, health and unemployment insurance...and, my lord, yes, votes for women over the age of thirty in 1918...like Her Ladyship, and all men like me, over the age of twenty-one."

"Yes, yes...to get more votes...to get more votes, Frederic. He thought people like you and women over thirty would vote for him and his radical policies... He couldn't fail. But I ask you, what do women of any class really know about politics? That's always been a man's world!"

"Now we have the Housing Act, Sir...for council housing and more homes fit for heroes, which everyone promised us. Surely working men who served in the Great War deserve decent places to live."

"To get more votes, Frederic! That's what it's really all about!"

"But we live in a democracy, Sir."

"Yes, yes, I know. How do you know all this then, young man? Did my wife tell you? She seems to tell you everything else."

"The lecturer from Army HQ, my lord, came to tell us all about the Versailles Treaty in June. We also had a couple of lectures to prepare us for the world outside when we were demobbed later, to bring us up to date with life in England today: poverty, unemployment, syphilis, influenza, tuberculosis, social unrest and so on."

"Oh do sit down, Frederic. This is not a board of enquiry."

"Thank you, my lord."

I sat down in front of the desk and relaxed. He closed the ledger in front of him and gazed at me.

"I really loved this country, Frederic. We had Queen Victoria, until alas, she died in 1901. We had the Empire... We had prosperity and stability. We didn't know just how lucky we were...and then David Lloyd George came along. Oh dear!"

He looked sadly at me.

"What do you want me to say, my lord?"

He leaned forward.

"Why should I care about England now when the Chancellor and the Inland Revenue are taxing me for all I'm worth, hey? So, we have the unemployment and health insurance, plus the old-age pensions you mentioned, but at what cost, young man? Half my colleagues – Their Lordships in the House of Lords with any land – are facing economic hardship, you know. Houses everywhere like this one are crumbling, staff being let go and farms neglected. Several of my friends in the Upper House lost sons and grandsons in the war, but for what Frederic? ... For what, hey? What price the conventions of polite society or Edwardian England now?"

"I was afraid you wouldn't like me any more, Sir, just like

Lord Queensbury reacted to Oscar Wilde when he found out about his feelings for Alfred Lord Douglas, his son."

"Well, I'll tell you, young man, after my latest tax demand from the Inland Revenue I care not that much for England or its sanctimonious, upper-class social values! Anyway, I hated Lord Queensbury – such a bad-tempered oaf! ... I think Britain was a better place after he died in 1900. Hurrah and good riddance, I said."

His Lordship snapped his fingers loudly, making me jump.

"Charles was afraid you would protest about us, my lord. I think he is afraid of you."

He leaned back in his chair again and stared at me. His Lordship clearly decided to change the subject.

"So what do you think, then, Frederic? How can we make ends meet? You and your generation are the bright young things. You have the youth and enthusiasm to tackle all England's troubles today. Tell me, young man. Do I sell up half the estate to make way for the new trunk road and the housing development they say we need now?"

"I think...Sir...I think..."

"What do you think, young man? I need to know."

"We could turn half the estate into a horticultural nursery in order to provide produce to sell by the side of the road – flowers, plants, seedlings and garden furniture for the new garden city everyone is talking about. What about a garden centre for a garden city, Sir...to make money and balance your books?"

"Charles mentioned it. He thought it was a good idea."

"We discussed it together, Sir. A grant might be available from Ebenezer Howard and the Garden City Association, which promoted the growth of Letchworth in Hertfordshire."

"What would I be able to do, then? Take children around the car park on donkey rides? ... Show them the way to the toilet?"

"Of course not, Sir. But Charles and I could try to make something out of the place...to stop it going bankrupt. It would be something we could do together...as we have been doing recently. Besides, I have a plan to develop hybrid roses for display at the Chelsea Hospital..."

His Lordship seemed fascinated.

"...The old gardener took me to the original Royal International Horticultural Exhibition in 1913, my lord. He was exhibiting some roses but they didn't win anything, so I thought I might take Charles there to the new Chelsea Flower Show next year. It might give us fresh ideas."

His Lordship sat back in his chair.

"My son really loves you, you know. You have brought him back from the brink... Without your love and devotion he would be locked up in a secure mental hospital, I am sure of it. His mother and I always assumed he would find some charming young lady to fall in love with..."

I smiled but His Lordship stared up at the ceiling.

"...But, Frederic, I ask myself, now: would such a daughter-in-law be able to deal with Charles as you do, repair the roof, mend the drains or attend to my Rolls? She'd probably only be able to arrange flowers, play Chopin prettily on the piano and do some light needlework. What do you think?"

He turned to me and smiled.

"We love one another, Sir," I said calmly. "That is the truth."

"Good. Her Ladyship told me all about it, you know. But you might have talked to me first, as Charles' father. I had a right to know but my wife has no secrets from me – nor from you, it seems, young man!"

He raised his eyebrow at me but smiled. By now he realised I was no threat like his sister-in-law's gamekeeper had proved to be.

"She only wanted to discuss Charles' health, Sir."

"This happened in South Africa, sometimes, you know. I was out there fighting in the Veldt in 1902. I myself became very close to a young African native man. He was so handsome and so graceful – just like you. He was from a peaceful African tribe and couldn't understand why European settlers were fighting over territories in South Africa. We both spoke a little Afrikaans – well enough, anyway. He was one of our domestics, you see. But that's history. I was fighting for king, queen and country. He was just trying to earn an honest living and buy some goats."

I was fascinated. I'd never heard about this before. The butler knocked on the door and entered.

"Luncheon is served, my lord."

His Lordship smiled at me, winked and then turned to the butler.

"Have we still got some of my best port wine left in the cellar?"

"Only two bottles, my lord. The wine merchant insists that his last bill must be paid first...and the tax has gone up again."

"Yes, yes. Now bring one bottle upstairs. Frederic and I will take port with our cigars after luncheon."

"Very good, my lord. The best cigars, Sir? Only two left now... The tobacconist's bill is still unpaid... and the tax on tobacco has gone up as well, my lord."

"Yes, yes, the very last Havana cigars."

The butler bowed his head and went outside again. His Lordship turned to me with a smile and then placed the ledger back on the shelf behind him.

"We'll talk again soon, young man. Sit by me at the table. And, Frederic, if you'll allow a compliment from an old soldier – as one soldier to another, you understand... May I say what a difference you are making to this household. The old gloom and doom seems to be thing of the past, now that my son seems to be enjoying life again – and that's all because of you, isn't it?"

"Thank you, Sir."

He put his hand on my shoulder and we went off to find lunch together.

"My wife and I are very proud of you, you know, Frederic.

We both want you to be happy here. I'm not like Lord Queensbury who you mentioned. I don't judge people before I have got to know them and I think we have got to know each other better this morning."

Chapter 4

1930 – Inside the refreshment tent at the grand opening of our third garden centre

"GOOD MORNING, VICAR," I said when Charles took John-Boy away to talk to his mother.

"Ah, Frederic. Splendid occasion, my boy..."

He turned to his wife.

"...The memsahib was just saying to me how lovely your new roses are this year. What did you call them in the end?"

"The blue one is called 'The Lordship'. The pink one is 'The Ladyship'."

"And are they the ones which won first prize at the Chelsea Flower Show?"

"Yes, we were very lucky. Now they are selling like hot cakes. The lady mayoress wants some planted outside the council chambers."

Out of the corner of my eye I caught sight of John-Boy, who now seemed to be arguing with Charles. He was gesticulating in my direction but I had no idea what on earth they could be talking about. The vicar coughed to draw my attention but I wasn't really following what he was wittering on about, just like when he was speaking from the pulpit.

"Splendid, my boy! Splendid. I told my lord bishop all about them. He is here, somewhere. He's from Leeds, you know. He has inherited some ancient pile in a picturesque valley. Now he intends to marry his young secretary to create an heir and a spare. That's what he says! Well, good luck to him, I say."

Now I was surprised by John-Boy, who reappeared beside me and took hold of my hand. I smiled at the vicar and led John-Boy aside.

"You mustn't do that," I insisted. "It just isn't done."

John-Boy looked worried.

"But I don't know any of these people, Freddy. I told you that I need a good seeing-to, I'm so bored..."

Now he turned back to look for Charles, who had just stormed out of the refreshment tent.

"Uncle Charles is just impossible. Freddy, I sometimes wish..."

He let go of my hand again. I led him to a quiet table in the corner, where we both sat down while I glared at him.

"I'm so angry with you," I insisted. "You've done everything you can to undermine my confidence today. I nearly lost my place in my speech because of you. Your uncle Charles should take you indoors for a really good spanking."

"My dad tried that, Freddy, but it didn't work. I really need a good man like you to love me, not beat me."

He didn't say any more but looked down on the floor. Suddenly I felt sorry for him and tried to think of a new idea.

"Well, John-Boy, now is the time to make some new friends."

"I want to be with you, Freddy. You know I only love you."

"How old are you now?"

"Eighteen. You know that."

"Well, try and find yourself a girlfriend, then."

"You know very well, I just don't like girls. I never have."

"What about a boyfriend, then?"

He stared at me.

"But," he insisted, "I only want to be with you."

"Look, John-Boy, I like you. Of course I do. But it just isn't done."

"You only sleep with my uncle Charles, don't you, Freddy?"

I didn't quite know how to respond to this challenge but I suddenly had an idea and turned to him once more.

"Young man, look around you. All our staff are here. What about that handsome young man over there, then? Is he your type?"

I pointed at one of our youngest greenhouse staff, who never seemed to talk to girls.

"Not my type," he muttered. "I like sexy older men – like you."

Charles walked over to us with his sister. I got up from the table to leave John-Boy with his mother, while I went to have a look at our display of roses for sale. The blue ones seemed to be very popular today. It had been several years before we had any further success with them at the Chelsea Flower Show. Of course, other more urgent issues had to be dealt with first, ten years before.

The 1920s – A New Decade

"Freddy, it is time to dig up the Christmas tree again... "

Her Ladyship and I were the only ones at breakfast on this cold and frosty morning. Charles was in the bath. His Lordship had taken to his bed after an exhausting parliamentary committee meeting the day before when they were discussing the state of the German economy.

"You know my husband and I are planning to visit my daughter in the New Year. It is time we saw our new granddaughter in America... Do you think Charles will be all right now? He seems to be so much better lately."

I went over to the sideboard to help myself to bacon and eggs from the hotplate.

"How long will you be away, my lady?"

"About six months, I guess. My husband is thinking of doing some business on Wall Street. He thinks his investments might do better over there because he doesn't like Lloyd George's government and says the Chancellor will increase the taxation in the budget to help pay for the last war. So His Lordship wants to put it where Lloyd George's lot can't get their hands on it... That's what he says, anyway."

"So," I asked her, "has he finished negotiating with the property developers who are preparing the site for the new estate?"

"That's the point, Freddy. Some of the money is about to be paid into the bank. His Lordship thinks it would be better invested on Wall Street. Besides, the winters here are so dreary, aren't they? I think all the excitement of New York will do us both good. You two boys will be alright now, won't you?"

Charles appeared in his dressing gown and went to the hotplate for his breakfast. Her Ladyship was looking at her son disapprovingly through her lorgnette.

"Charles! You could at least have bothered to dress for breakfast. Look at Freddy now. Superheroes like him are already dressed and ready for action."

Charles stuck his tongue out at me and then at his mother, who just giggled.

"Happy Christmas to you as well, Mother."

As Charles sat down, he put a hand affectionately on my shoulder and squeezed it.

"Time to dig up the Christmas tree again," I said.

"Freddy, dear..."

Her Ladyship was smiling at me.

"We have bought you something very special for Christmas. It was His Lordship's idea but using some of my savings. My husband hasn't got any left, you know – so, hard times, Freddy. "

"Yes," Charles added excitedly. "A lorry is delivering it this morning. It is rather large, you see."

"Only we don't want you to see it until Christmas Day," Her Ladyship continued. "Please will you not go into the old stable block where the Rolls is parked for the time being... We are going to get the men to move it in there. Send Charles if you need anything from the stables."

This was most intriguing. I knew His Lordship was grateful to me now that his son was better again but why should he buy me a Christmas present that had to be parked next to the Rolls? I smiled and said nothing.

So we dug up the Christmas tree together. Charles thought it might have grown too large to get into the Big House but I showed him how to trim it back to fit it in its usual place under the main staircase in the hall. Her Ladyship and her part-time maid then spent the morning decorating it. I kept well out of the way during the delivery later in the morning. I did see the van, however, but there was no name on the side so I was still left guessing.

On Christmas Eve there was a heavy frost. We were not able to do very much outdoors but my time was taken up by attempting to adjust the temperature in the greenhouses, where we were trying to keep plants through the winter. The gas heating came from cylinders, which were kept under pressure like the lighting in old-fashioned railway carriages. The gas arrived by lorry from the gasworks some distance away but our tanks were getting low and the new ones did not arrive in time for Christmas. There was no alternative but to try to relight the old boiler in the boiler house. This had not been used since before the war but fortunately we did have coal and a supply of logs from the estate.

Charles and I spent the afternoon trying to clean out the old boiler, filling the system with water and getting the fire lit. Apart from some drips from a leaky pipe it started to work, after a fashion. I had forgotten how labour-intensive the whole thing was but Charles said he would take his turn to stoke the boiler through the night and the boiler house was pleasantly warm with such a large fire in the grate. Eventually we decided to stay out there together and Her Ladyship found us a camp bed, where one of us could sleep while the other stayed awake.

"Like a night in our dugout," Charles suggested. "Only we didn't have a roaring fire to sit by in the trenches. Sometimes our water bottles froze up."

"Why do we always end up talking about life in the trenches, Charles? For so many of us it was hell on earth. I think it is time to forget and move on."

"Very well, I'll do the midnight watch until four, then you can take over, Freddy."

That was the theory but I didn't get a lot of sleep because it was so romantic lying beside the fire and we spent most of the time talking.

The following day on Christmas morning, we banked up the fire, hoping it would keep alight until lunch, and went off for the Christmas service in the village church. His Lordship had his own private pew, where his wife and son usually joined him. Until now I had sat with all the other servants and tenants from the estate but Charles insisted that it was high time for me to join the family. There was some discussion about this in the Rolls but I said nothing. However, by the time we reached the church door the matter had been settled and I took my place beside Charles, with Her Ladyship at my other side. A few heads turned but by now it was common knowledge that I was already living in the Big House as the young master's attendant. I sat and listened to the vicar's Christmas message and joined in the carols. Once again my mind recalled a similar service in the Somme when we were promised that God was on our side.

I really would need to start forgetting all about the war.

It wasn't until the afternoon that we got round to the Christmas presents. I still had no idea what I would find parked in the old stable next to the Rolls.

"Well, Freddy," His Lordship said after the Christmas pudding plates were being cleared away, "I think the time has come... "

Even Her Ladyship came out with us to the stables, where an old sheet covered over what looked as if it might be a motorcycle.

"Close your eyes, Freddy... "

I felt the breeze as the dust cover was pulled away. I had driven staff cars in France and serviced my officer's car but I had never ridden a motorcycle.

"Now!"

In front of me was a contraption I had never seen before. It had handlebars like a bike but underneath was a small petrol engine and another curious contraption.

"Do you know what this is?"

"No, Sir."

"Well, it is so new. This is one of the first out of the factory – good reputable firm, though. We've bought threshing machines, horse ploughs and binders from them before... "

I got down to have a closer look. There seemed to be a system of revolving prongs underneath, driven by a chain, which also seemed to be connected to the wheels.

"Still no idea...?"

I looked up at His Lordship and smiled.

"...You won't be able to use it until the frost has gone... It is a mechanical cultivator to dig the soil... to help you with the digging. It runs on petrol just like the Rolls... Charles tells me you are planning to start... what did you call it?"

"A garden centre, Papa."

"Good idea, too, I think... Don't you, my dear?"

His Lordship turned to his wife.

"Well," she said, "if we stay in the United States, you two boys can do what you like."

"What's this about the USA?" Charles asked his father.

"Your mother and I are thinking of going to stay a bit longer in New York so I can look after my investments. We also want to spend time with your nephews and nieces, don't we, my dear."

Charles now turned to Her Ladyship.

"How long will that be, then, Mama?"

"As long as your father thinks it will take."

His Lordship carried on.

"You two lads have settled down, now. It's time we left you to get on by yourselves for a while and make a go out of your... garden centre. Maybe the new decade of the nineteen-twenties will be the age for young people to come up with some new ideas. Who can tell? Lloyd George certainly thinks he knows what to do for this country. I'm sure he means well, like all these politicians, if it gets them more votes at the ballot box... but I'm not so sure England isn't going to the dogs... What?"

Charles nudged me but I managed to hold back a giggle.

"Anyway," His Lordship went on, turning to me again, "this should help you avoid a lot of back-aching work with a spade... Merry Christmas, Freddy."

"Thank you, Sir."

His Lordship led his wife back to the Big House.

"What did you think it was?" Charles asked.

"A motorcycle."

"For two? Well, one day perhaps, Freddy."

"We ought to go back and check that boiler," I said. "We mustn't let the greenhouses get cold."

"Yes, duty calls. What? How about a nice fuck in front of the open fire door?"

"Why not? Who will know?"

"It's Christmas! I'll bring some mince pies. We can warm them by the fire."

"But we need to go in to open the rest of our presents."

"Oh, yes. I was forgetting."

From Her Ladyship I got a suit. She said it had been her brother's and that's why it smelled of mothballs. From Charles I got a card, which just said "You wait!"

I made my excuses and went back to see if the boiler was

still alight and it was – just. I checked the thermometers in the greenhouses and returned to stoke up the fire. Charles was sitting waiting for me and had already thrown more coal into the boiler.

"Just like being back in the trenches," he said. "I was just thinking about France."

"Have you checked the boiler-level sight glass?"

"What's that?"

I showed him the way to check the water level and we topped up the boiler from the hose.

"What happens if it goes down too low?"

"The boiler might overheat and explode... Bang! ... Boom!"

"That would be too much like the trenches... You're joking!"

"No," I said. "You look up the history of the railways. In the 1860s there were several terrible explosions, often because the boiler of the engine was allowed to run out of water."

"I never knew that."

"One engine on the North Eastern Railway in 1860 ended up looking like a porcupine, with its fire tubes all poking out."

"How do you know that, Freddy?"

"My dad worked on the railways. He kept a scrapbook with old photos in it."

"You've never talked about your family before."

We sat down together and I opened the door of the boiler to rake the fire with the poker.

"My dad was a fireman on the railway," I said. "We lived in a trackside cottage and my mum opened and closed the gates of the level crossing outside. That was her job."

"Where are they now, Freddy?"

"The line was closed down and they emigrated to Canada."

"Why didn't you go with them, then?"

"I didn't want to go. Anyway, Canada was a long way away."

"So you stayed here and worked in the gardens... I'm so glad."

He put his arm around me and hugged me. We sat for a while, just staring into the flames.

"I started to grow sweet peas in the garden next to the railway line," I said, after staring at the flames for a while.

"So you didn't want to be an engine driver?"

"I was afraid of steam engines... I wanted to work in a garden, with plants and living things."

Charles kissed me on the cheek.

"So, where was this railway line?"

"Not far from here. Your parents might remember it... We might go out there some time to see if anything is left... I don't know."

I threw some more coal into the boiler.

"Where are the mince pies?"

Charles took a bag out of the pocket of his coat. I brushed the ashes off the ledge of the fire door and placed them in front of the fire.

"Watch they don't burn."

"This brings back memories," I said. "The walls of this boiler house could tell a few tales... "

"What tales?"

"One day, Charles. I'll tell you everything one day."

I reached forward to poke the mince pies, sat back on the bench and lay my head down on Charles' lap and he ran his fingers through my hair.

"You're the best thing... ever... Do you know that, Freddy?" he said after a while. I looked up at him and smiled.

"Charles, I think this is the best Christmas I can ever remember, since playing football with the German soldiers in no man's land. That was the moment I realised the Germans on the other side of the front line were just like us. None of them looked to me as if they would have eaten English babies for breakfast, so that was just a lot of stupid British propaganda."

We sat quietly for a while. I regretted mentioning my

memories of the front line yet again. It really was time to let go of the past.

"So do you think we will we be happy together, Freddy – now that the war is over?"

"Your mum thinks so."

"She said that?"

I suddenly thought about my grandma. I hadn't given her the Christmas card and her favourite chocolates I had bought.

"Charles, I want you to come and meet my grandma. Can we go now? We can leave the boiler for half an hour. You might remember her – she ran the village school, years ago."

"Why don't we take her some roses, Freddy."

"You give them to her, then."

So we went into the greenhouse to find some winter roses and walked off to the village together.

"Merry Christmas, my lord," said the postmistress as we walked by and she curtsied.

Charles stopped to talk to her.

"I was so sorry to hear about your husband, Ma'am," he said respectfully. "He will be much missed, I know."

"It was the influenza, my lord," she said. "But you are looking better again after your terrible time in the trenches. I dealt with all those depressing telegrams from the War Office, you know."

Now she turned to me with a nod.

"May I say, Master Frederic, how pleased I was to read about your Victoria Cross in the local newspaper. It does us all good to realise that our late Queen Victoria intended it for any rank, no matter how humble – not just the officer class. Anyway, congratulations."

Charles looked at me, smiled and then turned to the postmistress again.

"We are adjusting to England in peacetime once more, Ma'am. It is taking some of us a bit longer than others, that's all. Freddy, here, is taking good care of me now."

She nodded knowingly at me and winked. The postmistress had always been at the centre of gossip in the village. If she approved, then there could be no scandal. So many villagers had lost sons, fathers and brothers in the war, perhaps they were just glad to welcome those who had returned, with or without the glories of a medal. Besides, the deaths from influenza had been far worse in our village than the toll of deaths on the Western Front. It was quite different to grieve over the death of a neighbour who lived next door. For most people, France and Belgium were a long way away. But perhaps the locals had agreed that it was time for everyone to take care of the survivors of the troubles, both at home and abroad. So we walked on down the High Street, side by side.

"Happy Christmas to you!" shouted another passer-by I did not know. We both waved and turned the corner to find my grandma's cottage. I knocked at the front door, which was shut to keep out the cold.

"Fred! There you are..."

She held the door open and recognised Master Charles.

"...Do please come in, my lord. This is an honour, I'm sure."

He glanced at me and we went inside the parlour. I closed the door behind us. Grandma's bed still took up half the room. There was only room for one chair by the hearth.

"I don't know where you are both going to sit," she said. "I'm still resting on my bed. It is my bad chest, you know."

"We brought you something, Ma'am," Charles said, holding out the roses.

"There's a vase outside in the kitchen, Sir," she said, sitting down on the bed. "Freddy will find it."

I was holding out the Christmas card and the chocolates. Charles took the initiative and went into the kitchen to find the vase and fill it outside at the pump in the yard. Grandma pulled up the bed covers around herself to keep out the chill from the street. She carefully opened the card but passed me the chocolates to undo the packaging. So I sat down on the chair with her needlework scissors from the hook by the hearth. Charles returned with the roses in a vase, which he placed on the bedside table. Grandma waved at me to give up my chair, just as she might have done for a member of the aristocracy, but Charles sat down on the floor at my feet by the fire. My grandmother watched all this in amazement.

"Fred," she said, "the kettle needs water from the pump to make a pot of tea... Would you...?"

Instead, Charles got up, smiled at me again and reached for the old brass kettle in the hearth. With another nod at me, he took it outside to the pump in the yard. My grandma stared at him with her mouth open.

"...Well, Fred, I never thought I would live to see the day! His Lordship's son and heir making me a cup of tea. I told you to bring your girlfriend to meet me, Fred. That would be the sort of thing for her to do, you know – not the young master."

I had no idea what to say, so I said nothing while Charles returned with the kettle and placed it over the flames. Once more he sat down silently at my feet to watch the fire. Grandma and I continued to chat while she showed me all the Christmas cards from Canada. When the kettle boiled, Charles got up again to make the tea but discovered that the milk jug was now empty.

"Fred will need to go and borrow some milk from next door," she sighed.

"I can go, Ma'am," he said with a smile. "You need to spend time with your grandson at Christmas."

So he took the milk jug to go and talk to the lady next door while my grandma watched, spellbound. She pointed after him as he shut the front door behind him.

"It's him, isn't it, Fred?" she muttered, now turning to me again. "I told you to bring your girlfriend but you told me it wasn't like that...last time you were here... Oh, Fred, what are you doing, I ask you? ... He's nice and handsome, I know, but he's not from your social class, is he? And what future can there ever be for an illicit love affair like this?"

"Grandma, I love you and it is Christmas but that's our business, don't you think?"

She stared at me.

"Well, I never! Fred, you don't, for one moment, really think this can work out, do you? I mean you and him...from either side of the great social divide. This is England, not Italy or France. Anyway, you know what the Bible tells us about Sodom and Gomorrah."

I was upset already. I didn't believe some of the things I heard in church.

"Grandma, it is working out. We really love one another."

She pointed in the direction of the Big House beyond the village.

"Do they know? I mean His Lordship and Her Ladyship?"

We stared at one another for a moment while I decided what to say next.

"Please stop worrying, Grandma. We know what we're doing."

"So they do know, Fred... They must do or you would be in prison by now – doing hard labour... Well, I never thought I would live to see the day. But people do say so much has changed just because of the war. Now I know it must be true... Do the two of you sleep together then, like that Oscar Wilde and Lord Douglas? ... Imagine, my grandson bedding a member of the landed gentry..."

I nodded, not knowing quite what to say.

"...And Her Ladyship actually knows about this?"

I nodded again and watched Charles return with the milk jug. He pointed at it, smiled and proceeded to pour out the tea.

"I paid your neighbour for one pint of milk, Ma'am. She had more than enough for Christmas, she said. If you need sugar, she has some of that too. And she asked me to give you this."

Charles passed her another card and a hot cup of tea. Grandma looked at him.

"Fred has just told me all about it," she said. "You will look after him, won't you? He's a good boy really... Well, you know he's always looked after me."

"And now Freddy looks after me, Ma'am. I am very lucky."

"Well, Sir," she added, "I'm the last person to make judgements or to tell him how he should live his life, even if the Bible tells us it is wrong for two men... "

She gasped and seemed to run out of words when Charles sat down on the floor at my feet and took my hand to kiss it. Then he turned respectfully to my grandma.

"I owe Freddy everything, Ma'am, just like my cousin who he rescued from the crashed plane in no man's land. Without Freddy, neither of us would be here today, I'm quite sure of that. He is everything to me. Yes, I will look after your grandson, Ma'am... I do know what the Bible tells us, but both Freddy and I now feel differently about the Church since we served in the trenches. We need to find our own salvation, Ma'am. After the terrible bloodbath in the trenches, I am losing my faith in the Lord."

My grandma stared at us with her mouth open.

"Well, I never thought I would live to see the day, really I didn't... To hear Her Ladyship's son say he is losing his faith."

She pointed at the portrait of David Lloyd George on the wall above us. "Social reform was what England really needed. He knew that, didn't he? ... But, I ask myself, will England ever be a land fit for heroes like you two...where you and your kind can live happily together...?"

She glanced once again at the portrait of David Lloyd George.

"...Did he know what he was starting when he talked about equality in England? Equality for whom exactly? ... Well, Fred and Your Lordship, respectfully now, maybe you've never thought about that – only time will tell... Perhaps, one day, England will be a land fit for everyone...with or without God's good grace... "

She suddenly stared at me with an expression of horror.

"...But what am I going to say to them all in Canada now, Fred? I said on my Christmas card that you'd found yourself a nice young lady."

She said no more, sipped her cup of tea and stared into the fire. We left her with her roses, the cards and her box of chocolates. I think she was in a state of shock. She didn't even turn to watch as we quietly closed the door behind us and returned in silence to the greenhouse once more.

We sat in front of the fire in the boiler room to warm up after our walk. Neither of us had much to say now. Perhaps it was time for action, not words. We were quietly staring into the flames again and I turned to rub my face in Charles' groin. He slid his fingers under my belt to touch my buttocks inside my pants.

"I was listening to the vicar this morning in his Christmas sermon," Charles said eventually. "What on earth does that man really know about love? And why does it have to be about Adam and Eve or Mary and Joseph? Why can't it be about you and me? ... Why should you have to find a girlfriend just to please your grandmother? And why did the vicar read out the banns for the next couple to get married in his church, but such a thing is just not possible for you and I?"

"It is the vicar's job to say nice things at Christmas."

"Well, do you really believe all that stuff about the manger and the baby Jesus, Freddy?"

"I did until we got sent to France. I think life in the trenches killed religion for me... I used to ask myself, if God really was on our side in the war, how on earth could He allow such chaos and bloodletting?"

Charles started to rub his finger in between my buttocks and I began to get excited.

"Are you happy now, Charles?"

"More happy than you can possibly imagine. I never thought love would be like this – with someone really special like you."

I undid the buckle of my belt to allow Charles to get his hand inside my pants.

"Your card said I had to wait. What for, Charles?"

"Oh, yes, I forgot."

He turned round to take another bag out of his coat pocket and gave it to me. I looked inside. It was a leather harness and I took it out to have a better look.

"Put it on, then!" he said, laughing. "It's for you..."

I opened the fire door wider so that more heat would come out.

"It is adjustable – look...!"

Charles showed me how the waist size could be reduced.

"...We can always make another hole if it is still too big for you..."

I took my clothes off so I was naked and stepped into the harness. Charles started to do up the straps.

"...I'm going to fuck you, Freddy, now you're wearing this... Gosh! You look so good!"

"Where did you find it?"

"In Paris during the war. It was designed for a striptease dancer."

"You mean a woman?"

"No, a young man like you, Freddy."

"Well, I never knew places like that existed in Paris."

Charles said nothing but finished adjusting the strap around my chest.

"Look, now, that is fantastic. Turn around, Freddy!"

I swivelled on my heels in the light from the fire and Charles smacked my bottom, which was now clutched tightly by the leather straps.

"Ouch!"

"Just what the doctor ordered! Now I'm going to fuck you! Bend over, Freddy!"

I turned around to lean over the bench and Charles started to rub his fingers around my bottom.

"I think we may need to undo the strap a couple of notches... "

I felt Charles adjusting the buckle around my waist so that he could pull the leather strap out from between my buttocks.

"You are so sexy... "

He started to massage between my thighs and around my waist. I closed my eyes.

"A long slow, tender-hearted fuck... "

Suddenly we were surprised when the boiler house door opened behind us.

"Well, well! What have we here?"

We both turned to look as Her Ladyship stepped in through the doorway.

"Damn, I forgot to turn the key again!" I muttered.

"Mother, really! You should have knocked!"

We both stood up.

"I came to tell you the Christmas cake is on the table."

She laughed. "Now I really do see what this is all about!"

Charles went over to his mother and ushered her quickly out of the door.

"What on earth is that thing that Freddy is wearing?"

"Not now, Mother! You should have knocked and waited."

"I didn't think anything like this would be going on in the boiler house. I saw the smoke coming out of the chimney so I thought you were just stoking up the fire. I had absolutely no idea!"

"Well, you do now, Mother!"

She laughed.

"Yes, I do, only the flames of passion were not the kind of fire I had in mind at all, young man!"

It was Boxing Day morning. I was in two minds about going down to breakfast. His Lordship was still in bed. Charles was in the bath again. I decided that if words were to be had, there was no time quite like the present.

"So, young man."

Her Ladyship was looking at me through her lorgnette again.

"Good morning, my lady."

"No aches or pains today?"

"Pardon, my lady?"

"Oh, come now, Freddy. There have never been too many secrets between us!"

I spooned some scrambled egg onto my plate and sat down opposite her. I didn't know quite what to say except the obvious question.

"Do you want me to move out again?"

"Of course I don't, but Freddy, dear Freddy. It really is none of my business what my son does with you in bed or anywhere else. But really, do you think the boiler house is the right and proper place?"

"Sorry, my lady."

We continued eating in silence.

"Coffee, my lady?"

She nodded and smiled. I got up from the table to return to the sideboard.

"Tell me, Freddy, what was that thing you were wearing?"

"It was my Christmas present from Charles."

"And where on earth did he get that?"

"Paris, I think."

"Really!"

I passed the cup of coffee to her.

"I will ask Charles about that!"

"My lady, may I ask you a favour? I know him too well."

"Well, Freddy, it rather depends on what that is."

"May I ask you to say nothing to Charles?"

"Why is that, young man?"

"Because I don't want him to go back into his shell."

"Oh, I see what you mean," she muttered. "Mental illness again."

"It took him so long to emerge from shellshock."

"Yes, I should know and I'm his mother!"

"I don't think it would help if he thought that what he is or what he does is wrong."

"Well, Oscar Wilde went to prison. 'The Ballad of Reading Gaol' was all about it – yes, two years of hard labour."

"Precisely, my lady. I don't think it would help to remind

Charles of that, do you?"

"Well, Freddy. If you don't mind what my son does to you, then I'm sure it is none of my business. But, listen, young man. I did warn you that scandal of any kind had to be avoided at all costs."

"Trust me, my lady."

"I guess I'll have to..."

She turned to me and looked through her lorgnette again.

"...But you'll need to be more careful in future. Next time someone else could walk into the boiler room. I suggest you check the door is kept locked before you two..."

"Yes, I will see to it, my lady."

She got up from the table and left the room.

The New Year

"So, Freddy, make a wish... What will it be?"

Charles was looking quizzically at me while pouring out the very last bottle of vintage champagne from the cellar into four glasses.

"Let's make a wish together. The next ten years could be critical for business."

"What will we be thinking at this time, Christmas, in nineteen twenty-nine, Freddy?"

"Your father thinks that Wall Street in America has all the answers."

There was a cough outside in the hall.

"What's that? Did someone mention Wall Street? My son-in-law has an office there, you know, Frederic."

His Lordship came into the room.

"I was just saying, my lord, that we might look to America if we want to know what the next ten years might bring."

"Quite right too, Freddy. England is going to the dogs, I tell you... Lloyd George has got it all wrong... yes, quite wrong.

Where is Her Ladyship now?"

His Lordship turned to Charles, who pointed up the stairs, which is where his father went to find her, calling out that it was nearly midnight and time to see in the New Year. We both burst out laughing and picked up our glasses.

"To the dogs, Freddy!"

"The dogs and Lloyd George, Charles!"

Before I could stop him, he kissed me passionately on the mouth.

"Happy New Year, Freddy."

"Not here, Charles, please. Your mother says we've got to be more careful now!"

"You wait! We'll go off to bed soon, yes?"

I nodded and we hugged one another for a minute or two, just like a courting couple. Our secret marriage in the woods had only been a few weeks before.

Now I pushed him away because Her Ladyship soon appeared with her husband and we handed a glass to each of them.

"Will you give us a toast, Sir?" I asked.

His Lordship went to stand in front of the Christmas tree and puffed out his chest as if he was about to address the whole House of Lords.

"To the reform of all Lloyd George's meddlings, I say. To hell with his People's Budget, his bloody death duties, his Land Value Tax and his blasted supertax... May the devil take all his extra taxes on my port wine, petrol for the Rolls, my Havana cigars and any other fiendish little plots or intrigues he has up his sleeve..."

Her Ladyship frowned at him but we all raised our glasses.

"...And my greatest wish for 1920," added His Lordship. "The repeal of the Parliament Act and the restoration of the proper powers to our sacred House of Lords. That's what I say!"

"Come now, Father," Charles muttered, winking at me. "What about David Lloyd George's popular old-age pension scheme and his insurance schemes for health and unemployment... Surely there is something to be said in their favour? And what about votes for women, his Housing Act and all these new homes fit for heroes in the new garden city?"

"Damned meddling! Putting up the price of everything like petrol, my cigars and the port wine. That's what I call damned meddling. What? ... Damned fine country... going to the dogs, I tell you... "

Charles and I had to turn away giggling but fortunately His Lordship did not notice.

Still carrying our glasses, we soon stumbled upstairs to our room, where Charles shut the door and we both collapsed onto the bedspread in fits of giggles.

"Damned fine country going to the dogs, Freddy... "

Like his mother, Charles had perfected the imitation of His Lordship to a fine art.

I raised my empty glass but could not express the words for laughing. Charles collapsed on top of me and we lay like that for some time, gradually recovering our breath. Then he turned to me once again and stared down into my eyes.

"Freddy, I never knew life could be like this. Last night, well, I'll tell you. I woke up after another dream about the trenches. But you were there lying naked, beside me in the dark. I put my arms around you and you curled yourself round into the curve of my body. Your skin was so soft and warm. Your beautiful hair smelled sweet from that new shampoo. Even in your sleep, you are still giving yourself to me. I love you more than I can say. I will never forget 1919... So, Happy New Year, and let's make this a decade to remember as well, Freddy."

"Charles, you are going all sentimental again. I snuggle up to you when I am cold, that's all. You keep me warm and comfort me at night too. A relationship works both ways, you know... Besides, I could never sleep alone, not any more."

Now he got down on his knees by the bed to take my hand and look at the ring he had put on my finger. I had never removed it.

"Dearest, dearest Freddy..."

Tears filled his eyes as I stared at him.

"...Freddy, I told my mother, only the other day, that you are, quite simply, the most wonderful thing that has ever happened in my life. You are the fount of all my joys. You comfort me in your sleep. You honour me with your beautiful body. You inspire me with your wisdom and your insight. You startle all of us with your ability to solve technical problems and get things going again... Well, do you know, Freddy? She smiled at me and said she knew. You were, she added, also quite simply, the best thing that has happened in this house since she could not remember when. God was really smiling on us, she said, the day I fell in love with you. Now you know just how much you are loved."

I burst into tears. After the vintage champagne this was all too much.

"Now what's wrong, Freddy?"

He placed both his hands on my knees to look up into my face.

"Nobody has ever said such a thing to me before," I sniffed.

I sat up, rubbed my eyes and smiled at him. He leaned forward, kissed me, slowly and passionately on the forehead, and then looked at me once more.

"No regrets, Freddy?"

"None, Charles. We make each other happy – a sort of marriage between two men, from different walks of life and different social classes, I guess, all terribly secret and witnessed only by Stanley the horse...but a happy one, I think."

"My father also told me what he really thinks of you, you know, over port after luncheon, just the other day."

"And what's that then, Charles?"

"He said that if I'd found him a daughter-in-law, she'd probably only be able to play a little Chopin prettily on the pianoforte, arrange the flowers and do a little light needlework. He's so proud of you, you know. He says it is so much more useful when you mend the roof, unblock the drains and deal with his Rolls Royce. You were right about that, you know, Freddy. I saw the local policeman staring at the faulty headlamp and the wonky nearside front wheel. I guess we'll have to get it fixed. My mother says she doesn't feel safe in it any more and the knocking from the big ends in the engine is getting worse. She says it sounds like the engine room of the Woolwich Steam Ferry on a bad day across the River Thames."

"But," I said, seriously. "You forget the one thing I could never, ever provide is a grandchild for them – a son and heir."

"Freddy, why spoil everything with things like that now? Anyway, I really can't imagine you breastfeeding and changing nappies in the middle of the night."

I'd already been living in the Big House for more than six months. At first I feared it might turn out to be a passing episode in my life, like my short time as an officer's batman or my duties bearing stretchers in the trenches and burying the dead. One episode more than any other convinced me that my place in my new-found family would endure.

It was in the spring of 1920 when I was trimming back the privet hedge outside, before it started growing again. I had used the tall wooden stepladder since before the war but it was going rotten after all these years. So I was energetically cutting back the hedge over the high arch into the rose garden. Suddenly there was a splitting sound under my feet. I do remember flinging the hedge clippers aside so that I wouldn't land on the sharp end and I found myself flying through the air. The next thing I remember was waking up on the day bed in the hallway of the Big House to find Her Ladyship sitting on a chair and holding my hand. She looked worried.

"Thank God, Freddy," was all she could say before bursting into tears. "We all feared that we might have lost you."

Charles came in with a cup of tea on a tray and handed it

to her.

"No, Charles, Freddy needs this more than I do. You stay with him now. He'll want to be with you now, won't he?"

She ran her fingers through my hair and then got up rather stiffly but smiled at me as she went away down the corridor. Now Charles sat down and took my hand and started to play with my ring.

"Mama's been here since seven this morning, you know, Freddy. She took over from my father. He was sitting here with you since three o'clock this morning when he took over from me... "

I realised my head was swathed in bandages and I had a headache like nothing I'd known before. Charles passed me two aspirins and the cup of tea. I looked down at my feet but they were covered with a blanket.

"What happened?" I asked, unable to remember anything at all.

"The stepladder broke, Freddy. My mother has ordered a new one for you. That was the least we could do. You fell onto the grass but you hit your head on a big stone. You've been out cold since yesterday afternoon. The doctor has been twice. We were terribly worried... I thought I was just about to lose you as well as my batman..."

He sniffed. I gave Charles the empty teacup and lay back again when my head started to throb.

"...Listen, I sat here last night with my father for a while. I told him straight: you, Freddy, are the most wonderful thing that's ever happened in my life. I told him that if you died, I didn't want to go on living any more. He stopped me and said I shouldn't upset myself because he knew everything. So we left it at that. Then he went back to bed..."

I put out my other hand to hold his hand with both of mine.

"...Listen, Freddy, in case you don't know this, I'm telling you now. You're more important to me than Eton or my exhibition to study classics at Oxford University..."

Charles was clearly getting upset. I tried to stop him but

he carried on.

"...Night after night you give yourself to me, unselfishly, without an 'ouch' or any kind of complaint. When I wake up in the morning your beautiful body is entwined in mine. You always smile when I kiss you... Freddy, I simply could not live without you any more."

"We love one another, Charles," I insisted. "These things work both ways and we are together again."

He leaned forward to kiss me tenderly.

"Now, how's your poor head? I wanted them to X-ray all of you to check if anything was broken but the doctor insisted you'd come round safe and sound. Anyway, he was right, Freddy. Your skull wasn't broken. Only lots of bruises, he says. I want you to stay in bed for a couple of days."

I tried to sit up.

"For God's sake, Charles, help me up to go to the toilet or I'm going to piss myself."

He held out his hand and I put one arm around his shoulder so that I could hobble to the downstairs toilet. He had to come in to support me while I pissed in the bowl. That was the moment I realised our relationship would last – from opposite sides of the great social divide, maybe. However, it wasn't doomed, because we had now earned the respect of his parents. I could stop worrying – I wouldn't spend two years on the treadmill in the local gaol like Oscar Wilde. Our love affair wasn't doomed to fall apart after a few months. So, we were a couple from today, just like other more conventional couples, who might be blessed in a church – in sickness and in health.

Early in 1920, Charles had another appointment with the specialist in charge of his case. Her Ladyship took me aside at breakfast the day before while Charles was still in his bath.

"Freddy, I want you to accompany my son to see his specialist tomorrow. I telephoned him and told him all about you. Now he wants to see you and not me. Anyway, after that nasty accident, you need a proper check-up. Well, I told him that you are by far the most important person in Charles' life now. Apparently he'd already seen that bit in The Times about your VC and your heroic exploits out in France."

"What do you want me to say, my lady?"

"That's up to you now. Well, the specialist told me that the cure for Charles' shellshock was to find somebody to love. I told him the truth – he'd found you, Freddy – a national hero, no less."

I must have looked worried. Her Ladyship put her arm around my shoulder. This had never happened before.

"Don't worry, Freddy. He used to be an Army doctor but I don't think he's ever met anyone with a Victoria Cross. He sounded most intrigued."

"Do I have to go, my lady?"

"No, not if you don't want to. But listen, the doctor tried everything to help Charles to recover – medication, electro-therapy, psychoanalysis. He'd run out of ideas, except declaring him insane and having him secured in a mental hospital. Then you came along and suddenly...well, in the consultant's own words, Charles' recovery astounded medical opinion. I told him it was because of you, the warmth of human love, your devotion and kindness. Indeed, he mentioned this case at a conference on the subject in America."

"Do you mean everyone knows my name, my lady?"

"Of course not, Freddy. Now stop worrying. His consulting room is as confidential as the confessional in a Catholic church. Apparently there has been great interest in this case, which was described in The Lancet. You seem to have made medical history, Freddy, but nobody knows who you are, trust me. But, listen..."

She looked around the breakfast room to check that nobody was listening.

"...Sit down, please and listen carefully to what I have to say..."

She sat down right beside me at the table to whisper.

"... I am ill but I am telling you because I trust you. My husband doesn't know and Charles must never be told, at least not until I am ready."

"I am sorry to hear it, Ma'am."

"I have, well, what people call a woman's problem – it is still in the early stages and happens at my time of life. My doctor doesn't know how long it will ..."

She sniffed but put one hand on my arm.

"... One day, dear Freddy, and it might be in six months or sixteen years – nobody knows how long – I will need to leave my son in your care. Well, there is nobody else. Don't worry, I'm rewriting my will to leave some money for you to continue all your good work. It won't be a lot – well there's not much left after settling death duties we had to pay when my father..."

I smiled.

"I know, Ma'am. Lloyd George and the Treasury took it."

"Yes, Freddy, you know all about that. But do you understand now why I want Charles' doctor to meet you? I mean apart from checking you over after your fall."

"Yes, my lady, I will go tomorrow."

"It is already time for you to accept your role in loco parentis..."

I looked confused.

"... Oh, forgive me, Freddy. That means acting in the place of the parent. Well, my husband will not know what to do. One day it will be your job to take care of Charles for good, and possibly my husband as well if I... Freddy, we are all mortal...even heroes like you...and that dreadful old rotten stepladder was inexcusable."

She smiled at me.

"...Well, perhaps some people, like Lloyd George, seem to be immortal. My bomb was doomed to fail to blow him up, maybe, if the Lord God is on Lloyd George's side. The Welsh certainly seem to think so, anyway. I'm sure the Welsh claim that their hero, David Lloyd George, sits at God's right hand! ... What do you think, young man? Should I forgive him and forget the People's Budget in my declining years? ... He gave both you and me the vote in 1918, anyway."

We laughed together. She placed her hand on my arm.

"...But are you quite sure this is what you want to do with your life, Freddy? I mean – looking after my son."

She reached for the silver coffee pot I had just placed on the table.

"Charles makes me very happy, Ma'am."

"Truly? You're not just saying that?"

"I shall be happy to look after him. But we take care of one another. You see, this is what I've always dreamed of but never dared to hope it would come true."

"Well, he dotes on you, Freddy. He went white when we carried you in from your accident. Now you've fully recovered, I've never seen him so happy. I think he believes it was God's will that you survived unscathed. He told me that you would have died if the Lord God had decided your relationship really was sinful. Perhaps he has found his faith again."

She smiled and poured coffee into my cup first, then her own.

"So all those eligible young debutantes must look elsewhere, then, young man?"

We laughed together.

"Yes, my lady."

"You must say this to Charles' consultant. He needs you to say all this – in confidence, of course, dear Freddy. Then he will know it is true."

So, for the first time in my life I found myself with Charles in the waiting room of the consultant's posh practice in Harley Street. I was amazed when the doctor came out of his door to greet us in person. Charles turned to me.

"Freddy, my mother wants you to talk to the doctor on your own first of all."

So the door was closed behind me and I was invited to take a seat at the consultant's desk.

"Firstly, young man, let me congratulate you on your belated VC. Why did it take so long, then?"

"A matter of state security, Sir," I said. "There were issues which did not appear in the newspaper."

The doctor tapped his nose.

"Ah, hush-hush, what? ... Now, young man, Her Ladyship has been kind enough to bring me up to date with everything and I can assure you I do realise everything is sensitive and confidential."

"I am not the marrying kind, Sir, nor is Charles."

"My dear boy, you don't have to tell me that! But are you really prepared to give up your right to happiness with a wife and family for the sake of respectability in polite society? A handsome young man like you, received at court and honoured in the newspapers, must be attractive to many young ladies with money and prospects... There are many respectable men I know who would welcome you as a son-in-law, even in a white marriage."

"What is a white marriage, Sir?"

"One in which the partners refrain from sex – different beds etc."

I knew that would never do in our case.

"Charles and I love one another, Sir, and sex is very important."

"Well, young man, homosexual relationships are still strictly taboo – as Oscar Wilde learned to his cost... He was acceptable in London society just so long as he stuck to the rules – with his wife and children. I knew their doctor, you know. What a sad case! Reading Gaol is such a dreadful place."

"I don't want to be married, Sir, and I've read 'The Ballad of Reading Gaol'. I know the risks we take."

"I hear what you say, young man. But then, I would advise you both to move abroad, to France perhaps, where the Code Napoleon is more liberal when dealing with issues of homosexuality than the English courts..."

We sat in silence for a while. I did not know what to say.

"...Well, young man, she also told me about your accident with the stepladder out in the garden."

"I was out cold for twelve hours, Sir."

"No lasting problems, then – any headaches, dizzy turns, noises in the head? Any swellings that haven't gone down? Her Ladyship told me that you still look as fit as a fiddle."

"I feel fine, Sir."

"Well, Frederic, I've said everything I had intended to satisfy myself about. But I had to be sure that Charles wasn't putting you under pressure to engage in illegal activities you were not happy about. Some of these shellshock cases can be very difficult, you know. Some mental patients can confuse what is right and wrong – so that's why they have to be confined in Broadmoor and places like that."

"I am aware of all the issues, Sir."

"I'm sure you are, young man. But look, may I say what a wonderful thing you have done for Charles. I speak as a human being as well as his doctor. You have brought him back from the brink of insanity – that business with the grenade under the table. Yes, I heard all about it. Her Ladyship told me she had her doubts about you until then. You won your VC for a second time that night. I wish I could have seen it for myself. She says you occasionally have twinges from the bullet wound in your leg. Would you like me to look at it? She's happy to pay if another operation would make it more comfortable, you know."

"It is just a matter of time, the Army doctor said, Sir. I had to learn to play tennis and get more exercise to strengthen the leg, that is all."

"Very well. Perhaps it is time to ask Charles to join us but is there anything you want to ask me first? This is, after all, your consultation – paid for by Her Ladyship, I hasten to add."

"Do you think Charles is now fully recovered...or will the shellshock ever come back?"

"If it does, Frederic, it will be because you leave him. He may still suffer from flashbacks, at night probably when he's asleep – nightmares and so on. But if you are there, lying naked beside him in bed, then he may find comfort with you. Sex with you may help him to forget – that's what Her Ladyship thinks, in confidence. She gave me permission to tell you, by the way...and to say thank you for giving yourself so unselfishly to her son. May I add, Frederic, that I have dealt with only one or two cases of homosexual love...I have always assumed that young men who tempted the aristocracy from the straight and narrow were criminally inclined, immoral or just opportunists. Now I have met you, I know that I was wrong. So, maybe...just maybe, Frederic, it is English law which is at fault."

"Thank you, Sir. I take that as a compliment."

"And, if it is any consolation, I have examined Charles. He is not suffering from any venereal disease, by the way. I don't know about you, though. Her Ladyship wanted me to confirm your good health as well. Now, I need to examine you. Please lie down on the couch... As you may know, syphilis is spreading in all classes of society and as yet there is no cure although, we are assured, treatments may become commonplace one day in the future..."

I could have told him there was nothing wrong with me. We'd all had illustrated lectures from the MO in France about venereal disease and I knew the symptoms perfectly well. Nevertheless, I lay down on the couch for a medical examination.

"... No, young man. You pass A1 in my book. That bullet wound in your groin could be more troublesome in the future as you get older, though. Anyway, time will tell. Take my advice, if you want to live a long and happy life, avoid casual sex with anyone else. If you and Charles stick together and have sex only with each other, then the risk of infection remains zero. Now, young man, I'm telling you as a friend. Once again I would like to reassure you that this meeting is confidential. Her Ladyship alerted me about your worries."

Charles had been sitting outside longer than I had realised. Fortunately, the receptionist had brought him a cup of tea. The consultant invited him to join us and shut the door again.

"Well, Your Lordship, we've had a little chat, Freddy

and I."

Charles was looking worried now.

"You're not going to send Freddy away, Doctor?"

"No, why on earth should I do that?"

"I couldn't live without him – not any more. I've only been myself since Freddy said he loved me. If you send him away, I'm shooting myself with my pistol."

"Now stop worrying, my lord. Freddy isn't going anywhere. He's going to stay with you and sleep naked beside you all night, aren't you, Frederic?"

I smiled at them both and the doctor turned to Charles again.

"Look, you see, my lord, you do not need to worry now and may I say that you couldn't have found a more splendid, healthy and handsome example of young English manhood to share your bed with."

"Because we love one another, Doctor," Charles insisted. "You told me to find someone to love. Well, here he is – Victoria Cross and all. What more deserving partner could I find? I love this beautiful young man here with all my heart and I know he loves me."

"Yes, I heard all about it, my lord. You'll have to look after each other and keep it out of the newspapers. Make sure you always lock the door to keep things private and secret. Don't tell anyone of your relationship who you cannot trust to keep quiet about it. Never hold hands or kiss in public and things like that. You'll need to trust one another implicitly... I have found no medical reason why you should not be happy together. I will tell Her Ladyship, in confidence, of course."

We waited while the receptionist brought in a tray of tea and biscuits. She left and closed the door behind her. I was amazed when Charles got up to pour the tea and pass cups and biscuits to us both. He was taking the initiative once more, just as he did at my grandmother's house. His recovery from shellshock was clear. The doctor watched all this carefully, winked at me, placed his cup on the table beside him and smiled at us both.

"Well, Gentlemen, are there any questions you want to ask me while you are together?"

Charles was beginning to relax.

"Freddy's bullet wound, Doctor. It hurts him sometimes when we are having sex. I have to be careful how hard I fuck him."

The doctor turned to me now.

"Are you sure the bullet was completely removed – no shrapnel or anything like that? Has it ever been X-rayed?"

"I don't think so."

The doctor reached for his telephone.

"Alice, give me the X-Ray Department..."

He held the candlestick microphone to his chest and looked at me.

"...Best to get it done right now. Then we will know for sure, young man."

It seemed only a few minutes before I found myself lying under the X-ray apparatus in the private hospital next door. This gave the consultant time to chat to Charles in confidence and I waited for the X-ray plate to be developed and dried. Half an hour later, Charles, the doctor and I were looking at it on a light box in the consulting room. The consultant pointed at it. I'd never seen an X-ray plate before and it seemed even more amazing that we were all looking at my spinal column, my pelvis and my hip joints on the glass plate.

"So, did the Army hospital do a good job, Doctor?" Charles asked.

The consultant was studying it carefully.

"Freddy has no metal splinters, no fracture, no shrapnel and no infection in the joints. There are no suspicious shadows on the X-ray. The bullet was cleanly extracted, my lord... With time, and if you go gently when you fuck him...the irritation will disappear. Play more tennis, Freddy. Teach Charles how to be your partner on the tennis court. It will do you both good. That's what Her Ladyship thinks, as well. She told me and she's right. It only remains for me to wish you good luck in your lives together, strictly in confidence and off the record, of course. Let me know how you get on."

1930 – in the refreshment tent at the grand opening of our third garden centre

I found myself standing with John-Boy once again.

"Is there nobody you like here, then?" I insisted. "What about that young man over there – the one who looks after the greenhouses in our old garden centre? Do you like him, then? His name is Frank."

I pointed at a handsome, blond young man who was helping to lift the empty tea urn off the table and replace it with another.

"I bet he's married. All the best ones are," John-Boy giggled, "just like you are to my uncle Charles, only nobody is allowed to know the truth – just another of my late grandma's family secrets."

"Well, would you like to go and work with Frank at the other garden centre? You might learn a useful trade at the same time."

"You mean – to give me something useful to do and earn my keep?"

I was starting to lose my patience with Charles' nephew.

"Yes, quite frankly, John-Boy. You need something to take your mind off things like sex."

"And the day my dad jumped out of his office window, last year?"

I sometimes found it difficult to think what to say next.

"But you cannot go on blaming yourself because you couldn't stop him, can you now...?"

I stared very closely at John-Boy. I'd always had some doubts about his father's suicide.

"...He did jump, didn't he? It wasn't like that time when you pushed him out of your window into the swimming pool?"

John-boy stared at me for a moment. There was no emotion on his face. Was he putting on such a sweet and innocent expression just for me? We stared at one another. Then he changed the subject.

"But you did manage to stop Uncle Charles shooting himself or blowing himself up with the grenade."

"Yes, but I was just lucky... Listen, John-Boy, I do understand what you must have gone through...because, I know, your dad was such a bastard and hit you."

Yet again he refused to discuss the incident. Would he keep our secret if I kept his?

"Ok. I'll go for it now, just for you, Freddy. You know I want to be an actor, but I've got to broaden my repertoire. I was OK as Romeo in that local production of Shakespeare's play but I couldn't get any acting work in New York. You know I failed my audition. I can talk and recite Shakespeare but I can't sing in tune and I just can't dance. Broadway theatres all want actors who can sing and dance now, like Fred Astaire. Musicals are suddenly all the rage out there. Who wants Shakespeare any more?"

I leaned back and smiled at him.

"Who is Fred Astaire?"

"Oh, a hoofer dancer who was in Over the Top, Lady Be Good, Smiles and big Broadway stage hits like that."

"Well, young man, if I paid for you to go to drama college here, in London, would you like that, then? I think we could afford that now. Your grandma would have been proud of you. Perhaps you might even meet another handsome actor, like him."

John-Boy was looking Frank up and down and licked his lips.

"I told you not to do that!" I snapped at him. "You're in England now. This is not New York. We have old-world laws and social conventions over here, you know. One day, you might move back to the USA – somewhere like California, perhaps – where Anglo-Saxon inhibitions and morals are a thing of the past."

"Sorry, Freddy, but I would miss you. Of course, you could always come with me for wild sex out in the desert, while prowling dogs howl under a full moon. How about that?"

"You deserve a good spanking!"

"Oh yes please, Freddy!"

I made a point of ignoring such an impudent challenge.

"Well, will you do some work for us until you start at the drama school? There would be fetching and carrying to do – loading stuff into council lorries, planting more roses in the High Street and so on."

"With him?"

"Yes, if you like and promise to behave yourself."

John-Boy nodded and smiled at me with one eyebrow raised. I'd never seen him smile like this before. What did that gesture represent in New York, I wondered? Then he looked me up and down.

"Would you sit for me, Freddy? I'd like to draw you, I mean naked, just like my grandma told me, when you threw Uncle Charles' rusty German hand grenade out of the window."

"She told you about that? Did she really?"

"My grandma told me everything, Freddy. She was like that, you know. We had no secrets – well, not about you, I guess. She told me how good you looked with no clothes on – just like one of Michelangelo's famous sculptures or paintings, she said."

I decided to change the subject and waved at Frank to come over.

"Well, as you'd say, John-Boy, your grandma was some dame, yes Sir! I think you take after her... I'll introduce you to Frank in a minute."

I left him for a moment to lead Frank quietly aside and mention that His Lordship's grandson would like to learn more about gardening, now he was living here in England. Would he have time for an apprentice? I tactfully didn't mention the drama school. Anyway, John-Boy might not be accepted and he would still need to earn his living and be happy somehow.

Chapter 5

1920

So my great day arrived. I had told John I didn't want any ceremony and was rapidly turning into a pacifist now the Great War was over. There would be no military parade, no pomp, no circumstance and no Army uniforms. Everyone would be in civilian clothes at Buckingham Palace, or I didn't want to know. The British Army officials were horrified but it was my occasion and I would not have it any other way. During these negotiations I realised how much confidence I had gained since I had returned from the Western Front. Only His Lordship seemed to be disappointed because he would not be able to get his Boer War uniform out of storage, where it had been wrapped up with the mothballs. Her Ladyship said I should now follow my conscience and join the International League of Pacifism with her.

However, the day did not begin well. It was decided there was no ready money to stay overnight at The Savoy or Claridge's. The Rolls was not sufficiently roadworthy for a long journey, so we would all go to London by train. But when we turned up at the local railway station in the morning, there was a chalk sign saying a derailment was causing delays. Then a fire was lit in the waiting room for Her

Ladyship, and the stationmaster's wife brought a pot of tea while we waited. His Lordship telephoned the Palace from the station office to explain our late arrival in London. We were assured a car would be waiting at St Pancras Station.

The clock on the wall of the waiting room ticked loudly and a porter with a stepladder came to wind it up and clean the glass. Then one train arrived at the opposite platform. The porter came back to tell us it wasn't going to London but was only a slow train to the north. More minutes ticked by. The stationmaster's wife brought hot water. The teapot was topped up. Her Ladyship asked to go to the toilet. His Lordship was becoming more incensed by railway inefficiency and went off to talk to the local depot on the telephone. When he returned, he told us to get ready for the taxi. He had ordered one to take us into the next town, where trains on a rival line to London were running on time. So we were all bundled into the car and jolted on unmade roads into the city. We had a first class compartment to ourselves. Eventually, we reached Kings Cross but we were already four hours late. The car the King had provided had gone but John was waiting outside in his Rolls Royce. So we eventually arrived in The Mall and drove sedately through the gates to Buckingham Palace, where apparently my presentation had already been cancelled. We were informed Queen Mary had to leave on time in order to launch a new ocean liner in Belfast. Only King George was at home. My commanding officer in the Somme had left to attend a regimental dinner, but by now he had already convinced himself I had turned pacifist and would reject such an award, anyway.

However, the King welcomed John and Her Ladyship while His Lordship and Charles stood to attention by the door. Eventually, more tea was brought by a liveried footman. We were all invited to sit down around the fireplace, where John told His Majesty all about the incident in no man's land. Nobody had briefed him and the paperwork seemed to have gone missing – one more item in the catalogue of disasters on my special day. So, unceremoniously, and just as I had always wanted, King George handed me my Victoria Cross over a cup of tea. John insisted on pinning it to my jacket. The King then decided, because John and Her Ladyship were 'family', he would take us on a conducted tour of the Palace himself. He explained that a magnificent new front had been added to the building in 1913. He was proud of it but laughed when he said some critics still preferred the old one. I stayed silent as we were led from room to room, Charles at my side. Servants opened doors and then stood to attention until we moved on. I was in another world I could only have dreamed about before. But I still felt unworthy of my award, especially as my illicit lover was walking publicly at my side. It seemed that we were now being accepted by the very highest class of English society, where such things as illicit lust were never mentioned.

Eventually, we all said goodbye. I bowed in front of His Majesty just as Her Ladyship had taught me to do. His Lordship once again apologised for our late arrival but King George said it had been a relaxing occasion without tedious pomp or circumstance. Finally, we were conducted to the door and John's chauffeur drove us in his Silver Ghost to St Pancras Station. In the first class compartment, Her Ladyship removed her new shoes because she said they were killing her and she'd got blisters walking around Buckingham Palace. How could anybody be happy in a place like that when it was so large? she asked. What if you had to walk down so many corridors just to go to the toilet?

Charles made everyone laugh when he suggested that footmen still brought the royal commode on demand. So at last, about half past ten, as the last train puffed slowly into our local station, the day was judged a success and everyone said they felt proud of me. His Lordship offered to lock up my Victoria Cross in his fireproof safe to stop it getting lost.

Charles led me up the stairs to bed and pulled off all my clothes to kiss me all over, but I really did need to freshen up before we went to bed.

"I need a bath, Charles," I insisted. "Will you come and

wash my back with the loofah, like you did that first day?"

He followed me into the bathroom, where I lit the geyser to heat up some water. Charles sat down on the washing basket once more.

"My parents were so proud of you, Freddy. I could see it in their eyes. When the King passed you the VC and Cousin John pinned it to your jacket, I could see this was just what they might have expected for me. I was so terribly flattered to be your companion today."

I turned on the cold tap because the water from the geyser was far too hot now. I stooped down to feel the temperature of the water in the bath. Charles came up behind me to press himself against my bottom and rub his hands up and down my thighs.

"Yes, in a minute," I insisted. "We'll have sex again when I've had my bath."

I stepped into the water and passed Charles the loofah from the brass hook. I picked up the carbolic soap from the dish on the bath and started to rub lather around my groin. From behind Charles gently rubbed the soap between my thighs and in between my parted buttocks so that I would immediately develop a hard on. This was so erotic and he had learned just how to arouse me to make me ready for sex.

"Listen, Freddy...all that way in the train I was thinking about you – what it would be like to hold you close in the night, to feel your breath on my face, to hear your heartbeat when I lie with my ear against your chest. I need to know that you are really happy now – with me. Are you sure you don't want to go off to fight in another war overseas – to win some new gong for king and country, in the name of the British Empire?"

I turned to look at him while he rubbed my shoulders gently with the loofah.

"Surely you must know, Charles. By now you should know me well enough to see I am through with wars, the glory, the heroics and all that flag waving. I have a good mind to join the International League of Pacifists with Her Ladyship."

"But if the opportunity arose, Freddy...if the War Office were to offer you a commission now, would you go?"

"No, I feel just like T. E. Lawrence of Arabia, now the war is over. I only want to be a humble civilian, not some great political pawn in the game of international peace negotiations. Now it is time for people like your father, His Lordship, to sort out the world around the negotiating table."

Charles put down the loofah to put his arms around me and kissed me on the forehead.

"I will never know what I've done to deserve someone like you. So will you stay with me now, then?"

"If you'll still have me, Charles. I've nowhere else to go..."

I laughed.

"...Besides...where on earth would I find another prize fucker like you...?"

From behind Charles slapped my bottom hard.

"Ouch! ...What was that for?"

"I really love you, Freddy. You know that. Never leave me, will you? Now bend over. It is time for you to get another slow, tender-hearted fucking."

The sun was shining through the curtains when I heard a knock on the door. I called out loudly to find out who was there.

"Me!" muttered Her Ladyship outside. "Who did you think it was?"

I levered Charles off my chest and put on the dressing gown to go and unlock the door.

"I've brought you breakfast in bed, Freddy. It's half past eleven. You've both overslept."

She put the tray on the bedside table just as Charles yawned and turned over.

"Mama! What's this then? Where's the butler?"

"You've forgotten, Charles. It's just me now. Your father's bank account is empty. The butler, my maid and the cook have all had to go! Freddy, do you think you could give me a hand putting the washing out in the garden? My blisters from yesterday are still killing me."

"Yes, my lady."

"Listen, enough of that! My name is Elizabeth. After yesterday, you can call me Liz from now! ... By the way, the local newspaper is sending a photographer with a reporter to talk to you this afternoon. They telephoned again about that front page for next week. Can you manage that? Local people expect it, you know. They want a picture of you holding your VC. I'll go and tell my husband to get it out of the safe."

She looked at Charles, who had sunk back on the pillows again.

"Freddy, do something with that sleepy lump, will you? Go and play tennis or something! If he's not up to it, you can come and play tennis with me!"

She left us in peace again.

"Come back to bed, Freddy. I need you to warm me up again. Mama's breakfast has gone cold!"

So, as we waited for the reporter from the Gazette, I found myself playing tennis with Her Ladyship while Charles rummaged for lost balls in the shrubbery. The blisters on her feet were spoiling her game.

"It went over there, you idiot!" shouted Her Ladyship at him, laughing. "Honestly! Call yourself a ball-boy?"

Charles stuck his head up through the bushes.

"Now now, Mother. Any more rudeness like that and I'm going indoors! Really, Freddy, the language I have to put up with these days!"

We heard the noise of a lorry outside the Big House. Everyone thought it was the people from the local paper but Her Ladyship took me aside while Charles went to find His Lordship.

"Freddy, the men have come for the Beckstein grand piano. We're really broke, you know. I wasn't joking... I'm glad my father never lived to see this day. As they say, the financial crunch has come."

We put down the tennis rackets and walked together

around the front of the building, where the French windows into the music room were being opened so the men could wheel the piano out onto the grass. Her Ladyship put her hand on my shoulder to steady herself while we watched.

"Damn this blister. I thought it was better, Freddy. I should have stayed indoors. Still, you and I have had our first game of tennis together, haven't we? ... I'm sorry I'm no good at it any more... Ouch!"

She was trying to lever off her plimsoll. I stooped down to help her to remove it.

"That's better... Freddy, what would we do without you?"

I looked up at her.

"Are things really so bad, my lady?"

We turned to watch the workmen hauling the piano across the grass to the van.

"Well, nobody played it any more. Charles never learned, you see. We can't afford musical evenings nowadays. So what's the point of a Beckstein grand? It's so out of tune anyway. Damn! They would turn up right now!"

Behind the van, a car had pulled up and a man with a camera got out. Her Ladyship gestured at him frantically.

"Over here!"

He walked towards us, followed by another man with a notebook.

"What's this, then?" the reporter asked, turning round to look at the men heaving on the piano. Her Ladyship winked at me.

"It has to be serviced and reconditioned, my man," she muttered, trying to distract him. "Now this is the young man with the Victoria Cross. You've come to talk to him. If you'll excuse me, I must go and talk to my husband."

The reporter touched the brim of his hat respectfully. He scribbled notes with his pencil. I told him about the train the day before and the problems we'd had getting to London. I explained how I'd rescued a distant member of the Royal Family from the plane in no man's land but made no mention of the secret codebook which had to be kept from the Kaiser's cryptographers. Her Ladyship returned with my medal and the photographer took some photos of me holding it in one hand while waving the tennis racket in the other. The story would tell how a local boy, although wounded by a German bullet and honoured with this medal by the King, was now athletically engaged in the sport that I had learned when recovering from my wounds in France. It was to be a cheerful, uplifting lead story to distract readers from local bereavements after the influenza epidemic and so much post-war poverty, unemployment and general gloom and doom in the county today. After a quarter of an hour, the reporter and his photographer departed and Her Ladyship reappeared with the teapot again.

"Was that a terrible ordeal, Freddy? His Lordship is bringing the trolley outside. Well, I told him. The butler has had to go. There is nobody else left now, only Charles – he's gone to the dentist, by the way..."

His Lordship was having difficulty wheeling the trolley across the ruts in the grass. I got up.

"...Bless you, Freddy," Her Ladyship continued. "I said to my sister on the telephone what a nice young man you are – not a bit bigheaded after your presentation at court yesterday. She was jealous because she wasn't invited, you see. I had to promise to tell her all about it – well, we're sisters... Forgive and forget – that's my motto in life from now on, Freddy. You know all about my sister and the gamekeeper. Well, what right do I have to begrudge my sister a bit of slap and tickle in secret? Yes, just like you and my son, Freddy...but I didn't tell her about that, of course. I told her that she was so lucky our telephone hasn't been cut off, we owe the Post Office so much money."

I got up to help His Lordship to lift the trolley over the flowerbed to the garden table.

"Now I know what my butler did to earn his money, Frederic."

His wife lifted the teapot onto it.

"Have the builders phoned you back then, dear?"

"Yes," His Lordship explained. "They start the foundations for the new road next month. We have a deal, my dear. The first instalment of the purchase price for our land is being paid into the bank next week. I phoned the manager at the National and told him to extend our overdraft."

"And what did he say to that, then?"

"He says he wants to see the colour of their money first - such a nasty little man! I told him in your father's day, my dear, we owned the bloody bank."

"Did that cut any ice?"

"No! ... So we're bankrupt...except for rents due next month, my Army pay and your savings, my dear."

"Not under any circumstances!" she muttered.

His Lordship looked at me and winked.

"Such a hard woman... I suppose you've told Freddy about that, too, how I have left you destitute with my profligate spending."

"We have no secrets," she muttered, patting me on the knee. "Do we, Freddy?"

I just smiled while His Lordship cut the cake. He sat down again and passed me some on a plate.

"Well, young man, what do you say? You're part of this family now. You and my lazy son seem to like each other. Bankruptcy is the order of the day and the wolf is at the door. Lloyd George and the People's Budget have provided for the working man in time of need, but alas, not the aristocracy – what's left of us, anyway! ... So now it is the time for a council of war, as we used to say in South Africa."

"I'm sorry, Sir. What do you want me to say?"

"Tell us more about this garden centre idea of yours. The road is being built, after all. Progress is just around the corner. Henry Ford and his model T will provide cheap transport for the working man in the new garden city. The Housing Act will provide the houses fit for heroes – if I sell more land to make way for them... Is that what you think I should do, then, young man?"

"Yes, Sir."

His Lordship passed another bit of cake to his wife.

"Very well then. That's decided, my dear, and if you'll excuse the expression, bankruptcy has been the mother of invention."

His Lordship raised his teacup as if it was a glass of expensive champagne, and clinked each of ours in turn.

"Freddy? No swelling in the head after yesterday? Such a grand occasion! You've made me a proud man, my son!"

I sniffed. Her Ladyship turned to me and whispered.

"Now what's wrong, Freddy?"

"His Lordship has never called me 'Son' before."

The old man leaned forward and put his hand to his ear.

"What was that?"

Her Ladyship raised her voice.

"You've embarrassed him, that's all."

"Where are your folk, then Freddy? Still in Canada? It's a shame they couldn't have made it to Buckingham Palace yesterday. Well it made me a proud man, anyway...after my really pathetic son Charles' disasters out in France. What a waste of time that boy turned out to be. Why couldn't he have turned out just like you?"

"I'll send them cuttings from the newspaper, Sir. And if I may say so, Sir, now we are on friendly, talking terms..."

I stopped in case I was about to say something I might regret.

"Yes, go on, Frederic!"

"Well, Sir, I care about your son. You know that and it upsets me when you say things like that about him."

"Oh, I'm sorry, I'm sure. But can't you get him to do something with his life? It is not as if we will have a large estate to manage, tenants to look after, or lots of horses and hounds to take for a run."

Her Ladyship decided to defuse an awkward moment and put a hand on my arm.

"We all love you, Freddy. We'll never forget what you've done for Charles and for all of us."

"Well, my dear," His Lordship said, sitting back, "I have

decided. When the money comes through from the road building scheme and we've cleared all our debts, I'm taking you to America to visit our daughter and all your grandchildren."

Her Ladyship's face lit up and she turned to me again.

"Yes, Freddy, our latest granddaughter has just been born. We only heard yesterday... Goodness, my daughter has so many, now! They keep trying for another boy, you see."

This time His Lordship put his hand on my arm.

"Thanks to Freddy, Charles has someone to love him and take care of him now. We can leave him in your capable hands, can't we, Son?"

Once again I found myself standing on Grandma's doorstep. I knocked but there was no reply, so I went for a walk and found her queuing in the village bakery for a loaf of bread. It was baked in ovens behind the shop and the air was full of appetising smells.

"Oh, Fred, there you are. I'll come back later. I'm sure they will have some bread left after lunch..."

I took her arm and we walked slowly up the cobbled street to her cottage.

"Just like the old days with your grandfather, you know, Fred. You're so much like him, young man..."

She patted my hand.

"...I don't mean in looks, I mean in character: kind, generous, honest, strong and an ideal companion for a woman... with a mind of your own... Master Charles now, is he well?"

I opened the door of Grandma's cottage. It had never been locked as long as I could remember. The dusty key still hung unused on a hook over the fireplace, beside her collection of gleaming horse brasses celebrating the Royal Navy.

"Well, Grandma, we're still together, if that is what you mean."

She sat down in the chair by the hearth. The walk up the hill had made her breathless again. I placed the kettle over the flames once more. There was now a rustic three-legged stool at the side of the grate. I sat down on that and Grandma looked closely at me.

"You look well enough, anyway – no flu, TB or syphilis. Anyway, Fred, when you told me about you and him, the young master, I was afraid the Lord God might strike you down with a thunderbolt, like it says in the Good Book, you know."

"Grandma, really!"

"Well, I looked it up in your grandfather's family Bible, up there..."

She pointed to the shelf above us.

"...But I ask you, my boy, how can such a sexual relationship between two men flourish? If I asked the vicar, he would say it was an abomination in the sight of the Lord. If I talked to the village constable, he would warn me that it is quite illegal. Do you remember Oscar Wilde?"

"So what do you think, Grandma? For one moment, please forget about the Good Book, the Lord, the vicar and the village constable."

We stared at one another.

"Master Charles hasn't corrupted you, has he, Fred? I mean, you are his social inferior with certain obligations to the landed gentry and your social superiors."

"No, Grandma, there was no corruption, only love. Remember, the Bible also tells us about the love of one man for another."

"Well, I'm not sure that's what people around here would say...if they knew the truth."

"But what do you think, Grandma?"

"Me? ...Well, I think the young master should be courting a suitable young lady to marry and then provide the son and heir for His Lordship. You can't do that, Fred, can you now? That is a biological impossibility... And since you ask, young man, I think you should find yourself a nice buxom country girl to look after you. Everyone expects healthy young people like you to raise children – preferably boys – to provide a new generation for England, in order to replace the fallen on the Western Front... Some people might say that it is your duty,

Fred, my boy."

"Grandma, I've done my duty – to help keep England free of the beastly Hun...the ones we were all told would be eating English babies for breakfast. Now I'm going to live the way I want, thank you."

"With him...?"

We sat quietly until the kettle boiled. I got up to make the tea while Grandma stared at me.

"...Well, I don't know what your grandfather would have said."

"Does it really matter, Grandma?"

She seemed to be outraged.

"Of course it matters when my grandson sleeps with another man. Church and State condemn it. I cannot see any future for either of you."

I arranged the teacups on the table, trying to think what to say next. I had hoped my grandma would have accepted everything by now. Our intolerant Church of England religion had unsettled her mind.

"But I don't go to church nowadays, Grandma, so I don't believe in heaven, hell or sin any more. The war finished all that for me."

"Well, I really don't know why. You were brought up as a God-fearing boy."

She stared at me in horror but I had to tell her why I thought like this.

"When I was burying the dead in the cemeteries, I lost my faith on the Western Front... Lots of us did."

"That is a pity, Fred. I used to be so proud of you."

"I tell you now, Grandma. As I went around collecting English bones and body parts, I knew there could be no God. If there was any sort of God up there, no caring, loving God I had previously believed in, could ever have allowed such dreadful carnage."

"But we won the war in the end, Freddy."

"Yes, the padre always assured us that God was on our side too, but I no longer believed it... What did that man really know, I ask you? ... Looking back now, I think it was just a lot of propaganda. He was telling us what the authorities wanted us to believe so that we would not question their incompetence and stupidity."

My grandma was becoming more and more outraged.

"What incompetence, Fred?"

"I saw an awful lot of that, believe me. You weren't there, were you? Headquarters should have taken better care of the soldiers who were fighting for king and country on our front. What was the point of losing so many splendid young Englishmen just to capture a hundred feet of God-forsaken territory, when we all knew the Germans would take it back, about one week later?"

"It wasn't your business to question your officers' decisions, Fred."

"But we were not just expendable cannon fodder to be sent into no man's land on a whim. In all innocence we had presented ourselves at the recruiting desk, full of virtuous high hopes for a quick resolution of the conflict... Do you know how many French and English soldiers died on the very first day in the Battle of the Somme, Grandma? Twenty thousand souls – words fail me."

So Grandma and I drank the tea in silence. I got up to go and she finally turned to me, placing one hand on my arm.

"But are you really happy now, Fred?"

"Stop worrying, Grandma. I'm living the way I want. I'll bring Master Charles with me to see you again next time. Then, you can see for yourself that we are still happy together. I assure you there is no corruption – just the warm, wonderful and caring love between two human beings. I have never known such happiness before in my life, yes, just like you found with my grandpa up there."

"But my union with your grandfather was blessed in church, Fred. That was quite different. There is no comparison."

She waved at her fading wedding photo on the wall and I left her sitting quietly with her thoughts for the rest of the afternoon. I had quite forgotten to show her my Victoria Cross, and that was the reason I had knocked on the door in the first place. Other things had taken priority and I resolved to show her my medal when I could bring Charles with me. I needed her to see that he was important in my life now.

Soon it was time to say goodbye to Charles' parents as they set sail for America. Only a few years before this might have been a hazardous journey. Now, only a few unexploded mines were being fished out of coastal waters away from major shipping lanes, and a better watch was being kept on dangerous icebergs. Nevertheless, Charles was rather apprehensive but His Lordship promised to send a telegram as soon as the ship reached New York. His wife even gave me a cuddle. His Lordship became quite upset about leaving us behind and shook my hand. Suddenly he put both arms around me and hugged me.

"Look after my son, young man," he said quietly, with tears in his eyes. "We owe you so much, Freddy... yes, so much."

"We'll telegraph soon," Her Ladyship sighed, while the stationmaster held the first class carriage door open. "Come here, Son," she said to me and put her arms around me to give me another kiss. "Well, I'm so sorry all those eligible English debutantes really don't know what they'll be missing... Look after Charles for me, won't you? And don't let him lie in bed all day."

I stood beside Charles and waved until their train was out of sight, and then we went home to resume digging the flowerbeds for the roses.

So, at long last Charles and I were left on our own. I was rather apprehensive, in case it turned out to be a testing time for our relationship. The first thing I did, while Charles was again at the dentist, was to call in a favour. I phoned John, who I had not seen since I was presented with my VC at the Palace. Somehow the Post Office had still not disconnected the telephone in His Lordship's estate office. John's butler went to call his master to take the call.

"Freddy! Are you coming to work for us now?"

"No Sir, I'm sorry... I would like to call in the favour... You did say, any time."

"Of course. Name it, Freddy."

"You heard about His Lordship's little accident in the Rolls on the way home from the regimental reunion dinner last year?"

"I did hear something. So what do you want us to do, then?"

"To assess the damage to the chassis and get the Rolls back on the road."

"I thought the money had run out."

"I mean as a favour to me."

"For you?" he asked.

"They took me in and made me one of the family after the war, when others in my situation were out of work after the Armistice. It is just to say thank you to them, John."

We chatted about old times for a few minutes.

"Leave it with me, Freddy, can you? I'll talk to them all at the body shop in the Rolls Royce Department. Well, I can ask, can't I? Tell me,in your opinion, is this old wreck really worth doing up?"

I thought about the buckled chassis at the front, the white metal in the crankcase and the neglected rear brakes.

"Difficult to say, John. If I tell you we left the window open in the barn where the Silver Ghost was standing on blocks of wood. The chickens got inside and started using it as a hen house. Do you want me to go on?"

"What would Henry Royce have to say about that? I know him, you know, Freddy... But, look, it rather sounds to me that this Rolls has gone beyond economic repair...but, well, just for you, I'll come and take a look... No promises, mind!"

So one wet day John arrived with his chauffeur to take a look in the barn. I'd already got rid of the hens and done what I could to clean up the Rolls Royce. I pushed open the door. John let out a sigh. He could see immediately what the brick wall had done to the nearside front of the Rolls. I was afraid he would say the chickens should be allowed back inside again. Having got down on his hands and knees to take a closer look all round, he brushed the straw off his trousers.

"Well now, Freddy..."

I was waiting for the bad news.

"... When does my aunt arrive back from America?"

"About six months' time."

John consulted his diary.

"I tell you what we'll do. I talked to the advertising agency handling our publicity now. We are promoting our new motor body workshop and speedy repair service. Believe me, this is not the first Rolls to collide with a brick wall. We've had them waterlogged or left out on the beach to get swamped by the sea. We had one that had caught fire – a passenger left a lighted cigarette in the upholstery! Freddy, you wouldn't believe the mess! We even had one where the driver forgot to apply the handbrake when it was parked on top of the White Cliffs of Dover. That rolled backwards!"

"Oh no!"

"Oh yes, bad news! I had to go and tell them it was a write-off. The owner had bought it from us brand-new only one month before... Don't ask, Freddy! It really is time there were proper driving tests to get rid of all these stupid idiots who don't know what the handbrake is for."

"What about this Rolls Royce, then?"

I pointed over my shoulder and John sighed.

"Well," he said, "we'll take photos of it while we restore it, starting tomorrow. Can you move the chickens back inside, just for publicity? Then we'll move it to the workshop on the back of a trailer. We'll need exclusive rights to use the photos for our advertising and promotion: from chicken house to this and all that sort of thing... We'll remove the number plates and other identification first, of course. Nobody will ever know."

"How much will it cost, John? Could you add electric lighting all round? Acetylene lighting is such a dreadful fire risk in an accident and should have gone out with the ark. "

"How much was my life worth, you mean? Well, you saved mine out in France. I will never be able to thank you enough. I am here only thanks to you, Freddy! That night, nobody else could be bothered to do what you did. They all valued their own skins too much... Now are you sure my aunt and His Lordship would want to go ahead with all this?"

I nodded, and John returned with his chauffeur to his pristine Silver Ghost waiting outside.

The following day, just as John had arranged, a photographer turned up with the driver of the lorry to transport the Silver Ghost back to the works. I had to get the chickens to arrange themselves on the running board of the Rolls. That was easier said than done! The photographer decided there might be one shot they could use. The chickens were just too quick for him. So we tried another idea. I fed the chickens with grain laced with laudanum that a doctor had once prescribed for Charles. This made them rather drowsy and more co-operative, although two of them fell asleep! We found we could perch them on the window ledge, around the 'Spirit of Ecstasy' on top of the radiator and even on the steering wheel. At last the photographer was happy. His Lordship's Rolls Royce could now be winched onto the lorry and driven away to the works.

The next day, Charles surprised me by deciding to hold a party at the Big House.

"Freddy, while the cats are away, the mice – that's you and me – will come out and play. I'll phone John and ask him to bring his record collection. He might bring his fiancée to meet you. She might bring the glittering beau monde of London with her."

"Do you think that's a good idea, Charles? Won't people start to ask awkward questions about you and I?"

"Well Freddy, if they do, we just don't tell them anything, do we? You must meet the young lady I was supposed to marry before the war. She's nice. I think she'll like you."

But the party was not to be. In the middle of the night soon after, Charles creased up in agony. I thought it might be food poisoning and went to fetch a bowl from the kitchen, just in case. By the morning he seemed to be a bit better, so we resumed work in the garden, but after lunch his pains returned with a vengeance. I telephoned to the doctor from a public phone box and he immediately assumed Charles had suffered from another mental breakdown. I managed to convince him the symptoms were very physical this time. He arrived in his open-top Morris and I took him upstairs to see the patient.

"You must be Frederic," he said, stopping on the landing for a while. "Her Ladyship told me confidentially what a difference you have made here. In truth, I don't really approve of such sexual relationships between men. I believe that they go against the word of God...but under the circumstances... She was most anxious to emphasise that secrecy was essential and I agreed."

Our conversation was interrupted by a cry of pain from Charles' room.

"How long has he been like this, then?" the doctor asked me.

"The pains started last night."

The doctor soon made up his mind after a brief examination, during which I had to wait outside, but the door soon opened again.

"Charles must go into hospital at once. He has a nasty appendix. It could rupture any moment. I'll telephone the hospital before we are faced with peritonitis, Frederic."

"The telephone might have been cut off," I warned him. "His Lordship has been late in settling the phone bill, Sir. The Post Office is less generous than the old company, since they took over all the telephones, just a few years ago."

"Are things really that bad?"

"I'm afraid so. The money from the sale of land for the road building scheme has only just gone into the account."

"You seem to know a lot, young man. I thought you were just the gardener."

"Things change, Doctor. His Lordship said bankruptcy has become the mother of invention."

"I see. I thought Her Ladyship had booked a passage to New York."

"She has her own money, Doctor. They've been living on that."

"What about my medical fees, then? How will Charles pay for an appendectomy?"

"I will pay. His Lordship left me in charge of expenses. There is cash in the safe, Doctor. I have the key."

"Good. I'll just have to take your word for it. If we can't phone for an ambulance, I'll have to take Charles to hospital now in my car. There may not be much time before Charles' appendix bursts."

So the doctor and I helped Charles down the stairs and into the Bullnose Morris, which was driven away at speed. If I'd gone with them, I would never have been able to get back from the hospital. In 1922 the bus service only ran in the mornings and on market days. Suddenly, I found myself alone in the Big House. Of all the staff who had been employed here only a year or so before, now, at the age of twenty-five, I alone was left. So I went to have a look in the safe. If we were going to settle Charles' medical expenses and survive, we would need to start counting the pennies. I pulled open the heavy iron door. Inside were fifty pounds in bank notes and some coins His Lordship had left for us to live on. I noticed an envelope addressed to me in Her Ladyship's writing so I opened it. There was a letter inside:

Dear Freddy,

I am leaving you a cheque for emergencies from my own funds. Please find enclosed cheque for five hundred pounds, payable in cash to you if you need it. I suggest that you open an account at my bank in your own name. I've told the manager he may hear from you soon.

P.S. His Lordship doesn't know about this. He would squander it all just to repair the roof. Somehow, I think you might make better use of it. With love...

I was shocked. The most money I had ever had in my hands was a five pound note. I placed the letter and my cheque back in the safe and locked everything. So I walked around the house from room to room, just to check that the doors and windows were locked. This really was my home now and I was happy at last. The music room still looked empty without the Beckstein grand. Should I go and redeem it for Her Ladyship? But she could have done that herself. Clearly, she thought there were better uses for the money. What would I do with it now? I sat down on the window seat. The carpet still showed the dents where the wheels of the piano had stood for years. I moved on to the dining room. After the last of the servants had left, dust was settling on the table.

I had been neglecting my grandma again and took the opportunity to call on her once more. Anyway, it was time for me to put down more rat poison in the back yard. I found the front door unlocked as usual but my grandma had a guest today.

"Ah, Fred," Grandma muttered, without getting up. "You don't know Myrtle, do you? She's the new teacher at the village school..."

A young lady was sitting by the fireplace, holding a cup of tea. I pointed at my packet of rat poison, hoping to escape into the back yard.

"Now Fred, not so hasty... Let me introduce you."

Grandma turned to the young lady and smiled. I put down the rat poison to shake her hand.

"Are you the young man with the VC in the photo, then?"

I nodded. She fluttered her eyelashes and tried to hold on to my grasp.

"...Such an honour, I'm sure."

My grandma had reached for another cup and saucer from her sideboard and started to pour out another cup of tea for me. I hadn't expected this but did not want to appear rude.

"My Fred did well for himself out in the Somme, didn't he, Myrtle?"

Perhaps sensing that she was intruding and that I might need to talk privately to my grandmother, Myrtle got up and placed her empty cup on the mantelshelf.

"I should go," she said. "There are things to do at the school."

Grandma showed her to the door. I nodded goodbye and went out into the yard with the rat poison. Grandma followed me outside.

"I don't understand you at all, Fred," she complained bitterly. "There is an attractive, intelligent and unmarried young lady of your own age but you took no notice of her at all. Any other young man would have offered to escort her down the road and invited her out in the evening."

I made no reply but poured more poison into the earthenware pipe we had placed by the rat hole under the privy.

"You know quite well, Grandma," I insisted, looking up at her. "I already have a partner. You met him."

Grandma put her hands on her hips, ready for another go at me.

"So you're certain it wasn't a mistake then, Fred? Lots of boys have strong relationships with other boys. I've seen it at the school – much younger than you, of course. But they grow out of it soon enough."

"I'm not like that, Grandma. Your kind of sex is not for me."

She seemed to be getting annoyed with me again today.

"Then, I'm sorry for you, Fred. I'm sure your family expected better of you, really I do. Perhaps you should think about us once in a while, instead of just yourself all the time."

She turned to go back indoors. I closed up the packet of rat poison and slipped out through the back gate. I could not cope with another confrontation today. Already I was getting depressed. Why did I have to live up to my grandma's expectations? Sometimes I wished I'd never made it back from the

Western Front. I was quite certain that many men who fell in the bombardment were far more virtuous than me. Why then did I survive? What divine purpose could possibly have been served? Perhaps Grandma would be happier today if I was just another name on the war memorial outside on the village green.

With Grandma's criticisms repeating in my mind, I decided to go for a walk outside to see how far the construction of the new garden city was progressing. The driver of a steamroller was damping down the fire and cleaning out boiler tubes as I walked by. The new bypass was well underway and the men would soon be working to widen the country lane outside the Big House. As I climbed a stile to take a short cut, I came across a sleeping figure huddled in the hedgerow. Whoever it was coughed as I passed by.

"Freddy? Is that you?" he said in a broad Scottish accent. "I knocked at the door but there was no reply."

I returned to the figure, who sat up and coughed again. I recognised him.

"Jock?" I asked. "Whatever are you doing here?"

"I thought I'd try my luck at the address you gave me if I happened to be passing."

I'd met him in the military hospital out in France. He was a gas casualty, with whom I had actually played chess on a couple of occasions. So I sat down on a fallen tree trunk beside him.

"I'm walking to London to find a job, Freddy... Lots of us are."

He coughed again – a kind of painful wheeze I knew so well in the casualties of chlorine gas attack. His face was wrinkled like an old man of seventy but I happened to know he was the same age as me.

"...There's nothing for me in Glasgow – no work, no money, no prospects and nowhere to live except with my folks... But there are seven of us in one tenement flat on the fourth floor... Now my sister has a baby on the way."

He started coughing again. When he took his hand away from his mouth, there was blood on it. I passed him a handkerchief from my pocket.

"But they discharged you from the gas ward," I said. "I thought you said the doctor told you that you would recover in a month or two."

"That's what I thought...but it has been rough, Freddy... You and I, we fought for king and country but, I tell you, there's nothing for us ex-soldiers in Glasgow. That's why lots of us are walking to London to find work. My brother lives in Shoreditch..."

He coughed again and pointed across the field.

"... Is anyone going to shout at me if I sleep under that haystack over there for the night?"

"No, Jock, you're coming home with me."

As I helped him to get up, I realised there were no soles left on his boots. Wet newspaper was sticking out from the remains of the stitching. He was very lame, like people with trench foot out in the Somme. He put his arm around my shoulder to hobble along the path.

"Just like France," he muttered, and suddenly fainted. So I lay him down gently on the grass. There was nothing left of him at all, only skin and bone. He coughed again and came round. There was no alternative but to put him over my shoulders, as I had done so many times before with war casualties – at least the ones who could not be fitted onto a stretcher. Eventually, I staggered up to the steps of the back door of the Big House, where I left him leaning against the wall. I had no key for this door but only had the front door key in my pocket.

"Stay here, Jock," I said. "I'll go round and open the door from the inside. Then I'm making you something to eat."

He grasped hold of my hand.

"God bless you, Freddy! I'm nearly finished."

I left him coughing blood into my handkerchief. When I returned to him from the kitchen inside, he was already asleep.

"Jock, wake up," I said, but he did not respond.

I managed to stoop down to get him across my shoulders and carried him upstairs to a spare bedroom, where the maid used to live. There was only a bare mattress now and a striped pillow without a cover. I lay him down on that and sat down on the chair by the bed. So much for Lloyd George's land fit for heroes! Now I wished Her Ladyship was here to give advice about what to do next, but I was alone in the whole house. I took his boots off so he would get better sleep, and went to find blankets. Clearly, he needed sleep more than food. I left him and went off to bed myself.

It was a strange sensation to sleep alone in Charles' four-poster bed. I could not sleep. Old houses creak as wooden beams get cold at night and I woke several times, fearing burglars were breaking in downstairs. This was strange in view of the fact that I had eventually learned to sleep through a bombardment at night in the trenches. So I got up again to see how Jock was getting on. He was now wide-awake.

"Freddy, I had to find a toilet. Did I wake you? Is this your house?"

I sat down on the bed beside him.

"No, Jock, I'm just the gardener. The owners are in America, visiting family, and the son is in hospital after his appendix was removed. I'm just looking after the place until they get back."

"Aren't you lucky. So you had this to come back to after the war. You never talked about any of this when we were playing chess together."

"You need something to eat," I insisted. "When did you last have a decent meal?"

"Some old dear took me in, near Doncaster, and fed me for a day or two. That was...? Freddy, I just can't remember."

He coughed once again into the handkerchief. The blood was bright red and I already felt alarmed. I helped him down the stairs and went to have a look in the pantry, where we had some bread and cheese. I found some eggs, a few rashers of smoked bacon and one of Her Ladyship's fruit cakes.

The range in the kitchen was still warm and I managed to revive the fire with some dry wood. Jock was clearly feeling better after a few hours sleep and watched everything closely. I made us both a cup of tea.

"Where are the staff?" he asked, looking around.

"Only me left now," I said. "The family have fallen on hard times. The two cooks, the maid, the chauffeur and the butler all had to go."

I found the frying pan, lay four rashers of bacon into some lard and placed it over the heat.

"Why are you, alone, left on the payroll?" he asked.

"Best not to ask, Jock. It is such a long story – another time, perhaps. I was the lucky one, I guess."

I broke two eggs into the frying pan and they started to splutter.

"Sorry, I didn't mean to intrude... Boy, that smells good, Freddy – so much better than Army rations out in the trenches."

We continued chatting about old times until the food was cooked. Eventually, he ate a decent meal and we both returned to bed.

I thought I would be able to get some sleep now but the bed was empty beside me. That was the moment I realised how important Charles had become in my life. Now I needed him just as much as he needed me. So I lay there thinking. The war had changed everything for so many people today, including poor Jock. But England was at peace now and we still had Lloyd George to contend with. Until now, the jury in my mind was still out over the issue of social reform in England. Ways and means had to be found to make the estate pay. Suddenly, I decided to spend Her Ladyship's money to open the garden centre as soon as possible. Already, steamrollers were flattening the tarmac along the latest stretch of the new trunk road two miles away. It would be only a few weeks before the workmen cleared the terrain outside the Big House. Now was the time to put our ideas into practice.

Jock was still coughing blood in the morning and I called the doctor again. I reminded him that I had served in the trenches and said another former soldier was staying with us, but he was poorly and we needed medical care. About lunchtime he turned up once more in his Bullnose Morris.

After a very brief examination, while I waited outside Jock's room, the doctor came out to talk to me.

"Tuberculosis," he muttered. "Your Scottish friend really should be in an isolation hospital."

"I thought it was just the long-term effects of gas attack in France, Doctor," I said.

"I'm afraid not and he must be rather infectious. He has, what we might call, 'galloping consumption' – both lungs are badly infected. He is terribly malnourished and poor diet hasn't helped, Frederic. His overcrowded tenement in Glasgow, which he said he told you about, probably made everything worse. As you know, there is little I can do about TB..."

I sat down in a state of shock. The doctor looked worried.

"...There are no drugs, Frederic – one day, perhaps. I'm so sorry, young man. Your friend has only a few weeks to live, in my judgement. But you cannot risk your own health, Frederic. It is unsafe for you to continue nursing him yourself. I'll telephone the isolation hospital at once. He cannot stay here. There may be a bed in the charity ward."

So poor Jock was ferried off in an ambulance. I was told I could not visit him because of the risk of the dread disease spreading beyond the walls into the general population. I was warned he would never recover because the infection had infected both lungs. He might have only a few days, rather than weeks left to live. So, even in 1922 there was still no fit land for a Scottish hero like Jock to live in. He had served his country in its hour of need, but England could do little for him now.

I went to look up Her Ladyship's medical reference book in the library. I needed to know more about TB. I was astonished to discover that a large proportion of the population were likely to carry the bacillus but it threatened to flare up mainly where there was poverty, malnutrition and overcrowding, such as Jock's Glasgow tenement. My own family had emigrated to Canada to escape a similar fate. So, poverty, unemployment, social deprivation and poor healthcare would all contribute to Jock's early death, which had little to do with the gas in the trenches. I placed the book back on the shelf. How lucky I was to be fit and healthy, with a new adopted family, a decent place to live and a lover like Charles. Lloyd George was quite right, after all, I decided. Britain needed more courageous social reformers like him. The wealthy and privileged few should be taxed to provide for health and unemployment insurance, pensions and better housing for others like Jock. Now I felt like a traitor to His Lordship and his battle against the People's Budget and the Parliament Act. But I was a citizen of England now with a vote of my own since 1918, thanks to David Lloyd George. I was entitled to my own views and to make up my own mind. I was not an impoverished serf living in a tied cottage any more.

They say that troubles always arrive in threes – first Charles' appendicitis, then Jock's tuberculosis and, finally, a letter. That was the day an order arrived from the new Garden City Council. Our area around the Big House had just been designated a zone for housing only. No trading or businesses would be tolerated outside council-approved segregated trading and retail business zones in the new town. A map was enclosed. I stared at it and tried to line it up in my mind with landmarks I could recognise. The letter informed me that the Garden City Council was empowered by the 1909 Town Planning Act and the 1919 Housing Act. Yes, I thought – even more implications of Lloyd George's vision of England. So, I put the letter in my bag to read later and went for a walk into town. I had to think about what to do next. This was bad news.

I called in at the bank with my five hundred pound cheque to open an account in my own name for the very first time. Now

I knew I had really arrived. The manager invited me into his office, personally.

"Good Lord, Son. You are the young man in the newspaper photo with your VC and your tennis racket. Well done, young man!"

I was invited to sit down at his desk. A secretary brought tea and biscuits. I explained that I wanted to open an account with Her Ladyship's cheque.

"You have ideas for the future. Her Ladyship told me, young man."

"Yes, Sir. Charles and I had intended to open a horticultural centre on the new main road through the estate."

"Do you think you can make a go of it, then?"

"I already grow flowers, seedlings and vegetables, Sir. That has been my job. We have the greenhouses. We have space for a car park. The garden city will bring new residents who want flowers and pot plants. Ebenezer Howard and his Garden City Association have given their support but no money, unfortunately."

I passed a letter to the bank manager, which he read carefully.

"I can see you have done your research, young man. England needs more people like you – full of bright ideas and get-up-and-go. Too many bright young men were lost in the war – such a waste. Well, the National Bank will be pleased to support you. Her Ladyship reminded me that her father used to own it, you know."

Then I reached for the letter that had just arrived from the Garden City Council about planning permission.

"Unfortunately this letter arrived from the new town council this morning, Sir."

The bank manager read it once, glanced at me with a puzzled expression and sat down to read it again. He eventually turned to me.

"Can you understand this, then, Frederic?"

"No, Sir."

"Well, it doesn't make much sense to me either... I tell you what, Frederic. I happen to know the new lady mayoress. I'll phone her and see what she thinks. Would you mind waiting outside just for a moment?"

He picked up the telephone on his desk and asked to be connected with the council chambers, while I went to wait outside the door. Eventually the door opened again and the manager beckoned to me. He was still holding the telephone in his left hand.

"Yes, Your Worship, he is right here with me now – the young man holding the Victoria Cross in the newspaper photograph. Yes, the very same."

The outcome of all this was that the bank manager and I would have lunch with the lady mayoress later that same morning at the local hotel. I passed him the cheque. He gave me my chequebook and details of my new account, held the door open and shook my hand.

"We'll meet her worship at the George Inn later, young man."

The telephone was ringing on his desk. He picked it up and I shut the door. So, I returned to the Big House to find a suitable outfit in Charles' wardrobe. I didn't think he would mind when he was in hospital.

At one o'clock, I was introduced to her worship, the lady mayoress of our new garden city. The bank manager greeted her on first name terms.

"Margaret, lovely to see you... This is Frederic."

We shook hands. She fluttered her eyelashes at me.

"Yes, I recognise him – he is my friend Elizabeth, Her Ladyship's, gardener. I've been cutting out bits from the local paper to stick in my scrapbook, you know... Frederic, that photo really didn't do you justice!"

We laughed. A waiter appeared to tell us that our table was ready, and the three of us went into the dining room.

"Well, Your Worship," the bank manager began, "Frederic has done his bit for England out in the trenches of the Somme. Now Lloyd George has told us that it is time to create a land fit for heroes and here he is, but your planning department of the local council sent him this... Give her that letter, Frederic."

I passed it to her worship. She put on her reading glasses to read it carefully, put it down on the table and turned to the bank manager.

"This is quite ridiculous, isn't it? Do you know how much work has been done creating the Garden City Parks Department? Well, I'll tell you, Frederic – nothing...not a barrow, a fork, nor one spade. The money's run out. There is a total freeze on new expenditure – no more cash until the next budget in the new financial year. It was all due to the Chancellor's latest deflationary budget and the rise in bank rate, you know."

She stared accusingly at the bank manager, who drummed his fingers on the table but said nothing.

"So," I asked politely. "Your Worship, how can you create a garden city without plants to put in public parks and gardens?"

"Very good question. Frederic, can I hang on to this letter to bring up the topic at tonight's council meeting? You've just given me some useful ammunition."

The rest of the lunch was spent talking about the new council. Clearly, there were already problems regarding the political allegiances of different factions in the council chamber.

"The new Labour Party was formed in 1906, you know," she said. "Our members are very forceful in debates. They see council business as a war zone between the interests of capital and labour. But I ask you. This is supposed to be a new garden city, full of fresh air, beautiful plants and picturesque, rural-styled architecture – not an arena to act out the class war."

"But we have a coalition government, Your Worship," the bank manager suggested. "The same disputes must go on in central government, between the Liberals and the Conservatives, under Lloyd George."

"He won't last," the lady mayoress declared. "That man has made too many enemies and made too many mistakes, don't you think? Well, I agree with your mistress, Freddy..."

She turned to me now.

"...Lloyd George will be out on his ear before long. Mark my words, young man. The days of coalition government in England are numbered."

After lunch, her worship hurried off to attend another urgent meeting. I really hadn't said very much but I knew I'd made a favourable impression. Outside the hotel, the bank manager shook my hand before returning to his branch down the High Street.

"Well done, young man. She likes you. Come and see me again in six months' time to discuss a business loan on favourable terms – that is if you will need one, but somehow I have the feeling you won't. Perhaps you will need to discuss how to invest all your profits, instead, huh?"

Charles was sitting up in bed when I arrived at the start of visiting time in the men's surgical ward. Already, I was worrying if I might be carrying the TB bacillus after Jock had coughed blood over me, but what could I do about it? I'd burned the handkerchief I gave him. I'd changed all my clothes, had a bath with carbolic soap and gargled with some of Her Ladyship's patent mouthwash.

"Freddy!"

He took my hand with both of his. I gave him the telegram from his father.

"You open it, Freddy. I'm still rather sore under all these bandages..."

He pointed to his stomach.

"...You were right to call the doctor. The surgeon came in this morning. He brought my appendix in a jar of preservative for me to look at. It is in there if you want to look."

Charles pointed at the bedside table.

"No, I don't!" I insisted. "I've seen enough English body parts out in France and Belgium to last a lifetime!"

He laughed.

"Well, Freddy, another souvenir to add to my collection, then. This one nearly did go bang as well, you know. It would have been peritonitis, which is often fatal, even today. I might have died, the surgeon said. I think your prompt action saved me yet again."

I read the telegram he passed to me: 'Arrived New York stop give Freddy our love ma and pa'

"Isn't that nice, Charles? They think of you and me at the same time as if we are a couple already."

He looked around to check nobody was looking and gestured that he wanted to whisper in my ear. I leaned forward but he kissed me quickly instead. Then I told him about his mother's cheque and my visit to the bank. The National had given our garden centre enterprise its official blessing. We had the finance. It now only remained for Charles to recover quickly so that all the stitches could be removed and we could make a start to provide flowers for the new garden city.

"Freddy, I've been lying here and slowly waking up from my anaesthetic. But do you know what really cheered me up?"

"Tell me, Charles...but I've half an idea."

"That somebody really loved me, at long last, and would be sleeping in bed with me again soon. I feel a bit lonely in this narrow single bed here, you know."

1930 – The garden party at the grand opening of our third garden centre

"Here is the cup of tea for your lady wife, Vicar," I said as he turned round towards me. "One sugar, I think."

"Splendid, my boy! You timed your speech just right. The memsahib and I were just dosing off in the sun and that business with the blunt scissors made us all laugh, didn't it, my dear?"

He turned to his wife, who was talking to the matron in

charge of the TB ward at the isolation hospital.

"Congratulations, Frederic," she said. "I was just saying that we must invite you back again to give a talk next season to all our ladies at the Women's Institute. Some of them weren't invited this afternoon, you know. You should have consulted me about your guest list first."

The vicar put his hand on his wife's arm.

"I'm sure Frederic knew what he was doing, my dear. He wanted to invite people with money to spend, buying plants for the town hall, the council parks department, new businesses in the garden city and so on. Some members of our Women's Institute haven't got two pennies to rub together, have they? It doesn't cost much to make plum jam and sing 'Jerusalem', you know."

We all laughed politely at the vicar's little joke and I handed an envelope to the matron. I didn't want to do this publicly on the podium in front of the whole audience, because I had wanted to keep it quiet. Instead of placing it quietly in her handbag as I had hoped, she opened it there and then. She read it and gasped.

"What's that, dear?" the vicar's wife asked, looking over her shoulder.

"Frederic has presented us with a cheque for one thousand pounds to extend the tuberculosis ward for charity cases at our local isolation hospital. Well, Vicar, you are our chaplain. I think this is splendid news, don't you?"

"Good Lord, Frederic," the vicar gasped. "I take my hat off to you, my boy. God's wonders work in so many ways. Can I interest you in the fund for the war memorial garden, then?"

"A dear friend died of TB a few years ago," I said quietly aside to him. "This is in his memory, Vicar. We need to take much better care of the living survivors of the Great War, rather than the glorious dead, don't you think?"

I moved on to talk to the head of the Parks Purchasing Department about next year's contracts. Everyone was so polite and friendly today. Memories of the pong of ordure, the broken cesspit wall and threats of legal action about sewage in the vicarage garden had all been forgotten. If they'd known the truth about Charles and me, things might have been so very different. Then the bank manager came up to me and put a hand on my shoulder.

"Freddy, the lady wife and I must take our leave. The bank is like time – it will wait for no man."

I interrupted him briefly.

"Sir, let me introduce our local vicar and his wife... But they might ask you for another donation to mend the church roof or for the new garden around the war memorial."

Everyone laughed and I went off to see where John-Boy had got to now. I was getting tired of pretending to be so respectable and was starting to have second thoughts about his invitation for us to find somewhere quiet to have sex. I saw him talking to Charles. Suddenly Charles got up and seemed about to box John-Boy on the ears. Then he stormed out of the tent once again.

"What on earth was that all about then," I asked John-Boy.

"Uncle Charles said your speech was too boring. People in the front row were falling asleep. He said you should have passed the microphone to him. Anyway, he said you were taking all the glory. I stood up for you, Freddy. I told him if it hadn't been for you, there would be no garden centre to open. He didn't like that and stormed off."

"You shouldn't say that sort of thing, you know. It will only make him suspicious of you and me."

"So how about it, Freddy? What about my room back at the Big House? We could have sex there."

"That really is the first place he would look, isn't it?"

"Well, I'm not giving up, Big Buddy. You'll just have to think of somewhere else, then."

Now I saw the lady mayoress again and went to have another word with her, leaving John-Boy to drink his fizzy lemonade.

Chapter 6

1922

THE OUTCOME OF THE council meeting to discuss the shortage of money to fund the Garden City Parks Department was an exclusive contract for Charles and myself to supply the council's needs for decoration of amenities, parks and the town centre with roses and other plants. As the lady mayoress explained to me, she had made the point in the angry debate that no new residents would want to move into the streets of a garden city where plants were conspicuous by their absence. Nor would traders want to buy new properties in a city centre which looked as drab and uninspiring as the East End of London. So, within a few weeks, all the rows of pink and blue roses I had been propagating in an effort to perfect our hybrids, were transplanted wherever the builders had finished and moved on. There was no need for us to trade with the public outside the Big House, because the council was buying everything we could grow. Money started to pour into my new bank account at the National Bank. I even had to visit the new Labour Exchange to recruit two gardening staff to help us with the planting programme around the garden city. It was an exciting time. We felt we were doing our bit to decorate avenues of the new homes in the land fit for heroes, which David Lloyd George had promised in his speech after the Great War.

Four months later, John telephoned to say the Silver Ghost was finished. All the photography had been completed. The advertising agency was delighted with the pictures and they would feature in new literature to promote business for the new motor body repair shop at his factory. He laughed when he told me they now had one Rolls Royce to repair which had been squeezed flat between two tramcars in south London. It was actually in a worse condition than His Lordship's and that was saying something!

So Charles and I took the train to the works in order to collect his father's rebuilt Rolls Royce. His parents would be landing from the Aquitania at Southampton Docks a few weeks later and we planned to drive the Rolls onto the quayside to meet them and to give them a big surprise. When we arrived at John's north London business, we were greeted like royalty. All the staff who had worked on the restoration of the Silver Ghost were lined up for another photo opportunity. The photographer had to place his camera on the flat roof of the factory to get everyone in shot. The camera looked down on the scene, where John shook hands with Charles in front of the Rolls while I sat smiling in the driver's seat. When that was finished we were both introduced by John personally to each of the staff. More photos were taken for the brochure. The forge master and his handsome assistant had bent the chassis back into shape. The apprentice engineer had reconditioned the crankshaft of the engine. Three junior electricians had installed the dynamo, the batteries, an electric horn and electric lighting throughout. The Rolls engine had been cleaned and fitted with an automatic self-starter, which I could operate with a key on the dashboard. Here was real progress! That would save all the backache caused by swinging the starting handle under the radiator. A sweet little old lady had sewn new covers for the seats in the passenger compartment and a bespectacled painter had resprayed the bodywork damaged in the crash. I was introduced to each in turn. I felt like royalty, especially when John persuaded me to get out the newspaper photos of me holding my VC. Finally, there was another photo of me sitting in the driver's seat, while John shook my hand and the rest of the staff all waved goodbye in the background. He promised to send me a copy of the brochure when it was ready.

Well, it was like driving a new car and I treated the reground crankshaft gently at first! John had tied a notice to the rear bumper, which said 'Running in, please pass'. The polished bodywork gleamed brightly in the sun. Heads turned when we stopped at road junctions. Two constables saluted when I passed by them at a police station outside London. One bus driver actually halted to give way to us and Charles waved from the window as if he was Queen Mary on a state visit. So we had a whale of a time. When we returned to the Big House, dust from the streets gave it a recently-run-in, sporty look. I was sure His Lordship would be delighted when we met them for their arrival on the Aquitania in Southampton that day in 1922.

I decided to surprise my grandma with an invitation to a picnic. Charles and I would take her out for a spin in the Rolls. So I arrived outside her tiny cottage a few days later when the sun was shining. Neighbours came out of their houses to watch what was going on. I told the lady next door that the engine was still running in and we would take my grandma out and to see if the engine needed fine-tuning before His Lordship returned from America. Now I sat in the driver's seat. Charles would sit in the back with Grandma. It might give her the opportunity to get to know him better. She still felt nervous about our relationship.

So we drove to see the crossing keeper's house, where I was born. She could remember it years ago. Nothing remained of the railway line now and the level crossing gates had long since disappeared. Only the brick platform for the signal box remained. I stopped the Rolls in the yard, where the railway halt and the goods depot used to stand. I knocked on the door of the house and a lady in an apron appeared. I left Charles to do the introduction. He pointed at the Rolls Royce, gleaming in the sun outside.

"Ma'am," he said in his best Oxford English accent, "the lady's family used to live here before the railway line closed and they all moved to Canada."

"I remember them all," she gasped. "I used to live down the road there, before I was married. Do; please bring the dear lady in for a cup of tea."

We were soon seated in the parlour I remembered so well. I asked if I could show Charles the little room that used to be my bedroom. So we left my grandma chatting to the lady in the apron. My old room overlooked the cutting where the railway lines used to be. He pushed the door to, grabbed me and tried to kiss me.

"No, not here," I insisted. "This is not the place, is it, Charles?"

"Sorry."

He stood back and looked shocked. I smiled at him.

"I mean later, that's all."

"I really fancied kissing you in what used to be your bedroom, Freddy."

We took Grandma outside to remind her where the signal box and the station halt used to be. There were stinging nettles and bushes growing everywhere, except where soil had been dug for a vegetable garden. I still remembered the days when the railway was running. Everything looked so sad and neglected today. Nothing remained of the flower garden I had started as a teenager, which began my horticultural career. I felt rather upset. Too many memories were flooding back. I said I wanted to go. So we said thank you to the kind lady for the tea and climbed back into the Rolls to drive away. That's when the heavens opened and we were caught in another downpour, so we had to eat the picnic in the Rolls by the side of the road. I climbed into the passenger compartment with the picnic hamper and pulled down one of the folding seats to sit down.

"Well, Fred," Grandma said, looking outside at the rain, "man proposes but God disposes, yes, a bit like you two young lovers flying in the face of social convention... Well, it is not for me to pass judgement on other people's lifestyles. Some folk would say this downpour must be an act of God... to rain on your parade... "

She smiled and turned to Charles.

"...But where would England be without all this rain?"

We laughed. I passed her the cucumber sandwiches. Charles smiled at me. I think she was growing to accept the two of us at last.

"Just like Oscar Wilde's Importance of Being Earnest, you know," he added.

"Yes, yes," my grandma muttered. "I remember the line: 'Pass Lady Bracknell the cucumber sandwiches, will you?' ...You know, Fred, I do feel like Lady Bracknell in this Rolls Royce too. Won't Her Ladyship mind her car being used while she is in America?"

She turned to Charles, who thought for a moment.

"My dear mama would be pleased to know Freddy's grandma has helped us to give it a trial run – to test the rear springs, the brakes and the new back axle. What do you think, Ma'am? Can I send her a telegram to the Aquitania to say it has now passed its road test?"

My grandmother looked around the refurbished passenger compartment.

"If it was mine, young man, I wouldn't want to travel in anything else. The noisy local omnibus will never be the same again."

But we did not send a telegram to tell his parents about his Rolls. Instead, Charles wanted it to be kept a secret. His Lordship sent us a telegram to confirm their time of arrival at the docks. One surprise was that John-Boy, their eldest grandson, would be accompanying them to start school at Harrow in west London. Charles' reply made no mention of the Rolls Royce. They must have assumed we would all be travelling by train. In fact, he booked some rooms in a hotel halfway along our route because the liner was arriving on the high tide in the evening. I had no wish to drive the Rolls down unmade country roads after dark, even with the new electric headlamps. This Silver Ghost had already suffered one road traffic accident too many!

We were early on the quayside and stood side by side watching the four tall funnels of the Aquitania come into sight. Charles put one arm on my shoulder. Already we were behaving like a married couple. Seagulls swooped around the masts and the radio aerials of this enormous luxury liner, from which coloured bunting was now being unfurled by sailors. A brass band appeared beside us. It was clear some dignitaries were on board and two photographers positioned themselves on stepladders. I went to ask whom they were waiting for. I was told Charlie Chaplin was on board. He had just founded United Artists after earning one million dollars at the First National Film Studio – a record-breaking contract. Now Chaplin wanted to visit his home in London again, before going on a European tour. The lord mayor of Southampton would be arriving in his car to greet him and they needed exclusive pictures for the popular press. Charles joked that his father would probably just assume all this was specially laid on for him and Her Ladyship.

Crowds thronged on the quayside. They started chanting "Chaplin! Chaplin!" It was clear we might miss Charles' parents in so much confusion. I suggested I might pose as His Lordship's valet so that we could be allowed up the first class gangway to reach the cabin inside. So I queued up to talk to the bursar's representative and managed to get a special boarding pass. I waved it under the nose of the gangway staff, who were trying to stop movie fans, who only wanted Charlie Chaplin's autograph. We found His Lordship's cabin, where

Her Ladyship insisted on waiting for the Chaplin entourage to go away outside.

"Freddy! Freddy!" muttered Her Ladyship, smothering me with kisses while Charles sniggered behind me.

"Mama, really! Such North American self-expression is unseemly in a woman of your age!"

His Lordship wagged an accusing finger at his son.

"Well, look at him," she insisted, turning to Charles. "So gorgeous! ... Freddy could be an international film star like that Rudolph Valentino in Blood and Sand. My grandson insisted that we should all go to see it, you know... But, I think, Charlie Chaplin is such an ugly little man."

His Lordship shook my hand warmly.

"Her Ladyship has even bought a pin-up photo of Valentino. Can you believe that? Well, Freddy, I called him a faded pansy... How are you, Son? We'll take you with us next time! My wife missed you every day. Yes, she did!"

Her Ladyship ignored him and pressed the bell for the steward, who appeared very promptly.

"We'll have a pot of English breakfast tea, please," she instructed. "And where has my grandson got to now? Do you know?"

"Yes, Ma'am. The young man will be joining you in a minute. We have packed up his things now. English tea will be here shortly, Ma'am."

The steward touched his cap and left us. She turned to me again.

"Freddy, you just don't know how much I've missed my cups of Earl Grey tea! The Americans only know about coffee! ... Well! ... I've had coffee black, coffee white and coffee with cream but you'd think, by now, they could learn how to make a decent cup of English tea!"

She turned to Charles at last.

"So, has Freddy been looking after you, then? You haven't faded away after that operation to remove your nasty appendix?"

"No, Mama, I've never been so well cared for since my

batman in the trenches. Freddy has been feeding me up again."

He put one arm around my waist and made a point of hugging me.

"Such outrageous Californian self-expression, Charles," his mother giggled. "It really does not become a respectable member of the English aristocracy, but you're not respectable, are you? Not at all."

"What time is the train, Son?" asked His Lordship, changing the subject quickly.

"No train, Papa," Charles muttered. "Freddy has a big surprise for you...Yes, Papa, an enormous surprise! As your American grandson, John-Boy would say: 'you just ain't seen nothin' yet! No, Sir!'"

The door opened and a beautiful boy walked in, carrying two suitcases.

"John-Boy, this is Freddy," His Lordship said. "We told you, remember?"

"The real live war hero? Golly, gee!"

He put the suitcases down and came to shake my hand but clung on to it and wouldn't let go. I ignored him.

"We'll need to put him on a Metropolitan Line train to the school just outside London," Her Ladyship explained. "John-Boy's father thinks Harrow School will make a man out of him."

"Perhaps he won't need a train, Papa."

"What's that, then?"

Charles put his finger to his lips and looked at me.

"How thoughtful of Freddy to keep a taxi waiting," sighed Her Ladyship. "Charles would never have thought of that, would you now?"

There was a knock on the door. The steward entered with a tray of tea and set it down beside us. When His Lordship gave him a handful of American coins, he smiled, tipped his cap again and left us.

"No use to us in England now, are they?" muttered the old man. "So, tell me, has Lloyd George invented some new fiendish wealth tax to bankrupt what's left of the aristocracy? Or has he pulled the plug out to let England sink beneath the waves, which she just can't afford to rule any longer?"

I laughed and winked at Charles, who smiled.

"Lloyd George has fallen out of favour, even with his own party, Papa. I think, and if you'll excuse the expression, Mama, this time the shit really has hit the coalition government fan!"

Her Ladyship looked outraged.

"What a disgusting thing to say in front of my grandson, Charles! ... Can this be really true, Freddy...?"

She turned to me in amazement.

"... We read rumours in the American press, of course, what with the US presidential election and all..."

Then she turned to John-Boy, who looked rather puzzled.

"David Lloyd George was the British Prime Minister who your grandfather didn't like. Now let go of Freddy's hand now, dear, please."

"Times have changed, my lady," I said, shaking myself free of John-Boy's grasp. "Lloyd George should never have sent the Black and Tans into Ireland. People want peace now and his support of Greece against the Turks is proving to be Lloyd George's undoing. In fact, you might even call it David Lloyd George's inglorious Waterloo, my lord!"

His Lordship turned to his wife.

"He seems to know all about it, my dear. Freddy, this is music to my ears."

I smiled and continued.

"Then unemployed workers from Glasgow started a hunger march to London. More of them might be passing your house some time soon, walking down the new trunk road, my lady. I thought we could spare some fresh fruit from the orchard...or a loaf of bread or two. Some of them are terribly emaciated."

"Yes," Charles interrupted. "David Lloyd George resigned from Number Ten on the nineteenth of October. Andrew Bonar Law has formed a Conservative ministry but people say that he isn't feeling very well these days."

His Lordship's eyes lit up.

"Do you hear that, my dear? As the Americans would say, public enemy number one has been gunned down! Yes, and by his own party... There now, and I was worried that Lloyd George would introduce a new wealth tax! ... Freddy, you've made my day!"

"No, Papa," muttered Charles, putting one hand on my shoulder and squeezing it. "I told you, and as John-Boy here would say: 'You ain't seen nothin' yet! Not no way... Not no how... No, Sir!' So, how are all my nieces and my other nephew, then, Mama?"

Her Ladyship was pouring out four cups of tea and looked up.

"Well now, Abner is just fine, just like John-Boy here... But poor Hortense has a cold, and little Mary-Lou looks just like her grandma!"

I took a look out of the porthole to check if Charlie Chaplin was still drawing crowds on the quayside but everything looked quiet now.

"Come, my dear," His Lordship said, getting up. "We must disembark before we find ourselves on the way back to New York!"

So with John-Boy's help I pushed his grandparents' luggage on a courtesy trolley towards the Rolls Royce. Suddenly His Lordship caught sight of it.

"Good Lord! ...What's this, then? I don't believe it!"

Now Her Ladyship stood still, looking perplexed.

"Has my nephew John lent you his car for the day, then?"

His Lordship stepped forward and stooped down.

"Look at the number plate, Elizabeth, my dear! Do you remember that? This is your father's old car. So this is the big surprise Freddy had for us, then! ... I don't understand, at all, Charles! ... When I saw this last, the chickens had taken residence! But is that electric lighting I can see?"

He pointed at the brand-new headlights.

"Papa... Freddy, here, called in an enormous favour...for saving John's life out in France, you know."

Her Ladyship had opened the door at the back to look inside. She waved at John-Boy to get in beside her.

"Well, just look at this, now! New carpet and matching seat covers in my favourite colour! I don't believe it. They even cleaned out your Grandad's nasty, smelly ashtray."

She stepped up inside and sat down, feeling the fabric with her fingers. His Lordship climbed in too to sit down beside her, and started to look around. He switched on the electric interior lights and ran his fingers along the polished woodwork around the window.

"Freddy, I'm speechless!"

Charles pushed me inside, where the two of us pulled down the refurbished rear-facing seats and smiled at one another. Now Her Ladyship leaned forward to place one hand on my knee.

"As John-Boy here would say: 'Golly gee, baby!' Where on earth did all this money come from, Freddy?"

His Lordship looked at me in despair and then at his wife.

"You've missed the point, my dear. Your nephew John owes everything to Freddy for saving his life out in France and John's new Rolls Royce franchise in north London did all this for free. Isn't that right, my son? So, that's what Charles meant when he said Freddy called in a big favour."

There was a knock on the window beside us. A workman tugged his cap.

"Pardon me, my lord. You're parked on the railway lines and we need to back the train up beside the Aquitania – fresh meat won't wait, Sir. Would you be so kind as to get your chauffeur to move the Rolls?"

His Lordship tapped Charles on the shoulder.

"Go and swing the starting handle for Freddy now."

"No, Father, just look at this!"

I hopped into the driver's seat and turned the key for the electric starter. The engine immediately sprang into life and purred quietly while Her Ladyship listened carefully.

"Good Lord, John must have valued his own life very highly, then! Listen to those big ends on the crankshaft now. Not a rattle or a bang to be heard... Freddy, you have quite taken my breath away!"

His Lordship felt in his pocket and gave the engine driver some more American coins. Charles left his parents in the back of the Rolls and came to sit beside me, where the valet might have sat beside the chauffeur years ago. John-Boy sat between his grandparents on the back seat but I felt sure he really wanted to come and sit beside me. Now, while the steam engine backed the goods wagons up to the side of the ship, we drove sedately out through the gates of the dockyard and away to find our reserved rooms at the White Horse Hotel.

Her Ladyship patted the chair beside her when we sat down in the dining room for dinner. Once again, John-Boy clearly wanted to sit with me but he sat down opposite us to stare at me instead. His Lordship took Charles to the bar, saying he was desperate for a proper pint of real English beer. He outraged Her Ladyship when he complained that the damned Americans only sold bootleg cat's piss, because of Prohibition after the Volstead Act in 1920. She had put her hands over John-Boy's ears to save his embarrassment.

"Come and sit next to me, Freddy!" she insisted. "Well, His Lordship has been ogling American hussies. Now it is my turn to ogle you!"

Then she turned to me with a more serious expression.

"Listen, Freddy, did you find my letter enclosing the cheque in the safe? And did you open an account at the National?"

John-Boy leaned forwards to learn more about such family secrets.

"Yes, my lady."

"So how much money is left now, then?"

I turned to John-Boy and winked at him to make him smile.

"My lady," I insisted, "I have a confession to make."

"Don't tell me that you have lost the lot, Freddy! ... How could you?"

"No, not that, Ma'am. I've sold your Eros of Praxiteles to the Garden City Council – that old statue you hated, outside in the garden."

Now Her Ladyship turned to her grandson as if in outrage.

"Well, Freddy might have asked me first. My great-uncle Bartholomew brought it back from Greece, you know."

"But, my lady," I explained, "you did say you didn't like it – well, it was just sitting in the garden, covered in bird lime. The new council wanted a centrepiece for the enclosed garden in the middle of their new block of posh council offices. Your friend the lady mayoress liked it. She said the council should invest in artworks likely to accrue in value over the years."

She turned to her grandson once again.

"Oh well, never mind. Shall we ask Freddy what he got for it, then? What do you think, John-Boy...ten pounds? Now, I told you. In New York, your currency is in US dollars. Over here we have pounds, shillings and pence. Well, I never liked that statue. You see, one hand was missing."

I winked at John-Boy once more and turned to his grandma again.

"No, my lady. We had it properly valued by someone from Bonhams, the auctioneers... The council needed to confirm the exact value for insurance purposes, you see."

"Freddy, I must pop to the ladies to powder my nose...You look after John-Boy for a moment."

She got up from her chair but turned to me again.

"...So how much did you get for Great-Uncle Bartholomew's old Greek statue, as a matter of interest?"

"You'd better sit down again, my lady."

She sat down and put one hand on my arm.

"Well, Freddy, don't tell me – one hundred pounds?"

"No, my lady... Eight thousand five hundred."

She gasped and turned to her grandson, who was fascinated.

"How much?"

"Eight thousand five hundred pounds," I insisted. "The lady mayoress said the sight of it might help to raise the level of debate in committee and inspire boring speakers in the council chamber. All the rooms overlook the garden, you see. It is one of these new Bauhaus-type buildings with big glass windows around the central garden area, where Charles and I planted all the roses. You must ask the mayoress to show you, some time."

Her Ladyship was still gasping and staring at her grandson.

"Eight thousand five hundred pounds of ratepayers' money for a thing like that, with one hand missing, John-Boy? Can you believe that?"

Once again I winked at him and turned to his grandma.

"Yes, my lady. You can spend it on a new leaded flat roof for the Big House. While you've been in the States, the rain has been coming in again. You could also redeem your Beckstein grand piano from the pawnbrokers."

Now she ignored her grandson and turned to me.

"So, tell me, Freddy. That bank account you opened with my five hundred pound cheque – how much cash is in it now?"

I put my hand in my pocket to find the bank statement and passed it to her. She unfolded her lorgnette reading glasses and looked at the figures in amazement.

"Nine thousand, four hundred and eight-two pounds, one shilling and four pence three farthings, Freddy...?"

She looked at me with her mouth open and then passed the bank statement to her grandson, who stared at it and then at me again.

"...So what else did you sell to the council, Freddy?"

"Various bushes from your parterre rose garden, my lady. We ran out of plants from the greenhouses, you see. I will replace them, soon. The Garden City Council has bought everything I could grow, almost as fast as we could load it onto the lorries. A garden city needs plants to keep the new residents and all these new business people happy, you know. Otherwise it isn't a garden city, is it? That's what your friend the lady mayoress said to me, in confidence, of course."

She looked around and squeezed my knee with her hand again under the table but turned to her grandson once more.

"See this young man here, John-Boy? I gave him five hundred pounds and he's turned them into nearly ten thousand in six months... So, while your grandfather and I were standing around whining and complaining endlessly about Lloyd George and all his new taxes, only Freddy, here, worked out how to make a lot of money out of these new streets, full of Lloyd George's homes fit for heroes...What do you say to that then, my lad?"

"Grandma, I would say: Golly, gee, what a hero!"

"Freddy, thank you so much. I don't know what to say except to agree with John-Boy here – what a hero!"

Now John-Boy turned to me, winked and smiled. Already I had found a new friend and, much later, a younger and very passionate lover.

Charles returned from the bar with his father, carrying pints of beer and an orange juice for his nephew. His Lordship nudged Charles on the elbow but said nothing while his wife made a point of fondling my knee again. Her son pretended to be outraged.

"Mama, behave yourself! You're in England now! Anyway, he's mine! I saw Freddy first!"

She put her hands over her grandson's ears again.

"Don't you listen to that, my lad. Things like that are not for the ears of innocent boys like you."

Everyone burst out laughing while other guests turned to stare in our direction. His Lordship changed the subject.

"The Rolls is amazing, Freddy. We can't thank you enough."

I leaned forward to whisper, "No, I thank you, my lord. You took me in and made me welcome as one of the family when I was feeling run down in 1919. I'd just come back, wounded in the war... and you didn't have me locked up like Oscar Wilde...when Charles and I..."

Her Ladyship put her finger to her lips and pointed in John-Boy's direction just as the waiter arrived with a notepad to take our orders and then left again. Now she put her hand on my arm and squeezed it.

"We don't know how to thank you, that's all ... So, dear Freddy, we brought you a little something from the USA..."

She reached into her handbag, took out a small box and gave it to me. I gasped.

"...Well then, open it, young man!"

Inside was a beautiful gold watch. I'd never owned one in my life and slipped it on my wrist. I leaned over to show it to John-Boy, who noticed that the time was wrong.

"You'll have to readjust the time, Freddy. Even our clocks are different in the USA!"

His Lordship leaned over.

"Greenwich Mean Time just isn't good enough in America, any more, Son... It was the War of Independence, you know – something to do with tea leaves in Boston Harbour and the new, outrageous English purchase tax on tea. Wasn't it, John-Boy? The Yanks didn't want to pay that either, back in 1773! Lloyd George should have learned a lesson from history, what?"

Everybody laughed and the waiter brought the soup.

So Charles and I moved the Rolls into the old stables behind the hotel and the porter locked the door. Then we went to find our room. What were supposed to be two single beds turned out to be one double, so we would find ourselves sleeping beside each other again. I decided to have a bath first in the en suite bathroom, which was quite luxurious.

The bath was enormous – far bigger than anything I had ever seen before. So Charles and I locked the door and had a bath together that night. He put his arms out as I got in.

"Freddy, I love you! ... My mother loves you and, now...yes, I know it, after the Rolls Royce, my father loves you too. We are all so lucky."

"The Marquess of Queensbury didn't see it that way!"

"So, Freddy, do you mean about Oscar Wilde and his son, Bosie?"

I leaned back in the bath and lay my head on Charles' chest.

"Well, they should have kept it secret, like you and I."

Charles ran his fingers through my hair.

"But maybe, if Lord Queensbury had welcomed Oscar Wilde into his house, instead of having him locked up in Reading Gaol, then he might have been able to pay for Lord Queensbury to do up his own stately pile. He probably had leaky leaded flat roofs, too. So, perhaps he should have rejoiced that no-good, lazy Bosie had found a clever lover who knew how to make lots of money, just like you, Freddy."

"But it has been great fun, hasn't it?"

Charles continued to run his fingers through my hair.

"Listen, Freddy, my mother has designs on your beautiful brown flowing locks!"

"Whatever do you mean?"

"She told me that my sister cuts the kids' hair with a gizmo, into fashionable bobs – like John-Boy's. Now Mama has brought one back from the States to cut yours too! She says you've let it grow too long... but I like it just as it is, Freddy... Let him alone, Mama, I said. He's all mine!"

We burst out laughing.

"Stand up, Freddy. Let me look at you again! I want to fuck the most beautiful chauffeur in the world."

I stood up in the bath. Charles reached out to clutch my groin into his face.

"Mama would love to do this to you, Freddy! ... No Sir! ... I'll tell her to find a handsome young lover of her own!"

"You wouldn't!"

"Now turn around, Freddy! I think this is your best side! She doesn't know what she's missing, does she...?"

He started kissing my buttocks and sucking them hard

with his lips.

"...Now bend over and hold on to the bath taps!"

The journey by road back to the Big House was slow and eventful. Some of the roads were in a dreadful state. One or two were no more than cart tracks. The new Ministry of Transport certainly had its work cut out to provide Britain with a viable road network. We came across one bridge where a heavy traction engine had broken it and toppled into the canal below. This involved a detour through a smelly farmyard and a herd of cows, much to Her Ladyship's amusement. Even His Lordship could now understand the need for an extended system of first class roads across England. We finally arrived outside Harrow School, where I got out to fetch John-Boy's cases from the boot. He looked tearfully at me.

"Freddy, I wish I could stay with you. Listen, I'm like all the others. I really love you too."

"Well, young man," I said, pointing at the school gates, "there you are. Harrow School is all yours now. Behave yourself! And don't be rude to the teachers."

I gave the cases to him and was amazed when he leaned forward to kiss me and then walked away, kicking a stone on the pavement. I suddenly took pity on him, dashed after him, grabbed his cases and we went into the school together to register his name at the front desk. Then John-Boy gave me a hug and another kiss, much to the school porter's amusement. So I left Harrow School's tearful new boy with some English coins from my pocket, because he said he had none. By the time I returned to the car, I'd made myself another lifelong friend. Looking back now, this was another milestone in my life but I only realised the full significance a few years later. I'd also found myself another, but much younger and very secret teenage lover.

So I returned to the driving seat of the Rolls and we drove off while Her Ladyship cried into her handkerchief.

"Poor little mite," she sniffled. "It looks a horrid place. Thank you for taking care of him, Freddy. I think you've made another conquest."

"Really, my dear," His Lordship protested. "John-Boy is far too young to fall in love yet."

"Well," she protested, "none of us thought to take him inside, did we? Freddy takes good care of everyone in this family, doesn't he?"

When we finally arrived at the Big House, builders were now carting off topsoil at the back of the Big House to build a cutting for our village bypass.

"What about the lovely view from my window?" muttered Her Ladyship to her husband in despair.

"Tut tut, my dear, we talked about all this. I told you. Bankruptcy must be the mother of invention."

A steamroller was flattening the tarmac on the lay-by outside our driveway.

"Freddy got them to widen it as a new entrance into our garden centre, Papa," Charles explained.

"Did he, by Jove!"

I stopped the Rolls and turned around in the driver's seat.

"We need a proper entrance for the loading area, my lord. I thought it best to keep the lorries and vans away from the front of your house, my lady. But now the council has found us an empty shop to use for retail sales in the new town centre, so the public won't be bothering you at all."

Her Ladyship leaned forward and tapped me on the shoulder.

"Very thoughtful of you, Freddy, I'm sure. My husband would never have thought of that."

I was rather apprehensive about what Charles' parents would have to say about the interior of their house. They'd been away six months, during which time dust had started to settle everywhere because we'd spent our time in the greenhouses and neglected to dust the furniture.

"I'll go to the Labour Exchange and recruit a Mrs Mop," she decided, staring at her husband. "Well, I think we can afford some domestic help now, can't we?"

Charles put down the luggage he was about to carry up the stairs.

"Freddy has another surprise for you, Mama!"

"Really?"

"Yes, he has named a new hybrid rose after you. It is a deep pink one called 'The Ladyship'. Freddy and I plan to exhibit it at the Chelsea Flower Show next year. There is another blue one we intend to call 'The Lordship' but it isn't doing so well. Something seems to be eating it."

"Well I never!"

"The old gardener started propagating them before the war, my lady. We've been finishing the project, that's all."

"And Charles has been helping you? You mean you actually got him up? That lazy lump didn't lie in bed all day?"

Charles pretended to be outraged when she pointed at him, and laughed.

"It has been a joint project, Mama."

"Well, I never! ... Freddy, you've achieved wonders. "

"We've started selling seeds to distribute in paper packets by train, my lady. Charles placed a large advert in the new Country Gentleman's Estate Book. Orders are starting to come in and, if it does well at the Chelsea Flower Show, the 'Ladyship' rose will be distributed around the country by train as well."

His Lordship came to find out what all the excitement was about. His wife took him by the arm.

"Freddy has named two new roses after you and me..."

"And they really are something new?"

"The Lordship is the first blue rose anything like this one... but there are a few teething problems with an aphid, my lord. I'm trying an experimental insecticide powder derived from the roots of the Derris genus, my lady. With a bit of luck, it might start to take effect before the entry deadline for the Chelsea Flower Show."

His Lordship sat down on a chair in the hall.

"Well now, my dear, and we wondered if we were leaving the place in safe hands. Freddy, tell me, is there anything you're not good at?"

"Are there any more at home like you?" Her Ladyship demanded.

"They all emigrated to Canada," I said. "My father was unemployed and I became your junior under-gardener."

"Well congratulations, Son," His Lordship added. " I do remember Bill the old gardener was working on something new, years ago. It is amazing what you have achieved with Charles while we've been away. Isn't that so, my dear?"

Her Ladyship put her arm around me.

"Freddy, we're very proud of you. You've done wonders. I told my daughter all about you. She says there's a job for you over there in the States any time. Their garden is in a dreadful state because my son-in-law never does anything."

Charles pushed his mother away and embraced me himself instead.

"Freddy is all mine, Mama. He's staying here with me! Aren't you, dear boy?"

His father got up again.

"Well, I would never have believed it! The Rolls, the new roses and the progress on the garden centre – all this excitement has been a bit too much. But are you making any money, my boys? It is all about money these days! ... David Lloyd George has taught us that, at least! But can it be really true? That dreadful Welshman has fallen out of favour? He's actually gone now?"

This was the first time His Lordship had ever referred to us his boys.

"I've been keeping written accounts in your estate office, Papa."

"There is a considerable running surplus now, my lord, what with mail orders and people calling at the shop in the town centre."

"Is there really, Freddy. Is there really?"

The old man turned to his wife.

"Did you hear that, my dear? Freddy has running surplus

of cash in the funds! This young man here can teach us a thing or two! Don't despair... We might yet keep the wolf from the door..."

He turned to me again with a smile.

"I'm investing money on Wall Street through my son-in-law's firm, Freddy. You didn't know that, did you? Some of the money from the sale of our land for the road scheme outside is now invested on Wall Street – where Lloyd George or any other nasty, meddling, avaricious British politician can't get his hands on it. It is just as we said, Freddy! In 1923, Wall Street is the place to make a fortune. That's what my son-in-law says, anyway, and when we left, the Dow Jones index was up, up, up. The American economy is set to boom, I tell you, and now I've got a stake in Uncle Sam! ...Yes, Sir! ... Isn't that right, my dear?"

Her Ladyship turned to me with a wink.

"My husband has put his faith in Calvin Coolidge, the new President of the United States. He just doesn't trust any of our politicians. Well, my dear, I hope you know what you're doing! The Dow Jones index can go up, but, Freddy, dear Freddy...you and I know, what goes up can also come down, just like a downpour in the garden, can't it?"

Charles stepped forward to take my arm but His Lordship suddenly had an idea and looked at his wife.

"Talking of The Country Gentleman's Estate Book, my dear, tell Freddy what my daughter said."

Her Ladyship led me by the arm into the library across the hall. His Lordship and Charles followed behind us and they closed the door.

"Freddy, dear Freddy, the time has come to tell you about the family secret. It has obsessed generations of this family for ages, hasn't it, my dear?"

We all sat down around the library table. Charles leaned over to whisper in my ear.

"Freddy, you've never heard such nonsense..."

Her Ladyship pointed at me with her finger.

"Don't you listen to him, Freddy. Charles is just a doubting Thomas who hasn't got any time for stories about the Napoleonic Wars, Great-Uncle Bartholomew and buried French treasure."

His Lordship put a hand on my arm.

"Frederic, my dear wife will make you believe in fairies at the bottom of the garden next. Won't you, my dear?"

Her Ladyship wagged a finger at both of them and then turned to me.

"I was telling my daughter in the USA about our financial crisis here at home. She has so much money, what with her husband working on Wall Street, she thinks it is funny – stupid girl. Anyway, Freddy, my daughter said we should start looking for the family treasure again."

"Family treasure, my lady?"

"Yes, Freddy, what have you heard about the family treasure, then?"

"Bill, the old gardener, used to talk about it before the war. He said it was all a big joke. He'd been involved in exploring the deep water well behind the Big House, here. He told me it was just like that story in Robert Louis Stevenson's novel *Kidnapped* about the deep well in Carisbrooke Castle."

Her Ladyship's eyes lit up.

"That's right, Freddy. My brother – the one who died in South Africa – had a bee in his bonnet about it. He set out to explore all the stonework in the well by dangling himself from a rope. Well, my brother was a just bit mad, you know."

His Lordship started laughing and interrupted her.

"Freddy, he was addicted to laudanum. Her sainted brother was a complete loony. I think it was the result of inbreeding amongst the English landed gentry."

Her Ladyship pretended to be outraged and put her hand on my arm again.

"His Lordship should not speak ill of the dead, Freddy. My brother was a very sweet boy who liked motorcycles, teddy bears, drugs, naughty adventures and...well, I've told you already. He liked other men, just like you do. That's what got him into so much trouble, you see."

"Not that they're saying you're a loony as well, Freddy," Charles insisted.

"Get to the point, my dear," His Lordship interrupted again.

Her Ladyship wagged her finger at her husband and then turned to me once more.

"Before he died, Freddy, my brother left notes about his research into the whereabouts of our family treasure, in case he failed to return from the Boer War in South Africa, which he never did, as you know. He stuck everything into the 1901 Country Gentleman's Estate Book, for safekeeping, you see..."

She pointed at a high shelf over our heads in the library.

"Do you think you could climb up there and get it down for me?"

I climbed up the library steps to retrieve the dusty volume and opened it in front of us on the table. Her Ladyship rummaged through old newspaper cuttings inside the cover and found a pencilled note.

"Ah yes, page ninety-nine: 'Water supply for country houses'..."

She turned the pages to find it.

"My brother was convinced the treasure was still concealed in the well somewhere. He was going to have another look when he got back from South Africa."

She passed the book for me to look at. Scribbled in the margin of page 101, beside Figure 2, in a diagram marked 'deep well', was a sketch of what looked like a flower. I pointed at it.

"And what's this, my lady?"

She looked over my shoulder.

"A fleur-de-lis, Freddy, adopted by the French royal house of Bourbon. My brother said it had something to do with locating the treasure in the deep well – a sign, he said."

"A sign, my foot," muttered His Lordship. "A sign of the devil..."

I gasped and suddenly felt rather faint.

"My lord, I've seen this before somewhere."

Both Charles and His Lordship got up in excitement.

"Where, Freddy?" His Lordship insisted. "Where have you seen this fleur-de-lis before?"

"Somewhere in the garden?" Charles demanded. "Was it under the statue of the Eros of Praxiteles by the Temple of Love? Don't say the family treasure has been carted off to the council offices inside the stone plinth it used to stand on!"

"My brother always had his suspicions about that statue," Her Ladyship suggested. "He spent hours examining it with a magnifying glass. He thought the fleur-de-lis was cut so small, the naked eye would never see it – a cunning security measure invented by Great-Uncle Bartholomew, you see."

I was puzzled. I really had seen this fleur-de-lis on something recently, but where? I was feeling very tired after such a long day and pointed at the clock. Charles smiled at his mother.

"Mama, if you'll excuse us, I'm taking Freddy upstairs for a bath now."

"So why does he need you, then?" demanded his father.

"Hush, my dear. Freddy wants Charles to wash his back, doesn't he? That's all. They know what they're doing."

The old man had a sudden inspiration.

"Perhaps you could stand as the Conservative candidate at the next General Election, Charles. It would give you a new direction in life."

Her Ladyship grabbed her husband's arm.

"That would delight the Labour Party and the Liberals, wouldn't it? A conservative candidate who sleeps naked every night with his father's gardener! ... The press would have a field day! Questions would be tabled at Prime Minister's Question Time – 'Would the Conservative Party Leader care to comment?'"

His Lordship looked puzzled.

"Do they sleep naked together? Really? .... Well, my dear, it is none of our business if their garden centre has balanced our books! It is all about money, not morals, today! Lloyd

George has taught us that! I think he really did commit adultery, you know. That twenty thousand pound bribe must have been to hide something very sinful, don't you think? If those journalists at *The People* got it right, after all, that is. Anyway, he's gone now. Perhaps we'll learn the sordid truth from his memoirs one day."

Her Ladyship winked at me again.

"As he says, Freddy – money, not morals... But I don't think some of the other parties' politicians know much about morals in private, either! That's what I have heard... It is only a rumour, of course. But anything is better than what's going on in the USA at the moment, what with the prohibition of liquor, armed gangsters and corruption at Chicago City Hall. At least, we haven't got Al Capone's gun battles on the streets of our new garden city – well, not yet, anyway."

Charles and I carried all the luggage up the stairs to leave it outside his parents' rooms. Then he pushed me through the door into his bathroom and locked the door behind us.

"What do you think, Freddy? Can we fit in it together like the one at The White Horse?"

He pointed at his old bath, which was shorter than the ensuite.

"We can try!"

I turned on the geyser for hot water. Charles sat down on the linen basket to watch me undress again.

"You don't think I'd be any good in politics, do you, Freddy? I think my father was having one of his little jokes."

"It would be a disaster! Your mama was right. Do you really think he didn't know about you and I?"

"Come here, you gorgeous gardener boy...!"

I left my clothes in a trail across the bathroom floor. He put his arms around me and looked up.

"... Freddy, thank you for everything. Don't ever leave me, will you? Now if you sit that end of the bath, I think I can squeeze in under the taps."

I sat down in the bath and stared at the designs on the

ornate Dutch tiles around the bath. There were blue glazed windmills and tulips in ornate patterns. I thought of the fleur-de-lis pencilled into the margin of the 1901 Country Gentlemen's Estate Book in the library downstairs. I was still puzzled. Where had I seen it before? I knew it was just a year or so ago. But where were we? What were we doing when I saw it?

"Freddy?" Charles asked. "Are you alright?"

"I'm thinking. What did we do about a year ago?"

I was staring at the flower motif on the tile in front of my nose.

"Not the family treasure again, Freddy. My mother should never have told you. Listen, it wasn't the laudanum that drove my uncle mad, it was the treasure hunt. That's what did it. He became obsessed by it. I'm not going to let that happen to you! Take my advice – forget about it!"

I started to relax.

"Yes, I'll try to forget about it for tonight."

So the two us found ourselves squeezed into a bath for the second time in two days. I turned round to lie back on Charles' chest. It turned out to be easier side by side in this one. He placed a hand on my groin.

"I really love you, Freddy, more than anything or anyone I have ever known. I'm going to tell my father exactly that – after all, it is the truth."

"We've been lucky, that's all. But your mother is right. It could all end unhappily in the newspapers. Secrecy is essential."

"My mother has given up her idea to cut your floppy hair, by the way. Hands off, I told her! She fancies you, I'm sure of it. You know about her sister and the gamekeeper. Well, I think it runs in the family..."

He ran his fingers through my hair.

"... I think your hair is just gorgeous, like the rest of you. I'm so incredibly lucky... Freddy, I'm going to take you for a holiday. Well, my parents have just spent six months in the States while you and I held the fort."

"Paris?"

"Yes, you gorgeous gardener boy – Paris, here we come! Well, you don't know this – my nanny now lives in Montmartre in a guesthouse she inherited. It is very popular with English visitors. She does bacon, egg and sausage for breakfast with Earl Grey in the best china brought over from Harrods."

I sniggered and reached for the hair shampoo.

"My master had a French nanny? ... Oo la la!"

I waggled my hips to make Charles laugh but he slapped my bottom.

"Ouch!"

"Yes, my sister and I were brought up by Nanny Monique, who used to tuck me up in bed with my teddy and a bedtime story but now, well, I've got you, Freddy. Anyway, you're much more sexy than any French maid."

He kissed me while I tried to rub in the shampoo. Charles took the bottle from me and started to wash my hair but I tried to look at him.

"So am I a better fuck than your teddy in bed?"

"No teddy snores as loudly as you do!"

"I don't snore!" I giggled.

"Yes, you do...!"

Charles made loud gurgling noises.

"...Yes, Freddy, just like that!"

I turned to him seriously.

"You woke me up again last night shouting 'That's chlorine gas, boys, quick!' You were back in the trenches again."

"Was I? ... Sorry!"

"So I snuggled next to you and pulled your arm around me like I did last time. That seemed to make the nightmare go away so you slept better until this morning."

"My teddy bear wouldn't have been able to do that. I thank God I've got you now, Freddy."

He kissed me again and ran his fingers through the foam in my hair.

"So when do we go to Paris, then?" I asked.

"I'll telephone Cooks in the morning. We'll take the boat

train from Victoria."

"I was dreadfully sick on the troop ship from Dover in 1915. But perhaps the Channel will be calm this time – just for us. Can we go to the Louvre? I never did get to see that."

"Well, Freddy, you will this time. I have an idea we might look at statues."

"To sell in the garden centre?"

"Well, cheap copies of the more respectable ones, anyway."

"Do you mean some statues are not respectable? Why can't we market copies of those? I'm sure they would sell like hot cakes. Perhaps your father was right. It is all about money, not morals, in the 1920s."

"Freddy, wait until you see some of the male nudes. Then you'll understand why a garden centre couldn't possibly sell anything quite like that! ...The English ladies wouldn't like it. They used to go around tying up fig leaves, you know. The sight of erect male members was just too much for them, you see."

"Are they better-looking nudes than me?"

"Your bum's bigger!"

"Insults! That's all I get from you these days – You say I snore and now my bum's too big!"

"You've got a gorgeous round bum... Stand up, Freddy...!"

I stood up in the bath and turned around. Charles pulled me towards him to kiss my buttocks again while I rubbed the shampoo into my hair.

"... You saved me from the lunatic asylum and now I love every bit of you. You know that! Now bend over and hold on to the taps again."

"But I'll get shampoo in my eyes!"

"You'll get shampoo somewhere else in a moment!"

"Oh yes please, Charles. I need a long slow fuck, just like last time."

He started to massage my bottom with his hands, working soap deeply in between my buttocks once again. I quickly became very excited.

"Listen, Freddy. I've found something new just for you. It will help you to forget all about hidden treasure, secret signs and Great-Uncle Bartholomew's fortune in gold...well just for tonight, perhaps."

He got out of the bath, leaving wet footmarks across the bathroom floor, to collect something from the bedroom. He returned, holding a floppy but elaborate rubber dildo and waved it under my nose.

"Oh no, Charles," I insisted. "This man here only takes the real thing, now I've got you."

But Charles got into the bath behind me and pushed me down to hold on to the bath taps once more.

"I'm only going to open you up for a moment or two, Freddy."

He gently slid the dildo in between my buttocks. I had no idea this could be so erotic and my erection grew quickly in his other hand. Then I felt the dildo slide right inside me.

"Oh fuck!" I shouted. "Oh yes! ... Oh yes, Charles!"

"I thought you would like this, Freddy..."

Charles increased the pace of his thrusts with the dildo and his massage of my erection with his fingers.

"Now try to forget about the family secret, Freddy."

He started to turn the dildo round and round inside me.

"Oh... f u c k!" I shouted, louder still. "Oh... FFF U C K!"

Suddenly there was banging on the door of the bedroom. Charles stopped to listen. His mother was outside, giggling at all the noise I was making.

"Charles? I was just passing ... Whatever are you doing to poor Freddy now? You really shouldn't torture him like that."

He laughed.

"Go away, Mama! You can talk to Freddy about it all tomorrow! He will tell you when you are eating your breakfast in the morning."

But Her Ladyship knocked again.

"Now, Freddy, dear, are you alright? Answer me! I'm worried about you."

I giggled and called out, while Charles yanked on the dildo once again.

"Yes, I'm fine, my lady. We were just getting carried away, that's all... Huh!"

She waggled the door handle but fortunately the door was locked.

"Well, whatever my naughty son is doing to you, and with what, I really don't want to know. But I wish His Lordship, my husband, had tried it out on me! ... Good night, boys!"

I started giggling loudly again as Her Ladyship walked off down the corridor muttering to herself, "Whatever is Charles doing to poor Freddy now? He is not just an innocent stuffed toy in the nursery."

Heaven knows whether so much sexual excitement triggered the realisation of a subconscious memory in my sleeping brain. I woke suddenly in the middle of the night beside Charles and I was now absolutely certain that I knew exactly where I'd seen the fleur-de-lis before. I nudged him. He turned over.

"So, was I snoring again, Freddy? Oh, I do hope I didn't make you sore after all that business in the bath this evening. Is that why you cannot sleep?"

"No, Charles, go and fetch the lantern. We left it outside the gun room."

"What? Have you remembered something?"

"The ice well, Charles! It was in the ice well. That brick which had fallen out of the ceiling had a design on it. It was that same fleur-de-lis. Yes, I am convinced of it."

We both jumped out of bed. Charles went to wake up his parents. I looked at the clock. It was half past three in the morning. Very soon, the four of us were climbing down the embankment towards the old ice well. Her Ladyship carried the 1901 Country Gentleman's Estate Book. His Lordship carried a crowbar and Charles carried one lantern. I was carrying the Tilley lamp we had used out in the trenches.

"How exciting, Freddy." Her Ladyship giggled. "I feel like Bill Sykes going off with Oliver Twist to break into that house in Charles Dickens' famous story."

Charles and I levered open the iron door of the ice house. Then I climbed inside to locate the brick that had come down from the roof. I picked it up and took it back to the doorway, where Charles shone his lantern over it.

"Look!" I shouted.

Her Ladyship held open her book to compare the fleur-de-lis design, which I was pointing at, on one side of the brick. They were the same.

We all looked up to the brickwork high above our heads, where the brick had fallen down. There was obviously a hole up there.

"Get a ladder, my lord!" I said excitedly.

Charles and his father went off with a lantern to find it in the outhouse.

"Oh, Freddy!" muttered Her Ladyship in excitement. "Oh, Freddy, what have you found? So, it was in the ice well. My stupid brother was searching in the wrong place, all that time. It was in the ice well and not the deep water well by the Big House, after all."

We waited for the ladder to be brought down from the Big House. I placed my Tilley lamp down on the floor.

"Oh, Freddy," Her Ladyship said again. "The day my son fell in love with you really was the best day of our lives. Even if there's nothing left up there of Great-Uncle Bartholomew's treasure, after all these years, I want you to know that Charles couldn't have found a better lover."

"Thank you, my lady."

Charles and his father were rather out of breath by the time they arrived with the ladder. We manoeuvred it through the narrow doorway of the ice house and erected it inside. Charles held it steady. His Lordship pointed up to the ceiling.

"Your job, Freddy, my boy."

His Lordship held the Tilley lamp above his head while I carried the lantern with me up the steps. From the top of the ladder I could just reach inside the hole left by the fallen brick. I could feel what appeared to be loose change just inside. I managed to pull out a handful. They were gold coins. Everyone seemed to be holding their breath down below.

"What have you found, Freddy?" His Lordship demanded.

"Gold coins, my lord – pieces of eight or something like that."

I stuffed them in my pocket and climbed down the steps again, holding the lantern. I passed some to His Lordship, who produced a magnifying glass from his pocket and examined one.

"No, Freddy, my boy! These are not pieces of eight but napoleons – twenty-franc coins issued in the reign of French emperor Napoleon the First, 1769 to 1821, if my memory serves me right."

Her Ladyship was beside herself in excitement.

"Let me see that! ... Give that here! Are they real gold, then?"

I held one up in front of the light. It shone as bright as anything manufactured yesterday.

"Yes, my dear, our Freddy has found the family treasure. Look!"

His Lordship was sorting through two coins in his hand.

"Yes, here is a double-napoleon – a forty-franc piece. Now, Freddy, go back up there and bring us some more!"

I climbed up the ladder again. Instead of placing the coins in my pocket, I reached into the hole in the brickwork and scooped out dozens, letting them cascade down onto the brick floor, where Charles and his parents scooped them up like manna from heaven.

"Oh, Freddy! What have you found? Oh, Freddy!"

I climbed down the ladder once more. His Lordship threw his arms around me to kiss me and then passed me to his wife, who did the same. Charles stood back, pretending to be outraged.

"Papa! Really now. He's all mine, Mama. Well, I saw him first!"

"Charles, we're rich," shouted His Lordship. "No, no, I'm

an idiot! The government will claim tax, tax and more tax, plus supertax. They might even claim backdated death duties on Great-Uncle Bartholomew. We'll have nothing left, I tell you! ....Freddy, Charles and you, my dear, must come with me back to the Big House for a council of war. We really must stop the government getting their hands on this!"

"But Lloyd George has gone now, Papa!" Charles insisted.

His Lordship appeared to be dithering about what to do next.

"Freddy, listen to me. Are there any coins left up there?"

"I'm not sure, my lord. The ladder really isn't tall enough for me to see inside. I've only scooped out the coins I can actually reach."

"It's too late to do anything more," Her Ladyship insisted. "We'll pick up everything we can, put a padlock on the door and lock these up in the safe."

"Good idea, Elizabeth," His Lordship decided. "We'll go and find a longer ladder tomorrow and come back again. Freddy might be able to find more in the morning."

I suddenly stopped dead.

"Now what's wrong, Freddy?"

"The workmen, my lord. They'll be here again in the morning to do more work, constructing the extra, wider foul sewer along the stream down there by the vicar's garden – you know, beside the first one they built last year, which turned out to be too small and overflowed across the vicar's garden again."

"Oh damn! I'd forgotten that."

"Listen, everyone," His Lordship insisted. "Absolute secrecy is essential. We don't want workmen breaking into the ice well and stealing any more of Great-Uncle Bartholomew's gold – that is if anything is left. Freddy, go back, will you, to cover over any footprints or any trace to show what we've been up to tonight. Take Charles with you to hold the lamp."

So, once again, we found ourselves outside the ice house, covering footmarks with leaves and double-checking the padlock we'd fitted to the door. I just hoped the vicar hadn't woken up in the night and looked out of his window.

After the workmen had all gone home, we carried a much longer ladder down to the ice house once more. In what was left of the daylight I suggested to Charles that we might heap up soil around the entrance to hide our activities. It wouldn't be long before the vicar poked his head over the fence to see what on earth was going on. If he did, we could say that we were working on our sewer pipe again.

Eventually, we fitted up a platform inside the ice house so I could excavate in greater safety. It was rather unnerving to sway on top of the ladder when removing bricks from the ceiling. Also, we needed to support the roof in case too many bricks fell down. Eventually, our construction resembled something I'd built in the trenches of the Somme to keep the water out. By the light of extra Tilley lamps, I was, at long last, able to look deeper inside the hole and also to dislodge more bricks. There was an old metal box. The coins had obviously been held in a bag that had rotted over the years since Great-Uncle Bartholomew buried his treasure, but the box had stayed secure. What on earth could it contain? I got Charles to stand on a second ladder to help me, while his parents stood below to steady everything. I reached into the hole to grasp the handles and to check they were still sound. I moved it towards us. I held my breath and lifted the box. Slowly we carried it between us down the ladders. Charles used his crowbar to lever the lid open. We stood back. Well, it became clear that the coins I had found were just a taste of what the box contained when Charles placed the metal lid aside. There were several more bags full of golden napoleons, and jewellery encrusted with diamonds and other gems. Clearly, Great-Uncle Bartholomew had his own agenda when he took arms during the Napoleonic Wars! Her Ladyship gasped and stooped down to marvel at her family's lost inheritance.

"What is the value of this little lot?" His Lordship asked her.

"Millions, my dear, probably. Lloyd George would have done anything to get his fingers on this!"

"He's gone now, Elizabeth. But I don't trust any British

politicians any more. Once bitten, twice shy, I say."

"So what on earth do we do with it now, Freddy? Well, you found it. What do you think?"

"My lord, I think it must be carried up to the Big House and locked up in your safe overnight."

"Is that the lot, Freddy? Is there anything more you can see up there?"

His Lordship pointed to the top of my ladder.

"No, my lord, only brickwork and earth."

"Is that it, then?"

Charles pretended to be outraged.

"What more do you expect, Papa, the Crown Jewels?"

So, under cover of darkness, we carried everything up to the Big House to lock up in the safe. All we had to do now was to decide what on earth could be done with it. In the meantime, it would remain locked up in His Lordship's safe until a suitable, but secret, means of disposal had been determined, probably in the USA, where the British government couldn't get their hands on it. Her Ladyship decided that two pieces of jewellery could be sold quietly in Hatton Garden in order to raise ready cash. She was later surprised how much money they fetched. The whole operation was very secret, in case the Inland Revenue got to hear about it. She told the dealer that hard times caused her to sell some of the family heirlooms. Now that was quite true. This prompted Charles to announce that I really had earned a good holiday in Paris and Her Ladyship gave me some of her cash to buy tickets for the Channel ferry at Cooks. She took the opportunity to talk to me in private again over another cup of tea.

"Freddy, my grandson has written a letter to me from the school. He really loves you. Well, you know John-Boy took us to see Rudolph Valentino in Blood and Sand. Well, my son-in-law and John-Boy don't get on, you see – he's too outspoken and mimics his father's broad Texas accent, as you know. My daughter told me that his father said he should be enrolled at the West Point military academy to make a real man out of him. Anyway, the interviewing officer decided that John-

Boy would never make officer material and turned him down – that's why he's at Harrow now. I don't think my grandson wanted to go to West Point, you see, and he probably misbehaved at the interview. Apparently the relationship went downhill after that. Look at this...apparently he printed this himself in the Harrow School photo laboratory. Now he says he never wants to go home..."

She passed me a photo snapshot which John-Boy had made of his own buttocks, which clearly showed considerable bruising.

"...I don't think we should stand by and keep quiet about it. What do you think, then, Freddy? Perhaps he might come here and live with us instead of returning to New York. Well, young man, you know about my state of health. One day, you might even become head of this household. Charles just hasn't got what it takes."

I suggested that she should stay in touch with her grandson and wait to see how things developed. I guessed John-Boy was only going through a difficult phase. It was wrong to intervene too soon between father and son. That's how we left it. Were we right to do nothing, I wondered later?

So one very wet and stormy day I found myself once again at the mercy of wind and rain in the English Channel. The troop ship I had travelled on before had been twice the size of this rather decrepit paddle steamer. Consequently, my seasickness was twice as bad. Charles did not seem to be affected at all by the swaying and buffeting. I stayed on deck, not knowing when I might have to rush to the railings around the side. Eventually we reached Calais and, at last, this dreadful ordeal was over. Charles joked that a Victorian railway company had once tried to dig a tunnel under the sea but that project had ended in failure. I told him I was sorry about that because I was completely exhausted when we climbed into the express train to Paris.

Nanny Monique's 'Pension Anglaise' stood in a quiet side street with a splendid view across Paris. By the time we arrived, the Eiffel Tower was lit up against the darkening sky, but I was just too tired to take much notice. Charles explained to her that I was still suffering from a bad case of le mal de mer and would not want to eat anything for dinner. She led us up a winding staircase to the attic room, where I tumbled into bed and immediately fell asleep. Charles went downstairs again to talk to her about old times. I awoke late in the morning to the sound of pigeons on the balcony and Charles snoring in my ear. I pushed him aside and went to find my breakfast. I'd eaten nothing at all since the day before.

"Oo la la!" Nanny exclaimed when I met her in the hallway, still wearing the silk dressing gown Charles had given me. "You want the petit dejeuner anglais? Your appetite, it has come back? Oui?"

Charles had warned me that his nanny had been living in France so long now, she spoke what he laughingly called 'le Franglais terrible'.

She insisted that I should have breakfast with her, away from the other guests. It was so late now, she protested, the tables in the dining room had all been cleared away. She would cook my bacon, egg, sausage and toast herself. The maid had already gone home.

I looked around the parlour. On the mantelpiece over the iron stove were old photographs in wooden frames. I recognised one. It showed my employers before the war, holding two children while nanny stood at the side. Charles looked so cute in his little sailor suit. Here was all the elegance of Edwardian England, preserved by his nanny, across the Channel in Montmartre. Now a grey-haired Nanny Monique entered, clutching a bone china teapot just like Her Ladyship still used to brew Earl Grey in the garden.

"I remember you," she said, sitting down. "You were a little boy in the greenhouse with that grumpy old man, the head gardener."

"He died – influenza in 1918," I informed her.

She leaned back in her velvet chair and put her hands on her knees.

"But now look at you. Magnifique! .... A great hero of the war, medals and all, received at the court of the King in Buckingham Palace... But we in la belle France got rid of them a long time ago, you know...touts les aristos...pouah!"

She pretended to spit and gestured the blade descending to cut off a head. Then she got up to go to the kitchen but turned to me at the door.

"Oui, c'est ca! ... Madame la Guillotine!"

I laughed. I'd never known Nanny before the war because she left shortly after I arrived when Charles and his sister grew too old for the nursery.

"Stand up and let me look at you, Freddy...!"

I got out of the seat and turned around like Charles often wanted me to do in the bath.

"Yes, I do know why... de toute beauté!"

She set the teapot down on the table and returned to the kitchen to bring in two plates of bacon and egg. I was starving but she ate only half her breakfast and then scooped the rest onto my plate for me to finish.

"You eat like a pig," she joked, getting up again to make toast in the kitchen. "But he loves you so much... Charles, mon petit garcon, from years ago in the nursery at the Big House... We talked last night while you were asleep... We drank lots of wine. He smoked cigarettes. We laughed and talked about you... Oo la la! ... The grand amour anglais like that Oscar Wilde and his Alfred Lord Douglas. He told me all about it, you see! ... We have no secrets... Charles et moi..."

She pointed at her collection of English gramophone records on a rack on the shelf. The HMV labels showed iconic Nipper, the dog, listening to his master's voice on the horn of a phonograph.

"Charles says that you speak up for him when His Lordship complains about him. So, you are not only His Master's Voice like that record label up there. You, mon cher Freddy, are also His Master's Lover – oui, mon brave. I think you are, yes, ...

Master Charles'...your master's, lover."

She punched me on the arm.

"I know all about it, mon brave! ... He says you are his teddy bear, now come to life! You saved him from the madhouse..."

Now she sat forward and looked at me seriously.

"...But, mon cher Freddy, let me for one moment warn you about Master Charles' teddy bears, years ago in the nursery. One day the young master fell into disgrace and was sent up to his room. Eh bien, I went in later and there was his teddy bear, stuffed full of his mama's hat pins – like a pin cushion, mon Dieu! He had taken out all his anger on the innocent teddy... Later, he had an even bigger teddy bear and nailed that to the dartboard..."

Madame put out her arms and legs to illustrate how such an abused teddy might look when used for target practice with its tongue hanging out. I became hysterical. She stared at me.

"Freddy, next time you are between Master Charles and any dartboard, remember what happened to both your poor predecessors. Fortunately, they had no feelings..."

She picked up the teapot to see how much Harrods breakfast tea was left, swirled it round and put it down once more.

"...But maybe, mon cher, I worry too much. Last night he told me how you brought him back from the brink of madness... Now you love each other... You keep him warm at night. He kisses you in the morning. You giggle when he... does that to you..."

She raised one finger in the air and we both laughed.

"... And Her Ladyship knows all about it! ... Mon Dieu! What has become of stuffy, Edwardian England since I left? I think it must all have been because of the Great War...!"

Now I picked up the teapot to pour out more tea. She got up again.

"... Do you want more toast, Freddy? This is the best marmalade from Harrods, you know. Charles promised to bring me some more but he forgot! ... All those years I looked after him in the nursery and my new case of Harrods marmalade ... mon Dieu, tombé dans l'loubli!"

I had a very poor knowledge of the French language and had picked up very little during the war. I assumed this was just another local Montmartre obscenity and laughed.

"We'll send you a crateful of best Harrods English marmalade, Madame. I will see to it myself!"

"That's what he told me... You killed the beastly Huns with your own bare hands, Freddy, out in the trenches of the Somme, to stop them reaching our lovely City of Paris... Mon Dieu...!"

She gestured at the beautiful view outside the window.

"...Then you saved his cousin John, a relative of the King, from certain death in the trenches."

"It wasn't quite like that, Madame!"

"Now, you've got His Lordship's Rolls Royce Silver Ghost completely restored ...oui, gratuitement! Yes, free of charge... Recently you have developed new roses called 'The Lordship' and 'The Ladyship' to exhibit at the Chelsea Flower Show. And now, mon brave, you have balanced the books! ... Freddy? Is there no end to your achievements? Such a big head you must have! I'm surprised you can you get it through the door!"

We both burst out laughing again.

"Could I have some sugar, Madame? The sugar pot. C'est..."

I picked up the sugar bowl and turned it upside down to show her it was completely empty now.

"He said that too – you make him laugh all day! That is why he loves you so much. Oui, c'est ca! ... C'est la vie, la guerre, et l'amour! Mais, toujours l'amour anglais, mon garcon..."

I had no idea what she was talking about and laughed.

"But just think for one moment, Freddy. If Master Charles ever got tired of you like with one of his poor old teddy bears years ago... Where would you be then...n'est-ce pas? I've seen it so often, mon cher garcon. Whenever there is a crisis, all the aristocracy close rank. And when push comes to shove, the English aristos are the worst. They will always form a circle - just as on the battlefield. You will be out, and, as they say –

persona non grata. I've seen it too many times."

"But as you said yourself, Madame, Master Charles loves me. He says we will always be together until death do us part."

"I thought so too, Freddy, before the war – him and his sister. I thought they both loved me. I should have seen the day coming. Off to public school they went and I was out... oui, mon cher, unemployed. Pack your bags, Nanny Monique. Home you go to France!"

She got up to take the empty sugar bowl into the kitchen, but paused at the door to think for one moment.

"...Freddy, I'm about to write my testament...what do you call that in England...? When you leave a legacy for somebody..."

"Your will, Madame."

"Yes, Freddy, in my will I might just leave this old house to you, young man. I have no relatives. Why should the City of Paris inherit it? Well, Master Charles grew too old for me, his poor, long-suffering nanny. Suddenly I was thrown out."

She gestured at the rubbish bin at her feet.

"...One day you may grow too old for Master Charles, mon cher... Mon Dieu, the ingratitude of all these aristocrats! ... I told you about Madame la Guillotine, didn't I? ... Pouah!"

I thought that she was joking about leaving the house to me and quickly forgot all about it.

So I found myself being led around the legendary Louvre museum by my lover. I had heard it was vast and one would need much longer than a day to see everything. But Charles had been here several times before. He insisted that we would only go to see the best of what was extra sexy, masculine, erotic and romantic. I had only seen the naked Eros of Praxiteles in Her Ladyship's garden but this was like a dream come true. We found Rubens' Council of the Gods, painted in 1623. Here were semi-clad nudes of both sexes. Almost stepping out of the picture at the front was a gorgeous blond-haired youth with a red cloak and a bow as if about to fire an arrow at darkened, devilish creatures to the side of the canvas. Charles pointed at the helmeted soldier behind him, who appeared about to jab him in the bottom with a pikeshaft.

"High art can be painful stuff, Freddy!"

I stood back to look at the whole scene but Charles took my arm and hurried me away to see 'Cupid and Psyche' by Picot, painted in 1817. A youthful, naked and winged Cupid was shown stepping out of Psyche's bed while she lay swooning across the pillow in ecstasy.

"That's how I feel when you get up in the morning," Charles whispered.

"But what's happened to Cupid's sexy bits?" I asked, pointing at the almost microscopic sex object between his legs. "I feel insulted now!"

So we walked on, glancing at this and that. By now Charles had put his arm around my shoulder – something he would never have done at a respectable gallery in England.

By five o'clock I was hungry again. Charles reminded me he'd found a restaurant in Montmartre where Utrillo and other artists might be seen. He would treat me to a scenic ride in an open-top horse carriage because, he said, it was the only way to travel in Paris, apart from the Metro, but that was underground. So we trotted at a leisurely pace along the boulevards, up the hill, and eventually arrived outside *La Maison Rose*. The window boxes and the painted shutters gave it an old-world atmosphere behind the table on the pavement, where we sat down.

"Nanny Monique warned me what happened to your teddy bears years ago," I said. "You used one for target practice on the dartboard."

Charles pretended to be outraged.

"The minx...and she expected me to bring her more marmalade all the way from Harrods. Don't you listen to her, Freddy. She tells tales out of school."

"She warned me not to stand between you and any dartboards, Charles... just in case."

He laughed and just stared at me for a while.

"So, Freddy, tell me, what was the most beautiful thing at the Louvre? ... Which exhibit took your breath away?"

I thought for a moment. We had walked around so many galleries my feet were getting sore and I pushed one shoe off underneath the table.

"The Portrait of the Mona Lisa. That's the most famous, isn't it?"

Charles shook his head.

"Only two-dimensional dry paint on canvas, Freddy."

"Well then, 'The Dying Slave' by Michelangelo. I liked that, even if he was really a pouting rent boy – far too well fed to be a slave. That was three-dimensional marble... How about that, Charles, or Mercier's statue of David, perhaps?"

"Too cold – all that marble made me shiver!"

"Then, I don't know. You told me beauty was in the eye of the beholder... I really don't know..."

"Well then? I'll give you a clue, Freddy... It wasn't made of paint on canvas, or cold stone, iron, plaster or marble... "

"Then how about 'The Winged Victory of Samothrace' – that ship's figurehead. Was that made out of wood?"

"No, the most beautiful thing in the Louvre is right here!"

I looked around in the Rue de l'Abreuvoir, where we were sitting. I thought there might be the copy of some exhibit in a window behind me.

Charles sighed loudly.

"Well, I'll tell you about the most beautiful thing at The Louvre... That was you, Freddy...!"

I stared at him. He'd never said anything quite so romantic before.

"... When I look at you I see real beauty on the outside but also on the inside. You are gorgeous stark naked but you also have all the inner human virtues I have come to value so much – generosity, intelligence, bravery, passion, love, creativity...virginity? No, I stole your manly virginity; or rather you gave it to me, unselfishly. What more can I say?"

I was getting emotional. It was all too much.

"Charles, my virginity really wasn't worth much, anyway."

"You are missing the point, Freddy. No mere painting or sculpture has any of the values I can see in you. I can only say this canvas is two feet by three or that marble weighs half a ton. When we sleep together, you also have human warmth, sweet breath, tenderness and the most beautiful silky-smooth skin and gorgeous soft hair. No objet d'art has anything like that!"

"Do I really have silky-smooth skin, Charles?"

"Yes, when you've bothered to have a hot bath."

The waiter arrived at the table to take our order but I had started to sniff after so many unexpected compliments so I wiped a tear from my eye. The waiter looked at me and then smiled at Charles.

"Why does he weep, your friend here? Our menu can't be that bad, monsieur! Perhaps he'd prefer fish and chips out of yesterday's English newspaper... or how about baked beans on toast, then?"

Chapter 7

1930 – The grand opening of our third garden centre

I TRIED TO CATCH UP with Charles, who had stormed out of the refreshment tent after arguing with John-Boy. I found him sitting on a chair by the rostrum and sat down beside him.

"Your speech was much too boring, Freddy," he insisted. "Why didn't you discuss it with me first? I know far more about public speaking than you do, and you really should have given me the opportunity to talk at the microphone. After all, the garden centre has been a joint venture. Anybody would think you did all this by yourself."

"I didn't know you wanted to talk to them, Charles. You might have told me yesterday."

"Well, how did I know you were going to be so boring? ... People were falling asleep everywhere. You should have left it to those of us who are accustomed to public speaking. I studied classics at Oxford, you know, so I could have advised you how to grab the attention of the rowdy populace, even in Rome."

"Now you're being really pompous, Charles," I protested. "It is so easy to criticise people who never went to public school. Some of us had to earn our living. I wasn't born with a silver spoon in my mouth."

We stared at each other. I was already regretting some of the things I'd said in haste.

"And another thing, Freddy. You spend all your time with my nephew, John-Boy. He was even sitting at your feet during your speech, while I had to sit at the back of the podium. Anyone would think I don't matter in your life any more. What kind of relationship is this? I thought we loved one another."

I had no idea what to say now. Charles had dropped a bombshell.

"You're being overdramatic as usual," I protested.

"Well, even my mother warned me that John-Boy loves you too much. I tell you, Freddy, it is either him or me – one of us will have to go. We can't go on living under the same roof. That is quite absurd."

This was turning into a silly quarrel. I got up.

"How can you say that?" I insisted. "I can't stop John-Boy loving me, can I?"

"Freddy, you could push him away – to show him you don't reciprocate his feelings... You don't, do you? And what was on that note he passed to you at the start of your speech? It certainly seemed to have some effect on you because you completely lost your place in your notes – not that it seemed to matter very much... "

I started to walk away but Charles got up to follow me.

"...After everything we've been through, you and me, Freddy. I really should have put my foot down and prevented John-Boy from coming to live here in the first place. He has become an absolute pest. I could strangle the bloody brat."

I was getting upset and stopped to argue with him.

"Charles, that is quite outrageous. When your sister's life is still under threat from disgruntled and bankrupt clients of her late husband in New York, how could we turn them all away? Where could they hide?"

"But John-Boy should have been sent back to Harrow

School, where they could still knock some respect into him, or off to some God-forsaken Army barracks as far away from you as possible."

I could feel my temper rising after such a difficult day.

"That's ridiculous, Charles. Harrow effectively expelled him because of his bad record. You know that and John-Boy would hate life in the British Army, square-bashing at six o'clock in the morning... Listen...how can I love you any more when you are being so unreasonable? You are driving us both apart."

"Oh, now it's me, is it, Freddy? Your big success has gone to your head, just like Nanny Monique predicted. I'm not talking to you any more. You are quite impossible sometimes."

With that, Charles pushed me aside and walked off. So I returned to our guests in the refreshment tent because I needed an iced drink to cool off somehow. I was desperately trying to work out what had gone wrong today. Why couldn't it still be like the time we visited Paris together? In those days, life seemed to be so happy and exciting. Charles had opened up a whole new world for me to share with him. Had I been ungrateful?

1926

When I got up early one morning, some time after we had returned from Paris, I met His Lordship at the bottom of the stairs. He stood back to look me up and down, admiringly.

"Good morning, Freddy. Yes, very fetching. Is that one of my late brother-in-law's sailor suits my dear wife found up in the attic?"

"No, my lord. Charles bought it for me at a boutique in Paris last week. He said it was the latest fashion for young men out there."

"Did he, by Jove? ..."

I was amazed when he put one arm affectionately around

my shoulder.

"...How are you, Son? Charles isn't making too many nocturnal demands on your elegant and slender person, I hope."

"Not at all, Sir. You see – it is I who often exhaust him first."

Her Ladyship came into the hall. His Lordship coughed, took his arm from me quickly and turned to her with a smile.

"I was just saying, my dear, how charming Freddy appears in this new sailor suit, here. The outlook has certainly taken a turn for the better since he moved in, don't you agree? Much more cheerful and gay these days."

His wife looked me up and down.

"He'll have to be careful, that's all. With a figure like that he might be press-ganged into the British Navy... yes bottom up, like it often is in the Senior Service, I understand... But nothing like that ever goes on in our magnificent British Army, does it, my dear?"

His Lordship coughed again and I laughed. Her Ladyship had never made a crude joke like this before.

"Quite so," His Lordship snapped at her. "Now, if you'll excuse us, my dear, I really must ask Freddy for his advice in the library. We'll take our breakfast later... Yes, yes, in a few minutes – leave it on the hotplate."

His Lordship dismissed his wife with a flick of his hand, led me into the library and closed the door behind us.

"Listen, young man. I've been in contact, confidentially, with my son-in-law – the investment broker on Wall Street, you understand. He says he can get all the napoleons melted down into gold bars, secretly, over there and sell all the jewellery on the black market in Chicago. He says 'Scarface', Al Capone, you may remember, is in the market buying gifts for his lady friends, but he needs stuff which cannot be traced by the American IRS – the Inland Revenue Service – income tax, you know..."

I was amazed by such talk about secret dealings with

American gangsters and from His Lordship – an honourable member of the British House of Lords, too.

"...Well, Frederic, my sympathies are with Al Capone for once... That information is for you to keep under your cap, young man."

I gasped. I had been reading in the newspapers how 'Scarface' had taken control of Chicago this year and was even said to be bribing officials in City Hall. I was quite amazed by His Lordship's proposal.

"My lord, forgive me, but is that wise to have dealings with the American underworld?"

I sat down on the chair behind me, and His Lordship sat down opposite.

"Well, Freddy, I ask you. Why should I allow our family nest egg to fall into the hands of our British political gangsters, just like Lloyd George used to be, and whatever avaricious political party takes control of Downing Street, hey? We should be investing more on Wall Street. Have you seen what's happening to the Dow Jones index this week?"

He pointed at the latest headline on the newspaper lying on the table. Of course, I had come across similar ill-founded optimism amongst officers in the trenches of the Somme. Just because they said the sun was shining outside our dugout, they believed it to be so, even though I knew perfectly well that it would continue to rain all day, just by taking a look at the black sky outside the door.

"But, my lord," I said, "what your lady wife said was quite true. Things that go up can also come down. With respect, I do urge caution, Sir."

"The pound sterling will come down, Freddy," His Lordship insisted. "Mark my words. The political banners tell us to trust our Prime Minister, Stanley Baldwin... But I ask you. Do you trust him, young man? Well, since 1918, you and my dear wife have had the vote... I tell you, it is far safer to trust the US President, Calvin Coolidge. Now there's a man to lead us all to glory, yes Sir, hallelujah! ... That's what my son-in-law on Wall Street says anyway, and he has every faith in the President of the United States."

I had no idea what to say next. Surely, His Lordship could not be drunk at eight o'clock in the morning? I cast a glance at his bottle of port and noticed the level had gone down since yesterday.

"What do you want me to say, my lord?"

"Tell me, young man. We usually depend on your advice these days. How can we smuggle so much gold out of the United Kingdom and into the USA? It is far too heavy for Her Ladyship and I to carry through the customs barriers and onto the next boat at Southampton..."

I had a sudden idea and smiled at him.

"...Yes? Has an idea sprung to mind? I need to know, Freddy."

"A short digression, my lord, if you will bear with me for one moment... My second officer out in France brought his Rolls Royce Silver Ghost out with him from England..."

"Yes, yes, you've told us several times."

"Well, my lord, I discovered that under the rear seat, but above the rear axle, is a hidden cavity, which is only opened by taking up the floor and removing the whole leather seat. It is just like yours, Sir, now your Rolls has been rebuilt."

"And, what of it, Freddy?"

"Well, my lord, my officer used to buy exclusive perfumes, cognac and Napoleon brandy while he was on duty in France, you see. I secured everything in the secret compartment under the back seat of his Rolls, and my officer then drove the car back home on leave to England, where he was very popular with everybody, in view of so much austerity on the Home Front in 1917."

"I can imagine, Freddy."

"When my officer later returned to the battlefront, he brought tea, coffee, sugar and soap with pounds sterling for his mates; and other, similar national shortages listed by the authorities..."

"But not declared at the embarkation office... Good Lord, Freddy. Now I'm beginning to see what you are getting at."

"Would you like me to see what I can do, Sir?"

"You mean – to take the Rolls with us to the USA on the Aquitania across the Atlantic?"

"Lifted into stowage by the crane, Sir. Well, you must have noticed, last time at the docks, how other people took their cars with them. It is quite common for first class passengers. I could dress up as your chauffeur, my lord."

I got up to turn around and show him how an elegant chauffeur's uniform might look on me. I was being a shameless tease this morning but I really fancied another holiday. My grandma would have been outraged.

"You want to come too, don't you, Freddy?"

"Extra security, Sir. I have had experience of HM Customs and their little ways at the Channel ports, with my officer. And from 1917, I had to deal with the Americans on the Western Front. I know some of their Yankee ways... Americans do so many things differently, like their so-called English language, Sir. For instance, their petrol is called 'gas' or 'gasoline' and their pints and gallons are different, too."

"Freddy, it is a deal."

I sat down again and smiled at him like a friend. Now I was really certain that it must have been the war.

"Thank you, my lord."

"Time for breakfast, young man. Sit with me today."

I followed him into the dining room, where Her Ladyship had left our bacon, eggs and sausages on the hotplate. With my breakfast I sat down next to His Lordship at the table. Now holding an EPNS fork in his hand, he turned to me again.

"My dear wife may choose to keep the diamond brooch, since it is her family heirloom, I don't know. Now I must ask for complete discretion on your part, Freddy. My position in the House of Lords could become uncomfortable, to say the very least, if HM Treasury Department should discover our little plans. So, mum's the word, my boy, what? If you keep my secret, I'll keep yours, hey?"

I nodded. It was the seal on a silent conspiracy. Civilian life suddenly seemed to be much more exciting. Charles' sexual relationship with me was no longer secret like the old days, when it could only be conducted by the back door at midnight. Today I was grateful for a fresh challenge now that the war was over.

1927

So I set about modifying His Lordship's Rolls exactly as I had done in France. Bookings for the crossing were made. Space was reserved on the stowage deck of the Aquitania for the car, with a first class luxury suite, including accommodation for a servant – that was me – described as chauffeur/valet to His Lordship. At dead of night, the treasure was removed from the safe and locked up under the back seat of the Rolls. We even had the whole thing weighed at a public weighbridge, in order to calculate the correct weight of ballast to replace all the gold, in case questions were asked on the return journey back to Southampton. I tried to think of everything, in order to make the whole operation a success. Charles and His Lordship were most impressed by my military precision.

As it happened, on the day, no difficult questions were asked by the customs officers in Southampton when His Lordship, Her Ladyship, Charles and I boarded the Aquitania. So we steamed swiftly past the Isle of Wight and out into the Atlantic. Unlike our transport ship during the war, this enormous ship was fitted with the latest stabilisers and I did not suffer from a queasy stomach or seasickness, thank goodness. For the first time in my life, I was about to set foot onto American soil. Charles had been there before, of course, and teased me with crazy stories about the Wild West, and cowboys and Indians, which I had only seen in silent movies at the cinema.

Having double-checked that the Rolls was securely locked up below, my lover took me on a tour of this gigantic four-funnelled Cunard liner. The Aquitania was known as the 'Ship Beautiful' and I had never seen such luxury. He paused to show me the famous cutaway poster on one wall. It showed everything from the enormous boilers below the waterline up to the four enormous red funnels belching smoke into the sky. So, we went off to explore all eight decks above stowage. Just like the Louvre, Charles had been here before, of course. He assured me this was one of the first giant Atlantic liners to be designed with sufficient lifeboats for everyone. He warned me that I should never mention the you-know-what which hit an iceberg and sank on its maiden voyage back in 1912. That was always bad luck in the North Atlantic.

So we walked around the first class Palladian Lounge, which rose through two decks. He said it was modelled on the architecture of Sir Christopher Wren, who built St Paul's. Then we visited the Louis XVI dining room, which also rose through two decks. But he wouldn't take me in the Jacobean Grill, because, he said, even first class passengers had to pay extra to go in there. Finally, we sat down in the beautiful Palm Garden Lounge for coffee. There were wicker chairs, settees and tables. Fortunately, Her Ladyship had given us some spending money to share and we both had coffee with cream and the famous peach Melbas, named, he assured me, after Nellie Melba – the famous singer. I joked that perhaps such fabulous, creamy desserts caused her to become so large and rotund. I was still wearing the sailor suit Charles had bought me in Paris. So many heads had turned when I was walking around, that he became jealous and told me to go back to our suite to change into something more sober and less figure hugging. In truth, I had put on some weight, myself, but it was so much fun to be admired.

We eventually landed at the docks in New York, where our Rolls Royce was lifted by the crane onto the quayside. Our passports were in order. The American immigration department waved us through and so we went to collect the car. But, just as we drove out of the dock gate, a uniformed official hailed us to stop.

"Now what, Freddy?" His Lordship demanded. "Have they been tipped off by the new Atlantic telephone from England?"

"Leave it to me, please, my lord," I reassured him. "You forget. I've dealt with Yankee officials before, during the war."

So, I got out of the car and followed the officer to his desk. I gave him my passport to look at and casually dropped my Victoria Cross on the floor, as if by accident.

"What's this?" he asked, picking it up.

I got the old newspaper cutting out of my pocket. It showed me holding my VC in one hand and the tennis racket in the other. Behind me, in this photo, were Charles and his parents. The officer beckoned to his colleagues to come and look.

"Guess he fought alongside us in 1917," one of them said. "Can I have your autograph? Sorry to hold you up, soldier. We had a tip-off from the Prohibition Navy that a consignment of Scotch whiskey was about to be unloaded from either Canada or England today. Your master doesn't carry anything illegal in his hip flask, by way of illicit liquor, does he? You know about the Volstead Act of 1920, of course. No liquor is permitted here in the USA these days, soldier."

There was a giggle behind me.

"Well, apart from the speakeasies downtown, controlled by you-know-who."

I smiled at everyone innocently.

"Actually," I suggested. "I don't actually think Al Capone would have his liquor delivered in an automobile that's nearly twenty years old, do you? I tell you, the radiator will boil over at fifty-five miles per hour with the FBI in hot pursuit."

They all laughed. I signed a piece of paper, shook hands all round and was allowed to return to the Rolls, where everyone seemed immensely relieved. The officer actually came out and saluted as we drove sedately through the gate. Charles waved to him, just like Queen Mary, out of the window, much to his mother's amusement.

"Remember to drive on the right, Freddy," Her Ladyship insisted nervously, tapping me on the shoulder.

"Hush, my dear," His Lordship reassured her. "Freddy learned to drive out in France. He knows what he's doing."

"Oh yes, dear. I forgot. How silly of me."

Charles did his best to direct us with the aid of a street map his sister had sent him, and eventually we pulled up outside her house in Queens on Long Island. By now I was suffering from nervous exhaustion. The New York City traffic with the street cars crossing junctions in front of us had undermined my confidence, but there was no collision. This was not like Paris in wartime. I slumped down in an easy chair in the hall.

"Poor Freddy's quite exhausted," Charles explained to his sister.

She shook my hand but I was nearly asleep already.

"The very same national hero?" she asked, laughing at me. "They told me all about you, Freddy."

She waved at her husband, who was talking to His Lordship at the door.

"We'll leave Freddy to rest," Charles suggested quietly to his sister. "Time to take up the back seat of the Rolls. Have you left room in your safe?"

"Best leave everything until after dark," she whispered, pointing at the neighbours opposite. "Prying eyes, you know. Drive it in the back yard. We'll lock the gate."

John-Boy was already here, having returned from Harrow School on another ship at the start of the long summer vacation. He'd already told his sisters and younger brother about me – well, the respectable things, anyway. I was introduced to each of the children and had to show my Victoria Cross to each one, who gasped and said things like 'Golly, gee – a real, live war hero!' They hugged their grandma and John-Boy whispered in my ear that he wanted to talk to me alone sometime soon.

Charles took me to have a look around his sister's house. In the kitchen was something I'd never seen before – a black woman in an apron, kneeling in front of an electric icebox which hummed in the corner. There was a chromium-plated electric food mixer on the dresser. But we, in England, didn't even have mains electricity at home, only the gas supply. Outside, in the enormous garden they called the back yard, was a swimming pool complete with a diving board. He said this was heated in the winter. I was stunned.

At long last, I tumbled into bed, upstairs in the attic. It was a single. Charles locked the door and pushed his bed right next to mine. Her Ladyship had told us to watch our manners, in case one of the children walked in and caught us unawares. But I was far too tired for sex now.

When I came down late in the morning, His Lordship took me aside to whisper that the family heirlooms had all been removed safely in the night. Even now, the napoleons were being melted down into shiny gold bars, down by the dockyard. I was not to ask any questions. He looked relieved. Then John-Boy came to talk to me. He wanted to take me upstairs to his room in order to see his Valentino collection. I asked Charles' sister if this was all right and she waved a hand in the direction of the stairs.

I was amazed. John-Boy's bedroom walls were covered in posters and photographs of the late Rudolph Valentino, the movie star. I had assumed that only teenage girls, who suffered from the notorious 'Rudy mania', would collect anything like this and build a shrine. John-Boy had also copied some images of Rudy in his own pencil drawings, and one or two really were quite good. Down one wall was an enormous pencil sketch of Michelangelo's David but with Valentino's head. I did notice that the penis had been considerably enlarged and only a small fig leaf had been stuck to the wall to cover it. John-Boy seemed immensely proud of that. Over his bed was the official poster of Valentino dressed in elaborate costume as Julio Desnoyers in 'The Four Horsemen of the Apocalypse'. There was also a signed portrait of him dressed as 'The Sheik' and another dressed as a magnificent bullfighter from 'Blood and Sand'.

"Well, Freddy, what do you think?" John-Boy asked. "What a shame he died, and from a ruptured appendix last year, so he was not an immortal god after all... Our Rudy was no great hero quite like the real thing, of course..."

He looked me up and down admiringly and licked his lips.

"... My father calls Valentino a painted pansy or a pink powder puff, depending on his mood and says I'm on the same path to hell and damnation, Freddy. He often gives me such a bare-butt whopping that I can't sit down."

I looked at John-Boy, who was now staring at me. He clearly knew more than I had imagined but he also craved for my approval. I walked over to the French window of his room, which overlooked the swimming pool in the back yard. He followed me and, standing very close at my side; he opened the French window and showed me how he could dive straight down into the water – about twelve feet below. Of course, in England, a safety rail would be fixed outside to prevent accidents but I made no comment. Anyone could fall too easily. I told John-Boy that his grandma had shown him the photo he had sent to her from Harrow. It showed his bare bottom after his father gave him a beating the year before.

"Pop wanted a hero just like you, not a son like me," he said. "That's why I've just been taken for an interview at West Point. But, buddy, can you see me happy, stuck out in some boring military academy? I was a bit too disrespectful to the interviewing officer. But, I ask you, how could I stick stuff like this up on the wall of the dormitory...?"

He turned around and waved his hand at everything.

"...Freddy, I wish I could have had a pop just like you. You don't look like a Great War hero in your fancy chauffeur's outfit – I really love it – but you are the real thing... My pop never served on the Western Front. By the time he got out there in 1918, the war was over... He dresses up like a war hero, you know. He goes to his regimental reunions wearing the full uniform...to salute the Stars and Stripes and sing the glorious praises of the Union."

I was amazed when John-Boy put one arm around my waist.

"...I love men in general and Rudy in particular, Freddy. My dad doesn't know I'm queer. I'm like you. My pop sees me as inadequate, effeminate and an insult to his own masculinity, you see. He thinks that by dragging me out to the woodshed down there to whack my bare butt, he will change me – look...!"

John-Boy turned around and dropped his pants to show me the results of his latest session in the woodshed with his father. I ran my finger along one painful welt. He suddenly turned around to stare at me. I really should not have been so innocent, and seen this one coming.

"...So, Freddy, would you like to fuck me, then?"

"I beg your pardon!"

"What if I were to open the window there and shout 'help'? I could also tell them all downstairs what I heard you getting up to with Uncle Charles last night! I heard everything, Freddy. These houses are made of wood, not brick. The walls and the ceilings are cheap... You love my uncle Charles. Now I want you to love me too. Let me give you a blowjob first please, Freddy – just a little one. This is one thing I'm really good at...!"

I sat down on the chair behind me. I felt faint. John-Boy was looking down at me and folded his arms.

"Well, Freddy, it is your choice. I don't think you'd last long in the New York State Penitentiary. I understand that pretty young men like you have a really rough time in there. Let me give you a blowjob please, Freddy and we'll say no more about it."

John-Boy locked the door and then knelt down to undo the fly buttons on my trousers, and started to suck while his pants were still around his ankles. Then he lowered himself down on my erection and we fucked, gently at first. At the back of my mind I could hear my grandma making strongly disapproving noises but I tried to put her out of my mind. John-Boy just stared at me, smiling all the while. But he became very excited and we finally climaxed together. Then he leaned forward to smother me with youthful kisses. John-Boy had discovered my weakness. My life would never be the same again.

When it was all over he just laughed as if he didn't care a damn, and quickly pulled his pants back up again.

"But my dad won't change me, will he, Freddy? You see, I will never love girls but, listen, I will always love you. I will never be the hoot'n', root'n', toot'n', go-getting, all-American, masculine son my father always wanted."

"I've never met anyone like you, John-Boy."

"Listen, Freddy, I promise you I will never let you down, Big Buddy. I'll keep your secret if you'll keep mine. That is a promise. Let me give you another kiss and no hard feelings. I will always love you now."

He took me in his arms and gave me a very long, intense kiss. I was quite overwhelmed. Finally, I felt deeply honoured to be called John-Boy's 'big buddy' and relaxed once more, when he let go of me and looked at his watch. He was suddenly very excited and said everyone would be going to the cinema that night. There was a new movie. I just had to see the latest sensation. People spoke words right out of the screen. It starred Al Jolson and was called 'The Jazz Singer'.

So Charles' brother-in-law drove us in his enormous station wagon into town to go to the movies. I had no idea what to expect. I'd only seen Rudolph Valentino, Charlie Chaplin and the Keystone Cops at the local fleapit in England. The New York Warner Theater was vast and bathed in glittering limelight. Uniformed flunkies conducted us to our seats in the gallery upstairs. The lights went down. At first, I felt disappointed because this movie began with title cards and seemed rather slow. Then, suddenly, the electric horns by the screen crackled and Al Jolson started to sing to his mammy, while everyone in the audience listened. Charles grabbed hold of my left hand in the darkness. John-Boy took hold of the other and I suddenly found myself in the middle of two lovers. By now, my poor grandma would have been apoplectic in moral outrage.

We were all in tears when the curtains closed at the end. Hollywood movies had finally been liberated from deathly silence. Great technical progress had been made. I was awestruck by the American Dream.

So I had made a friend of Charles' nephew, John-Boy. I was his great English buddy and his secret lover. He insisted on coming to sit beside me at the dinner table, and just like his grandma, he fondled my knee under the tablecloth where his father couldn't see. He explained that he had told all his mates that a British war hero was staying in the attic at his house. Could he borrow my Victoria Cross and the newspaper cutting to take the following day? I gave it to him, on condition I would get everything back. Her Ladyship seemed to approve of our growing friendship, but I rather thought Charles was becoming jealous. Later, he took great delight in assuring me that John-Boy really wasn't my type. Anyway, he was far too young! I pretended to be offended.

Eventually, while the children were at the swimming bath with their mother, we were taken on a conducted tour of Charles' brother-in-law's skyscraper in Wall Street. I looked out of the window of his office, which clearly had a sheer drop down to the street below. People looked like ants so far down on the sidewalk. There was no sound of traffic, but only the wind whistling through the ventilator above the window. I felt dizzy. It was unreal. I was amused by the drinking water dispenser in the corridor and the Otis safety lift, which descended so fast that my stomach seemed to have been left behind, up on the twenty-seventh floor.

One evening, a few days later, Charles said he would take me out for a night on the town. We would need our best suits, which meant I would need to wear one of his with the waist drawn in. So, no sailor suit today. A yellow taxicab arrived and we were off.

"Charles," I insisted, sitting next to him in the back seat, "where are we going then – to meet the President?"

"Carnegie Hall," was all he would say. "Your night out, Freddy."

When we arrived, I could see this was a glittering occasion. New York's beau monde were all out in force with the great and the good. Women in fashionable outfits stood elegantly with their gorgeous men, who wore the sharpest suits. Noisy crowds thronged the staircase. I had never heard of George Gershwin but gathered that he was playing the piano himself tonight. It would be an historic occasion.

"Freddy," Charles insisted, "you will remember this music for the rest of your life. George Gershwin is the newest thing in American music. He writes instant classics."

We found our reserved seats and sat down. Clearly, the performance had sold out. At the side, an angry dispute was going on where the ticket office had inadvertently double-booked a whole row. Two groups of people were arguing over who should sit where. Eventually, spaces were found after a cancellation elsewhere in the hall and the audience started to settle down. The lights dimmed. A tall, slim young man hurried onto the platform towards the piano in front of the orchestra. The illustrated programme told us this was George Gershwin's revolutionary piano Concerto in F of 1925.

"He wrote everything," Charles insisted. "This man is a genius of the twentieth century – a Franz Liszt of his time."

The pianist bowed and sat erect at the piano. When the music started, I could feel the whole audience's attention focussed on the stage. The first movement sparkled like the jewels on the ladies' costumes in the seats around us. The second movement was slower and more wistful. It reminded me of foggy days and drizzle in London while we were waiting for the troop train in 1915. But when the horns started, accompanied by a soulful distant trumpet at the back of the hall, it sounded to me that Gershwin was sounding the last post over the trenches of France. Suddenly I was in floods of tears. This was all too much. A lady in the row behind passed me a paper handkerchief. Charles turned round to thank her quietly.

"My friend was wounded in the trenches of the Western Front, Ma'am. He also left several friends dead out there."

I think that was the moment I realised he had finally recovered. There would be no more flashbacks now. The lady nodded and Charles took hold of my hand until the break. The third movement had the whole audience enraptured. Finally, I was deafened by applause. Charles pulled me to my feet when the audience erupted into enthusiastic cheering. I can't say I had really understood this music – it was so new. I had only been used to 'Lili Marlene', 'Land of Hope and Glory' and 'God Save the King' at home. We would need to buy a set of gramophone records so that I could hear it all again. Classical music would never be the same again.

During the interval, I had time to look around. Charles and I were not the only couple comprising two men. One very elegant character swept down the stairs beside a young man who was quite clearly wearing make-up. I even saw two young women who sat gazing into each other's eyes over their coffee cups. Charles whispered in my ear, "None of the devil's drink here, Freddy. Prohibition since 1920, you know. We'd have to go round the corner to the speakeasy for any sinful booze – later, perhaps."

"What would respectable England make of all this?" I asked him. "I'm glad your father, His Lordship isn't here."

We both gazed in amazement as two men kissed in front of us while an elderly woman, the spitting image of my grandma, looked on in horror. Suddenly I felt elated. America was leading the way to liberation.

"I wanted you to see what's happening over here, Freddy.

This is the future. Would you like to come and live over here one day?"

After the interval, Gershwin's 'Rhapsody in Blue' certainly had a different effect on me. By now, my mind was starting to tune in to the new ideas of syncopation and the interplay between percussion and piano. I closed my eyes and imagined scenes from years ago – a circus, a fair in my childhood, and triumphant scenes from Armistice Day in France, only a few years before. All too quickly such excitement came to an end.

"Well, Freddy, what did you think of that, then?" Charles demanded in the taxicab on the way back to Queens.

I just smiled and took hold of his hand again under my coat, which lay across our laps, but said nothing. New York was a dream come true.

Too soon, it was time to go home to England again. I put on my newly-cleaned and pressed chauffeur's outfit, which John-Boy took endless photos of with his Kodak Box Brownie. A family snapshot of everyone was made for posterity, around the Rolls Royce, which was washed down with the jet hose outside in the yard, especially for the occasion. Then, under cover of darkness, when all the kids had gone to bed, two sandbags were measured out and inserted under the rear seats, just in case the lost weight of the family heirlooms caused comment from any suspicious customs officers.

The following morning, in order to meet the sailing deadline set to coincide with high tide in New York Harbour, we took our leave. Charles' mother hugged and kissed her grandchildren, who then shook hands ceremoniously with His Lordship. John-Boy gave me a big, sloppy, lingering kiss on the cheek, which caused quite a sensation all round, and at which Charles pretended to be outraged. I heard John-Boy's father mutter something about the woodshed under his breath. I really did wish we could have taken the boy with us, rather than leaving him to his fate. Finally, singing our praises of the New World, we drove sedately through the traffic to the dockside, where United States Customs waved us through and saluted us with a smile.

Once again we were on an ocean liner – a brand-new one this time. Charles had obtained a copy of the elaborate gold-covered booklet all about this latest flagship of the French Line, launched in 1927. It showed the huge public rooms; and lady passengers carrying feather fans and even smoking cigarettes on the uncluttered sun deck. No old-fashioned tribute to Sir Christopher Wren here. This was a celebration of the new, the moderne and everything 'art deco'. Charles told me the interiors were inspired by the Paris Exposition des Arts Decoratifs et Industriels Modernes of 1925. I suggested we should raise our glasses in a toast to Paris and the way we had both fought to keep it safe from the Germans. But Charles reminded me that we would have to wait for the liner to move outside US territorial waters before the cocktail bar opened up. Thirsty passengers would already be sitting on art deco chairs, cursing Prohibition, and looking out of the windows in eager expectation, he said.

The 'Ile de France' was the very latest in chic Atlantic fashion. Decorative flags fluttered above us from the masts, fore and aft. Black smoke belched from the forward funnel out across the skyline. So, Charles and I went to explore the ship. The turbine engines were very quiet but suffered from vibration. Nevertheless, we glided effortlessly through the Atlantic waves with four propellers. The splendid, brand-new French interior displayed the latest art deco finesse in accommodation and decorations. The first class dining room was far more spectacular than anything on the Aquitania. This one rose three decks high and had a grand staircase down which elegant ladies could make an impressive entrance. We found the chapel, which was decorated in a chic, neo-gothic style; and the grand foyer, which rose up to the height of four decks. There was even a shooting gallery, where I challenged Charles to a match later. It was a long time since we had taken aim at the Germans and we might be a little rusty today. There was a gymnasium, where I would be able to hang upside down on the latest elaborate equipment. We even found the merry-go-round but Charles assured me that both of us were too old for that sort of thing now. We left it to the children and went to find the famous first class lounge to order our café au lait.

As we approached the doors, I heard a sound I thought I recognised. Someone was tinkling the ivories of the grand piano. We went in quietly to find George Gershwin once more, now dressed informally in a shirt and slacks. He sat at the keyboard as he had done in the Carnegie Hall, but seemed to be experimenting with something new. He looked up, smiled at us, closed the piano lid and walked off. What was he playing? I wondered later. Were we privileged to hear preliminary sketches of 'An American in Paris'? But we'll never know now. By the time our café au lait finally arrived, a beautiful young man had started to play the piano. He was the official pianist today and we were being serenaded with George Gershwin's music once more – his 'Three Preludes' for piano. I looked round the room. Around the walls and across the ceiling were dozens of bright strip lights. There was an ornate art deco clock over the door. Behind the piano, on the wall, was an enormous painting of some classical French scene I couldn't really understand. His Lordship certainly had nothing quite like this on the wall of the Big House. The chairs and the table where we sat down were sumptuous and beautifully upholstered with circular designs in the latest fashions. I was thrilled by all this elegance and luxury but I was comforted by the thought that Charles and I had both done our bit to keep such exciting French art deco design free from the dead hand of the Kaiser, back in 1915.

The latest English language brochure in our first class suite boasted that this ship was also the very peak in French marine engineering, with the latest stabilisers. A note tucked inside this brochure announced that a fancy-dress ball would be held on board when the ship reached mid-Atlantic. Outfits could be hired on a first-come-first-served basis from a new costume department and a society photographer, Madame

Rianne, would be covering this event with her team. She was also available at the liner's new portrait studio to make photographs of passengers during the voyage. There were numbers to dial for further details and bookings could be made on the telephone in our suite. An added bonus for Charles and me was the second double bed, on the other side of a sliding door – no bunks aboard the 'Ile de France'. Charles and I declared that we would share this double bed together. We were in a French ship now and the Code Napoleon did not outlaw two men sleeping in a bed together. Charles reminded Her Ladyship exactly why Alfred Lord Douglas and Oscar Wilde went to live in France in 1897. So, at last, both Charles and I felt proud that we had done our bit to keep Paris really safe from the Germans.

After dinner, we wrapped up in warm coats, found deck chairs and went to sit outside in the shelter at the stern, overlooking the wake of the propellers, to stare into the sunset. Charles and I now needed some time to ourselves. The first class suite was comfortable but rather too hot. His Lordship could not find the thermostat and had to ring for the steward to adjust it.

"Freddy," Charles said eventually. "I want you to know..."

A waiter appeared with our cocktails. We were out of American territorial water now and the bars had just opened. At last, prohibition of the devil's liquor was far behind us.

"What did you want to say?" I asked as the waiter walked off with his empty tray.

"Thank you, Freddy. That's all... You make my life wonderful... If the 'Ile de France' were to hit another iceberg and I was to drown tonight, I want you to know you have made me the happiest man alive."

"Sh...! Sh...!" I insisted. "You mustn't say things like that on a new ship... But I suppose this one has already sailed its maiden voyage, on the twenty-second of June, Charles. So, we're all safe now and the brochure assured us that there really are more than enough lifeboats on this one, too. The French learned that lesson from a certain historic disaster, I think."

So we both raised our glasses and drank a toast to Penhoet, the ship's builders at Saint Nazaire in France, and wished her a long and profitable life with the Compagnie Generale Transatlantique.

"Freddy," Charles said, putting down his glass, "without you... I'd be nothing, if I was still here at all... Do you know that?"

"Well," I said, "without you I wouldn't be here either, would I...? I shan't forget this journey in a hurry..."

I looked around to check nobody was listening and moved my deckchair closer to his. Under the travel rug, which was draped across our knees, he held my hand and I turned to my lover once again. But it suddenly struck me. I was now a man with two lovers. I was sexually active with John-Boy and, sometimes, still passive with Charles. Who was it who said 'love the one you're with'? And I did. I was embracing every new secret opportunity for love and illicit sex. My poor grandma would have disowned me by now.

"You know, Charles," I said, "smuggling gold into the USA was a bit like taking coals to Newcastle but it's done and dusted. Will your father be happy now?"

"He trusts my brother-in-law, our very own stockbroker on Wall Street, implicitly, you know. What do you think, Freddy? You saw the Dow Jones index lit up in lights. Can it really go any higher? Our family fortune is invested in that now, you know. All the melted-down, ancient, family you-know-what, which you heroically discovered in the old ice well, now rests with Uncle Sam... Well, God Bless America...I hope!"

I laughed and raised my glass to make a toast.

"Here's to Uncle Sam...blessed by God...we hope!"

We clinked our glasses together, but I had reservations about the Dow Jones index.

"...Your mama has a way of putting these things – what goes up can also come down, Charles."

"Don't you dare say that again to my father! ... Promise me now!"

We watched a large seagull swoop overhead and then turn back to the coast behind us, where a thin trail of black smoke from the boilers disappeared into the distance. After the excitement of smuggling so much treasure safely across the Atlantic, I was relaxing at last.

"So, Freddy, of all the sights and sounds of New York, what will stay with you for ever?"

"Al Jolson singing 'Mammy, Mammy' out of the movie screen. I will never forget that or George Gershwin on the piano playing his 'Rhapsody in Blue' or, indeed, in the lounge today. But that second young man on the grand piano in the first class lounge was much better looking, don't you think? I prefer my men well built, like you, Charles."

He ignored this.

"Well, Freddy, the second movement of Gershwin's 'Concerto in F' had you in tears."

"Yes, but the one thing I will never, ever forget is John-Boy kissing me so passionately in front of everyone. Nor will I ever forget his father making whispered threats about extra discipline in the woodshed behind us. We really should have brought him with us, you know."

"John-Boy loves you, Freddy, like we all do. But we'll have to keep an eye on that one. He will break a few hearts one day, I think."

"Do you mean a girl's or a boy's?"

"No, Freddy, I mean yours."

This took me by surprise. Just how much did Charles know, or had he just guessed?

"But he's too young for me," I insisted, trying to forget what my grandma might have thought. "You said so yourself the other day."

Charles and I sat quietly and we finished our cocktails, staring at the red, setting sun, sparkling in the wake of the sensational 'Ile de France', as America slipped further and further behind us. I was left thinking about John-Boy. If I'd ever had a son, I wish he could have turned out to be just like him. It distressed me to think we had just left him there at the mercy of his hostile and increasingly violent father. Somewhere, at the back of my mind, was a growing suspicion that we might soon be hearing more about the relationship between John-Boy and Charles' brother-in-law, especially as the boy would very soon become a strong young man with a will and the strength to fight back.

Charles surprised me by arranging a session with the ship's portrait photographer in her studio the day before we reached Southampton. He would hire an English soldier's uniform from the costume store and I would wear my own sailor suit. He said he wanted a photo of the two of us together in the pose usually reserved for a courting couple. The lovely Madame Rianne was elegantly dressed in a chic black-and-white gown of the latest art deco design. She seemed to me to personify a modern and liberated French Lady – like a great heroine of the barricades during the Paris Revolution. Perhaps one of Madame Rianne's ancestors had actually sharpened the blade of the guillotine or sat knitting with the other tricoteuses, in eager anticipation of the next aristocrat's demise.

In the studio, Madame Rianne had no time for tired old Anglo-Saxon inhibitions about photographs of two men together. She was quite happy to oblige and so we were seated under her studio lights while she arranged us in the appropriate pose for a loving couple. She snapped her fingers at her assistants, who then moved studio lights up or down until she was happy. Several frames were exposed on her Leica camera until she had got what she wanted. For one, Charles even put his arm around my shoulder, and in another, I was posed gazing up into his eyes. Finally she put down her Leica.

"Eh bien messieurs," she said. "Is there anything else you would like?"

Charles looked at me and winked.

"Something a little more avant-garde, Madame...just one, perhaps, to remind me what Freddy looked like in his prime."

"Take off your shirt, mon brave," she suggested, looking at me.

I left the sailor top on the floor. Madame raised my screw-top seat. We were repositioned under the lights so that I was lying back suggestively on Charles' chest. I was now naked from the waist up. She said that in France it was quite common to be asked to photograph two men together like this. Only in old-fashioned and stuffy England did Victorian prudery make such intimate male photography unlikely. Madame took another glimpse through her viewfinder.

"Oo, la la," she muttered, moving the camera closer. Finally she pressed the shutter. "Magnifique! L'amour anglais, plus illegal."

I went back later to collect the proofs and to select our enlargements, one of which we ordered in several sizes. We presented a small one to Charles' mother, who tucked it away safely in her handbag, where a sniffy British customs officer might not find it. Here was one photo my grandma would never approve of.

All too soon, our holiday was over and we returned to our garden centre business. The shop in the town centre had sold out of so much stock that the staff were reduced to buying plants in from a neighbouring nursery. The backlog of orders for packet seeds was becoming impossible for them to manage and I asked His Lordship to apply his military expertise from the Boer War to sort out the order book and devise a plan of campaign. This he did with enthusiasm, welcoming a worth-while project to keep his mind off his increasing dependence on port wine. So after all the excitement of America, I had to come down to earth and make the business pay once more.

I called in to see my grandma again and ask if her post-card had arrived from New York. I also intended to give her the miniature Statue of Liberty for her mantelshelf and the box of American cookies I had brought back for her. When the front door opened, I found her entertaining two guests.

"Oh, sorry, Grandma," I said. "I'll call another time."

"No, no, Fred," she insisted. "Come in, come in..."

I stepped inside. Nothing had changed. My grandma pointed to a young lady with her mother, sitting by the hearth.

"...Fred, dear. This is my friend the butcher's wife, and her lovely daughter Maudie..."

The buxom wench turned to smile at me and fluttered her long eyelashes, while her mother looked on with pride.

"...Maudie's boyfriend died on the Western Front, Fred. Isn't that sad?"

"Yes," added her mother, "he was one of Master Charles' men, you see. He and his mates all joined up together in 1914. Of course, they're all dead now – so sad – just names on the vicar's war memorial."

I tried to change the subject.

"Grandma, I've brought you some cookies from New York."

She assumed I was being terribly rude by ignoring her guests.

"Well, Fred, offer one to Maudie then, please..."

I started to undo the package and passed the Statue of Liberty to my grandma. She showed it to her friend.

"...Look, Agnes, what my Fred's brought me from America – I think it must be a candle... Fred is His Lordship's chauffeur, you know. He had to drive the Rolls Royce for him in New York on the wrong side of the road. Fancy that now. Americans can't even get that right..."

The women laughed but I was still trying to open the packet of cookies.

"...Oh Fred, do give it to Maudie. She can use my needlework scissors."

I passed the packet of cookies to the young lady and her mother looked me up and down admiringly. I knew I was being assessed and felt rather uneasy. My grandma poured out more tea from her antique teapot. I noticed that only the best china had been brought out of the cabinet today. She passed me an elegant cup of tea.

"So how did you find New York, Master Fred?" the butcher's wife asked. "We just haven't got the money for holidays, have we, Maudie?"

Her daughter had now opened the package and put it on the table.

"Very crowded, Ma'am," I replied. "The traffic in Manhattan was dreadful."

"Fred sent me a postcard, Agnes," my grandma added. "He went to see a talkie film. Imagine that, Maudie... What was it called, Fred? Wasn't it something to do with this decadent music called jazz?"

Over the cup of tea, I described Al Jolson singing 'Mammy, Mammy' out of the movie screen. The women were fascinated and Maudie stared at me with her mouth open. But soon it was time for Grandma's guests to take their leave and I was left alone with her. She waved after them out of the front door and then turned to me in excitement.

"There, Fred, my dear. Isn't Maudie such a lovely girl...?"

I looked at the clock on the wall, trying to think of an excuse to leave but Grandma would have none of it and stared at me.

"...Young man, I think Maudie would make you a splendid and devoted wife. She has nobody, you know. All the nice local young men of her generation died on the battlefields... except you, Fred. So, what do you think?"

"Grandma, really," I insisted. "We've talked about this before. I'm Master Charles' partner now. We really love one another...seriously."

I'd been through this before. Grandma had often mentioned one eligible young lady or another to bring to my attention but now I'd had enough. So I showed her the gold ring on my finger. Grandma gasped and stepped backwards to sit down by the hearth. She was obviously quite shocked today and started to mutter.

"You wear another man's ring? Oh, tut tut, my boy... But this isn't right, at all, young man... What happened to you over in France, Fred? Was it all the bromide the British Army put in the soldiers' tea?"

I smiled. I'd heard silly rumours that Army tea was doctored to put us off the local women out in the Somme.

"No, Grandma, it has nothing to do with bromide in the tea."

"I don't understand, at all. When did Master Charles give you that ring? Was it in the States, then? They say New York is such a wicked city – like Chicago, full of gangsters, bootleggers and sin. Maybe it warped your mind."

"Grandma, it's got nothing to do with America. I've told you. I'm not the marrying kind. I don't want a family. Maudie seems like a nice girl...but...she's just not for me."

"Then where is she going to find a nice husband when all her male contemporaries have died serving their country?"

I put down the empty teacup and got up to go.

"Grandma, I don't know. That really isn't my problem."

"Then whose problem is it, Fred? Hey? ... I really don't think Lord Kitchener, Herbert Asquith or even Lloyd George thought about this one at all."

I left her trying to decide where to put her Statue of Liberty candle. I suggested that heat from the fire would make it melt if she stood it on the shelf above the hearth, so she put it in the window, where people might be able to see.

When, shortly after, the short lease on the town centre shop was due for renewal, I applied for planning permission for a new garden centre to be purpose built on the edge of the new estate of houses. I made the case that car parking in the town centre had been badly planned and that our customers would need to drive their cars right into our premises to allow bigger items to be transported. A dedicated car park was essential to our expansion plans and a new site somewhere on the council's new southern bypass would be appropriate. This was but a couple of hundred yards from the estate of the Big House and the greenhouses where all our plants were growing. Ironically, this was where I had originally intended to open a garden centre anyway, had it not been for the prohibition notice issued by the council a couple of years before.

I made this case in a stiff letter to the planning department, countersigned by the lady mayoress, who clearly supported our application. The new garden centre would finally open in 1930.

I had a picture postcard of the Statue of Liberty from John-Boy in New York, wishing us well and saying how much he'd enjoyed our visit. There were lots of kisses at the bottom. He asked if he could come to stay with me. I decided to talk to Charles about this. I was concerned that he might become jealous of John-Boy's obvious feelings for me. Charles' decision was vague, as usual, but he said he'd think about it.

A few days later another letter arrived for me from Paris. I began to think I was extra lucky to have two letters in one week. However, I was quite unprepared for the news that this letter would bring. I was sitting with Her Ladyship once more, while we ate breakfast together. She passed me the butter knife to slit it open. It was in English but from a French solicitor. I was chewing a piece of bacon at the time and nearly choked.

"Freddy, dear, are you all right? Not bad news, I hope."

I cleared my throat.

"Yes, my lady; listen to this, my lady. Nanny Monique has died – peacefully in her bed, apparently."

"Oh dear, Freddy. I had a note from her, you know. She really liked you and wanted you to go over there to stay with her again. But I suppose it is too late now. Funny, I haven't heard anything. What does your letter from this Paris solicitor say then?"

I turned to the next page and suddenly stood up, sending my chair toppling backwards.

"Now what, Freddy? Have you won the French lottery?"

"No, my lady, You should read this bit for yourself."

She unclipped her reading glasses and I passed her the page to read. Then she placed the letter on the table.

"So, Freddy, the guesthouse has a new owner. Congratulations, Son. You, of all people, deserve a gift from the gods once in a while, but I never guessed she liked you that much..."

She passed me the letter to read again and then looked at me.

"...Maybe you really were the son she always wished she'd had herself – received at court by the King of England after your gallantry on the battlefields, helping to save Paris from the Bosch. That's what she told me in her letter, you know."

I picked up the fallen chair and sat down once more.

"I only chatted to her once over breakfast, Ma'am."

"Perhaps she fell in love with you, Freddy, like we all did in this family. I can't think of anyone in this house who has not loved, or been so fortunate as to be loved by, you. I include His Lordship, my husband, by the way...and my grandson, John-Boy, too. He worships the ground you stand on, just like my nephew – the one you saved in no man's land."

"Thank you, my lady."

She looked intently at me over her reading glasses once more.

"You know, there are some fortunate people – and you are one of those – who go through life and change things around you for the better. People feel blessed because you are in the world, Freddy, like an angel, perhaps...but certainly a great hero. Other men of your age grow fat and ugly, downright difficult or dangerous to know..."

I sniffed and wiped a tear from my eye.

"...Sorry, I am embarrassing you but I do know why Nanny Monique has left her house to you... So, what will you do now that you are a young man of means? I rather think I asked you the same question when my nephew John asked you to join his Rolls Royce franchise. But what did you do? Well, I have only to look in the barn to see our rebuilt Silver Ghost to know what you did. Now I know you were sent down from heaven, Freddy. That's why everybody loves you...so much."

She leaned forward to touch my hand.

"And we really do, you know. But perhaps my grandson John-Boy loves you too much... Freddy, you are his great hero... But let me tell you about the hero of Homer's Iliad, Achilles – it was a classic Greek legend, you know. The great hero Achilles had only one week spot – his heel...and because of it, he was vulnerable and it proved to be his downfall... Well, dear Freddy, I do hope my grandson, John-Boy, won't prove to be your very own Achilles' heel... So Greek legend would warn us that all great heroes like you have at least one weakness... "

I rushed out in floods of tears, quite unlike any hero I'd ever heard of. This was all too much. She knew my weak spot instinctively.

Shortly after this, however, Her Ladyship was thrown into a state of anxiety by a letter from her daughter, John-Boy's mother. She opened it at the breakfast table when we were sitting together again, before the others came down.

"Freddy! ... Listen to this now. My poor daughter says that relations between John-Boy and his father have sunk to an all-time low..."

She readjusted her reading glasses and tried to read the next passage once more.

"...My daughter's handwriting is dreadful. She says she's suffering from nervous exhaustion and the doctor has put her on tranquillisers, oh dear... Freddy, what are we going to do? They have every modern luxury you can buy in North America but are they a happy family? ... Listen to this now, Freddy. She says here...can you read this? Your eyesight is better than mine."

I got up from the table to look over her shoulder. Her daughter's scribble seemed to be going all over the place. I took the notepaper and read aloud:

"Mummy, the doctor's pills make me all dizzy. I hope you can read this!"

Her Ladyship snatched the paper out of my hand.

"Silly girl," she muttered. "Of course I couldn't read that bit...!"

While I leaned over her shoulder, Her Ladyship just about

managed to read the next line:

Mummy, now I'm pregnant again...

She turned to me in outrage.

"...Well, young man, what do you think of that? Another grandchild on the way but she's got four already - you met them all... My son-in-law really should exercise more restraint. I read Marie Stopes' book 'Married Love' in 1918, and went to meet her, you know, Freddy, when she opened her birth control clinic in London back in 1921. That service was set up in the face of much hostility, I might add. Snooty people said she was interfering with the will of God – such stupid nonsense! ... But she really ought to open a clinic for the middle classes in New York. How on earth is my daughter going to cope with child number five? ... I ask you."

Her Ladyship turned to the next page of the letter.

"...Now listen to this, Freddy..."

She readjusted her glasses.

"John-Boy has had a terrible fight with his father...It all started when he planted a lot of pink pansies in the back yard and bought a hideous something-or-other. I can't make it out...You read the next bit again, Freddy . My eyes are going squiffy."

I took the notepaper from her again.

"My lady, your daughter says here, I think: John-Boy bought a hideous, pink, porcelain lamp for his room to burn an eternal flame in the sacred memory of Rudolph Valentino. This so outraged his father..."

Her Ladyship burst out laughing and I couldn't read for a fit of the giggles. Charles came in to see what all the noise was about and leaned over my shoulder to squint at his sister's handwriting as well. I pointed at the next line of scribble to show him what we were laughing at and I continued:

"Mummy, this so outraged his father that he went out into the back yard and trampled all over John-Boy's pink pansies in a fit of temper, muttering outrageous things about poor Valentino and pink powder puffs..."

Now all three of us were laughing, when His Lordship came in.

"My dear," his wife declared, "you've never heard such a tale. Your eldest grandson has fallen into disgrace. Read the next bit, Freddy."

I tried to make out the following line.

"My lord, your daughter says here: In retaliation, John-Boy got hold of the teddy bear, which is the regimental mascot that my husband has been entrusted with. This enormous teddy bear was presented to my husband's US Army regiment by Theodore Roosevelt himself, in 1917, you know. Anyway, in revenge for what his father did to all his pink pansies, John-Boy took the teddy bear into the shed, cut all its paws off with the garden shears, pulled its eyes out and then slashed it mercilessly with a hacksaw."

His Lordship seemed to be outraged.

"Desecration of a company mascot was a flogging offence in my day – in front of the whole platoon."

I continued reading his daughter's letter.

"My lord, listen to this now: Since then things have gone from bad to worse.

John-Boy and his father had a big fight in his room overlooking the swimming pool. My husband was threatening him with another beating but John-Boy said he wasn't putting up with it any more. So my enraged husband grabbed John-Boy's pink lamp and hurled it out of the window and broke it."

"I knew this would happen," insisted Her Ladyship. "I could see this coming when John-Boy became older. He's almost a man now... I told him to stand up for himself when we were over there last time, didn't I, my dear?"

I turned back to the letter.

"Either John-Boy pushed his father out of the French window into the swimming pool or he slipped and fell – I don't know. Anyway, Mummy, I can't stand it any more. John-Boy will just have to go or I'm afraid this baby may be still-born like the last one."

"I never knew that!" exclaimed Her Ladyship. "My daughter should have told me about the dead baby. So, carry on reading, Freddy."

So I continued:

"Please, please could John-Boy come to England to live with you for a while? He won't be going back to school at Harrow because his end-of-term report was dreadful. So his father won't pay any more for John-Boy's education. He gets on with you, his grandma, and he really loves Freddy. Can you ask his uncle Charles what he would think about this idea? If nothing is done soon, I can see John-Boy ending up in the New York State reformatory for young offenders or my husband will be put on a murder charge for slaughtering your eldest grandson. I'm not sure which is most likely. Either way I'm going to lose this baby... Please, Mummy, what else can we do? ... Your loving daughter...etc."

Her Ladyship was in tears.

"Time for another council of war..." announced His Lordship.

We all sat down around the library table.

"Charles, what do you think?" he said, looking at his son. "It was perfectly clear to me that John-Boy showed considerable affection for Freddy. But we all love Freddy now. Isn't that so, my dear?"

I passed a tissue to Her Ladyship, who blew her nose, placed one hand on my arm and squeezed it while His Lordship seemed to be deliberating.

"...Anyway, my dear, I think it is our duty to take care of John-Boy, as we are his grandparents, don't you know... What do you think, Freddy? Could you find work for him in the greenhouses? Well, he seems to be trying to grow things out in the back yard already. Pink pansies aren't really my taste in flowers but..."

He ran out of ideas so I spoke up.

"My lord, we need every pair of willing hands we can find at the moment. At least John-Boy wouldn't need to be paid much, if he's family. Maybe our horticultural business might inspire him to mend his ways – if he gets involved in caring for living things like seedlings, roses and saplings in the plantation outside. Growing pink pansies was at least a start, my lady, even if your son-in-law doesn't approve of things like that."

Her Ladyship sat up straight.

"Freddy is quite right, as usual. I think we should send for him today...Well, before it is too late and either John-Boy kills his father or his father slaughters him. Anyway, I don't want my daughter to be faced with another stillborn child... Freddy desperately needs a secretary – somebody he gets on with and someone to trust. John-Boy is bright, good at maths and, did you know that he has taught himself to type on his own Olivetti? He is local branch secretary of the New York State Rudolph Valentino Memorial Society... That's something he has kept secret from his father. But he did, at least, tell his grandma all about it."

We all sat quietly for a moment.

"Well now," His Lordship decided. "I think we should vote on this. Thanks to Great-Uncle Bartholomew and Freddy, we are solvent once more. But mostly thanks to Freddy, I think, since it was he who found whatever we've invested with Uncle Sam. Well, everyone who wishes to invite John-Boy to live here, with us, will you please raise your hand."

Only Charles' hand remained down on the table. We all looked at him.

"So, Charles," Her Ladyship asked. "Why don't you want John-Boy to live here?"

"Because I don't want to lose Freddy, that's why. John-Boy fancies him too much. I could see."

I put my hand out to take hold of Charles'. I had never done this in public in front of his parents before. Her Ladyship looked over her reading glasses at us, and His Lordship shuffled for one moment.

"But, Charles," I insisted, "as you said yourself on the 'Ile de France', John-Boy is far too young for me. I'm thirty and he's only sixteen. He's cute, of course, but you are my partner and I love you... You must know that by now. So, honestly, Charles, your nephew is not a threat to our relationship...but he and his father have become a terrible threat to each other. We must do something. Please."

His Lordship turned to his wife and smiled at her.

"Well," Charles muttered under his breath, "if he makes another pass at you, Freddy, I'll throttle the brat myself."

Her Ladyship was outraged.

"How can you say such a dreadful thing, Charles? My grandson is not a brat. He's a sweet, gentle boy who loves us all... He's just been terribly misunderstood, that's all. OK, so he's besotted with Rudolph Valentino this year, silly pink lighting and fancy pansies in the back yard. What's wrong with that? We're all different. I think his father is at fault. Beating John-Boy black and blue in the woodshed will not make a West Point hero out of him, will it? No... Putting my daughter in the family way once more was really irresponsible of my son-in-law. He should take better care of the four children he has now, before creating another one."

"Very well," Charles decided, holding onto my hand. "We'll tell my enfant terrible of a nephew that he's here on approval and subject to his good behaviour... and keeping his thieving little hands off my Freddy, then."

His Lordship laughed. I don't think he'd ever heard his son and heir speak like this. Her Ladyship folded up her glasses and placed them on the table. John-Boy's transatlantic rescue had been decided by a new democratic process, which I'd never witnessed at the Big House before. I felt relieved. We had to take better care of the living today. Neither John-Boy nor his father would be remembered very long after they were dead, or so I thought.

So, one wet and windy day, Her Ladyship and I found ourselves waiting for the liner to berth at Southampton. Charles had stayed with his father to deal with the latest order for packet seeds and the despatch of more roses for the

Garden City Council. Eventually, we found John-Boy, who had been sent via the cheapest steerage class. Such was the low value his father placed on him now. However, he was in good spirits and had even found a friend on board, with whom he exchanged addresses before saying goodbye. His grandma was a bit put out by the way John-Boy hugged and kissed me first before saying hello to her.

On the way home, John-Boy sat in the back seat of the Rolls with his grandma, so I never heard what they were saying. When I glanced in the rear view mirror, they were always deep in conversation. Some new trunk roads had been completed and our journey to London was quicker than before, so we arrived at the garden city in time for evening dinner. Her Ladyship had just reappointed the cook and His Lordship's butler had now returned from an unhappy period whilst staying with relatives at a dreary guesthouse in South Wales. New money had made all the difference. I called in at the kitchen to talk to the cook and found her having a tea break with the butler.

"Master Freddy," the butler said excitedly, and getting up. "You are the first to know. I have just asked the cook here to be my lawful, wedded wife and she said yes. How about that, then? Do you think Her Ladyship will mind?"

I shook hands with both of them. They had both been here since I joined the staff in 1912.

"Sit with us a moment," the cook insisted. "They're all unpacking the young master's things from America, upstairs. You deserve a break after driving the Rolls all the way from Southampton, doesn't he, my love?"

She kissed the butler tenderly and I was touched. I had no idea that romance had been brewing belowstairs.

"How are things, Frederic?" she asked. "When we saw you last, you were still one of us – the servants. Then your big presentation at Buckingham Palace for your VC...and photos in the national papers – a great hero of the war, no less. Now look at you, young man!"

I smiled at them both, while the cook poured out a mug

of tea for me. I was astonished. She'd found the one that still said 'Junior Gardener' on the side. Everyone laughed. It was just like old times.

"Well, Frederic," the butler continued, "Her Ladyship told us all about it but asked for our sworn secrecy... That was a condition she made for paying both our wages again, you know. So you are 'His Master's Lover'. Charles told his mother what Nanny Monique christened you, you know. She said he took you to Paris that time to visit the Louvre art gallery. I bet that was a sight for sore eyes, too."

I was astonished. Now there seemed to be no more secrets in this house, which had kept 'abovestairs' apart from the lesser mortals 'belowstairs' in Edwardian times. Yes, I thought, it really was all because of the war. We all laughed and I put two spoons of sugar in my tea from the open bag on the table.

"What she said, Frederic," the cook continued, "was that you saved Master Charles at least twice from potential suicide with his pistol and his hand grenade."

I pointed at the butler.

"You came with your lantern to find me, didn't you?" I reminded him. "That dark night, before my cottage was demolished to make way for the new road."

"That's right, Master Frederic. But I never knew the whole truth until much later. Well done, Master Frederic. That's what I say. Isn't that so, my dear? ... We never know in this life who the real heroes turn out to be. As they say, some ordinary folk like us even have greatness thrust upon them. And even ordinary folk find someone to love in the end."

The butler took hold of the cook's hand and held it.

"True love, Master Frederic," she added. "That's what makes the world go round, isn't it? Abovestairs or belowstairs... Well, I think love occurs where we least expect it – between a junior gardener, yes, like you, and our young master...and, now, even between His Lordship's butler and the family cook, yes?"

I smiled at them both.

"...Frederic, we both want you to know that we are not a threat to your happiness. If you love Master Charles and he really loves you, that's good enough for us, isn't it, my dear? And I don't care a damn what they might say at the Women's Institute."

The cook passed a home-made biscuit to the butler. She looked at the clock and then passed the plate to me.

"But, more important than anything else, Frederic, she told us that the turnaround in the family fortune – new roof, new drains and Rolls Royce now back on the road – was almost entirely due to you. So our wage packets are also thanks to you. She wanted us both to understand who we really need to thank, you see... So, Freddy, thank you..."

"Are you living in upstairs again?" I asked the cook, who turned to the butler again.

"For the moment we are, Master Frederic, yes, but we've put our names down for a new little house over the road in the garden city development – such a nice place, too. After we're married, we're going to retire there, aren't we, my dear, and sit outside in the garden to admire your blue roses we've all been hearing so much about. So, at long last, we will be able to live in one of Lloyd George's homes fit for heroes. Well, Master Frederic, the butler here has always been my hero. Now he tells me I have always been his heroine."

"Now, Frederic," the butler added, "sniff that dinner in the oven. That's why she's always been my heroine. Well, I tell you – when I was still living with my sister, until last week, in that dreary guesthouse in South Wales, I got to know what horrid, boiled cabbage smelled like..."

I laughed and the butler continued.

"... Another thing – talking of homes fit for heroes and my heroine, here – in that guesthouse, over every fireplace in each room, was a portrait of David Lloyd George. He is a great hero of the Welsh, you know. He stood up against the English and fought for Wales, and then in 1909 – heaven be blessed – he gave us all old-age-pensions, and in 1918, the vote to determine our own futures. Now that is what I call a great hero...

not quite like you – rescuing you-know-who from an aircraft in no man's land, Freddy – but a great, national hero of all the Welsh people."

The cook leaned forward to say to me quietly, "Master Frederic, don't you dare say anything about Lloyd George to His Lordship. The butler doesn't want to lose his job again. Really, my love! Lloyd George a great hero – what heresy is that? And in His Lordship's kitchen, too...!"

We looked at each other and laughed. I was already part of another silent conspiracy belowstairs as well.

"...Anyway," she continued, "we'll grow your lovely new roses in our garden, too – pink Ladyships for me, and my hubby-to-be says blue Lordships for himself. Fancy me being a respectable married woman at last, Freddy. Well, better late than never, we say."

It was rather late. I was sure dinner should have been on the table by now.

"How is Master Charles, now, then?" the butler asked me. "They tell me he is a new man again, all thanks to you."

"Well," I said, "you must have worked out that something romantic was brewing – that day you brought us two cups of tea in bed..."

All three of us laughed together.

"...Was that the day the roof sprang a leak or was it the drains again? I can't remember, can you?"

"Well, Master Frederic, if it wasn't one thing it was the other – hard times they were, too! And then, Master Frederic, you took charge, turned around the family fortunes and, the rest, as they say, is history."

The cook and the butler looked at each other and smiled.

"Bring Master Charles down with you for a cup of tea next time, Freddy," the cook insisted, turning to me again. "We'd like to see you both happy together, wouldn't we? Well, I tell you, after everything he went through in the trenches, he deserves some tender loving care now, doesn't he?"

A bell rang on the wall above our heads. Now the butler got

up and went to see what Her Ladyship wanted in the library upstairs – probably to ask when dinner would be served. The cook found her oven gloves and opened the oven in order to remove the steak and onion pie, the roast potatoes and parsnips, which had filled the kitchen with delicious smells of our dinner tonight.

"Poor John-Boy," the cook said as I paused at the door. "He looks as if he could do with some feeding up. What have they been giving him to eat out there in New York, then, just bread and water? Look, Master Frederic, how lovely your King Edward spuds and these parsnips which you grew, look now – straight from the oven. Yes! Tell them all upstairs that dinner is ready!"

Chapter 8

1930 – In the refreshment tent at the grand opening of our third garden centre

"FREDDY," JOHN-BOY WHISPERED, SITTING down beside me and placing one hand on my knee to squeeze it. "Let's go somewhere quiet for a moment. I need you, Big Buddy."

Most of our guests had already left. The last ones were shaking hands and saying their farewells.

"Now what?" I insisted as John-Boy whispered in my ear.

"What better time for another fuck than this, the ending of your great day..."

I gasped. He certainly chose his moments.

"...Well, Freddy, I'm eighteen now. I am almost an adult. Now I can talk to you as an equal."

I waited quietly until one of our guests waved and walked out of earshot.

"You want me to fuck you now?" I whispered, already getting excited. I had teased him mercilessly by playing difficult to get. He leaned closer to my ear.

"Yes. You deserve a special treat after such a great day, now it is all over. The new garden centre is open. You should sit back and relax now... Where can we go for a quickie, just you and I?"

I got up from the table and John-Boy followed me outside

the marquee. There was nothing left for me to do today. I decided to take John-Boy up on his offer and pushed him in the direction of the path to the privacy of the boiler house once more.

The old boiler house was just as we had left it last. I locked the door securely behind us and cleared a cobweb from the grating in the roof to allow in some extra daylight.

John-Boy came to throw his arms around me and we kissed. He was far more passionate and a better kisser than Charles had ever been. Somehow, after all the stresses of the last few days when everything had to be made ready for the grand opening, I desperately needed an emotional release. I undid his tie and started to undo his shirt. Then I moved stuff off the bench behind us.

"Get up there and lie down," I said.

First of all John-Boy threw off all his clothes, laid some on the bench behind him and lay back on those. He held out his feet and I placed them in the leather straps above us that I had fixed to the ceiling. He was starting to enjoy this routine and seemed to find it amusing. With my fingers I started to massage his buttocks tenderly and rubbed my thumbs deep between them.

"Huh! ... Do that again! ... Oh, Big Buddy, you're something else!"

The dappled light from the grating gave his youthful skin the look of a young fawn lying in a shady glade in the forest. He knew he was quite beautiful – just like a young Nijinsky, dancing in L'apres-midi d'un faune of 1912. I'd kept an old newspaper picture somewhere.

"Oh, Freddy," he muttered, holding out his hands, "my English buddy – I really love you. Now fuck me...What did you say last time?"

"A tender-hearted fucking, but you really deserve a good spanking, you know," I insisted.

"Oh, yes! Another time, Freddy, bare butt over your lap. I could go for that. I'd take anything from you... But come here..."

He put his arms around his legs to hold me as I penetrated him very gently. John-Boy lay back on his coat and groaned while we fucked. In this position we could gaze into one another's eyes. It was very romantic and he had become so handsome now he was older.

"Huh!" he muttered and then laughed. "Oh, Big Buddy, I love you so! ... Since that time in New York when I took you upstairs to see my Valentino collection. How do you say it over here? Yes, Freddy, I took you upstairs to see my etchings. Now fuck me again, please!"

Anyone standing above the grating in the ceiling above us would have heard tell-tale grunts and groaning loud enough to give our game away. John-Boy was far noisier in the sex act than I had ever been.

"Oh yeeesss! Jesus! ... Huh! ... Oh... Freddy, I fucking love you."

Suddenly we climaxed together and I leaned forwards so that he could smother me once more with youthful kisses.

"...Big Buddy, I really needed that!"

We stared into each other's eyes and smiled. It was the look of love – no longer just sexual passion and illicit lust.

"Well," I said, getting up again, "before you and I are missed, we'll have to go back to say goodbye to the last of our guests."

"So this was just an intermission, then?"

I helped him down from the bench.

"No, much more than that. You must know by now."

"So, do you really love me, Freddy?"

"Yes, I do," I said, cupping his beautiful buttocks in my hands once more.

He turned round to put his arms around me and kiss me passionately once again.

This fast became one of many secret sex sessions in the old boiler house. Charles and I never came in here now. While my activities as a passive object for Charles' sexual passion subsided, my new-found role as an active partner for John-

Boy had increased. Recently he had calmed down and had become a happier and more contented eighteen-year-old. John-Boy was no longer an enfant terrible as Nanny Monique might have said. Somehow, I hoped that my loving attentions had contributed to this sea change. Was it that he felt valued, when he realised I really loved him now? But there was little evidence of this when he first arrived to live with us only two years before.

1928

In those days, I was still playing hard to get after our first sex session in New York. We might have been forgiven for assuming John-Boy had left his troubles behind him in America, but he continued to court controversy almost from the moment he set foot in England. Everything started when Her Ladyship gave him a new bicycle for his birthday. She told Charles it would enable her grandson to get some exercise and see something of our magnificent new garden city. He might even meet an English friend somewhere, but it so happened that the brand-new Garden City Theatre was opening. The construction of this had been funded by a mystery millionaire whose identity had already caused much speculation in the Garden City Gazette. His Garden City Repertory Company had been established with the brief to promote challenging, revolutionary and avant-garde theatre for a new community.

John-Boy told me later that he happened to be cycling past this theatre and noticed a poster advertising auditions for a new production of Shakespeare's 'Romeo and Juliet'. So he went along to see what was happening and to find out if he could get a part. What we didn't know was that he took his cue from the life of his hero, Rudolph Valentino, and walked onto the stage for his audition entirely naked except for a diaphanous shawl, which he had borrowed from Her Ladyship's wardrobe, draped round his waist. The result was his immediate selection in the lead role to play Romeo himself.

The first we knew of this potential outrage was when His Lordship returned from one of his rare appearances in the House of Lords in a state of high dudgeon. In this session, the Lord Chamberlain, no less, challenged His Lordship to explain how it was appropriate for his grandson to appear on the stage of an English theatre in a state of undress. John-Boy was immediately summoned to the library with his grandma, to explain himself. But she stuck up for him and surprised His Lordship by confessing that she had been coaching John-Boy to learn appropriate and sensational extracts of speeches from Shakespeare for weeks. These he had been practising for the audition in a full-length mirror, inspired by dramatic poses struck by Rudolph Valentino in some of the production photographs from John-Boy's extensive collection. Finally, after some heated debate to which neither Charles nor I were invited, it was agreed that John-Boy should be allowed to take his first step on the English stage. When news leaked in the Garden City Gazette, of course, the first week of Romeo and Juliet was a complete sell-out, especially when the theatre critic speculated whether Juliet herself might be similarly seen in a state of undress in the sensational and supposedly avant-garde bedroom scene.

We were later advised by the local paper that the mystery benefactor of the theatre had now intervened personally. A legal team had been appointed and...'no expense would be spared in challenging the ridiculous powers of the Lord Chamberlain to supervise propriety and nudity on the English stage in 1928'. This revival of a pivotal work by the English bard...'might even shake the very foundations of classical English drama'. Within a few weeks, the entire production was a complete sell-out and even had to be extended. Such was the eager expectation of the public for John-Boy's first appearance on the stage.

Anyway, His Lordship was persuaded not to interfere, and allowed his grandson to continue to attend all the rehearsals and to be coached by his grandma to learn such a large part.

So, his uncle Charles and I waited for the first night with bated breath. When this finally arrived, I was reminded of our visit to the Carnegie Hall in New York. The front of the theatre was bathed in electric light. The great and the good, plus the press reporters, arrived in motorcars at the door and we took our places in the private box at the side, with John-Boy's grandma and even His Lordship. At first he said he would never set foot in the place, but was persuaded at the last minute not to miss his eldest grandson's first step on the stage.

The lights went down. The curtains opened. We were amazed to see the orchestra behind a see-through net at the back of the stage. Here was no traditional, painted backdrop but only a black wall, a scaffold balcony and some white-painted wooden boxes set around the stage. The theatre programme advised us that the design had been influenced by the revolutionary, continental designs for Bertolt Brecht in Germany. The lighting involved a bright top light throwing a circle down on the boards of the stage, into which stepped the narrator, highlighted by a follow-spot, who pointed out at the audience. I shall never forget his opening lines: "Two houses, both alike in dignity...in fair Verona, where we lay our scene..."

We were entranced. The costumes were all traditional and brightly coloured. The sword fights had been beautifully rehearsed, the dancing in Juliet's father's Palace was sensational and Romeo's scene with Friar Lawrence had us all in tears. I could not believe that we were watching Charles' nephew on his stage debut. His grandma had helped him to tone down his American accent but his stage presence was as magical as Rudolph Valentino on the movie screen. The way he fluttered his eyes and gestured suggestively in the direction of ladies sitting in the front row of the stalls was all copied from 'The Sheik', 'Four Horsemen' and 'Blood and Sand'. I had seen some of these at the fleapit cinema down the road, of course. But everyone was waiting for his, by now, notorious and much-hyped bedroom scene with Juliet. I had no idea how he would cope with this, since, from what he had said, he did not like girls. The lights went down. We all held our breath. In very dim top light we saw Romeo with Juliet lying on one of the white-painted boxes on the scaffold balcony above the stage. They were both covered by a colourful bedspread. Romeo cast it aside and got up, clutching a sheet to cover his nudity. There was a loud gasp from all parts of the audience. He tucked the sheet around his waist while Juliet watched him from her bed saying, "Wilt thou be gone? It is not yet near day: It was the nightingale, and not the lark... "

As Romeo climbed down the scaffolding, the lights went out completely and so nobody could see if he was entirely naked or not. I think the audience was a bit disappointed. By the time he had reached the floor of the stage, he was hidden from the waist down by another pile of boxes while Juliet dealt with her nurse above. That was it and the lights came up again. So, the dead hand of the Lord Chamberlain had prevailed after all. There would be no outrageous nudity today. The audience took a collective sigh of relief and sat back in their seats to watch the rest of the show.

The death scene was similarly underlit and an awful lot was left to the viewer's imagination, but it worked. Modernism had reached our new garden city. The heritage of Bertolt Brecht and German theatrical innovations would never be forgotten. Charles and I stood and cheered. Even His Lordship got up out of his chair to shout "bravo!" Her Ladyship almost fell over the balcony when her grandson took his bow and blew a kiss in our direction. He had three curtain calls with Juliet and then two all to himself while blowing more kisses, just like Valentino used to do, at the swooning women in the front row. Another chapter in British theatre history had been written on this opening night. Charles and I were amazed. His brat of a nephew from New York had fallen on his feet.

We tried to get to the stage door to collect John-Boy and take him home but the pavement was besieged with excited young women, just like the crowds who used to wait for Rudolph Valentino. I looked around. Unfortunately for Her

Ladyship's grandson, there didn't seem to be a single sexy boy in sight, only girls holding up theatre programmes for him to sign. But I had overlooked a sharp-suited young man sitting in his sports car by the curb. Nor did we know that one of the more mature ladies at John-Boy's side was a theatrical agent who had come down from London specially, just to see what all the fuss was about. By the following morning he even had the offer of a lucrative contract and was about to start a professional career on the English stage. But also in the audience that night was the young sculptor who had just set up her studio in the garden city. She was still looking for a suitable teenage boy from whom to strike plaster casts to produce brand-new statues of a twentieth-century Eros, the boy god of love.

In 1928, it was clear to me that John-Boy had every intention of renewing his sexual relationship with me but I tried to convince him that this just wasn't possible – he would have to look elsewhere.

"Don't you want me any more, then, Freddy?" he asked when we were alone together in the greenhouse. "Was my love not good enough?"

"You know I don't mean that at all. This is England, not New York. You are still a minor here until you are twenty-one. It is just not possible for us to have sex. There are English laws to prevent that sort of thing."

"Well, Freddy, one day. One day I'll change things – that's a promise, Big Buddy. You'll see."

I had no idea just how prophetic these words might turn out to be. In the meantime, John-Boy completed his sensational season as Romeo at our new Garden City Theatre and, almost as quickly as he had arrived at the Big House, he went off to London. Here he would appear in the London release of this revolutionary production of Shakespeare's play, care of his new theatrical agent. She took him under her wing and acted in loco parentis, because John-Boy was still a minor. I think his grandma never got over it and seemed bored with life for a while. Charles seemed to be relieved. He still harboured suspicions that his nephew fancied me.

John-Boy's departure refocused my mind on my other family obligations. I had not been to visit my grandma for some time and was feeling guilty about neglecting her, so I took her some flowers and chocolates from the village store. I found her sitting in the back yard enjoying the sun. Clearly she had recovered from her latest chest infection.

"Oh, Fred, there you are," she said, looking up from her knitting.

I passed her the chocolates and the flowers.

"How are they all at the Big House?"

"Her Ladyship isn't well," I said. "The doctor comes and goes."

My grandma put down her knitting for a while.

"Well now, Fred, all that wealth and the power of the aristocracy has failed her in the end. She can't take it with her, can she? I mean, when she moves over to the other side...to talk to Saint Peter at the pearly gates... "

I laughed but Grandma turned to me with a serious expression.

"...I'm leaving the parish church, Fred. Our local vicar has become far too wishy-washy for my liking. Sometimes he witters on about the world today in his sermons but I'm sure we've heard it all before. Is he losing his grip, Fred, do you think?"

"I don't go to church very often now, Grandma, except on special occasions – Christmas and Easter – and only if Charles is going."

She resumed her knitting once more but glanced up at me from time to time over her glasses while she knitted one stitch and pearled the next.

"Fred, I've a good mind to join my friend at this new chapel that's opened up down the street – my friend Agnes – you met her. She goes there with Maudie just for the fire and brimstone sermons, you know. She says the new minister has come over from the USA with fresh ideas about sin and what is good and bad in the world. That's what we need today – firm guidance... I think our local Church of England vicar has gone far too soft on sin, Fred."

I sat and smiled, not knowing what to say. I had long since reconciled myself to what Grandma would call sin, because of my sexuality. If I went to church to embrace all parts of the Bible, I would surely feel uncomfortable about my sexual attraction to other men. In the hymns, I would feel too hypocritical to sing too many hallelujahs.

"Grandma, you know that all the death and destruction on the Western Front killed religious faith for me."

"That's a pity when your parents sent you to Sunday school every week. Young people, just like you, need more moral guidance today so that you do not stray from the straight and narrow when confronted by so many temptations of the devil. There are far too many of those around today, I think – like this new jazz music, for instance... I see some girls around here now wearing make-up and lipstick, Fred, as if that is going to make a silk purse out of a sow's ear..."

I got up to fetch a vase for the flowers. I felt unqualified to discuss the attractions of local girls like Maudie, but my grandma continued to lecture me about the latest sensation at the new mission hall down the street.

"...My friend says the new gospel minister has been warning his flock about some of the worst radio broadcasts in the United States. There are advertisements tempting you to spend money you haven't got and radio programmes with irreligious popular music and wanton songs about sex, immorality and lust... As for this new jazz music of jungle rhythms, Fred ... temptations of the devil, he says."

"But this is England, Grandma."

She put her knitting down to look at me once more.

"Well, he warned everyone to beware these new BBC radio broadcasts from London, lest we be tempted by the devil himself. He says those dreadful gales in February last year were to warn us of the Lord's displeasure at the first regular programme of popular music broadcast by Christopher Stone at the BBC. He says it was all about propaganda for the devil – over the ether from London. My friend Agnes thinks I ought to go along with her next Sunday to judge for myself."

I finished filling the vase at the pump and handed her the roses to arrange. I had no wish to hear any more about sin and the devil's work.

"Why don't you open your chocolates, Grandma?"

"Perhaps you ought to come along with me next Sunday, Fred. The minister is going to tell everyone about the tidal wave of sin on the silver screen. He says the movie studios in Hollywood are making far too many films about fallen women, moral turpitude and other things too dreadful to mention on the Lord's Day. Agnes says we should all be protesting against that new cinema they are building to show talkies down the road, which might even be open on Sundays."

I was starting to feel depressed at the thought already.

"Grandma, I must go. Things to do, you know."

So I returned to the greenhouses to resume packing another delivery for the garden city. Business was booming. Charles and I had to cope with the urgent task of providing the Garden City Extension - Phase Two with more and more plants, because of its status as a real garden city. This was, once more, being called into question by the Garden City Association, whose founder, Ebenezer Howard had just died. Still no official municipal parks or gardens department seemed to have been established. We were only told that it had once more been delayed because of planning and financial problems. The loss of John-Boy's low-cost pair of extra hands made new staff essential. Once more, I found myself at the Labour Exchange to place an advert for experienced and apprentice gardeners. I also had to deal with the town council, the architects and the Garden City Planning Department about our third garden centre, to be opened in 1930. In retrospect, it seemed to me that my duties as a batman out in the trenches of the Somme had brought me far less worry and frustration!

Without Charles' support and comfort, particularly at night, when I often suffered from insomnia, I might have given up. Her Ladyship found me some soothing herbal bath salts and massage oil for Charles to rub into my skin to smooth my cares away at the end of each day. To such an extent our roles in life were further reversed. Now my lover was healing me.

"Well, Freddy," Charles said, as I lay down naked on the bed at the end of one particularly frustrating week, "what on earth did your accountant have to say to you today?"

"Don't ask," I said with a sigh. "It was all about tax."

We were already halfway through a new financial year and somehow the taxman's figures weren't making sense at all. I rolled over to put my arms around him.

"You'll get massage oil on the bedspread again, Freddy."

"I don't care," I insisted. "I need another cuddle now, please."

So we rolled around naked on the bed, leaving stains everywhere. Suddenly there was a knock on the door.

"Freddy!" shouted Her Ladyship excitedly outside. "You must come and look at this! The sculptor has just delivered the first statue of our John-Boy as Eros, the youthful god of love."

We had been promised this new product for our display of upmarket garden ornaments for weeks. I had also secretly ordered one to replace Her Ladyship's statue of the Eros of Praxiteles in her rose garden. That was still standing in the centre garden of the council offices, just down the road. Charles and I put on our dressing gowns and followed her into the yard by the back door, where His Lordship was waiting.

"What do you think of your grandson now?" I asked him.

We walked around the statue together while Her Ladyship followed with her son. This statue was cast in bronze and stood lifesize, which was five feet tall. His Lordship poked the buttocks with his walking stick.

"Good-looking boy, just like you, Freddy"

Her Ladyship pretended to be offended and muttered under her breath. I turned to her.

"This one is for you, my lady."

She gasped. "For me?"

Charles now stepped forward.

"Freddy has had this one specially cast in bronze to stand in your parterre, Mama. He still feels guilty about selling yours behind your back when you were away in New York."

She gasped but said nothing.

"Well, my dear," His Lordship reassured her, "you won't miss your grandson, John-Boy, any more now. He will always be with you in the rose garden and lifesize in his prime, too. I dare any pigeon to shit on this one!"

"I'll shoot it with your blunderbuss, my dear," she muttered. "Freddy, I just don't know what to say."

"Well, my lady, it is to say thank you for all your many kindnesses over the years. I'll get it moved..."

I was astonished when Her Ladyship burst into tears and cried on her husband's shoulder. He turned to me.

"Freddy, my dear boy. It is quite beautiful. We just don't know what to say, do we, my dear?"

He took his wife indoors, leaving Charles and myself to walk around the bronze and admire it once again.

"Shame about the fig leaf, Freddy," Charles said, with his hand on my shoulder. "I suppose we'll never know."

"Well, Charles," I giggled, nudging him, "nobody could possibly be as well endowed as you! ... And you thought I would go for anything quite as small as that!"

Charles now put his hand inside my dressing gown.

"I tell you, Freddy, you've still got a much better bum than his."

A few days later Her Ladyship remained in bed and did not come down for breakfast. We were told she was unwell and that the doctor would call. I was in the greenhouse when His Lordship came to find me.

"Freddy," he said, "she wants to see you – not me, nor Charles, not the butler or the cook. Only you will do, she says."

I washed my hands, went upstairs and found her door open.

"Come here, Freddy, and sit with me a while," she insisted.

I had never been so privileged before, shut the door behind me and sat down. She lay on her chaise longue by the window, overlooking the rose garden and the statue down below.

"I see you've installed the new Eros now. John-Boy looks splendid in bronze down there, doesn't he? Listen, I've had another letter from him..."

She unfolded some writing paper, which she'd hidden up her sleeve.

"His writing is just as bad as his mother's. I can hardly read a word without new glasses..."

She held the letter out for me.

"...You read so beautifully, Freddy."

I stared at the scribbled handwriting. John-Boy might have taken pity on his grandma and used his Olivetti typewriter.

"My lady...your grandson says, I think: Dearest Gran, I have met someone in London. Well, there have never been any secrets between us, so you are the first to know. I'm living with my boyfriend, who is a real life viscount, no less..."

Her Ladyship asked me to read that bit again, and I did. She turned to me in outrage.

"A viscount? ... His boyfriend? ... But John-Boy is still a minor! ... I thought his theatrical agent was going to take care of him! Can this be true, Freddy?"

I checked that I had not misread the scribble.

"These things happen, my lady."

"In England? This is not New York, you know... Carry on reading, Freddy...please... Perhaps my son-in-law was right about John-Boy all along and should have spanked him harder!"

I smiled. Was Her Ladyship in a bad mood today?

"Well, Your Ladyship, your grandson says here the viscount owns an art gallery in Chelsea. They understand that the Eros statue is now finished. Can he bring his boyfriend in the Hispano-Suiza to meet you at home and to inspect the statue outside?"

"And what, pray, Freddy, is this Hispano-Suiza?"

"A very expensive Swiss sports car like movie stars drive in Hollywood, Ma'am."

"I see, Freddy. Presumably the viscount drives it, not John-Boy, I hope... Well, if he's a driver anything like his grandfather, His Lordship, that won't last long, will it? ... When it collides with another brick wall."

"I can't say, my lady. Your grandson doesn't say who drives it."

"Go on, Freddy."

I squinted at the next line and turned the page to the window to get more light.

"Your grandson says here, I think: 'Grandma, I hope you'll like him'. That's it, Ma'am, except for 'Give my hugs and kisses to Freddy'."

"Give my love to Freddy, indeed! ...What about me, then?"

"Oh, yes," I said, looking at the PS added at the bottom of the page. "'You are the world's best gran. Love you lots! Phone me on this number at the top, first page'."

Her Ladyship reached for the letter and tucked it back inside her sleeve.

"Well, Freddy, what do you think of that, then? Should I challenge his theatrical agent? In loco parentis, indeed! All she wanted was her percentage and then she let him loose in the wicked city... Freddy, will you help me down the stairs, now? I want to sit out in the parterre rose garden with you for a while. Fresh air would do me good, you know."

She seemed to be in some pain as I helped her down the stairs and outside into the garden. She grabbed my arm once more at the steps down from the back door.

"Let's sit in the 'Temple' again like we did years ago. Then I can see the lovely statue more clearly. It must have cost a fortune in bronze, Freddy. I think it is so beautiful... Beautiful just like you, young man..."

She took hold of my hand to squeeze it for a moment, when she felt another spasm of pain.

"...Now Freddy, please go and telephone my grandson, will you? Tell him to bring this viscount, his boyfriend, here for afternoon tea – yes, soon. I'm going to make up my own mind, Freddy, just like I did when my son fell in love with you. Maybe I might even know this viscount's mother. Were we, perhaps, suffragettes together – sisters in adversity?"

I'd brought two cushions to make her comfortable. She patted my hand as I helped her to sit on the seat inside, out of the sun.

"Yes, Ma'am, shall I telephone him now?"

She handed me the first page of John-Boy's letter and I got up to return inside.

"And," she added, "Please tell the butler to bring us Earl Grey tea with scones and some strawberry jam. I have a mind to travel down memory lane with you this morning, Freddy."

I left her and went to telephone John-Boy, who actually answered the phone at the other end in Chelsea.

"Freddy, is that you?" he said excitedly. "What do you think, then. Will my grandma meet my boyfriend, the viscount?"

"Yes, she wants you to bring him over for afternoon tea,"

"Some dame, my grandma, yes, Sir!"

We set a date for the following week and I returned to the rose garden to discover the butler setting up the garden table. He went back inside the house to fetch the Earl Grey tea.

"Well, Freddy?"

I told her the date I'd arranged.

"And, my lady, your grandson said, if I my use the expression: 'Some dame, my gran, yes, Sir!'"

She laughed.

"So, what's this viscount's name, then?"

"Sorry, I didn't ask."

"Well, Freddy, you turned out to be my son's secret lover,

all those years ago. I guess I will have to wait to find out more about my grandson's titled beau now."

At three o'clock on the appointed day, John-Boy did indeed arrive in the sports car, driven by his viscount. Her Ladyship was already seated, just as before, in the rose garden by her bronze statue. Once again, she only wanted me at her side for afternoon tea. The viscount was a handsome, blond young man, taller than John-Boy, and immediately took Her Ladyship's hand to kiss it. She blushed. He had apparently made another conquest already.

"So," she said, "What's your name then...Viscount...?"

The viscount clicked his heels together and said, "Viscount Landauer, meine Dame."

Her Ladyship sat up with a jolt and stared at John-Boy, who had already sat down and picked up a fruit scone from the plate in front of her.

"Not the German bankers, surely?" she muttered. "Please, excuse my grandson..."

She turned to frown at her grandson.

"...Really John-Boy, anyone would think you had no manners at all. Offer a fruit scone to Viscount Landauer, then, please."

John-Boy put his hand out to touch his grandma's arm.

"Yes, Grandma, the British branch of the German Bank Landauer. What do you think of him now?"

The viscount clicked his heels again and smiled at Her Ladyship.

"At your service, my lady. Is that the statue of John-Boy as Eros, then...?"

He pointed at the bronze outside the 'Temple of Love'. Her Ladyship turned to look and nodded at it.

"Ausgezeichnet!" muttered the viscount. "Pardon me, Your Ladyship, this statue is excellent – so schon ein nackter Junge!"

The viscount stepped outside to take a closer look while John-Boy continued to scoff another fruit scone and ignored his boyfriend, who was walking around the statue, making appreciative noises.

"Were these Freddy's strawberries you used, Grandma?" John-Boy asked, now helping himself to the jam.

"Well," she asked, pointing at the statue again, "what do you think of yourself now you're cast in bronze, then?"

"He'll want to buy it for our garden in Chelsea, Grandma," John-Boy insisted, pointing at the viscount and picking up another fruit scone.

"Haven't you been eating at all in London?" his grandmother demanded. "I'll get the cook to put some more scones in a bag."

The viscount was still walking around the statue, now feeling the surface of Eros' bronze thighs with his fingers.

"Wunderschon!" he kept muttering. "Come, John-Boy, hubscher Liebling, look at this!"

Her Ladyship watched while her grandson stuffed the fruit scone in his mouth and went to join the viscount. She turned to me and whispered, "Freddy, what do you think? Can this be real? Am I dreaming?"

I shrugged my shoulders. This was so bizarre. I felt shocked that this German viscount, who I could well have been fighting somewhere on the Western Front a few years ago, was now, apparently, her grandson's boyfriend, no less. Not only was John-Boy technically still a minor, this was clearly a homosexual relationship with a German national who, only a few years ago, was probably one of England's national enemies. Was he actually related to the German Kaiser, I wondered? The implications were, quite frankly, mind-boggling. All I could do was smile at Her Ladyship and wave my hands in the air. I was at a complete loss for words.

"For God's sake, Frederic, go and tell His Lordship not to let Charles come out here...or World War Two could break out this very afternoon...!"

She beckoned for me to stoop down close to her ear.

"Are you absolutely certain Charles is not hiding another hand grenade, somewhere?"

I put my hand on her arm and squeezed it.

"Don't worry, my lady," I said. "I'll go and tell Charles I need another body massage in bed now. Trust me. I'll take him safely upstairs, out of the way."

"Good, I'll tell John-Boy to take his viscount back to London as soon as possible."

Early the following day I met Her Ladyship at breakfast once again. She smiled at me and pointed at the headline in the daily paper.

"Look, Freddy – votes for all women between twenty-one and thirty years of age on the fifth of July 1928. There were times I never thought I'd live to see this day. Emmeline should have been a happy woman today. We have equality at last, in theory, anyway. But for many women, I fear, real freedom to be independent – more than just their husbands' goods or chattels – might take a while longer."

I was tempted to ask if she was happy now the objective of the suffragette movement had finally been fulfilled. However, in view of Her Ladyship's declining health nowadays, I thought better of it.

"Well," I said, sitting down with kippers from the hotplate. "I heard nothing more yesterday afternoon. World War Two didn't break out, then."

"No," she said, smiling and turning to me in excitement. "I was astonished. After you took Charles to bed, His Lordship came out with a bottle of schnapps and shared some booze with the viscount – a common bond of the nobility – the noblesse oblige..."

She laughed.

"...Now, would you believe it, Freddy? My husband had met him a few weeks ago, you see. You know His Lordship is on some House of Lords subcommittee. Well, they are investigating the effects of the Treaty of Versailles on the German economy. This viscount actually gave evidence... Well, I had absolutely no idea, Freddy."

"So John-Boy sleeps with the German viscount who His

Lordship had met before in the House of Lords? Life is queer, my lady."

In spite of her spasms of pain, Her Ladyship still read the daily papers to keep up with the news. Perhaps it helped to provide her lively mind with distractions and put her own problems in perspective.

"Anyway, Freddy, so they told me all about it... I'm so glad that we don't live in Germany... You know that in 1920, the Supreme Allied Council decided that Germany would make forty-two annual reparations to Britain, France, Italy and Belgium. Then in 1921, this was fixed at one hundred and thirty two thousand million gold marks – that was six thousand six hundred and fifty million pounds, Freddy! ... Think of that...!"

My mind was dazzled by Her Ladyship's memory for figures.

"Then, in 1923, the exchange value of the German mark dropped to ten thousand million Marks to the British pound. Imagine living with an exchange rate like that, Freddy."

"Ten thousand million marks to the pound, my lady?"

I felt sure she must have made a mistake.

"Yes, I had no idea! ... I hope I've got the figures correct... Anyway, in November 1923, the exchange rate plunged again to four million two hundred thousand million marks to the US dollar, and the Rentenmark was introduced. Well, I forget any more of the details... Anyway, all this time, John-Boy sat scoffing more scones with your strawberry jam. That boy is such a pig."

I laughed. Was Her Ladyship getting fed up with her grandson?

"My lady, I remember your comment about the women at the Treaty of Versailles, who were only allowed to lay out tables, arrange flowers and make the tea. Do you think, if you'd been there to challenge all the men around the negotiating table, the women might have got it right?"

"Yes, Freddy, I do. In 1921 some upstart called Adolf Hitler got in charge of – what did the viscount call it? ... The Nazi

Party...sounds like a nasty party to me and they are growing in popularity, Freddy, because Hitler says Germany should not pay one single pfennig more. Of course the viscount says the Treaty of Versailles should have seen this coming back in 1919 –the same year the Nazis first got together. I could have told them this sort of thing would happen! I have a very nasty feeling, Freddy, just like Wall Street. I don't like this at all."

Things happened so quickly after this. In lieu of war reparations still outstanding, the London offices of the Bank Landauer were seized, along with the viscount's garden flat in Chelsea and his art gallery. The viscount was declared persona non grata and repatriated by the British government. So, John-Boy found himself homeless once again and, instead of returning to stay with us, disappeared on the next boat back to New York to meet his latest and youngest brother, of whom he'd only seen snapshots made at the christening. I think his poor grandma gave a sigh of relief and I was spared any further temptation, for the time being.

1929

In spite of protests by some local zealots, the new garden city talking picture house opened a few miles down the road with Al Jolson in 'The Singing Fool'. Contrary to my grandma's fears, the sky did not fall in. Moral turpitude did not spread like wildfire through our village. Maidens were not ravished on the village green. The cinema even showed Britain's first talkie 'Blackmail', directed by Alfred Hitchcock, which Charles took me to see. But Grandma's prophesies about the Lord's displeasure might actually have come true where money was concerned. What can I say about 1929? The first we heard about the big financial crash on Wall Street in October was when His Lordship was summoned to the telephone. A friend of his in the House of Lords had seen the ticker tape about the crisis. He came into the library as white as a sheet.

"Whatever is the matter now, dear?" asked Her Ladyship, who was lying on her chaise longue, reading Country Life.

His Lordship went straight to his bottle of port and filled a tall glass. He sat down beside her.

"Wall Street has crashed, my dear. They are already calling it 'Black Thursday'. I must telephone our son-in-law at once."

He got up to go outside, while Her Ladyship turned to me.

"Freddy, did you hear that? Do you remember what I said about the Dow Jones index?"

"Yes, my lady. You said whatever goes up can also come down, like the rain in the garden."

"Thank goodness I kept back most of that jewellery you discovered in the ice well. Otherwise we'd be completely ruined, wouldn't we now? Certainly it is helping to pay for my radiotherapy and all these pills."

"But, my lady, the garden centre business, which you helped to finance, is booming. Phase two of the new garden city development is well underway."

She reached out to take my hand.

"Bless you, Freddy. How many times have I asked what we would have done without you? Perhaps only a few of the gold bars will be lost. Wall Street might bounce back on Monday. What do you think?"

But Wall Street did not bounce back after the weekend because of Black Monday, 28 October, when the telephone rang again from New York. Her Ladyship's daughter was in tears. Her husband had just jumped to his death from his office window on Wall Street. The whole family was ruined. The bank had already foreclosed and she did not know where to turn next. She said some of his clients had made death threats after the trust funds he was entrusted with had collapsed into the abyss. What was she to do? Her Ladyship telephoned Cooks at once to pay for the family to emigrate to England at the earliest possible moment, as soon as the paperwork could be completed. As if to cap this disaster, Black Tuesday was followed by Black Wednesday. His Lordship's investments on Wall Street were worth nothing whatsoever. Of all the golden napoleons I had packed away under the back seat of the Rolls, not one dime was left. Uncle Sam had had the last laugh. Maybe, after all, God had failed to bless America in October 1929.

So, once again, I found myself parked in the Rolls Royce at the quayside in Southampton, waiting for the Aquitania with Charles. Her Ladyship was still unwell and unable to travel. His Lordship had gone to a meeting of the House of Lords Finance Committee to discuss the world situation and the affect it might have on the German economy.

The liner was late today. We were advised that storm force winds had caused a delay. But this was nothing compared with the storms on the world financial markets. I was beset with fears that phase two of the garden city development would be cancelled and our garden centre business would crash too. Who would want to buy trees, flowers and shrubs if the pound sterling was worth nothing at all? So we waited. Charles had brought his wind-up clockwork gramophone and we listened to George Gershwin recorded at the Carnegie Hall in an attempt to keep our spirits up while we waited. Eventually the Aquitania came into sight. No colourful bunting or flags on show today – just leaden skies and general gloom and doom.

Only John-Boy was happy. The other children seemed quiet and subdued. None of them had been to England before. Charles' sister was nursing yet another baby. She looked exhausted as they all climbed into the Rolls. The passenger compartment was bulging full of kids, cases, baskets and whatever could be salvaged from the house in New York before the bailiffs moved in. Charles sat in the back to nurse the baby while his sister fell asleep. Fortunately, John-Boy came to sit beside me in the front. I wound up the passenger compartment window situated behind the driver's seat so that the two of us could talk.

"Freddy, you just can't believe the chaos at home," he said, reaching across to touch my knee.

"Don't do that when I'm driving," I insisted. "Or it may be more than Wall Street crashing today!"

He looked upset.

"Sorry, Freddy. I've missed you so much. It is good to be in England again and the best part is seeing you again. I'll make it up to you, you know, if you still want me."

I did not say anything but concentrated on the road ahead, to take everyone safely back to London. We arrived after dark. Cook was waiting for us all and had left a cold supper out on the table. I silently blessed her because everyone was starving. The children had eaten nothing all day. While everyone wolfed down the cold roast ham, the potato salad and the pickles, His Lordship came to sit with us to say Her Ladyship was asleep and should not be disturbed. Finally, the younger children followed their mother and her suckling baby to bed, and John-Boy sat with me while Charles and his father supervised bedroom allocation, pillow cases and disputes over who slept where. I shared a bottle of beer with John-Boy.

"Freddy, I'm sorry. I wasn't very well behaved today."

"It doesn't matter," I insisted.

"Can we have sex again soon – you and I – like New York?"

I looked around. Fortunately we were quite alone. I sighed and said nothing. But this young man had just lost his father, who had jumped to his death on Wall Street. Maybe he was now looking on me to fulfil that role. I hesitated.

"...So I guess not, Freddy. But can we still be friends?"

I turned to him and this time put my hand on his knee.

"Yes," I said, "I'll be your English buddy."

He smiled and looked relieved.

"Thank you. I couldn't stand anything else now. My pop has gone but, well, I'll be honest with you. It was either him or me."

This had me puzzled for one moment but after the long drive back from Southampton, I was far too tired to think much about it now.

The following day, Her Ladyship came downstairs to meet everyone. She looked drawn and was clearly in pain. She asked me to help her back to her room, where I sat for a while. She didn't seem to want to talk to anyone else today. By now her health was failing. His Lordship called in to check how she was. He mentioned the dread word cancer and a nurse was employed a few days later to take care of her. We were later warned to prepare ourselves for the worst. The Wall Street Crash could not have come at a worse time. She still blamed herself for not standing firm and stopping Great-Uncle Bartholomew's golden napoleons from being shipped off to the States.

One day she rallied and asked to be brought down to sit in the garden with the children beside her bronze statue of John-Boy. She insisted that I should sit with her and watch the fireworks on Bonfire Night. But it turned cold and she had to return indoors.

January 1930

Not long after the New Year, Her Ladyship was confined to bed. A resident nurse was engaged full-time and lived in the adjoining room. Her Ladyship could ring the bell to summon help at any time of the day or night. One morning the nurse came down to breakfast to tell me that I was required upstairs.

"Ah, Frederic," muttered Her Ladyship, "now shut the door. We need to talk privately, you and I."

The nurse came in but Her Ladyship waved her aside.

"What can I do for you, my lady?"

"What's this I hear about you and my grandson, John-Boy?"

"How do you mean, my lady?"

"Well, it is obvious, isn't it? John-Boy kisses you but you don't protest. You never push him away. When Charles sees it, he gets jealous."

"It is only an innocent little peck on the cheek, my lady."

"That's not what my son says. You should be more assertive, Freddy. I know John-Boy is my grandson but I think you should push him away. Be a man, Freddy. Show him that you don't reciprocate his feelings..."

She stared at me for a moment.

"...Freddy, be honest with me now. Have you ever done things with John-Boy? I know he dotes on you..."

I did not reply but looked down on the floor.

"...I see! Like that, is it?"

"You said there should never be secrets between us, my lady."

"Oh, Frederic, how could you? John-Boy is underage and he is my grandson... But now his father has gone, I know, you feel responsible for the poor kid. He needs a bit of love sometimes and he doesn't get that from anyone else after his viscount got sent back home."

I sniffed.

"He really loves me, my lady."

"And, be honest with me now. Do you love my grandson?"

"Yes, my lady."

"Well, are you going to take care of him for me...and my son Charles as well?"

"Yes, my lady, I will try."

"Oh, Freddy, how on earth are you going to do that? Now ring the bell, please."

She suddenly felt a pang of pain and turned away. I rang the bell and left her with the nurse, who brought her pain-killer ready dissolved in a glass.

The very next day, the family lawyer was summoned. Her Ladyship intended to change her will but nobody had any idea what it might involve, except me. I suddenly realised that I should have protested my innocence where her grandson was concerned. But it was too late now. Anyway, I might have been imagining Her Ladyship's change of mind about suitable beneficiaries and her promise to leave me something to help look after Charles. I did think of asking her direct but I never had the chance to talk with Her Ladyship again. She died in her sleep two days later. I felt I had lost more than a friend. For years she had been more like a mother – replacing my own, who had emigrated with the rest of my family to Canada when I was only fourteen. I only knew for certain that it was Her Ladyship's wish to be buried in the family mausoleum beside her father's monument on the estate.

The day of her funeral brought back to my mind everything Nanny Monique said to me in Paris when I had breakfast with her. She warned me that the English aristocracy would close ranks in a crisis. The hearse for Her Ladyship's coffin was drawn by two black-plumed horses. A black limousine turned up to carry His Lordship, his daughter, Charles and the children. I was asked to drive the Rolls a respectable distance behind, to carry the butler, the cook and two of the other staff to the mausoleum. Because he was His Lordship's grandson, John-Boy would travel in the limousine. I already felt I was being excluded from the intimate family. The writing was on the wall. Only Nanny Monique saw this coming, just a few years before. The cortege started to move off and I followed slowly with the Rolls.

At the gates on to the road, suddenly the limousine stopped. John-Boy jumped out, waved at me to halt and he jumped in the passenger seat beside me. I turned to him. He looked angry.

"Freddy," he snarled. "Please don't ask..."

I turned around to check the glass window behind the chauffeur was closed so nobody would hear us in the passenger compartment. John-Boy reached across to place one hand briefly on my knee.

"I don't belong in there, do I? I'm yours now, Big Buddy."

The cortege moved on slowly once more. He sat in silence, glaring ahead through the windscreen, saying nothing.

My exclusion was confirmed once again when we reached the church for the service. Charles sat at the front with his father, his sister and the children. But John-Boy refused to sit with his family in the church and insisted on coming to sit with me, the cook and the butler. In the pews behind us were the staff from the garden centres and the nursery; tenants from the estate, including my grandma; and other villagers. What they made of the seating arrangements, I really do not know.

1930 – In the refreshment tent at the grand opening of our third garden centre

His Lordship came across to talk to me. He still wore a black armband in memory of his late wife.

"Freddy, where's Charles? I haven't seen him for a while."

"Isn't he with his sister or talking to someone over there?"

"No, I've just asked them. They haven't seen him either."

He took me aside for a moment to talk privately.

"You shouldn't let John-Boy kiss you like that, you know. You must be aware how much it upsets Charles."

"I can't stop him," I insisted. "It was just a harmless little peck."

"Well, Freddy, you should do something. Tell him that sort of thing just isn't done here. This is not New York. What if the vicar, the lady mayoress or the bishop were to be watching? How could I explain what is going on to my lord bishop – a colleague in the House of Lords? He's very hot on proper Christian morals, don't you know?"

"Should I go and apologise, then, my lord?"

"No, Freddy, I'm sure he didn't see anything this time. But next time you might not be so lucky... I know he is my grandson but John-Boy is still technically a minor – under twenty-one, you know. I feel responsible for the lad, now that he has lost his father."

"My apologies, my lord. I will tell John-Boy not to do it again but sometimes he catches me unawares, Sir."

"Quite so, Freddy. Quite so. I'll go and see if Charles has gone back to the Big House. Maybe he's feeling unwell or is upset about something."

"Yes, my lord, I'm so busy here. I need to talk to the head of Parks Purchasing before he leaves. He is so difficult to get hold of on the phone these days."

His Lordship went off to locate his son and John-Boy reappeared beside me. I took him aside again to a quiet table.

"Listen, young man," I insisted. "You and I must have words..."

He looked worried.

"I know," I smiled at him. "You like me and you like to give me a kiss but your grandfather says next time the lady mayoress, the vicar or the lord bishop might be watching – still worse, somebody from the Garden City Gazette. How would we explain that to your mother?"

"Sorry, Freddy. You know I love you. One look at you and I go weak at the knees, especially after our visit to the old boiler house earlier."

"Listen to me, John-Boy. If you don't behave yourself your grandfather might send you away somewhere – back to school, perhaps. Your uncle Charles says it must be either you or him from now on. I warn you. He wants to send you to a tough public school to have some decent respect knocked into you – either that or the British Army."

John-Boy sat back and appeared shocked for once.

"Freddy, please, no... Don't let them send me away. I couldn't stand it. I love you. You know I do. I'd do anything for you, any time, like today in the old boiler house. That was just amazing. I'm really sorry I have nothing else to give you – only myself and my special love. You know that!"

There seemed to be tears in his eyes. I was touched.

"Well, promise me you will never kiss me again in public. It gets embarrassing sometimes."

"Ok, Freddy, if that is what you want. But can I see you again in secret tonight?"

"You know that's difficult. Charles so gets jealous if he even sees us together."

He got up but leaned forward.

"Leave it to me, Freddy. I will find a way."

I should have asked him just what he meant by that but I saw the head of Parks Purchasing in the distance and rushed off to talk to him.

Chapter 9

1930 – Some time later in the refreshment tent after the grand opening of our third garden centre

HIS LORDSHIP REAPPEARED BESIDE me and put one hand on my arm. He led me aside but I was still talking to the head of the Parks Purchasing Department before he went home.

"Freddy, I couldn't find Charles anywhere so I went in the Gun Room to check. His old Army revolver is missing. Have you got it?"

"No, Sir, why would I remove it?"

"I don't know, Freddy. I've just got a nasty feeling something may have happened. You forget, before you came on the scene in 1919, we went through this before."

"But why now, today of all days?"

"I don't know, Freddy. Perhaps he saw John-Boy kissing you just now. You know how jealous he can get."

I immediately thought Charles might have overheard John-Boy and me in the old boiler house. I made my excuses to the head of Parks Purchasing and followed His Lordship outside the tent.

"We need a plan of campaign, Freddy, before it is too late."

"Where have you looked, my lord?"

"I've been in all of the rooms in the Big House, including the cellar and all the attics."

"Oh, God..."

Now I was starting to panic.

"...What about the outbuildings?"

"No, not yet. That's why I came to find you. I'll need to sit for a few moments – the angina you know. It gets me at times like this... Yes, yes, I've had another pill, Freddy."

"Where's John-Boy, Sir? We could do with him now. He could run or cycle around the estate and check everywhere in half the time it would take you and I."

His Lordship sat down on a garden seat to rest, and mopped his brow with a handkerchief.

"I thought the lad was with you, Freddy. But didn't I see him talking to my daughter, his mother, a while ago?"

I stooped down beside him while he undid his shirt collar.

"Damned hot today, Freddy... Yes, yes, damned hot."

"Will you be all right now, Sir?"

"Stop worrying about me! Go and find Charles, Freddy. I have a bad feeling something's happened."

I got up and tried to think of all the places Charles might have got to. I hadn't seen His Lordship so upset since Her Ladyship's funeral, and passed him a glass of water I happened to be carrying.

"Thank you, Freddy. Now go and find Charles, please."

I ran along the gravel driveway we had made from the new garden centre to the Big House. I saw the cook hanging washing on the line at the back of the kitchen and went over to her.

"Have you seen Master Charles?" I asked.

"No, Master Frederic. Whatever is the matter? You look all peaky."

"We've lost him. He's disappeared. Could you ask the butler to fetch His Lordship's angina tablets and take them to the refreshment tent... Yes, now please. Then he needs to be brought back here to lie down for his afternoon rest..."

She turned to hurry indoors.

"...And, Cook, have you seen John-Boy? We've mislaid him too."

"Why, he's with the butler in the kitchen, Master Frederic. They've been talking about America."

I followed her through the back door into the laundry and then to the kitchen, where John-Boy was showing his pictures of Rudolph Valentino to the butler.

"Have either of you seen Charles?" I asked.

"Why, whatever is the matter, Master Frederic," the butler asked.

"Have you seen Charles, either of you?" I insisted.

The butler looked at John-Boy.

"Well, we thought that he was with you and the lady mayoress in the refreshment tent. Now what's happened?"

"His Lordship is having another angina attack," I said. "He needs his medicine and your help to come back here to rest, please."

The butler hurried out, leaving me with John-Boy while the cook went outside, leaving us alone together.

"Have you seen Charles?" I asked him. "You haven't made him really angry as well, have you?"

"No, Freddy. What have you said to him now?"

This wasn't the time for a confession.

"Well, your grandfather is getting worried. John-Boy, I need you to run or cycle around all the places you know Charles might go – the greenhouses, the old stables, the barn, the old boiler house, the temple in the rose garden and then the woods as far as the new road."

"What's happened, Freddy?"

"Your grandfather says Charles has taken his service pistol from the Gun Room, that's what. You haven't seen it, have you?"

I caught hold of him and turned him around to look him straight in the eyes.

"Let go, Freddy! Why would I break into the Gun Room

and pinch that, for Christ's sake?"

"Well," I said, "put on your running shoes and get going, please. Yes, now."

"All right, Freddy. Keep your hair on!"

John-Boy hurried out to the hall cupboard to find his plimsolls. I sat down to think and grabbed a hot biscuit from the cooling tray on the kitchen table. The cook came back from the garden. I turned to her.

"Where would Master Charles go if he was really upset, do you think? Well, you've known him longer than I have."

She sat down beside me with her washing basket.

"The old ruin in the woods, Master Frederic. Why don't you take the horse from the stable and go to look for yourself?"

"Yes," I said. "Bless you. That is the best idea. John-Boy will never run that far."

I got up and grabbed another hot biscuit from the tray and hurried off to the stables. However, I found the stable door was open and the horse had already gone. I looked in the tack room. The saddle and the reins had gone too, so I hurried back to the Big House to see if Charles' riding clothes had gone from our wardrobe. On the stairs I met the butler, helping His Lordship up to bed.

"What did you find, Frederic?" he muttered.

"The horse, Charles' saddle and the riding tackle have all gone, Sir," I said. "He must have gone off for a ride."

His Lordship paused for a moment at the top of the stairs to catch his breath while the butler held one arm.

"And why would he do a thing like that in the middle of your great occasion, huh? You need to follow the hoof marks, Freddy, like we did in Africa. He can't have gone far. If we still had two horses, I'd come with you."

"You must rest, Sir. You know the doctor has advised you not to go out riding any more."

The butler helped his master into his room to lie down. He often talked about his experiences when tracking the enemy in South Africa in 1902. To follow the trace was actually the natural thing to do but it never occurred to me to follow the hoof marks out of the stable. So I abandoned any thought of returning to our guests in the refreshment tent and returned once more to the stable to look at evidence on the ground. The weather had been dry for several days recently so any fresh hoof marks were difficult to find but I thought Charles must have ridden the horse down the old drove road. It was the path we always took from the stable. Sure enough I found fresh horse droppings and they were still warm so I followed, but any further traces disappeared in a ploughed field by the railway line to the north. On the way back to the Big House I came across John-Boy, who was now jogging slowly and seemed to be out of breath.

"Charles took the horse, Freddy," he muttered breathlessly.

"I know," I said sadly. "I lost the hoof marks by the railway. But I don't think he would have gone far today, do you?"

"I thought my uncle would stay with you and the guests in the refreshment tent. After all, this is your big day."

John-Boy put his arm around my waist as we walked back along the track. I was now grateful for his affection and didn't protest any more.

"Did you upset him?" I demanded. "Are you sure you haven't said anything about the two of us. You know how jealous he can get."

"No, why would I do a thing like that?"

"Well, you must come with me now in the Rolls and keep your eyes open while I'm driving. At least we know the direction the horse must have gone - north beside the railway line."

"Ok, Freddy, let's go."

So we both returned to the Big House, found the cook and told her where we were going. I also asked her to send the butler back to the refreshment tent to apologise and tell the last guests that the garden party was now over because I had to go.

John-Boy stared out of the side windows of the Rolls while I drove along the narrow country lanes, but we saw nothing. We found His Lordship's binoculars under the back seat and stopped on a ridge overlooking the valley through which the railway line curved to the north. I helped John-Boy to climb up on the roof of the car to get a better view over the hedges.

"What can you see?" I asked anxiously.

He was scanning the railway line carefully.

"Nothing, Freddy... There's another express train coming. The signal's just gone up. Would my uncle Charles have ridden the horse to the railway station, do you think? Well, it is just along the line from that ploughed field where you lost the hoof marks."

We climbed back in the Rolls and drove down the lane to the railway station to see what we could find.

"Are you sure you haven't said anything to your uncle Charles to upset him?" I asked John-Boy once more. "Well, you know he gets suspicious if we are together too long."

John-Boy moved across the front seat towards me while I drove.

"Like now, do you mean, Freddy? You don't think he heard us fucking in the old boiler room. What happened to that silly note I gave you this afternoon? You didn't drop that somewhere, did you?"

"I put it back in the pocket of the suit hired from Moss Bros, I'm certain."

"Are you sure? Anyway, we'll have to remove anything like that before it goes back, won't we. My uncle Charles wouldn't have gone through the pockets of your hired jacket, would he?"

I didn't want to think about it any more and said nothing. John-Boy put one hand on my knee but I was past protesting now.

"Do keep a look out the side," I insisted. "You never know, the horse might have thrown him so that he is lying in a ditch."

I still had my suspicions about John-Boy. Was he a teenage murderer? Exactly what had happened on Black Monday in his father's office on Wall Street, 28 October 1929? He had never told me, although he'd apparently given a statement to the New York State Police. I decided to ask him about it as we drove along.

"Do you think I've murdered Uncle Charles then?" he insisted.

"I didn't say that, did I?"

"Listen, Freddy, I'll tell you what I said in my statement: you saw my father's office. The ticker tape machine was in the lobby by the door to the corridor outside and it was churning out doom and gloom about the stock market. When I called in to see my dad, he was sitting in his office, arguing with a client on the telephone. One of the companies my dad's fund had stock in was demanding extra cash from investors to stay afloat. I could hear the shouting on the phone from the lobby. The man was refusing, in no uncertain terms. But I was watching the ticker tape to see how my own stock was doing."

"So you had your own stock, John-Boy? How was that possible when you were so young?"

"It was registered in a false name but I knew it was mine. My American grandfather had given me some stocks and shares. He said I needed to learn how the American Dream operated. Now my stock was going down, like everyone else's. Then I heard the window of Dad's office open. I felt the draught under the door by the ticker tape machine. I couldn't understand why my father should open the window, in case the wind should blow papers around his office. When I returned to see what was going on, he was standing on the window ledge outside. Well, Freddy, what would you have done?"

I gasped but had no idea what to say. I knew I'd killed at least two Germans in that machinegun post by throwing the grenades during the Battle of the Somme, but could I push my own father out of the window?

"Freddy, I asked you what you would have done? You know how often he beat me black and blue in the woodshed."

"So you pushed him."

"I gave him a helping hand, but that wasn't in my statement to the New York State Police. I'm being honest with you, Big Buddy. I owe it to you because I love you..."

I was shocked. How could an eighteen-year-old be so cold hearted as to push his father to his death?

"...The client was still shouting dreadful things on the phone on Pop's desk. I didn't touch anything but took a look out of the window. Traffic had come to a halt by the sidewalk down below. Passers-by were gathering around the body. Then I knew I was free of my father. Now he would never abuse me again. That's when I ran outside into the corridor and told a secretary to call the cops. Now you know the truth. So what would you have done?"

I said nothing but put my hand out to squeeze John-Boy's knee. He was getting upset. I did believe this was the shocking truth at last but I really wished he'd told me all this before.

I drove the Rolls into the town and parked in the yard behind the local police station.

"Now what are you doing?" John-Boy asked. "I'm not turning myself in to the Feds, you know."

"I'm not asking you to. I think I would have pushed your father out of the window a long time before, if he'd done all that to me."

"I did, Freddy, but instead of landing on the concrete, he fell in the swimming pool outside my bedroom in Queens. You know that."

I really wanted to ask him more questions. I could not believe that someone with whom I'd recently engaged in illicit sex had just admitted such a potentially serious crime as patricide. But John-Boy was my passionate lover now and it was time to take care of the survivor of the old conflict between father and son. If he had really murdered his uncle Charles to get him out of the way as well, would he have made such a confession?

"Stay there and look after your grandfather's Rolls," I said, getting out of the car.

I went into the police station to talk to the desk sergeant.

"No, Master Frederic, we've heard nothing. Perhaps Master Charles will return on his horse this evening. I'm sure he can't have gone far. Perhaps he will walk in the front door before sunset, wondering what all the fuss is about. People don't often just disappear into thin air, you know, except in the movies. Did you see that one last week – what was it called?"

I didn't want to chat and hurried outside. So I returned to the Rolls but got out the local map from the locker to have a closer look at the local paths leading north out of our stable. By now we were sitting side by side on the front seat with the map across our laps. John-Boy turned to me.

"Freddy, I must say it. Whatever happens...I love you so much. You know that. If I kissed you at the wrong time or if my note upset Uncle Charles, I'm really sorry. But this is life, Freddy. I've loved you since you picked up my suitcases and came with me into Harrow School. That's when I knew."

"What was that?"

"That you and I are destined to be together – like right now, Big Buddy. It just feels right when you and I are side by side."

Under the map he rubbed his thigh against mine but I wasn't in the mood.

"Not now, John-Boy. We're supposed to be searching for your uncle Charles, remember."

John-Boy laughed.

"But we could hijack my grandfather's Rolls and drive off together into the sunset – just you and I – like the ending of a Hollywood movie. How about that, Freddy?"

I folded up the map to restart the engine but made no reply. So we drove back slowly along another lane parallel with the railway track without finding anything. At the bottom of the driveway into the rear entrance into His Lordship's estate, I stopped the car and switched off the engine.

"We'll walk along the track to the stables," I suggested.

"To check we haven't missed anything?" John-boy asked

cheerfully.

If he really had murdered Charles, he was being incredibly calm about it.

"No, I want to talk to you seriously," I said, "before we go back to the Big House. It is not so easy with everyone around."

So I locked up the car and the two of us walked along the track slowly. John-Boy turned to me.

"Well, here we are, Freddy. What is it?"

I think he was expecting more questions about what happened on Wall Street.

"Are you really serious about loving me?" I asked. "You didn't give Charles a helping hand to commit suicide as well, did you, to get him out of the way? ... Well, it worked for you once in New York."

John-Boy seemed outraged.

"What kind of guy do you think I am, then?"

"You are only eighteen. I think you found how easy it can be to get someone out of the way – by pushing your father over the edge of the window physically or, perhaps now, emotionally, so that Charles might go and blow his brains out in the woods."

"It is all very well for you to talk, Freddy. What did you do with the hand grenades in the Battle of the Somme?"

"They were enemy Germans preventing me from rescuing a British casualty in no man's land. That was quite different in wartime."

"But your action resulted in two deaths, just the same. You had to get rid of them – to get them out of the way... Nowadays, when England and Germany are at peace once again, you would be charged with murder, wouldn't you, Freddy?"

"Well, if you'd been eighteen years old in 1917, you might have found yourself fighting alongside other Americans on the Western Front. Things are very different in wartime, you know – kill or be killed."

"Well, Big Buddy, I told you it was either my dad or me."

We walked quietly for a few moments. John-Boy was actually quite right. I had acted on impulse too, out in no man's land. If I'd thought too hard, I might not have done anything, but left the dying officer to his fate in the crashed biplane. At the time I had no idea that he was actually related to the King. He was just an ordinary injured airman who desperately needed help. I had no way of knowing about the secret codebook sewn into his flying jacket.

"I'm sorry if I have shocked you, Freddy, but I have not killed my uncle Charles to get him out of the way, just because he loved you. Please will you believe that?"

"I guess you've seen too much of life in eighteen years," I sighed. "But, listen, some British soldiers were actually younger than you in the Great War, you know. They were underage when they signed up."

"I'm nineteen tomorrow, Freddy."

"Oh yes, I forgot. But why do you love me, then – not some all-American hunk like we see on the movie screen playing Tarzan?"

John-Boy kicked a stone.

"Life is like that, Big Buddy. I like beautiful Englishmen just like you. I saw you that day in my grandma's cabin on the Aquitania. Woof woof, I said – look at that! You were wearing your old sailor suit, Freddy – like the one Charles bought for you in Paris. For me, it really was love at first sight."

We were approaching the stables again but from the other direction now. We were amazed to see the horse standing outside its stable door, which was still open. I ran across to grab the reins.

"Look," John-Boy said, pointing at the horse's shanks. "Spurs have dug in and cut the hide. It must have thrown Uncle Charles."

I stooped down to look. Stanley was still wearing Charles' saddle, the reins and stirrups he always used. Somehow this horse had found its way home but Charles was nowhere to be seen.

"I saw this old silent cowboy movie," John-Boy said. "The Indian brave followed Champion the Wonder Horse back through the mountain pass and found his injured rider just in time. He had been bitten by a rattlesnake. Anyway, that was the Hollywood version. Let's see what this horse does now, Freddy."

I let go the reins. John-Boy patted the horse's neck.

"Did Charles get on with this horse?" he asked me. "Was there an emotional attachment – like you and I, Big Buddy? Did they love each other like Champion the Wonder Horse and this hero in the movie, bitten by the rattlesnake?"

The horse turned back to the lane.

"Stanley...go find Charles!" I said. "Where have you left Charles?"

So we followed, slowly at first. The horse stopped briefly to check that we were following and then continued along the drove road while we walked on behind.

"Freddy," John-Boy said, taking my arm, "does my uncle Charles really know how lucky he was to find you?"

I didn't push him away this time, but together, arm in arm; we followed the horse, which stopped from time to time to check that we were right behind. We reached the level crossing at the railway line. I looked and listened but no train was coming so we followed the horse further still. The sun was starting to go down now but Stanley trotted onwards. At the other side of the railway line was the station where we had called earlier, but there was no sign of Charles. Finally the horse stopped at a gate and looked over it. Another horse appeared from the other side and neighed excitedly.

"I think he's found his girlfriend," I suggested.

"So where's my uncle Charles got to?" John-Boy asked, looking around. "I think this mare is in heat. Stanley the horse must have brought Uncle Charles in here to meet his girlfriend – this mare which is in heat and getting so frisky."

So we went to have a look. I shut the gate behind us to stop either horse escaping. Then John-Boy and I started to walk across the field. We were interrupted by some excitement behind us, and turned to see Stanley mounting the mare.

"I've got it!" John-Boy said. "Uncle Charles was thrown

because Stanley mounted the mare. So he must be lying here somewhere. I think that was also part of another Hollywood silent movie – was it Valentino's 'The Four Horsemen of the Apocalypse'?"

I was still having doubts about this young man who admitted he had actually pushed his father to his death on Wall Street. So, how did he know Charles was lying in this field unless he'd actually been here before? Exactly where was John-Boy when I couldn't find him earlier? Had he actually managed to run so far in such a short time? Perhaps he had used his bicycle. So had John-Boy now pushed Charles to his death too? Would the murderer now be the one to find the body? Which Agatha Christie plot was that? I couldn't remember. But I actually had no reason to suspect my youthful lover of any involvement whatever.

"We must take a closer look while the light lasts," I said.

So we left the horses to themselves and walked around the field, but found nothing. I tried to think what Sherlock Holmes might have done when investigating the disappearance of an experienced rider in a field with two amorous horses in it. Would he have got out his magnifying glass and examined the hoof marks on the ground? But maybe he would have cross-examined a boy of eighteen who has just admitted pushing his own father to his death. When Holmes later turned to the faithful Doctor Watson to declare the solution was 'elementary', what might his explanation have been in this case? And where was Charles' old service pistol which His Lordship had found missing from the Gun Room? So did this young man have it all the time?

But John-Boy was someone I had grown to love and already had sex with several times. I tried to dismiss any doubts from my mind and concentrate. We had actually been brought here by Charles' own horse. So, had Stanley the horse been responsible for Charles' death and not his nephew? Or had Charles actually left the horse here and then gone off into the woods to shoot himself with his pistol? Maybe he had just discovered the truth about John-Boy and me. Had he found the note

John-Boy handed to me at the start of our opening ceremony? If I had carelessly dropped that note, maybe I was actually responsible for Charles' death, if indeed he was dead. We just did not know that yet.

In the middle of the field was a pond covered in thick slime and duckweed but I couldn't see anything underneath that. John-Boy had found a long stick and was poking the water with it. Nobody knew how deep the water was and I really needed a rowing boat, but there was nothing like that. It was starting to get dark and we would need to start walking soon before the sun disappeared completely.

"I guess he's just disappeared," John-Boy said. "Didn't Agatha Christie disappear in 1926 for ten days when her husband fell in love with another woman? Perhaps my uncle Charles has done the same because he's found out that you have now fallen in love with me. When I was at Harrow School, we used to read whodunnit paperback thrillers out loud to each other in the dorm after lights out, using torches, you know."

Just like John-Boy, I'd read Agatha Christie thrillers as well as Conan Doyle's, and now tried to think like a famous fictional detective.

"Let's think. What would Hercule Poirot have done if this was 'The Mysterious Affair at Styles', do you think?" I asked. "Your grandmother, Her Ladyship, told me all about that after she read it. Agatha Christie had her glued to that book for days on end. She was trying to work out who did it."

John-Boy stopped prodding the weed with his stick and tossed it aside.

"Hercule Poirot would go home to activate the little grey cells, I guess, Freddy. Perhaps we ought to go back and do the same. I'm sure Poirot would have thought to bring some sort of lamp with him, anyway."

"No," I said, "he would have left poor old Japp of Scotland Yard to think of practical things like that."

I started to wonder if this was the kind of casual conversation I would be having right now, if John-Boy had actually murdered his aristocratic uncle Charles. Even that idea sounded like the plot of a famous thriller, but I really couldn't remember which one it was – or was it in a movie at the cinema, instead?

"Look!" I muttered, pointing at something lying in the mud.

I stooped down to look. There was Charles' service pistol. John-Boy was about to pick it up.

"No!" I insisted. "Don't touch that – fingerprints, you know. We must contact the police."

Neither of us had thought to bring a lantern. We retrieved Stanley and he walked reluctantly through the gathering darkness back along the drove road to the stable, where we now found the butler, who was looking worried. He was now carrying a lantern.

"Master Frederic," he said. "We were getting worried about you, too, in the darkness. Is that Charles' horse?"

We explained everything and followed the butler back to the Big House, where I telephoned the police station to bring them up to date with our discovery. The desk officer even identified the owner of the field where Stanley led us to his girlfriend and said a search would take place as soon as possible. But he insisted Charles might even now be finding his own way home, having abandoned his mount in the field. We waited through the night but he did not turn up. We telephoned the police station in the morning. They confirmed that a search of the field and surrounding land had started at dawn but so far nothing had been located.

John-Boy went to sit with his grandfather, who was still suffering from angina and hadn't slept at all during the night. I had to go and supervise the dismantling of the refreshment tent and to get the previous day's party cleared up. During the morning, Charles' sister sat by the telephone to give the latest news to friends and the press reporters. The mayoress called in to see if she could provide any extra help but we assured her that the Garden City Police were now searching the pond in the horse's field. Finally, John-Boy came to find me after his grandfather fell asleep and we went to sit in the rose garden by the statue of Eros.

"Freddy," he whispered, "if it is any comfort to you, I meant everything I said yesterday in the Rolls. I do love you. I could not have wished Uncle Charles any harm, not even because he loved you too. Anyway, I'm telling you so you know the truth, just like the facts about my dad."

That was the moment the butler appeared, looking rather upset.

"The police have just telephoned. I regret Master Charles has just been found by the police frogmen under the weeds, gentlemen. They say the horse threw him into that pond, where he hit his head and drowned. I'm so sorry. The police say it was clearly a riding accident, judging by his spurs and the matching marks on Stanley's hide. They say that hoof marks in the mud and stones around the pond may provide the proof. They have been examining the horse's shoes for evidence of a struggle."

The butler shuffled away again. John-Boy came to sit right beside me, exactly where his grandma had sat so many years before.

"Freddy, I'm sorry. I don't know what to say."

"Did you have any hand in that?" I asked angrily.

"No, Freddy."

"Are you sure?"

John-Boy was clearly upset by my doubts, but I had to be sure.

"Listen, Freddy, I know it is difficult for you to believe now you know the truth about my father falling to his death on Wall Street, but I swear I am not responsible for Uncle Charles drowning in that pond. This was an accident. If you love me, you must try to believe that."

Suddenly the whole situation became too much. I had just lost one lover and was now needlessly accusing John-Boy of murdering him. So I buried my face in John-Boy's lap and cried. Finally I looked up at him.

"Sleep with me tonight, please," I whispered. "Now I really need you. Otherwise, I won't get any peace at all."

His face lit up. He looked around to check nobody was looking and kissed me tenderly.

"I'll come to you after they've all gone to bed."

"Yes please... Your nineteenth birthday treat, John-Boy. I'm all yours now but we've got to keep everything secret. You're a minor until you are twenty-one, you know."

"You must learn to trust me, Freddy. I'm not going to let you down, Big Buddy. From now on it is you and me against the world."

How prophetic this was, I had no idea at the time. I put my hand on his knee and got up again to go inside, but happened to look up towards the window overlooking the garden. His Lordship was staring disapprovingly down at us from the floor above and had probably been watching everything. Now he turned away with a look of disgust.

Shortly after midnight the door of the bedroom opened and John-Boy came in quietly. I got up to lock the door and then we cuddled one another for a while. I'd never slept with a nineteen-year-old before and was rather nervous. Should I tell him to go away? But he seemed to need me just as much as I needed him. He took off his nightshirt and we climbed into bed.

"Listen, Freddy, I love you. This is the best birthday present I've ever had."

"I just don't know what I would have done without you," I sighed.

We lay quietly together in the darkness. Only a pale shaft of light from the crescent moon fell across the bed. After all the tragedy of the last twenty-four hours, I was starting to relax. I leaned over to kiss John-Boy but he was already thinking about the future.

"Listen, Freddy, when the funeral cars line up again for my uncle Charles' funeral, just as they did for my grandma, I'm not even getting in the car with Grandpa, I coming with you and the staff in the Rolls. I'm telling them straight. My place is with you now, Big Buddy. Fuck the lot of 'em, I say!"

I gasped.

"John-Boy, you mustn't say things like that. They are your family."

"The only one I love is right here, Freddy – that's you. Now fuck me gently. I need another tender-hearted fucking."

When I woke up in the morning, John-Boy had already gone back to his room. In his nineteenth year he was becoming more sensible and had started to think for himself. Was this because we had consummated our love in bed at last? I lay there thinking. Suddenly, it struck me, after His Lordship, there was only one clear descendent in line to the title and the hereditary seat in the House of Lords, and that was John-Boy himself – His Lordship's eldest grandson. Now I decided that it was best not to say anything, in case there was another male descendent I did not know about. We would have to take life one step at a time.

Ten days later, just as John-Boy had predicted, the funeral cortege lined up in the driveway outside the Big House. The hearse and the limousine were exactly the same ones as before. I already knew the form. The aristocracy would close ranks once again, just as Charles' nanny had predicted, and I had been the one he loved. But, just as before, there would be no room for me in the front pews of the church. I would be expected to sit at the back with the butler, the cook, the villagers and tenants from the estate.

I could not have born the ingratitude and the shame if John-Boy had not, once again, come to sit between me and the cook. She seemed to expect it and moved aside on the pew seat for us both to sit, without comment.

"A life cut short..." the vicar began, in his appreciation of Charles' life from the pulpit. There followed a catalogue of his achievements at Eton and Oxford University, followed by his tour of duty as an officer in the Great War.

"I knew it, Freddy," John-Boy whispered to me. "I saw this coming. There will be no mention of you in Charles' life at all. I think we should go now, before you get all upset."

"Wait!" I insisted.

He sat back and we waited but he was quite right. The vicar was already talking about Charles' new-found energies in building up the garden centre business, without any mention of my part whatsoever. I marvelled at Nanny Monique's foresight. She had seen this aristocratic ingratitude coming. My part in Charles' life was being completely denied. So much for the English noblesse oblige that she hated so much. I stood up. The vicar paused and looked over his glasses from the pulpit. John-Boy followed me quietly out of the church while His Lordship turned round to glare at us both. I could not stand the service any longer. I just had to go outside.

"Calm down, Freddy," John-Boy insisted, putting an arm around my shoulder while we sat on a fallen yew tree. "It is the English way. Nothing must be allowed to tarnish the family escutcheon. In death, we learn that Uncle Charles was a saint, not a sinner. You know we saw it coming."

I looked across the churchyard towards the horses. They had drawn the hearse and were now being fed from nose-bags by the groom. The uniformed chauffeur of the limousine was also polishing the paintwork for the journey towards the family mausoleum.

"We'll go away," I said, placing one hand on John-Boy's shoulder. "Just you and I. Yes, in your own words, fuck 'em. After everything I've done for this family since 1919, not one single word from the vicar – nothing about my role in Charles' life or my part in the garden centre business – nothing, not one single word."

"Calm down, Freddy, you've got me now."

"Yes, bless you. It was as if I'd never existed."

"Lets go, Freddy. Leave the Rolls outside. My grandfather can drive it for himself. You are far too upset, anyway. I'm walking you home to the old boiler room for a really good fuck. Besides, they'll all be coming out of the church soon. I don't want them to find us here."

We got up slowly, while the sound of the organ drifted across the churchyard from an open window. Not caring what anyone would think, we walked arm in arm across the fields, back to the Big House. Everywhere was quiet when we arrived at the old boiler room. I knew the house would be locked up, awaiting the arrival of the mourners for the wake. John-Boy and I would face that challenge soon enough.

"I love you, Big Buddy," John-Boy said, locking the boiler room door behind us. "Now calm down."

He came to sit beside me on the bench and put one arm around my shoulder.

"Would you like to go to Paris?" I asked him, all of a sudden.

"Your house? What was it called now – the Pension Anglaise?"

"Yes," I said, "the one Charles' nanny left me. Let's go and see what I've inherited. Well, I won't inherit anything here, will I? It is just as Nanny Monique predicted. She said the English aristos would close ranks in a crisis. I would be out, just like she was, years ago. I didn't believe her at the time."

John-Boy stopped me saying anything more with a youthful kiss. He started to undo my tie and then my shirt. Then he threw all his clothes onto the shelf behind us. In the nude he was stunningly handsome.

"If you get up there," I said, "you can stick your feet up in the stirrups hanging from the ceiling like last time. Then we can look at one another. That's what I used to do."

He gasped.

"You got fucked in here by my uncle Charles, didn't you?"

"It was our secret hideaway."

John-Boy hopped up onto the shelf to lie on his back and raised his feet for me to place inside the straps once again.

"Oh yes, Freddy. I've always dreamed of something like this – a secret dungeon to hide in. I think Rudolph Valentino would have loved it. Which movie was that?"

I leaned forward to kiss him while he undid my shirt to reach my nipples. Then I reached under the bench to find the hand cream for John-Boy to lubricate himself.

"Do you still dream about Valentino?"

"Not now I've found you, Big Buddy."

I suppose anyone else might have been shocked at what John-Boy and I got up to in the old boiler house while his uncle's funeral service was finishing in the local church. But I desperately needed John-Boy's youthful affections now. At least I felt better prepared for the wake and, just as we had anticipated, the family gathering after the funeral was a nightmare. John-Boy stayed at my side throughout. He tactfully explained that I had become too upset in the church so we had left early to sit outside. Now His Lordship kept his distance from us because I think he was embarrassed. Perhaps it was just an accident that any mention of me had been left out of the vicar's address. But I wasn't in the mood to eat anything with the other mourners. So I took John-Boy downstairs to talk to the cook in the kitchen. We found her clearing up the table and piling things by the sink. John-Boy rolled up his sleeves and I reached for a tea towel.

"Bless you both," the cook said. "Nobody else would have thought to come downstairs to give me a hand, would they?"

So while Cook received trays of dirty glasses from the butler, John-Boy and I did the washing up. We felt happier to be useful. If we'd stayed upstairs, whatever would I have said? I didn't know all those people. There were some from Charles' regiment on the Western Front. I wondered if they'd actually read the despatch from Headquarters which had urged him 'to be relieved of duty at the earliest possible opportunity'. There was no talk of his failings as a soldier now, only speculation about his horse rearing up and throwing him into the pond to drown. Suddenly His Lordship walked into the kitchen. The cook curtsied, as etiquette demanded.

"The lawyer is about to read Charles' will," he announced to John-Boy and myself. "I think you should both be there, you know. Well, even I don't know what's in it. Not that my son had much to leave to anyone."

He didn't invite the cook or the butler. Presumably he knew enough about the contents of the will to assume that neither of them would be beneficiaries. I passed my damp tea towel to the cook and she hung it on the rail in front of the stove.

"Thank you," she muttered. "I wish I knew what to say."

"We're moving to Paris," John-Boy said to her. "We're going to run Nanny Monique's guesthouse together. You must bring the butler for your Paris honeymoon when you get married. I'll write."

Her eyes lit up.

"Bless you both. Now hurry upstairs, Master Frederic, or you might miss the lawyer's meeting. Come and tell me what Master Charles left you later."

The library was silent when John-Boy and I sat down by the door. The lawyer opened his briefcase, untied the red ribbon from a slender document and laid it out on the table. Then he looked around.

"I have here the late Master Charles' last will and testament..."

I should have guessed. Nanny Monique must have seen this coming too. I remembered how she sneered at 'those English aristos'. Once more John-Boy led me quietly out of the door. I had inherited nothing – not a pin, a single keepsake or anything else to mark our relationship since 1919. John-Boy had inherited his horse, the tackle and contents of the stable, which he whispered to me he didn't even want because he didn't know how to ride. Everything else had been left to His Lordship or the family estate.

We went to sit outside in the rose garden by John-Boy's statue. I looked up at it. I had paid a lot of money for this. Was it mine, now? Nothing concerning me had been mentioned in Her Ladyship's will, either. But did I really care after all this?

"Don't get upset, Freddy," John-Boy sighed. "You have me... I've given myself to you – body and soul. Can that be enough? I'm sorry I have nothing else to give you – not a dime, I'm afraid, Just myself, Big Buddy."

I put my hand on his.

"Thank you," I said. "I really don't know what I would have done if you were not here."

Shortly, after all the potential beneficiaries had gone away, His Lordship summoned me to return to the library without John-Boy. No friendly invitation for me to sit down now, so I stood to attention. I was beyond any further insult and waited silently. He snarled at me.

"So, Frederic, what now for you, huh?"

"I don't feel I belong here any more, Sir."

"Quite so. Quite so..."

We stared at one another. I waited for him to make the next move. He eventually opened a box file in front of him and looked up.

"Perhaps your duty is done here now, young man..."

Was that it? Perhaps, just like our demob ceremony at the Army barracks in north London in 1919, I was being told that I had done my duty now. Thank you. The door is over there. Goodbye. I only found out about my Victoria Cross much later. Now His Lordship handed me my cards, as if I was being sacked or made redundant, just like Nanny Monique had been.

"But listen, Frederic. We don't want John-Boy to live here any more, either. His mother and I have both decided. She's fed up with him. He only brings her grief... For my part, I think he only brings death wherever he goes..."

I was so outraged, I did not know what to say.

"...Well, think about it, Frederic. First his father jumped to his death on Black Monday, from the office window in Wall Street. Then my dear wife, his grandmother, died and now my son Charles – all dead. I think death follows some God-forsaken souls, like my grandson – in his shadow, you know. So who next, Frederic, huh?"

I sat down, feeling shocked. How could his loving grandfather ever say such a terrible thing? His Lordship glared at me because I had dared to sit down uninvited, but I wasn't getting up again.

"That was unkind, Sir."

"That's for me to judge, young man."

"Then I wish to leave as soon as possible to go and live in Paris, my lord."

"But I order you to take John-Boy with you. There is no place for either of you here now. Exactly what caused my son Charles to ride off and get drowned, I don't know. The death certificate implies a riding accident. Perhaps we will never know exactly what happened... but I would not put it past my grandson to have had a hand in that as well, somehow... Frederic, I have my own private doubts about what actually took place in my son-in-law's office to cause him to slip or fall from the window on the twenty-seventh floor – because John-Boy was the only witness. Was that really suicide, I ask you?"

"But, my lord," I protested. "Her Ladyship died from cancer. What possible hand could John-Boy have had in that?"

"He caused her lots of grief, Frederic, in the same way that he always upset his mother. Neither of them ever had the strongest constitution. I think my late wife's cancer was brought on by so much worry and stress. His mother would be next. I am sure of it. I need her here to look after the other children."

"I can't believe I'm hearing this," I muttered.

We stared at one another again.

"If you really love my grandson...Young man, I have heard various disturbing rumours and I know what I saw going on in the rose garden from my window. I think my son Charles knew about it all along..."

He raised his hands in despair.

"...Now, Fredric, you must take John-Boy with you to Paris, where the Code Napoleon is less harsh in dealing with sexual attraction of this kind. That's all I have to say. My disreputable grandson is all your responsibility now. My daughter and

I both wash our hands of him..."

I suddenly felt relieved. I would not have to challenge His Lordship. He had decided for himself. Now he got up out of the chair.

"...We will expect you to be gone as soon as possible."

So that was it. John-Boy and I were dismissed dishonourably, without any thanks, just like Nanny Monique had been, all those years ago. But afterwards I was angry with myself. I should have discussed financial compensation – the cost of all my work on the garden centre business, the rebuilding of his Rolls and the cost of the bronze statue in the garden, at least. But I let the opportunity go. Anyway, he had given me his grandson – the only person who loved me now. Perhaps that was enough. I shook hands only with the butler and the cook. Now I had to go and deal with my grandma, who I had been neglecting again, but I needed my young lover's support today.

"John-Boy," I insisted, "I want you to come and meet somebody in the village."

"Your grandma?"

"Yes. I've got to say goodbye. I'm leaving for Paris early in the morning."

"What about me, then?"

"I'll send for you when I've got things sorted out in Montmartre."

"But I can't stay here, Freddy. Now Grandpa thinks I killed Charles and he's told my mother that he saw us kissing down in the garden."

I got up but he took hold of my hand.

"Freddy, I must come with you. I don't care if your house in Paris isn't ready. Let me come with you to help you get things together."

"You should wait here for me to telephone when I'm ready," I insisted curtly.

John-Boy was really upset and now got down on his knees to cling tightly to my hand.

"No, Freddy. You must take me with you – now or never,

for better or worse, for richer or poorer. I'm not staying here."

Even I was starting to get upset again.

"OK, OK," I sighed. "The house might be in a dreadful state and dreadfully dirty but...well, I could do with some support right now."

John-Boy let out a long sigh and stood up again to kiss me.

"You'll never regret this, Big Buddy. I'll make it up to you, sure thing. We'll have sex every day and...I'll learn to cook ham and eggs for our English guests and take care of you as well."

"Very well. Now I need you to come and help me say goodbye to my grandmother. I warn you, it may be a difficult scene. You said that you wanted to be my consort. Now is your chance to prove it. Anyway, I've just bought her a radio set for her birthday. I want her to be able to listen to the programmes now her eyesight is getting worse. I hope this might help to change her mind about radio broadcasts by the BBC, when even the King is speaking over the airwaves nowadays. Listen, I'll need your help to string up the radio aerial in the yard outside."

So John-Boy and I carried the radio, the aerial wire and the accumulator battery to my grandma's cottage, where I knocked on the door.

"Fred!" she exclaimed. "You've been avoiding me. Who's this?"

She looked at both of us with a look of disdain.

"John-Boy has been helping me to carry your Christmas present, Grandma. Here's a radio set so you can listen to His Majesty the King."

My grandma had never met His Lordship's grandson from New York and she obviously assumed he was just a junior technician who had come to install the apparatus.

"Oh, Fred, I heard about poor Master Charles... Was it murder or just an accident, then? I haven't heard the latest."

"Just a moment, Grandma..."

I asked John-Boy to go outside into the yard and start to

string up the radio aerial from the roof of the privy to the window into the parlour. I also needed to talk to Grandma privately. He took a kitchen stool to stand on and went outside. I closed the back door so he wouldn't hear anything.

"Grandma, I'm moving to Paris. Someone has left me a house in Montmartre, so I'm leaving. I'm sorry it is so sudden."

My grandma sat down, looking shocked.

"Oh, Fred. What have you done now?"

She obviously suspected me of murdering Charles.

"Nothing, Grandma. You must have heard that Charles had died falling off his horse – the police say it was an accident. Now I need a change..."

"I knew it!" she muttered. "The Good Lord saw your relationship as an abomination and He put an end to it!"

We stared at one another for a moment.

"So who's this John-Boy, then? I thought he'd come from the hardware store to install the radio set."

"No, Grandma, John-Boy is His Lordship's grandson from America. He's coming to live with me in Paris."

Grandma stared at me with her mouth open in horror and pointed to my grandfather's Bible on the shelf.

"Your sins will find you out – first His Lordship's son and now his grandson. I don't believe this, Fred."

"Love can also be a good thing, Grandma," I insisted. "You know what the Bible tells us."

"Beware Sodom and Gomorrah, the Good Book says. That's why those cities were destroyed by fire and brimstone, you know, Fred. But the Lord moves in mysterious ways. So Master Charles was thrown by his horse and drowned in the pond. You'll be next, my lad, or this young man outside. Perhaps you'll both be drowned when the Channel steamer sinks in another storm on the way to Calais."

"Grandma, how can you say such a dreadful thing about someone I used to love or someone I love now?"

She stared at me in moral outrage once again.

"What about him, then – His Lordship's grandson? Have

you corrupted him too, now?"

She pointed outside the window, where John-Boy was attaching the radio aerial to her window frame. I was already regretting my decision to bring him to meet my grandma today.

"Listen, Fred, you are my grandson, I know, but I have failed. I should have boxed your ears a long time ago and dragged you down to the local mission hall to hear all the sermons down there about hell and damnation... Because that is what is in store for all homosexuals like you. Poor Master Charles has learned that to his cost. And now you tell me that you are absconding with His Lordship's grandson outside. How old is he then?"

"John-Boy is nineteen."

She gasped in outrage. I'd never seen my grandma like this before.

"I should turn you in at the local police station, my lad."

"But we're moving to Paris, Grandma. The Napoleonic code does not outlaw people like us. That's why Oscar Wilde went to live in France with Alfred Lord Douglas in 1897."

By now John-Boy had finished wiring up the radio aerial and brought the kitchen stool back into the parlour. My grandma turned to him.

"Well, young man, I'm sorry to put you to so much trouble but you can go and take all that wire down again. I don't want the radio set, not even if the King himself is going to speak on it. Our new minister at the mission hall has just told us that radio, and this new television contraption that Mr John Logie Baird has just invented, is all the devil's work to spread sin far and wide...on the airwaves over the ether!"

I stood up and looked at John-Boy.

"I thought you were going to give her the radio for Christmas," he said. "Doesn't she want it now?"

"No I do not!" Grandma insisted, wagging her finger at him. "Now take it all away. I won't have any more of the devil's work in my house! You two have been quite enough for one day! I'm quite disgusted! ... And to think poor Master

Charles is not yet cold in his grave."

So we left Grandma's cottage behind us and carried the radio set away once more.

"Cheer up, Freddy," John-Boy said. "We'll give this to the cook and the butler as their wedding present. What do you think?"

I was carrying the heavy lead accumulator battery, trying not to slop sulphuric acid on my fingers.

"Would you like me to carry that, Freddy? You're far too gorgeous to get your fingers burned any more today. Your grandma's wrath has done enough damage for one day, I think."

"Sh! ... Sh!" I insisted. "People might hear and assume you and I are eloping to Paris, just like the plot of one of those dreadful women's novels your grandma, Her Ladyship, used to read."

John-Boy laughed.

"She really was some dame, my grandma, yes, Sir! But she really loved you, Freddy. She told me, several times. You were her hero, you know – her knight in shining armour. But she also told me she thought I might turn out to be your Achilles' heel. She insisted that every true hero had one of those... Perhaps she was right, Big Buddy. Do you really think I have ruined your life...?"

I did not reply but blew a kiss at him instead. It was time for action, not more words. I put the battery down on the path to rest a moment. John-Boy placed one hand on my arm to whisper, "I'm coming to bed with you again tonight, Big Buddy. Wild horses won't be able to drag me away."

We stared into one another's eyes.

"Do you know, John-Boy?" I sighed. "For once, I really don't think anyone would care a damn."

"Let's go right now," he said. "The two of us will have a bath together, just like you said you used to do with my uncle Charles."

"Yes, we'll do just that. Nothing we can do will make the slightest difference any more."

"My grandfather, His Lordship, has washed his hands of both of us now, Big Buddy... We are out, cast into the wilderness – Depart from me, ye cursed! ... Yes, just like your grandma, Freddy. Fancy her being on the same side as the aristocracy."

We both laughed together. This time he carried the heavy battery.

"Nanny Monique warned me the aristocracy were all the same," I said, "whether they were in France or England. But I thought that she was joking. Do you know? I think that, in a former life, she might even have sharpened the blade of the guillotine at the Place de la Revolution before Marie Antoinette and the Marquise de Brinvilliers got the chop."

John-Boy suddenly thought of something.

"Back home in the States, George Washington wasn't fond of the aristocracy either, Freddy – I mean the English sort. He preferred to put them to the sword or fire cannon balls at them. He certainly didn't want them on American soil. Of course, that's why the French sent us the Statue of Liberty in 1884 – a great symbol of American unity against oppression by the English aristocracy, I think."

I suddenly turned to him.

"You do realise you might have to eat your words if your grandfather, His Lordship, dies?"

"Why's that, Freddy?"

"Because, John-Boy, when he does, you will become the next lordship. You are next in line to inherit the ancient aristocratic title. You do know that, don't you?"

"Well, if I do, Freddy, can I count on you? I'll need you at my side. Without you, I'm nothing, am I? Just an enfant terrible."

"Yes, I'll be your consort, my lord."

Before we set sail from England, I decided to try to seek a reconciliation with my grandma. I did not want to move to Paris and leave her alone in the village, so I knocked on the door once again, hoping to find her in a better mood today. I noticed the curtains twitch in the window by the door but she did not open it. This would not do at all and I went along the side passageway through the back gate into the yard.

"Hello," I called, pushing the back door open. "Grandma, it's me."

She was sitting in the chair by the hearth and looked up without a smile.

"Oh, it's you, is it? You haven't brought His Lordship's nasty American grandson with you today, I hope."

"No. You didn't seem to like him at all."

"I don't like you either, Frederic, not any more. To think of you indulging yourself with that young man almost half your age. I think it is disgusting, really I do. I don't even want to think about it. The preacher at our local chapel keeps telling us about all the horrors of hell and that is where you are going, Frederic, unless you mend your wicked ways...to spend eternity in hellfire and brimstone, my lad..."

I felt shocked and had no idea what to say to her now, but she would not let me get a word in edgeways.

"You are nothing but an abomination in the sight of the Lord... You have become a servant of the devil and His Lordship's grandson has become your slave of sin. I know that whenever you force that poor young man to engage in your illicit lust – the devil's work – you drive another spear into the side of our dear Lord Jesus."

I was outraged. I could not understand how any intelligent person could ever embrace such radical and disagreeable beliefs. I was tempted to tell my grandma to go back to the parish church on Sundays and avoid the depressing mission hall.

"Grandma, I love you but this is most unfair. I am not a servant of the devil. I do know the difference between right and wrong but my sex life really must be my own affair."

"Not when your shocking and illicit lusts go against the word of God, Frederic. You bring dishonour on your whole family... You must repent all your sins, I beg you, for the sake of your grandfather..."

She pointed over her head at the portrait on the wall.

"He must be spinning in his grave. I have a good mind to give you up to the village constable. I cannot understand why His Lordship has not already telephoned the police. You and this poor young man are just filthy beasts wallowing in the mire... That is what decent people say."

Grandma was running out of choice words.

"I'm sorry you feel like this, Grandma," I insisted. "I'm sure I don't know what I can have done to upset you so much. Was it not enough for me to take care of you during your attack of flu and collect your pension from the post office?"

She was refreshing her memory with choice rhetoric she had recently learned in the chapel down the street.

"Frederic, you are now...serving the devil and all his legions... Yes, the Lord God must be looking down on you in despair...yes, while Satan stokes the fires of hell ready for God-forsaken sinners like you. Doesn't this young man's mother care about him any more?"

"No, she doesn't," I snapped. "She wants me to take John-Boy with me to Paris."

"Well, I don't know what the country is coming to – allowing sinners like you to go free when you should both be locked up."

I wasn't going to endure this tirade any longer.

"Grandma, listen to me. John-Boy and I are leaving England for France tomorrow, possibly for good. I only came to say goodbye to you."

"Well, Frederic, goodbye. I'm glad your parents moved to Canada. They have been spared the disgrace you have brought upon the family."

She turned away to stare into the fireplace and ignored me. I was deeply hurt. After all the times I had come to care for her during her influenza – fetching her medicine, her groceries, her pension, moving her bed downstairs and so on, I was in despair. Her new religion had poisoned her mind against me. So I got up quietly and left her with her angry thoughts.

When I returned to the Big House to talk to John-Boy I found him packing his things into a steamer trunk and trying to close the lid.

"Freddy, please sit on the top to squash my things down so I can do up the clasps..."

I sat on it as he suggested and then he noticed my face.

"...Whatever has your grandma said to you now?"

"That you and I are on the slippery slope to hell, that's what."

"Oh, my American grandmother used to say things like that about sin and devil's work. She joined the New York fundamentalist church after the war, Freddy. You know the fundamentalists tried to outlaw the teaching of things like evolution in Tennessee back in 1925. My grandma hated anything modern, you see. She used to tell me not to go to the movie theatre, in case my soul became contaminated by all the sin on the silver screen. So I went anyway – just to see what she was afraid of."

"Well," I sighed, "even my grandma has joined the local radical chapel down her street. She has started spouting dreadful insults about you and me. I think it is just as well we're moving to France tomorrow."

John-Boy sat down on the trunk beside me and took my hand.

"Freddy, listen to me. I have loved you ever since that first time in my bedroom in New York. I mean really love – all the way..."

I turned to look at him. Only John-Boy knew how to cheer me up today. I put his hand to my lips and kissed it.

"...Freddy, I had to learn to ignore all the nasty words people threw in my face. You must learn to do the same. We have each other, Big Buddy, and that's quite enough for me. Now it is time for you to finish packing your stuff. Do you want me to come and help you?"

"Yes please. You can help me to be ruthless about all the junk, otherwise we'll never get it up the gangplank onto the paddle steamer."

John-Boy smiled and put one arm around my shoulder.

"We're going to make a fresh start at your house in Paris – just you and me, Big Buddy. Let's not spoil everything now, Freddy please... And when we reach your new house in Montmartre I want you to pick me up and carry me over the threshold. Isn't that the sort of thing English heroes are supposed to do in the movies?"

So the following day, we found ourselves standing by the rail around the deck of the paddle steamer to Calais. Towering above us were the famous white cliffs of Dover, which we were finally leaving behind us.

"Listen, Freddy," John-Boy said, picking a book out of his hand luggage. "I found this book of quotations when I was packing yesterday. The German viscount gave it to me for Christmas."

He leaned over the handrail beside me and thumbed through the pages to find Macaulay.

" By those white cliffs I never more must see,
By that dear language which I spake like thee,
Forget all feuds, and shed one English tear
O'er English dust. A broken heart lies here...
My uncle Charles' I think, Freddy."

He put down the book to place one arm around my waist. Sea mist was wafting across the Channel and gradually we lost sight of Macaulay's white cliffs.

"But my heart isn't broken, John-Boy," I insisted eventually. "I lost one lover but I still have you. We buried your uncle Charles in the family vault..."

"No we didn't, Freddy," he whispered quietly. "You and I were fucking in the boiler house, remember?"

We smiled at one another – one of those long, sexually-charged glances which must have left other passengers guessing around us. But we would be in French territorial water very soon, where the Napoleonic code prevailed. It just didn't matter any more.

"Ashes to ashes, dust to dust. Don't you see, Freddy? We

must forget all about the nasty things your grandma had to say about us being the devil's own. It is up to you and me to make our own happy life together, Big Buddy... United we stand, divided we fall... Who said that, I wonder?"

John-Boy turned around.

"Look, Freddy!"

I turned to look ahead in front of the ship, where the sea mist was clearing ahead of us to reveal the distant coast of France. Now I put an arm around his shoulder. John-Boy turned to me again.

"Do you know what Shakespeare wrote in Measure for Measure? I think your grandma might even approve of it. Perhaps, even now, she is nailing the Bard's framed words above her hearth beside her portrait of David Lloyd George..."

I needed John-Boy's cheerful banter right now. Grandma's painful insults were still reverberating in my mind.

"Well, Freddy, Shakespeare wrote: 'Some rise by sin and some by virtue fall'..."

I turned to him with a puzzled expression. The English aristocracy were so fond of quoting Shakespeare. Now John-Boy had played Romeo on the stage of the Garden City Theatre, he had learned lines of other plays as well.

"Don't you see, Freddy? Shakespeare could have written it about you. In the Battle of the Somme, your colleagues – the virtuous who gave their lives for their country – fell all around you."

"Twenty thousand died on the first day in 1916," I added.

"Yes, Freddy. I am so glad that you survived. But your grandma would add that you rose from the ranks of the working class by becoming my uncle Charles' illicit lover... Hence all the sin – according to all her tin chapel moral standards, you see."

"Yes, very clever, John-Boy. Now please put that book away before I throw it over the side."

He laughed and stuffed the book in his pocket. So we stood side by side on the deck in silence as the outline of

Calais cleared through the sea mist straight ahead. Suddenly the ship's siren deafened our ears as a sailing barge came into sight and the engine room telegraph rang loudly in the throbbing space below to slow the heroic splash of the paddle wheels at either side. So my new lover, Master John-Boy, and I would join the ranks of English expatriots in Montmartre, who were sheltering either from the British police or, more often, in hiding from some outrageous tax demand by His Majesty's Inland Revenue.

The End